A SNATCH OF TINSEL

A drug courier is arrested; the drugs s
a way to repay their Dublin dealer for the l... ̆
seize a Hollywood star currently in Ireland making a movie, and
demand a ransom for her return.

The kidnapped star is hidden while waiting for the ransom to be
paid by her Studio – itself a front for a Mafia boss in Las Vegas. He has
the ransom delivered by his own men as he has an ulterior motive –
their job is to retrieve the money after the actress is released.

A Dublin police superintendent and his crew arrive to take charge
of the investigation.

**But Kilbracken is Scobie Tierney's territory and while they try to
sideline him, he goes about things in his own inimitable way!**

... ALSO BY THIS AUTHOR

RANDOM NUMBER...
This was the chance they had gambled on...

The bomb was hid deep in the hotel's basement. – Now the
Washington hotel is to host a US government Middle East peace
conference. Ten year-old Hussein Shaffeed's father and his stepmother
are members of a group of radicals planning to activate the bomb!

In a small town just outside Washington DC, ten year-old Abi Swenson
is at home, recovering between bouts of chemotherapy treating her
cancer. A new telephone is installed to relieve her isolation and
boredom. Abi experiments calling random numbers and connects with
Hussein. An unlikely friendship forms, and he relates words his
parents' use in late-night secretive conversations. Soon both are certain
that something evil is being planned...

But who will believe two children?

THE SCHIAPELLO CROSS...

Santini watched in awe as his father took the Christ figure and laid it on the cross. With delicate manipulation of the plunger, he soldered the figure to the stem without allowing any excess molten gold to drip from the joint.

Leaving the cross aside, he picked up the small golden band and with the same painstaking precision, attached a circle of diamonds, taking great care with each. The band was then fixed to the cross over the head of the crucified Christ. Finally, he soldered the red rubies to the body – one to each hand and another to the figure's feet.

Santini knew the German officer who had commissioned the work, would soon call to collect the cross. What he did not know was that his father would never part with his masterpiece … it was their heritage. It was the *SCHIAPELLO CROSS!*

A *maelstrom of international murder and intrigue, something quite new to Detective Sergeant Scobie Tierney of the Irish police. But when it comes knocking on his door, there's no better man to take it on!*
'

*****

PETRA

Murder and Injustice...
Petra Kailno, a young Latvian immigrant works two jobs in Ireland to assist in supporting her family back home.

When she develops strong feelings for the husband of an invalid woman, she must keep them to herself. – But when the woman is found dead in the nursing home where Petra is a cleaner, her mundane life spirals into a terrifying orbit which threatens her very existence.

– '*Everyone is a moon and has a dark side which he never shows to anybody…*' *Mark Twain.*

ABOUT THE AUTHOR

Sean Burke was born in Athlone, Co. Westmeath in Ireland. His forty-year marriage to his wife Mary has resulted in four children and six grandchildren. Educated in the Marist Brothers College in Athlone, over the years he has worked in the aviation, pharmaceutical, engineering, and service industries. A sportsman all his life, he represented his country at all levels in his favoured sport of basketball. A voracious reader, his preferred authors cover most fiction genres. Over the years, he published short stories and poetry in magazines and newspapers and has only lately ventured into writing novels.

Already with four books to his credit, each feature his hero, Detective Sergeant Scobie Tierney of the Irish police. Sean still lives in Athlone.

To my wife, Mary

A Novel

by
J.P. BURKE

A
SNATCH OF
TINSEL

To Amanda.

Hope you enjoy JJ,
Best Regards

Joe Burke

CHAPTER 1

The two horses jumped the second last hurdle side by side, as if they were joined together like the horses on a kids' carousel at the fairground.

Gerry swung his feet onto the side cross braces of the high stool and stood up, his posture like that of a jockey standing up in the stirrups, his eyes glued to the large television screen. 'Will ye give it a feckin' wallop, ya dozy git ya! You're supposed to be a feckin' jockey and not a bloody statue!'

As if his words had somehow passed through the screen and winged their way into the brain of Teddy Reynolds, the young seven-pound claimer astride the 6/4 favourite on the sunlit Gowran racecourse, the jockey gave his horse a few cracks of his whip and as they approached the last hurdle, he had moved on by half a length. He winged the last like a stag and while the second horse kept on his tail on the run in, there was still that half-length between them as they flashed past the post.

Gerry sat back down on his stool with a relieved sigh and reached to the counter and took up his pint of Guinness and took a deep draught which finished it off. He waved the empty froth stained glass at McCluskey's. 'Fill us another one Macker. Help to wash down that last one.'

The bar owner picked up a clean glass and put it under the tap and began filling the fresh pint. 'How many winners is that you've had?'

Gerry grinned. 'That's the third in a row. One of me better days and that's for sure. Although I thought for a minute that last one had a jockey who thought his whip was only for knocking the shite off his boots. If he'd gotten turned over by that other yoke, I'd have hopped in the car and gone over to Gowran and rammed that feckin' whip up his arse. Gobshite had the best horse under him by a mile but he was riding it like a muppet.'

McCluskey left the swirling pint on the drip tray. 'Ye must be up a fair few bob so, Scobie. Ye've been doubling up your bets, haven't you?'

Gerry grinned again. 'Arra they were all short-priced favourites, but I still had a hundred and ten going onto that one so yeah, the auld chipper will get a right rattle on the way home. It'll be a lot more than a battered sausage and chips.'

McCluskey topped off the pint and left it down in front of him. He took the fiver Gerry handed him and gave him his euro change. He rested his elbows on the bar. 'You hear anything about this movie they're supposed to be making here?'

Gerry took a swig from the new pint and licked the creamy froth off his upper lip. 'Heard the rumours all right. But that's all they are. Only rumours. Where'd you hear it?'

'Tommy Stokes was telling me. He said he heard it from your woman who works in the tourist office. What the hell's her name? Tuohy. Yeah, Lucy Tuohy.'

Gerry took another pull from his pint. 'Well if Lucy Tuohy has it, there might be some truth in it. That one has a nose that can sniff out anything that's going on in Kilbracken before it even happens. If you were to have an affair, she'd be telling everyone about it before you'd even dropped your pants. If it is true, there'll be an awful lot of feckers preening like peacocks, hoping to get their mugs into it.'

'Tommy was saying Lucy told him Sabrina Metcalfe is going to be in it.'

Gerry let out a low whistle. 'James Street! If she's going to be in it, I might try and get in it meself. She's one fine piece of stuff. Sex on legs. And they're some feckin' legs too. Like a feckin' giraffe. Go all the way up to her arse.'

'Aye,' McCluskey said. 'She's a looker all right. But isn't she married to your man Richard Tremayne. The fella who was in that one that was on in the Adelphi a few weeks ago. The Gregorian Affair. He played the British doctor who operated on the president and saved his life after the assassination attempt.'

Gerry gave him a wide-eyed look. 'James Street, Macker! I didn't know you were such a movie buff.'

'Ye didn't see it so?'

'Haven't been in that place since I took Eileen Cleary there one night shortly after coming here. And that's not today or feckin' yesterday. And I wasn't there to look at the picture either, if you get my drift. The back row in the balcony of that place could tell a tale or two. There were more spits swopped and hands dropped there than in a bleedin' leper colony.'

McCluskey gave him an incredulous look. 'Eileen fuckin' Cleary! Jesus, Scobie! That one had more rides than Lester Piggot.'

Gerry grinned and took another drink from his pint.

'Arra sure I was new in town, wasn't I? Didn't know anybody's history.'

McCluskey laughed. 'I bet you found out hers fierce quick. We used to call her the Kilbracken Tandem. Anything in trousers was fair game to her.'

Gerry took another pull from his pint. 'Yeah. I found that out that night all right. She nearly sucked the tonsils out of me head and pulled the willie off me.'

He fiddled with the near empty glass. 'Where did she end up anyways? I know she left town a few years ago.'

McCluskey pulled at his nose. 'Fucked off with some big Nigerian fella as far as I know. Guy was about six foot six tall. Worked in Tumelty Chickens until they closed. I think they went to London or Manchester or somewhere like that. Poor bollocks is probably only a shadow of a man now if he stayed with her. She'd even wear out King Kong himself with a packet of Viagra in him.'

Gerry stood up and drained the last of his pint and wiped a hand across his mouth. 'Yeah. She had some engine for it all right. She had Duracel batteries long before they were invented while we poor sods only had yellow pack ones. I think the film in the Adelphi that night was called The Wrecking Crew. Dean Martin was in it. Played a sort of yankee James Bond if I remember correctly. Well I can tell you after that night with Eileen, I called her the Wrecking Screw. I was knackered for weeks afterwards.' He hitched up his trousers. 'Well that's me finished for this afternoon. Going to pick up me winnings from Paddy P's and then hit Luigi's for some of his fine soakage. I might drop back later tonight if I don't fall asleep. I'll see you, Macker.'

The publican waved a hand. 'See you, Scobie.'

Out on the street, Gerry took a few minutes to get himself together. Six pints wouldn't normally affect him at all, but they had been on a virtually empty stomach and he was feeling a little light-headed. Satisfied that he was on an even keel, he walked down the road, heading for the Italian chip shop.

There was a minibus parked outside with the driver leaning against the front, smoking a cigarette. He nodded to Gerry. 'Hope you're not in a hurry.' Gerry understood the comment when he went into the shop. There were about fifteen women mingling in front of the counter, all wearing pink T-shirts emblazoned with the words 'Chrissie's Hen'. One of the group had a large L-plate around her neck and a small white veil on her head – obviously the chief hen, Chrissie.

He recognised two of the group. Orla Hickey nudged her friend Freda Bannon when Gerry walked in. 'Will ye look at what's just walked in, Freda.' She waved a hand at the group. 'Look girls. It's Detective Sergeant Scobie Tierney, the Garda Siochana's answer to yer wan Agatha Christie's French detective, Hercules Parrot. Bonjour, Scobie. How are they hangin'?'

Gerry grinned. The two worked in Dempsey's Dry Cleaners where he brought all his stuff and he always enjoyed the banter with them. 'How's it goin' ladies? And it's Hercule Poirot, Orla. Not feckin' Hercules Parrot. And he's Belgian, not French.'

She laughed, the sound deep and throaty which was no surprise considering her obese size. 'There y'are, girls. Not only do ye get the best chips in Ireland here, but ye also get a lesson on literature from one of Kilbracken's finest.' She walked over to Gerry. 'It's me cousin Chrissie Geary's hen, Scobie. That's her with the veil. She's from Finglas and these are all her Dublin mates. We were in Gowran at the races and we're heading up to McCluskey's after we eat the grub and then onto the Cloisters night club.'

Gerry made a quick decision that he wouldn't be going back to Macker's. He nodded at the group. 'I'd say yis are all feelin' no pain now by the look of you.'

She laughed again. 'You're right there. We had a rake of Prosecco on the bus and a clatter of drinks in the bar where we had our own room and private barman. And then some of them began ordering shots. Half of them won't see the night out. They're pissed as pounds already.'

'Did ye back any winners?' he asked.

She laughed again. 'What? Ye mean there were horses runnin'?'

He grinned at her and then nodded to her jeans which were ripped at the knees, displaying two big knobbly kneecaps. 'Did you get attacked by a dog or climb Croach Patrick on your knees or what?'

She gave his arm a playful puck but he still felt it. 'Arra ya big gobshite ya, Scobie. Sure, that's the fashion nowadays. The ripped look.'

He made a face. 'Pity I didn't know that all them years ago when me mother reddened me arse for tearing the knees out of me pants. I could have told her I was just being fashionable.'

He was about to say something again when there was a cry from the group. They were all huddled in a circle and he could see a pair of feet sticking out with the toes sticking up. Someone was on the ground. He heard one voice shout in a loud Dublin accent. 'Deirdre! Get up ya dozy mare ya and stop pissin' around.' And then with more concern. 'Deirdre! Jaysus! Are you all right?'

He pushed his way through and knelt down beside the collapsed girl. She was about nineteen or twenty, flat on her back, her eyes closed. He could see the sheen of sweat on her brow and she was white and ashen looking. He could sense the growing panic around him. He looked up. 'Anybody know if she has a medical condition?'

One of the others pushed forward. 'I think she's a diabetic.'

He spoke as he reached for the bag around the girl's shoulder. 'And was she drinking everything?'

There was a general shaking of heads. 'She doesn't drink,' the same girl said. 'All she had were bottles of orange.'

He opened the bag and upended the contents onto the ground. He immediately spotted the insulin pen. Grabbing it, he took off the top, pulled up her T-shirt and jabbed it into her stomach. 'Her sugar levels are probably gone too high from too many soft drinks. Hopefully that'll sort her out. Now move back and give her a bit of room. Let her get some air.'

They widened the circle around her as Luigi came around from behind the counter, a glass of water in his hands.

Gerry saw the eyelids flutter and then the eyes open. He put a hand behind the girl's head and propped her up a bit and then took the glass of water and put it to her lips. 'Here. Take a drink of this. You fainted for a minute. Probably from all that orange you drank. I've given you your insulin. You'll be all right in a little while.'

He helped her to sit up and when some of the others huddled down around her, he stood up.

Orla came over to him. 'Jesus, Scobie! Thank God you were here. None of us would have had a clue what to do.'

He grinned at her. 'Well then would ye mind if I got my order in first? If I've to wait until Luigi does all yours, I'll be fainting meself.'

She turned to the little Italian. 'Luigi. Give us a quarter pounder with all the trimmins', a go of french fried onions and mushy peas and a big bag of chips for Scobie here. And we're payin', aren't we girls?'

There was a chorus of yeses followed by a few whoops and general laughter. Now that the girl was up on her feet and the crisis over, they were back in hen mode. The girl came over to him, the colour now back in her face. She smiled shyly at him. 'I want to thank you, Mr. Tierney. I shouldn't have drank so much orange.'

He waved a hand. 'It was nothing, love. Just watch that auld condition. It's a bummer I know but you have to be careful.'

She nodded. 'I will. I won't drink any more. And thanks again.'

Luigi put a large brown bag up on the counter. 'Your food, Scobie. He waved a dismissive hand when the girls collectively started to root in their handbags. 'No money. No money. I do this.'

Gerry took the bag from the counter. 'Thanks, Luigi. You're a decent auld skin.' He looked at the girls. 'Enjoy the rest of the hen, ladies. And take it easy on the poor fellas in the Cloisters. The fellas down here are fierce innocent ye know. Wouldn't be up to ye Dublin ones at all.'

One of the group sidled over to him, a drunken smile on her face. She was about five-foot six inches tall, probably in her mid to late thirties with a heavily made up face, short black hair and a body which was lean and muscular looking in the pink T-shirt and skintight blue jeans she was wearing. The t-shirt sleeves were tight over solid looking biceps and one of her wrists bore a blood red rose tattoo. Her breasts were small but solid looking, the prominent nipples pressing against the t-shirt advertising that she wasn't wearing a bra. The face didn't match the body though. She had eyes which were a bit too close together and her facial bones were very prominent, giving her a slightly gaunt look. She was certainly no oil painting, but he had seen worse looking in his day. The voice was a bit slurred. 'You wouldn't consider going to the Cloisters yourself, detective sergeant, would you?' She slowly rolled her tongue over her lips, the movement slow, lewd and suggestive. 'Wouldn't mind being frisked by you later.'

Freda Bannon came over, an open bag of chips in her hand. Like her friend Orla, she was far removed from being catwalk material, unless it was to act as ballast. 'You met Chloe here, Scobie?' There was a slight wrinkling of the nose. 'She's into all that body building malarkey.' She stuck a pudgy hand into the bag and took out a wedge of chips and stuffed them into her mouth. 'Wouldn't be my cup of tea, all that humping and grunting. Just so you can look like one of them Chinese bodies with all the skin gone off them. The ones that were in that exhibition in Dublin.' She looked at the other woman. 'That's what ye look like, you know. Like little wiry men with tits.' She turned back to Gerry. 'Ye men like a bit of flesh, don't ye, Scobie? Ye like to have something to get a grip of.' She held up the bag of chips. 'These are the only kind of weights I like lifting. That and a good big glass of sauvignon blanc.' She gave the other woman a smirking look and walked away.

7

The two small eyes were back on Gerry. 'Scobie? Wasn't there a jockey called Scobie once?' The look deepened. She tried to inflect the words with a sexy timbre but all she managed to do was get more slurred. 'You do any riding, Scobie?'

Gerry weighed up the blatant innuendo. She wasn't too bad looking. He grinned to himself. Not quite a wiry little man with tits but it wasn't too far off the mark. But he could only imagine what it would be like having those long muscular legs wrapped around him. As Smithy had once said when he had made a slagging comment about the looks of one of his dates, 'you don't look at the mantelpiece when you're poking the fire.' But she was as near as pissed as damnit. Another few drinks and she'd be blotto. He might get to poke the fire all right, but the flames would be gone out. He'd bet all his winnings that she'd be snoring in a corner before they even got to the Cloisters. He wasn't going to take those odds.

'Maybe some other time, Chloe.'

He walked out, the burger already up to his mouth.

*****

CHAPTER 2

Richard Tremayne walked out to the heart shaped pool where his wife lay sprawled on a towel laid out on the small patch of manicured green lawn beside it. She was wearing a deep blue bikini which highlighted her hourglass figure and long legs; a big floppy hat and large round sunglasses which covered nearly half her face. A small table beside her had a bound manuscript which was open face down on the glass top, a cocktail glass with a small amount of clear liquid in the bottom, a large tube of suntan lotion and her watch laid flat on the table, a thin delicate band of linking gold hearts with a round faced dial which boasted a circle of small diamonds around the edge which sparkled in the bright sunshine. He had spent over fifteen thousand dollars on it for her thirtieth birthday six months ago. It had nearly been all his fee for his part in The Gregorian Affair.

He walked over and stood looking down at her. 'That was Sam Brookman. He told me to tell you there's a pre-production meeting at the studio at three o'clock this afternoon. He wants you to be there.'

She said nothing for a while, her eyes invisible behind the dark glasses. He waited. He was used to that. Of the two of them, she was by far the biggest star who brought home much bigger paychecks. And that, in her opinion, put her top of the tree. He knew his place. Eventually she sat up and removed the glasses. 'I hope you didn't tell him I'd be there.'

He shook his head. 'I told him I'd give you the message. That was all. He wants you to ring him back.'

She picked up the glass and drained the last of the gin. 'That man can be so bothersome. Well if he thinks I'm going to waste my afternoon sitting around listening to him waffle on, he can think again. I don't know why the studio picked him for this one.'

'Probably because his last two pictures were hugely successful,' he said. 'Made big bucks at the box office.'

She gave a little snort. 'It wasn't him who made them the success they were. It was the actors, despite him directing. The man's a moron.' She held up the empty glass toward him. 'Get me another drink.'

He took it from her, despite his increasing annoyance. She was in her Cleopatra mode as he called it, and when she was like that, everybody including himself, was her lackey. And it was Conchita's day off, so she only had him to boss around. He walked back through the open patio doors and over to the small bar counter on which an array of bottles stood. He picked up the bottle of Grey Goose gin and filled out a small measure and then opened a small bottle of tonic and tipped it in. He went across the big room and into the kitchen and pressed the glass against the ice maker on the door of the large fridge, allowing two cubes of ice to plop into it. He carried it back to her.

She took the glass from him and took a sip and then looked up at him and held it out, an annoyed expression on her face. 'That's too bloody weak. Put another drop of gin into it.'

He took the glass from her but didn't move. 'Do you think you should be drinking this early? It's only one o'clock you know.'

Her face clouded over. 'When I drink is my business. Now – are you going to get me a proper one or will I have to get it myself?'

He went back in and added another shot of gin to the glass and brought it back out to her. She took it from him without a word.

She took the script and put it on the towel in front of her. He watched as she flipped over a page. 'When do you go to Ireland?'

She took off her sunglasses. 'Tomorrow week.'

'I might go with you if that's all right.'

She looked up at him. 'Why? We're going to be there for nearly two months and it's not a city we're going to be in. It's only a small town I'm told. You would be bored silly after a few days.'

He shrugged his shoulders. 'I've been to Ireland before. We could do a few tours when you're not working. Explore some of the country. It's very nice. And sure if I get bored, I can always pop over to England and see the old man for a few days. I've nothing else on anyways.'

'No, you haven't, have you,' she said, making no effort to hide the sarcasm in her voice.

He let the slight pass. She was always making snide comments about the fact that he only ever got small supporting parts. Even in his last picture, The Gregorian Affair, he had only been on screen for less than ten minutes. His name was featuring lower and lower on the roll of credits and he knew and accepted that it wouldn't be featuring at all if he wasn't married to the glamorous Sabrina Metcalfe. She knew this too and she never let him forget it. Sure, he had the looks – that was one of the reasons she had married him – but his acting ability was mediocre to say the least. One critic had likened him to an Indian totem pole – physically very attractive but wooden nevertheless. And more and more producers and directors were forming the same opinion, despite his marriage to the current queen of Hollywood. The Gregorian Affair had been over eight months ago, and he hadn't got a sniff of anything else since then. He resented her stardom, but he kept the resentment to himself. It paid all the bills and merited the best of tables in all the restaurants and deferential treatment from the maître d's. Even when she wasn't with him, he still got directed to one of the better tables. And she was on first name terms with all the top film people and the cream of Hollywood society. They were on the top of everyone's party list. So her caustic remarks every so often was a small price to pay for the lavish lifestyle and the glamourous circles they moved in.

He was half relieved when he heard the phone ring again. He went back into the house and picked up the handset. It was Brookman again. 'Richard. You tell Sabrina about the meeting?'

He glanced out to where she now sat cross legged, the script resting on her legs. 'I'm not sure she's going to be able to make it, Sam.'

He heard the exasperation in the voice. 'Can I talk to her?'

'Hold on,' he said.

He walked over to her and held out the phone. 'It's Sam. Wants to talk to you.'

She gave him a murderous look and then snatched the phone out of his hand. 'Sam darling. I was just about to call you. I don't know if I'm going to be able to make the meeting this afternoon. I have an awful headache at the moment.'

'I'm sorry to hear that, Sabrina. Hopefully it will get better soon. We would really like if you could come. It's very important. We want to go through the shooting schedule and all the travel arrangements as well. Syl is going to be there.'

She allowed herself a small smile. Syl Carpenter was playing the male lead opposite her. A six-foot four inch Canadian, he was considered one of the hottest males in all of Tinseltown and had the reputation of being a fantastic lover. He was never out of the magazines or tabloids, always with a different beauty on his arm. He was the subject of quite a few kiss and tell stories by some of the young starlets he dated but none of them criticised his love making abilities. She had never worked with him before. 'I'll do my best, Sam. I'm so excited about working with you and Syl. I think between us, we're going to produce a great movie. Hopefully the pain killers will kick in soon and I'll be able to make it. Bye, darling.' She pressed the off button before he could reply.

She flung the phone down on the towel. 'Now look what you've got me lumbered with.'

He said nothing, just stooped down and retrieved the phone. He walked towards the house. 'I'm in the study if you want to be driven."

She sat looking after him. They were married nearly five years. She had been introduced to him at a studio party. He was the quintessential Englishman and her interest in him had heightened when she found out that his father was a Lord back in England and as the only son, he would inherit the title when the old man died. To a girl who had been born a plain Mary Harte on the wrong side of the tracks in Bixby, Oklahoma, this was heady stuff and, so she had set her sights on him. He had been as equally mesmerised by her and they had soon become the golden couple on the social circuit. They had married in a blaze of studio generated publicity six months later, the queen of Hollywood marrying the future Lord Richard Tremayne of Wiltshire, England. But now five years on, she was still only Mrs. Tremayne and not Lady Tremayne of Wiltshire. The eighty-five year-old Lord Tremayne hadn't obliged by dying as quickly as both she and Richard had expected, despite all his ailments.

She closed the script and took another drink. She thought of Syl Carpenter and smiled. While he was five or six years younger than her, that shouldn't be a problem for their on-screen romance. Or for what she hoped might be an off screen one too. The thought excited her. She was blessed with a sultry look which was ageless, the one good thing she had gotten from her mother, who – despite working twelve hours a day in a truckers' roadside diner – still looked considerably less than her fifty-five years. She herself looked the same as she had in her early twenties.

She had never known her father. He had done a runner when he had learned of the pregnancy. Her infancy had been spent in a basket in the diner's kitchen and when she had started to walk, she had been left in the care of an old black woman who ran an unofficial creche in her ramshackle home. The woman had eight other kids in her care, all from single mothers working menial jobs. They were all put into a large room with only a handful of old broken toys and she had quickly learned that if you wanted something, you had to fight tooth and nail to get it. A lot of the time, if they soiled themselves, they were left dirty. At fifteen dollars a day per child, the old woman didn't consider changing diapers and cleaning bums to be part of her responsibilities.

As a teenager, she had been rebellious, missing school on a regular basis and hanging around with a small group whose main activities were shop lifting and smoking hash. But it was on one such shoplifting expedition when sixteen years of age that something happened which had changed her world around completely. Four of them had gone into a large department store called Brambles. The two boys had gone to the music department while she and another girl went to the ladies clothing department. They wore the uniform of shoplifters, loose tracksuit bottoms with overlarge hoodies. Their modus operandi was simple. One of them would ask an attendant about some item or other and while she was distracted, the other would stick an already identified pair of designer jeans or pants and top under the hoodie and go into the ladies' toilets where she would cut the security tags off the clothes and put them on under the tracksuit and hoodie. She would then pick up some other piece of clothing outside and casually walk into the fitting room, showing the item to the attendant.

Back outside again, she would shake her head and comment about it not fitting properly or something like that and leave it on the rail. She would then stroll out of the shop a short while later. It always worked because they only ever took the one outfit and they never went back to the same store. All had gone to plan, and she had emerged from the fitting room wearing a body hugging pair of gold coloured pants and a black and white polka dot blouse under the tracksuit and hoodie. All in all, $800 worth according to the tags now stuck in the toilet cistern. She had lingered for a while examining some other items while her accomplice left. They never left together. She had just reached the door when she had felt the hand on her arm. It was one of the store detectives. She was brought into the manager's office and made to take off her tracksuit and hoodie, revealing the high-class outfit underneath. And that was what had saved her. The store manager had been so taken with how well she looked that he had called in his publicity manager and after a short-whispered conversation, they had made the propositon to her. No charges would be brought against her if she agreed to pose for some shots in different outfits. Naturally, there would be no fee. She had been quick to agree, and they had then taken her to their make-up section where two of the attendants had worked on her face and hair. A few weeks later, she was the face of Brambles department store on large in-house pictures and in local newspaper ads. And that was when Imogen Meyers had come into her life.

A spinster in her early fifties, Imogen Meyers was a casting consultant to Global Pictures. She had stopped off in Bixby on her way back from a meeting in Oklahoma City and had gone into the coffee ship across the road from Brambles. While sipping her coffee, she had idly looked across the road and a large full height cut-out of Mary in the shop window had immediately caught her eye. It had caught it for two reasons. Firstly, her professional eye had spotted an image which oozed sultry sex and if that could be generated by a cardboard cut-out, she could only imagine how potent the sexiness would be in the flesh. And then the second attraction. Imogen Meyers was a dyke. A dyke who had a penchant for younger women and who had no qualms about using her powerful position to fill her bed. She had made a few enquiries and after getting the address, had called to the Harte two-bedroom house and as they say in the best of Hollywood stories, the rest was history. Although her daughter was only sixteen years of age, Tina Harte was only too happy to have the cost and the responsibility of a growing and troublesome teenage daughter taken from her and had readily agreed to Mary leaving with Meyers.

Mary Harte had only been too happy to flee her dead-end life for the bright lights of Hollywood. She was more than happy to allow the older woman to initiate her in the ways of lesbian love making and while it never held any attraction for her, she considered it a small price to pay for getting into the movies.

Meyers had changed her name to Sabrina and to her mother's maiden name of Metcalfe. She had started her movie career playing a schoolgirl who seduces her teacher and her performance had generated a lot of favourable press. She had been only too happy to allow the studio bosses to create an image based around her looks and sexiness and after only two more pictures, she was getting leading roles. Her lead role in a remake of Cleopatra had firmly established her as the sexiest actress in Hollywood and elevated her to Hollywood royalty. She ditched Meyers shortly afterwards, gotten Marty Klugman to take her on as a client and her career had been on a sharp upward curve since.

She got up and picked up the script. The meeting was a nuisance but at least Syl Carpenter would be there. No harm doing a bit of pre-filming groundwork. She would get Richard to drive her in and she could get a studio car home.

*****

14

CHAPTER 3

Syl Carpenter acknowledged the fawning welcome from the receptionist with one of his trademark gleaming white smiles and felt the smug feeling he never got tired of feeling when she looked like she was wetting herself. He strode down the corridor to the conference room and walked straight in without knocking.

There were eight other people in the room, seven of them sitting around one end of a massive sized table made of polished mahogany. He did a quick identity check.

Sam Brookman sat on one side, along with Harold Zwimmer who was the producer for this new movie. Brookman, whom he knew was thirty-nine years of age, was no more than five feet three or four inches tall with a widening girth, a bald head with a bad combover and a face in which quite a few of the blood vessels were broken. Probably from heavy drinking for which he had a reputation, though he always claimed it was a skin condition called rosacea. Beside him, Zwimmer looked like a beanpole. Around fifty years of age and over six-foot tall, he was as thin as a rake with a bullet head and gold rimmed glasses. Beside him was Ruby Lipman whom he recognised from one of his previous movies. She was the studio's head costume designer.

On the other side of the table were Stuart Flinter, his own agent and Corby Goldstein, the studio's chief financial officer. A tall man in his sixties with a head of wavy grey hair and a black woman whom he estimated was in her mid-twenties, neither of whom he knew, sat beside them.

Standing at the head of the table was Enrico C. di Angelo, head of Global Pictures and reputed to be closely associated with some leading figures in the American mafia. It was him he directed his high wattage smile at while acknowledging everyone in the room. 'Gentlemen. Miss Lipman. How we all doing?'

There were general handshakes for the men and a peck on the cheek for Lipman and the other woman who introduced herself as Faye Knight, assistant on this picture to Sam Brookman and Harold Zwimmer. The grey-haired man whom he didn't know, introduced himself as Marty Klugman, Sabrina Metcalfe's agent. di Angelo was the recipient of a great big back slapping hug which he accepted, albeit, with some rigidity. He slid into a seat beside Zwimmer.

Di Angelo looked at his watch and then at Brookman.

'You did tell her three o'clock?'

Brookman glanced at Marty Klugman and then back at di Angelo. 'Yeah, three o'clock.' He gave a shrug of the shoulders. 'She was complaining of a headache but said she would try and get here.' He looked over at Klugman again. 'You hear anything from her, Marty?'

Klugman shook his head. 'When you told me you had called her, I didn't bother ringing her.' He gave a little grin. 'But sure you know Sabrina. A watch is only a piece of ornamental jewellery to her. The fact that it tells the time wouldn't even enter her head.'

di Angelo picked up the phone beside him and punched one of the keys. 'Any sign of Sabrina Metcalfe?', his voice grumpy and impatient. He obviously got a positive answer as the 'good' that followed had less grump in it. He put down the phone. 'She's here.'

They all looked to the door as the receptionist opened it and stood aside to allow Sabrina Metcalfe sweep in. She was wearing tight black leather pants, a blood red blouse and a black leather bolero type jacket. She had a black silk scarf knotted around her neck and a pair of gypsy style hooped earrings which hung nearly down to her shoulders. Her stiletto heels were almost six inches high, but her stride was still rock steady and full of swagger. She walked straight over to di Angelo who had risen to his feet and air kissed both his cheeks and then stood back a bit and pouted. 'I'm so sorry, Enrico. Richard drove me in, but we were late leaving because his father, Lord Percival, rang. And when Percy rings, it's very hard to get the old dear off the phone.'

Syl Carpenter stood up and pulled out the chair beside him.

She gave him a beaming smile as she walked over. 'Why thank you, Syl. Such a gentleman.'

He slid it deftly under her perfectly shaped bottom as she sat down and then took his own seat again. He had never seen her in the flesh before and he had to readily admit that the live version was even sexier than the celluloid one he had watched a few weeks ago when he had heard she was going to be his co-star. He could get the strong scent of her perfume, but he knew he was smelling something else as well. She was emitting a very strong sexual pheromone which he could feel affecting him already. Mixed with the scent of the perfume, the combination was quite heady. He felt his body heat up and the blood pound in his ears. He had never experienced this feeling before, despite the endless parade of young starlets he had put through his hands and his bed. He felt a shiver of anticipation rush through his body. The two months filming in Ireland now looked a lot more promising. He just hoped she didn't bring that ponce of a husband she was married to. He shook himself to focus on di Angelo who was speaking. He was saying something to Sam Brookman about the shooting schedule.

'Six weeks max, Sam,' di Angelo said. 'Anything over that and the budget is in trouble.' He looked at Goldstein. 'Isn't that right, Corby?'

Goldstein nodded. 'We've got two other movies being shot at the same time, so we've got a major amount of the studio's cash being swallowed up in sizeable chunks, all at the one time. We just can't afford any of them to go over budget.'

Brookman looked at Zwimmer. 'I thought we agreed a two-month schedule, Harold? I don't think we can do it in six weeks.'

Zwimmer glanced at di Angelo who was now smoking a cigar, the thick blue smoke swirling in front of his face. If di Angelo said six weeks, then six weeks it had to be. He looked at Brookman. 'It's doable, Sam.'

Brookman shook his head but didn't say anything. He knew those three words translated as 'end of discussion.'

Zwimmer opened a file in front of him and took up the top sheet of paper. 'The Irish government are going to do everything they can to facilitate us. Got this letter from their Minister for Arts. ...' He glanced down at the sheet. 'A Mr. Risteard O'Duinn.' He took a while to get his mouth around the name and it came out sounding like *Ris-tarred-o-do-in*. He made a face. 'Goddamn it! Why do these guys have to write their names in that leprechaun language! Anyways, they're willing to let us use some of their army guys for the fight scenes.'

Di Angelo blew out a swirl of smoke. 'We gotta pay them or are they giving them for free?'

Zwimmer shrugged his shoulders. 'Don't know that.' He looked over at Faye Knight. 'You might check on that, Faye. Ring this guy and ask him if the soldiers come free.'

She made a note in the pad in front of her.

Zwimmer took out another sheet. 'All the travel arrangements are made. Production crew fly out in two days' time with the cast following three days later. Stan, myself, Faye here, Syl, Sabrina and some of the cast are booked into the Cloisters Hotel in Kilbracken, where most of the shooting will be done. The rest of the cast and crew will stay in the Intercontinental in Kilkenny city. It's only a thirty-minute drive from Kilbracken. The container with all the equipment, props and costumes is scheduled to arrive in Dublin port tomorrow and will be on location when the crew arrive.'

Di Angelo stubbed out his cigar and looked around the table. 'So? We all set so? Nobody got anything else?'

Sabrina Metcalfe gave him a wide smile. 'Richard was talking of coming over, Enrico.' The smile disappeared. 'I don't think that would be a good idea. He would be a distraction to me. Don't get me wrong. I would love to have him there, but I can't have anything compromise my focus on the movie and my part as Eloise. Do you think you could have a word with him, Enrico? Maybe suggest the studio doesn't think it would be a good idea. I know he respects your opinion on everything.'

She wasn't the only one to look expectantly at di Angelo. Syl Carpenter was also waiting for his reply.

Di Angelo stood up. 'I have to agree with you, Sabrina. We don't want anything getting in the way of getting this movie shot and in the can in the six weeks. It's going to mean a tight schedule for everybody so there'll be no room for husbands, wives, boyfriends or girlfriends for anybody. I'll tell him that.'

She stood up and walked over and gave him a peck on the cheek. 'Thank you, Enrico. I just don't want to have any distractions doing this movie, even if it is my darling husband. It's such a great script and I just love the part of Eloise. She's so ....so me.'

Zwimmer closed his file and stood up. 'Right so. We meet here at the studio in five days' time. We fly out from LAX at 9.30 so everybody should be here by 6.' He gave a grin. 'I know it's an early start but with just a six-week shooting schedule, it won't be the only one.'

Marty Klugman came over to Sabrina. 'You need me to do anything, Sabrina?'

She shook her head. 'No, Marty. Not for now anyways. I'm happy with the contract. The only thing I'm not sure of is this hotel in whatever the name of that place is. I'm told they don't have suites so if the room they give me is not to my liking, I'll be looking to move somewhere else.'

'I wouldn't make too much of a deal about it, Sabrina,' Klugman said. 'You're flying first class, you're going to be chauffeured to and from the set and if you don't mind me saying, your fee is substantially bigger than Carpenter's. And from what I've seen on their website, it's quite a good hotel. Has a four-star rating.'

She was about to say something else but stopped as Carpenter came over after finishing his conversation with his own agent. He beamed at Sabrina. 'I just want to tell you, Sabrina, that I consider it a great privilege to be starring in this film with you.' He took her hand and kissed it and then looked up with hooded eyes. 'I just know we can produce something great together.' His voice said he was talking about the film, but his look implied he was referring to something else. She felt a frisson of sexual excitement. Richard was probably the worst lover she ever had, with no imagination and very little staying power. And lately, he had been having problems with erectile dysfunction. The only thing he could maintain stiff now was his upper lip. The prospect of locking legs with her virile co-star was something she was looking forward to. But it would be on her terms and not his. She would pull the strings, not him. After all, she was the queen of Hollywood. The woman countless men around the world queued up to see on the silver screen and then dreamed about when they went home. The face and body they focussed their minds on when making love to their plain looking and shapeless wives. Women around the world should be thanking her instead of being jealous of her. It was her image which gave their husbands the libido they brought to their beds. She looked at him, the gleaming white toothed smile still on his lips. She gave him a much tighter one. 'I'm sure I will bring out the best in you. As I do with all my leading men.' He could read into that whatever he liked. She tapped Marty Klugman, who had his back to them and was now in a conversation with Corby Goldstein. When he turned around, she said. 'My headache's coming back. Will you bring me home, Marty?'

She didn't wait for an answer, turning on her high heels and walking briskly to the door.

*****

CHAPTER 4

Ratser Whelan picked a dried wizened boogie from his nose, studied it closely for a few seconds and then flicked it off the tip of his index finger with his thumb. Thirty-three years of age and a criminal all his life, he had been in and out of prison since the age of 15. He had a three-day stubble on his small ferret face and his long black hair was greasy and matted looking. He was wearing blue denim jeans and a black leather jacket over a black t-shirt which had a large skull and bones emblazoned on the front. He looked at the other four men lounging in various positions around the room.

Danny Corbett was sitting in the opposite armchair to his, one jean clad leg arched over the arm. His stockinged foot dangled loosely over the side, his big toe poking out through a hole in the wool sock. He was twenty-nine, over six feet tall but didn't boast an ounce of surplus flesh. His body was muscled and toned looking and he would be considered good looking were it not for the large strawberry birthmark which ran from under his right eye to the corner of his mouth. He had a smoking cigarette dangling from his lips with about an inch of ash ready to drop off and disappear into the thick carpet pile like the few before.

He had a rubber ball in one hand which he was squeezing in and out, his finger action regular and constant, like a metronome.

Sprawled full length on the couch was Fatty McGivney. Forty-five on his next birthday, he was only a little over the five-foot mark but what he lacked in height, he more than made up for in girth. He was nearly as wide as he was high, a great big slab of hairy fat hanging down from under the green Irish soccer jersey which apart from the 3 logo, bore quite a few other markings which had nothing to do with the sponsors or Irish soccer. A few food companies could well lay claim to them though, particularly one of the ketchup companies. The preponderance of this particular garnish testified to his insatiable appetite for burgers which constituted the main part of his daily diet.

Leery O'Leary was sitting at the small breakfast counter which separated the living area from the small kitchen. He was eating his second cream eclair and his bushy beard was flecked with blobs of cream and small pastry flakes. The counter top also boasted a covering of the pastry flakes. He was thirty-four years of age, been brought up in the same block of council flats as Ratser and the two of them had mitched from the same school. Unlike his friend, Leery had yet to see the inside of a prison. He always just seemed to manage to get away from the coppers whenever a job went sour. He took off his heavy black rimmed glasses and faced over to the wall to the right of the open door leading into the hallway. Though facing the wall, he was looking directly at the fifth man in the hallway, a phone up to his ear. And that was why he was called Leery. He was as cross-eyed as Clarence, the lion similarly afflicted with errant eyeballs in the 1960's film.

The man on the phone in the hallway was Billy O'Driscoll, thirty-eight years of age and leader of the gang. He was of average height with a passable face despite the long scar running down one side, a full head of prematurely greying hair and a pencil thin moustache which he incorrectly thought made him look like Errol Flynn. But at least it was still black. His face now also sported a very worried look. He too was a lifelong criminal but like Leery, he had never gotten caught either. He now spoke with a heavy Dublin accent. 'I fuckin' told you. You'll get your money. I just need a couple more weeks.'

Leery watched him pace up and down the short hallway. He knew O'Driscoll owed one of the capital's main drug dealers for some supplies which the cops had subsequently found when they stopped the car belonging to the gang's sixth member, Lugser Brennan. And Lugser was now cooling his heels in Mountjoy, waiting for what would be his twelfth appearance in court, despite being only eighteen years of age. This would be his first as an adult, so they expected he would be out of commission for another five or six years at least. But O'Driscoll still had to pay for the drugs. That was the unwritten law. Failure to do so could be fatal. Particularly when you were dealing with Arthur Spence.

They all looked over to him as he came back into the room and slammed the door. Leery spoke to him though his eyes were looking at Ratser. 'Well? What did he say?'

O'Driscoll glowered at him. 'What the fuck do you think he said? He wants his fuckin' money and he doesn't give a rat's arse how we get it. We have two weeks.'

Danny Corbett unhooked his leg from over the arm of the chair, scrambled the Nike trainer over with his foot and, after pulling the sock out a bit and folding it over the exposed toe, pulled it on. He looked over at O'Driscoll. 'We could hit a few houses.'

The look he got was laced with contempt. 'For what? Fuckin'

peanuts. We could do the whole of fuckin' Howth and we still wouldn't get enough.'

McGivney pulled himself into a sitting position. 'How about a jeweller?'

O'Driscoll shook his head. 'Wouldn't be able to fence it in time. No – this has to be a big payoff with a short turnaround.'

Ratser started picking at his nose again. 'How about one of them bankers? Grab their family and hold them until they grab the dosh from the bank.'

It was O'Leary who answered. 'Too risky now. All them feckers are being watched closely. And their houses are wired straight into the cop shops.'

There was silence for a few minutes and then O'Driscoll broke it. 'Well? Has none of ye any ideas? If we don't pay Spence, it's not just me who's fucked!'

Danny Corbett looked around him. 'Any of you see the news last night? About that film they're going to make down in Kilkenny?'

McGivney grunted. 'Yeah. So what's that got to with this and the price of monkey nuts?'

Corbett grinned. 'It's a Hollywood crowd making it. Not your bog Irish film makers. And the one coming over to take the lead part is Sabrina Metcalfe.'

Ratser whistled. 'Jeez, I'd love to give that one a touch of the old Whelan feelin'. She's some sexy broad.'

Leery sniggered. 'You! Are you fuckin' mad or what! I'd say she'd suck you in like a hoover and blow you out in little bubbles.'

O'Driscoll hammered a fist off the counter. 'For fuck sake! Will ye listen to yerselves! Spence is threatening to cut our balls off and then fit us all out with wooden suits and all you bollocks' are doin' is swopping notes on some bit of quiff from Hollywood.'

Corbett shook his head. 'Not just any bit of quiff, boss. She's one of the top actresses in the movies at the moment and worth an awful lot of money to her studio. And she's married to an English guy whose father is a Lord something or other over in England.'

O'Driscoll looked hard at him. 'Are you suggestin' what I think you're suggestin'? That we lift her and look for a ransom?'

'Why not?' Corbett said. 'Nobody would be expecting that and I'm sure it would be easy enough to grab her.'

McGivney snorted. 'And after we've grabbed her. What do we do with her then? The whole fucking place would be crawling with cops. We'd be in bracelets before we got halfway back to Dublin.'

Corbett grinned and tapped the side of his nose. 'But we don't have to take her back to Dublin, do we?' He looked over at O'Driscoll. 'Remember Lugser was telling us about an old step uncle he has somewhere in Kilkenny. The IRA sympathiser. Didn't he tell us once about him hiding some activists from the cops for over a week. A secret cellar he has under one of his cow sheds.'

O'Driscoll's eyes widened. 'Jesus, you're right. He did.'

He looked at Corbett, a smile forming on his lips. 'It's visitin' time in the Joy tomorrow. You get your ass in there and find out all you can from Lugser. Where this old uncle lives, what he's like and anything he knows about this secret cellar.'

He switched his attention to McGivney. 'You can work a computer, Fatty. You get on and find out all you can about this actress one and this film they're makin'. I want to know everything there is to know about her and it.' He clapped his hands. 'Right lads. This could be it. We meet here tomorrow evening at five. After Corby has seen Lugser. And then we plan.'

Ratser laughed, his leering look making him even more rat faced. 'Yeah. Plan to snatch a snatch.'

O'Driscoll cut him with a look. 'She's a package, Ratser. Just a fuckin' package. We grab her, hold her and then we sell her back. That's it. Now, who's for a pint? All of a sudden, I'm feelin' a lot better.'

*****

23

CHAPTER 5

Gerry lugged the black plastic bag up onto the counter. Freda Bannon came out through the strip plastic curtain and grinned at him. 'Howya, Scobie.'

'Bit of auld laundry here for you, Freda,' he said. 'A few shirts, pants and jackets for washing and a few underpants that need the skid marks removed.'

She made a face. 'Ye can fuck off with yer dirty skivvies, Scobie Tierney.'

He laughed. 'Arra I'm only coddin' you, Freda. There's none of them in there.'

She pulled the bag down off the counter. 'Well thank God for that. You should see some of the stuff we get here. There's some right dirty fuckers out there. And who they are would surprise you.'

She leaned over the counter and then glanced around as if checking that there was no one else in earshot. 'Ye know yer man Andrew Horan, the councillor.' Her voice dropped lower. 'He brings in his skivvies. Now there's no skid marks on them but there are other silvery stains on the front, if you get my drift. Sometimes they look like a clatter of snails had done a few laps around them. And the fronts can be a bit hard with all that stuff dried in. He's a fuckin' wanker. And I mean that literally.'

Gerry grinned. 'Maybe he was a bit of a boyo when he was young, and his father told him to take himself in hand and he misinterpreted what his father meant.'

She snorted. 'Yeah, right. He should get himself a woman and give his hand a rest. Sure he's only what? Early fifties?'

Orla Hicky came out from the back. 'What are ye two whispering about?'

'Handy Andy,' her friend said. She grinned at Gerry. 'We call him that here. You can guess why. I was just telling Scobie he should get himself a woman and give his hand a rest.'

'That prick,' Orla said. 'You'd want to be fierce desperate to go out with him. He's a fucking creep. He was coming out of the Cloisters when we were going in the other night. Ye should have seen the way he eyed us all up and down. I'd say the minute he got in his car, he was at it. And it wouldn't have been the gear stick he was pullin' at. And I've heard, he does it with fellas too.'

'How'd it go in the Cloisters?' Gerry asked. 'Did ye have a good night.'

'Arra it was all right, I suppose,' she said, looking to her friend who nodded.

'Most of us were pissed anyways. Don't remember half of it.'

'And how about the body builder? Chloe whatever her name was. How did she get on?'

Freda Bannon gave him a sly look. 'You think you missed out there, is that it, Scobie? Well ye needn't worry. She puked her ring up all over herself before we even got to the hotel and then conked it in the back of the bus. She was still snorin' her head off and smellin' like shite when the bus left at three, heading back to Dublin.'

Gerry mentally paid himself his bet.

'You hear about this movie that's being made here, Scobie?' Orla asked.

'Yeah' he said. 'Sure the whole town is talking about it. I hear they've booked the top floor of the Cloisters and also a good few rooms in the Intercontinental in Kilkenny. I heard down at the station that O'Duinn, the Minister for Arts, is coming down for a civic reception the council are throwing for all the Hollywood bigwigs tomorrow.'

Bannon snorted. 'Feckers will be tripping over each other trying to get their mugs in the papers. 'She laughed. 'I'd say when Handy Andy sees yer woman, Sabrina Metcalfe or yer man, Syl Carpenter, his hand'll be going like a jackhammer.' She laughed louder. 'Jackhammer. Get it?'

Hickey laughed. 'Yeah. When you see his photo in the paper, I'll bet he'll have his hand in his pocket and his face will be all scrunched up.'

He saw her look behind him and then she put a hand to her mouth to stifle a laugh. 'Oh fuck!'

Freda Bannon let out a long snigger and then she clamped a hand to her mouth as well.

Gerry turned around to see what they were reacting to.

'Detective Sergeant Tierney. How are you?' Councillor Andrew Horan said as he closed the door behind him.

Gerry glanced at the two women. Their cheeks were puffed out, both obviously struggling to keep from laughing.

'I'm fine, councillor,' he replied and then coughed to hide the little burst of laughter he himself couldn't keep in.

'And how are my two favourite ladies?' Horan said as he left the sportsbag up on the counter.

Orla Hickey was the first to compose herself. 'Ah we're fine, Mr. Horan. We were just talking about this movie that's going to be made here.'

Oh yes,' he said. 'That's going to be something, isn't it? The handsome Mr. Carpenter and the gorgeous Miss Metcalfe. Hollywood royalty no less. And all here in our own little Kilbracken. Great for the town. Just great.'

'You know what the movie's about?' Freda Bannon asked.

He tapped the side of his nose with his finger. 'Can't say anything yet, my dear. But all will be revealed tomorrow when we have the civic reception. The minister wants to be able to announce it himself.'

'Arra give us a clue,' Orla Hickey said. 'Sure it's not the third secret of Fatima, is it?'

He gave her a condescending smile. 'Well I'll tell you this much. It's going to be a period piece. I can't say any more than that.' He nodded to the bag. 'Do you think you could have those ready for me tomorrow morning? It would be great if you could.'

Orla pulled the bag in front of her. 'What is it? Shirts and things?'

'Yes,' he said. 'A half dozen shirts, a couple of t-shirts, a few pairs of socks and some underwear.'

She looked over at Freda with raised eyebrows. 'Nothing too hard there so, is there, Freda?'

'No,' Once there's no major stains, should be all right for tomorrow morning.'

Horan gave them a smile. 'That's great, girls. I'll pop in around ten.' He gave Gerry a pat on the back. 'See you around, Tierney.'

He went out and had no sooner closed the door when the two women burst out laughing. 'Nothing too hard there so,' Freda said. 'I nearly wet meself when you said that.'

Orla gave her a friendly slap on the arm. 'And when you mentioned stains, God, I thought I'd burst out laughing right into his face.'

Gerry stood grinning at the two of them. He was just glad he washed his own smalls. 'Right, girls. I'm off before ye reveal any more dark laundry secrets. I'll pick my stuff up in a couple of days.'

'See ya, Scobie,' they said in unison.

He was just back outside when Boss O'Connor came walking up, his two big dogs straining at the leashes and pulling him at a much faster pace than his bulky body was normally used to.

Horan jumped into the roadway as they passed by him and then stood looking back, shaking his head. He would have to check up and see if O'Connor had a license for them. Knowing him, he probably hadn't. And then he thought a bit more about it. Boss O'Connor was not a man to get on the wrong side of. He had a hair trigger temper and never let what he considered a slight or criticism go unanswered. There were plenty in Kilbracken and further afield who had found that out, much to their regret. He wasn't going to be another one. He walked off, his thoughts turning to the film actress he would be close to in the morning at the civic reception. He felt his face flush.

The prospect of being in her company was making him a bit light headed. She had to be one of the sexiest looking woman on the planet. Sultry sinful looks, a great body and those legs that just seemed to go on and on. He stuck his hand into his pocket and through the hole he had deliberately poked in the lining.

O'Connor stopped at the pole outside the laundry and tied the dogs to it. He wiped the sweat from his brow. 'Jaysus, boss. These two fuckers have me worn out. Normally I'd bring them out to the forest and let them run loose but the entrance is closed off this morning and there were a few security guys there. Told me that it's out of bounds for the next four or five weeks. Whatever the fuck that's all about. You any idea, boss? '

Gerry shook his head. 'That's news to me. These security guys? Were they local?'

O'Connor shook his head. 'Naw. They were from Dublin. Armour Security according to the name on their jackets. I was goin' to tell them to fuck off. That it was our forest, but there were six of them.' He grinned, displaying his stained teeth. 'And that might be a bit too much, even for me, boss.'

'I'll check it out,' Gerry said. 'Could have something to do with this film that's starting here soon. Maybe the forest is going to be part of it.'

They both looked as Billy Hamilton, a retired postman, came over to them. Billy had a dreadful stammer and people did their best to avoid him because it could take him five minutes just to say hello. It was said he knew everybody's secrets, but most people found hearing a juicy titbit just wasn't worth the frustrating wait. But they were caught now.

'Heh-heh-heh hell-le- le- lo ma -ma- ma- ma-men. D-d-d-did ye see -see-see-see a-a-a-a-Alfie t-t-t-t-t-Tum-mel-mel-melty? I wa-wa-wa-was to m-m-m-m-meet h-him ar-ar-ar-around h-h-here.'

Boss looked at Gerry and grinned and then looked back at the old man, a serious look on his face. 'Well now, boss. He was here when you started talking but I don't know where the hell he is now.'

The old man gave him a scathing look. 'T-t-t-t-think yo-yo-yo-you're a sm-sm-sm-smart a-a-a-a-arse, d-d-d-don't yo-yo-yo-you, b-b-b-b-boss.'

'Arra I'm only teasin' ye, boss,' O'Connor said. 'Sure me own auld man had a bit of trouble with the auld words as well. The ma told me it took him five minutes to say, 'I do' when they got married. She thought he was changin' his mind, it took him so long. He just managed to get it out before her auld lad thought the same and bate the shite out of him.'

Gerry could see that Boss' attempt at appeasing the old man wasn't working.

'I saw him about fifteen minutes ago, Billy,' he said. 'He was going into the Perk Me Up coffee shop just up the road there. He's probably still there.'

'T-t-t-t-ta-ta-ta-thanks, Sco-Sco-Sco-Scob-b-b-bie.'

He threw another baleful look at O'Connor and then shuffled off down the footpath.

Gerry grinned over at Boss. 'Don't think Billy will be adding you to his Christmas list.'

Boss was untying the dogs. 'Arra I'll drop him in a bottle of poitin one of the days. That'll take the starch out of his lip.' He yanked the leashes. 'Come on ye pair of feckers. I'll get ye back to the house before ye pull the fuckin' arms from me shoulders. I'll see ya, boss.'

Gerry watched as he took off back down the footpath, the two big dogs again pulling hard, people stepping quickly onto the roadway to avoid them. It was a toss-up which of them people found more frightening, Boss or the dogs. But Gerry would never hear a word against Boss, or the dogs. Only for them, he might not even be around now. They had saved him from the East European heavies who had him at their mercy in the same forest only a few months earlier. When he had been investigating the trafficking of women from Eastern Europe into Ireland. He grinned as he saw another couple grip each other and hop out onto the road to avoid the two straining dogs and their lumbering owner. Whistling tunelessly, he headed off for the station.

*****

CHAPTER 6

The flight landed at Dublin airport at 8 o'clock on the Saturday night. They had flown from Los Angeles to London and then London to Dublin. And now they had another hour or so by car, to get to Kilbracken.

Sabrina was feeling tired and cranky from all the travelling and the fairly large amount of champagne she had consumed on the transatlantic flight wasn't helping either.

Syl Carpenter came over to where she stood inside the arrivals building. 'Sam and Harold have gone to sort out the luggage. They said we should clear immigration and then wait for them inside. They're arranging for us to exit through a side entrance so that we can avoid the public area.'

Sabrina nodded. She just couldn't face any more requests for autographs or photos. It hadn't been too bad on the Los Angeles to London flight. A few of the other passengers in first class had come up to her but it had all been civilised. But not so the flight from London to Dublin. There had been a technical problem with the private charter and with no other aircraft available for a few hours, the decision had been made to take a commercial flight. There had been no first class and she had never felt as uncomfortable in a plane before. As plain Mary Harte, she had never been on a plane and as Sabrina Metcalfe, she had never flown anything other than first class so flying economy was a whole new experience to her. And it was an experience she hoped she would never have to repeat again. It was like being in a sardine can. To make matters worse, there had been a constant procession of people up to herself and Syl looking for autographs and to have photos taken with them. By the time they had landed, her nerves were frazzled, and she was ready to hit the next person who approached her.

She reached the immigration counter and passed her passport to the man sitting in the cubicle. He looked at it and then at her, a great big smile on his face. 'Miss Metcalfe. You're very welcome to Ireland. I've always been a big fan.'

She forced herself to return the smile but hers was thin and fleeting. 'Thank you,' she said. She took the passport and put it back in her bag. Syl followed behind and when he too got the big welcome, he accepted it with a lot more grace.

Faye Knight came over to them. 'The luggage is all loaded and already on its way and the cars are outside. If you follow me, I'll take you to them.' They followed her out through a door marked 'Private'. It brought them into an office which was empty and when they passed through another door, they were in a short corridor and when they passed through the door at the end of that, they were outside the building. Sam Brookman and Harold Zwimmer were already in one of the three Mercedes cars which stood parked in a line just outside. Behind them was a luxury coach which would take the rest of the cast and crew who had still to exit the arrivals building through normal channels.

Faye Knight opened the back door of the second car. 'This is for you two. Harriet, Jerome and Harvey will take the other one and the rest of us will be on the bus.'

Harriet Taylor, Jerome Scott and Harvey Rockwell were the three main supporting actors whose status also merited special transport.

Sabrina stood at the open door. The car in front had just pulled away. She looked at Syl Carpenter who stood behind her, waiting for her to get in. 'Would you mind, Syl darling, if I had the back to myself. I'm just so tired. You don't mind travelling up front with the driver, do you?'

Carpenter gave a little bow. 'Of course not, Sabrina. You get in and make yourself comfortable.'

When she slid in, he closed the door and then got into the front passenger seat.

The driver, a man of about forty-five, glanced back at her and then turned to Carpenter. 'We good to go so, sir?'

'As we say in Hollywood – sorry, I didn't get your name?'

'It's Sean,' the driver said. 'Sean Donovan.'

'Well, Sean Donovan. As we say in Hollywood, that's a wrap.'

He sat back as the driver eased the car out and soon they were out of the airport and speeding down the brightly lit road.

Sean Donovan couldn't believe he was sitting in the same car as Sabrina Metcalfe and Syl Carpenter. Particularly Sabrina Metcalfe. Like a lot of men, he had lusted after her on the screen. And here she was lying across the back seat of his car. Well, not quite his car – it belonged to the chauffeur service he worked for – but tonight it was his car. And with Syl Carpenter sitting right beside him. He sneaked a sideways glance. The big man had his eyes closed and his head back against the headrest. Certainly as handsome in real life as he was on the screen. He reached up and slightly tilted his rearview mirror until the prone figure snuggled down on the back seat filled it. She too had her eyes closed. He felt the blood pound in his head. God, she was so beautiful. Even more beautiful in real life. And so sexy. And her voice. When she had spoken to Carpenter. Slightly deep but oh so sensuous. Kind of like Lauren Bacall's voice. And even from the front seat, he could smell her perfume. A rich intense scent which only enhanced her sexiness. She was the epitome of every man's dream woman.

He quickly focussed his eyes back to the road ahead as an oncoming car flashed its headlights. He jerked the wheel roughly to correct his drift across the centre line and exhaled a relieving sigh. That's all he needed. To crash the car and be responsible for killing the sexiest woman in the world. He straightened his rearview mirror to its correct setting. He would have to settle for her scent and just knowing that she was only two feet behind him. He drove on in silence, the only sound in the car, the regular breathing of the man beside him.

An hour later, he pulled up in front of the Cloisters hotel.

Syl Carpenter felt the car stop and opened his eyes.

'We're here, sir,' the driver said.

Carpenter looked behind him. Sabrina was lying on the back seat, still asleep. He opened his door and got out and then opened the back door. 'Sabrina. Sabrina. We're here.'

Sean Donovan got out from behind the wheel and walked around to the passenger side. He wanted to see her get out of the car.

Sabrina opened her eyes. She rotated her neck a few times to try and relieve the stiffness. She could see Syl Carpenter and the driver waiting outside. She swung her legs off the seat and then slowly got out, one leg first and then the other.

Sean Donovan thought he would pass out. Her dress had ridden up her thigh and for a brief second, he had caught the glimpse of red satin. And that first leg! Long and perfectly shaped. Like a shop mannequin's. His own wife's image intruded on his mind. Dora was a size 16 with short plump legs, a big bust which was rapidly heading south and a voice which was more often than not, spouting one criticism after another at him. Not for the first time, he cursed himself for getting her pregnant all those years ago. But she hadn't been half as fat then and marrying her hadn't seemed too bad a price to pay for his lack of control. And it had been her fault anyways. She was supposed to be on the pill. But she had tricked him. And in those days, you got a woman pregnant, you married her. He had been paying for it ever since. The only thing she exercised over the years was her mouth. A two-strand programme. Eating anything and everything and bitching at him the whole time. If the rest of her body was as active as her mouth, she would be as lean as Twiggy. They had only had the one child. The accident. Dympna, now twenty-three years of age and as useless as her mother. Nearly as fat and with the same acid tongue. But at least she had moved out recently. Moved in with her boyfriend, a forklift driver in a glass making factory in Carlow. He could now have the pleasure of her moaning and whining. At least with Dora, it was just single sound. When Dympna had been at home, it had been surround sound.

He felt his legs go weak as Sabrina Metcalfe came over to him and gave him a peck on the cheek. He breathed in hard, taking in as much of her scent as he could fit into his lungs. He could smell her. Sure, he got the smell of her perfume, but he could smell her as well. A musky odour which set his heart pounding in his chest. He was disappointed when she didn't speak. To have that voice speak solely to him, well that would have been the icing on the cake.

Syl Carpenter stuck out his hand. 'Thanks for the ride, Sean Donovan.'

He shook the large hand and his own came away with a twenty euro note in it. 'Why thanks, Mr. Carpenter,' he said. But he knew the peck on the cheek was the much greater tip.

He stood watching as Carpenter took Sabrina's arm and together, they walked into the hotel. When they were out of sight, he pocketed the twenty euro note and then opened the back door and got in. He pretended to be searching the floor but put his nose to the leather seat and inhaled deeply. He could still smell her off it. He slowly got out and got in behind the wheel and drove off.

Inside, Jeremy Clarke was shaking hands with the two new arrivals and welcoming them to Kilbracken and the hotel. He had already shown Brookman and Zwimmer to their rooms. As manager, he normally wouldn't be in the hotel at such a late time, but this was Hollywood royalty. It was expected. He looked at Sabrina Metcalfe. She was certainly a stunning looking woman. Probably the best looking he had ever seen. But he was more than happy with Helga to whom he had been married for eight years now. She was enough woman for him.

He smiled at the two. 'If you're ready, I'll show you to your rooms.' He led them over to the lift and pressed the button for the top floor. He opened the door to room 415, the biggest bedroom in the hotel and stood aside to let her pass in. It was the one they gave to newlyweds for the night of their wedding. It boasted a large king size bed, two comfortable easy chairs, a writing table and straight-backed chair, a large dressing table and padded stool, a 48-inch television on one wall, a walk-in wardrobe and a large bathroom with bath and separate waterfall shower. The room also had a fairly large mini bar which was fully stocked. There was a large colourful vase of flowers on the writing table along with a bowl of fruit, a large bottle of champagne and a plate of handmade chocolates, all compliments of the hotel. All her luggage – six large suitcases and a small vanity case – was neatly stacked against one of the walls, delivered earlier from the airport. He watched as she did a quick appraisal and it was evident by her facial expression that she wasn't overly impressed. He handed her the key card. 'Anything you need, Miss Metcalfe. Please do not hesitate to ring down to reception.'

He left her standing in the room and closed the door.

Syl Carpenter lay lounging against the wall in the hallway, waiting to be shown to his room.

He opened the door to room 417 and stood aside as the actor went in. It was a smaller room than 415 but did have the same king size bed, dressing table and stool, large television and a bathroom which had the waterfall shower but did not have a bath. It also did not have a walk-in wardrobe but had instead, a standard built in unit with a garment rail on one side and four large shelves on the other. There was a small table with two padded chairs with arms. There were no flowers on the table, but it did have the bowl of fruit, the bottle of champagne and the chocolates. The four suitcases were lined up against the wall. He handed over the key. 'Anything we can do for you, Mr. Carpenter, please do not hesitate to call.'

Carpenter nodded. 'Will do. Might just have me a glass of that champagne there and then I'm hitting the sack. It's been one hell of a long day.'

Jeremy Clarke wished him a good night and went out and closed the door. It had been a long day for him as well.

Downstairs, he walked over to the reception desk where Tommy Reilly, the night manager was sitting. He looked up as Jeremy came over. 'All tucked in for the night?'

'Well they're in their rooms,' Jeremy said. 'Hopefully they're all tired and will go straight to bed. Mr. Brookman, Mr. Zwimmer and Miss Knight have all asked for an alarm call at 7.30. Miss Metcalfe and

Mr. Carpenter didn't so don't call them. The others should be arriving soon. There's three more coming by car and five more from the bus. The list of names is there. I'll let you look after them. Now, I'm going home. I've been here since 8.30 this morning. Unless there's a major problem, don't call me either.'

'No bother, Jeremy,' Reilly said. 'What time's the civic reception ?'

'Three o'clock. The councillors and the other invited guests should be here around two thirty and then the Hollywood brigade will make their entrance at three. Should be an interesting spectacle.'

'You want me to come in early?'

The manager shook his head. 'No. There's no need, Tommy. I'll see you.' He paused as the door slid back and then walked out.

*****

CHAPTER 7

Gerry arrived into the station at half past nine. He'd had a quiet day yesterday, staying in the station all day and clearing up a lot of outstanding paperwork, something he hated doing. But at least it was done now. Flann was already at his desk as was Elsie Masterson who was on the phone.

Gerry walked over and sat down beside him. 'Anything stirring, Flann? Need to get out and about today. Nearly went mental yesterday. Think I've blisters on me arse from sitting down all day.'

'Nothing that needs your expertise, Scobie,' his friend replied. 'Think the local felons and scumbags are taking a bit of a break. It's been very quiet lately. Not that I'm complaining mind.'

Gerry nodded to the stairs. 'Doyle in?'

Flann nodded. 'Think so. His car is here anyways.'

Gerry stood up. 'Arra feck it! I'm going to Supermacs for a fry up. If he comes asking about me, tell him I'm gone out to check up on something.'

'Check up on what? What'll I tell him if he asks?'

'Tell him I'm gone to take a statement from Billy Hamilton. That he rang in with a complaint.'

Flann laughed. 'Feck sake, Scobie! Billy Hamilton? Sure a statement from him would take the whole day.'

'Met him yesterday,' Gerry said. 'I was talking to Boss O'Connor when he came up and asked us if we'd seen Alfie Tumelty.' He laughed. 'Boss told him he was there when he started talking but he hadn't a clue where he was now. Billy was f-f-f-f-f-feckin' m-m-m-m-mad.'

'I'd say that was funny, God love him,' Flann said. 'He gets very embarrassed about it at times, poor bugger. He drinks in Harty's Bar and he doesn't ask anymore. Just points to the tap or if it's a short, to the bottle. It was Alice Harty's suggestion. She got pissed off standing around waiting while he ordered.'

Gerry grinned. 'Isn't Billy very religious? Wonder what Father O'Mahoney does when he goes to confession. And he would be just the type to go every feckin' week.'

'Arra sure what would he have to tell?' Flann said. 'I'd say it's only as long as it takes him to say, 'Bless me Father for I haven't sinned.'

'Well he called Boss a smart arse yesterday. That would be nearly a mortal sin to him. He's probably been and confessed it already.'

Elsie Masterson came over. 'What are you two talking about?'

Gerry looked at Flann and winked and then as one, they said, 'B-B-B-B-B-B-Billy Ha-Ha-Ha-Ha-m-m-m-milt-t-t-ton.'

'Bloody bastards the pair of you,' She said, although she was grinning herself. 'You shouldn't be slagging off poor Billy like that. Mocking is catching you know.' She pulled in a chair from a nearby desk and sat down. 'I hear the Hollywood crowd arrived last night. Either of you see any of them?'

Flann shook his head. 'Not me anyways. Didn't even know they were coming last night.' He looked at Gerry. 'Did you know, Scobie?'

'Yeah. Jeremy Clarke had told me. But I think it was late and it was supposed to be all hush hush. Not that I'd be too bothered anyways.'

Masterson raised her eyebrows. 'Not even for the beautiful and sexy Miss Sabrina Metcalfe? Apparently, the woman that most men in the world would like to sleep with if they got a choice.'

Flann sniggered. 'If I got that one into bed, I wouldn't be doing much sleeping, and that's for sure.'

'And how about you, Scobie?' Masterson said. 'Do you think you could withstand the alluring Miss Metcalfe – or should I more correctly say – Mrs. Richard Tremayne?'

Gerry made a face. 'Don't suppose I'd kick her out to make room for a hot water bottle.'

He stood up and winked at Flann. 'Well I'm off to check out that complaint we received. Should be back in an hour or so.'

But he didn't get too far as Inspector Freddie Doyle, now acting superintendent at the station, came down the stairs. He was only in the temporary position two weeks and would return to his permanent post in the Santry station in Dublin as soon as someone was appointed full time. He nodded to the three and then addressed Gerry. 'Have you much on today, Tierney?'

Gerry shook his head. 'Not really, sir. Just heading out now to follow up on a complaint. Shouldn't take more than an hour or so. Nothing else after that.'

'Good. I want you to attend this civic reception that the council are holding for the film crowd in the Cloisters this afternoon. Be our representative there.'

Gerry feigned disinterest. 'Do we have to be at it, sir? It hasn't really anything to do with us, has it?'

Doyle laughed. 'I thought you would be jumping at the chance to rub shoulders with the Hollywood set. We have to establish relations between ourselves and them, their security people and the local security liaison they have hired. He will actually be the conduit between us and the others. He's one of your own in fact. Served a long time at this station.'

Gerry gave a wide grin. 'Eamon Clancy? Our ex-superintendent. Sure it has to be him.'

Doyle shook his head. 'No. That's not the name. It's a Dick Larkin.'

'Ah for feck sake!' Gerry said. 'Moby feckin' Dick! And they've hired him as their security liaison?'

Doyle gave him a surprised look. 'It's him all right. I believe he was a detective Garda here. You don't seem too impressed.'

Gerry snorted. 'That feckin' Luder has a body the size of an elephant and a brain the size of a pea. He's as useful as a fork in a bowl of consommé soup.'

'Well be that as it may,' Doyle said. 'He's the man we have to deal with and I'm appointing you as our liaison officer, so you will just have to put up with it.'

He turned to go and then turned back. 'The reception is at three.'

The others watched as he went back up the stairs.

Flann slapped Gerry on the back and laughed. 'Look on the bright side, Scobie. Sure you can just ignore Moby the same way you did all that time he was here. And sure he'll probably be too busy mooning at all the women and stuffing his face at the catering truck.'

'Don't know about that,' Elsie Masterson said. 'Moby will be so full of his own importance, he'll want to be seen to be the main man. He'll be eying the women all right and eating anything that isn't nailed down, but he'll also be looking to impress. You mightn't get it all your own way with him now, Scobie.'

'Feck him,' Gerry said. 'The day Moby Dick Larkin gets the better of me, I'll shave me head, tie a knot in me willie and go off and join one of them enclosed monasteries. Now, I'm off to Supermacs.'

'I thought you were going off to investigate a complaint?' Masterson said.

'I am,' he answered. 'Me feckin' stomach's been complaining all morning that it needs a proper bit of grub. And that's one complaint I take very seriously.'

Five minutes later, he walked through the door of the fast food restaurant. The place was virtually empty with only two tables occupied, a quartet in builders' garb at one and two women at the other, probably getting together for a natter after doing the school run. The four builders were tucking into full plates of sausages, rashers, egg, beans, black pudding and hash browns. The two women were sipping from large cardboard cups of coffee.

'Yes, Scobie?' Tina Dolan said as he got to the counter. 'The usual, is it?'

He grinned at her. 'Arra ye know me too well, Tina. Stick on an extra egg as well. Instead of the hash browns.'

'I'll drop it down to you,' she said and then turned away and picked up one of the plates stacked on the counter behind her.

He sat down at one of the tables.

She was out to him a few minutes later with his food. 'You heard about this film they're making here?' she said as she left the tray down on the table.

He took the large plate off the tray and she took off the small plate of toast and the cardboard cup of tea and put them down on the table along with a few sachets of salt. 'Is the whole bloody town talking about this feckin' film?'

She stood with the empty tray in her hand. 'Well you have to admit, Scobie. It's the biggest thing to ever happen in Kilbracken. And it has your man Syl Carpenter in it.' Her face took on a dreamy look. 'He's a fine thing, isn't he? He could throw a leg over me anytime.'

Gerry stabbed his knife into one of the eggs and then speared a sausage, dipped it into the oozing yoke and then stuffed the lot into his mouth. He looked up at her as he chewed. 'And what would Larry have to say about that?'

She sniffed. 'Might just focus his friggin' attention.'

Gerry grinned. 'Yeah. How long is it now? Must be four or five years.'

'It's bloody six,' she said. She held up her left hand. 'Still no ring.'

Gerry took a bite of toast and then another mouthful of egg, sausage and pudding. 'Maybe it's time to review your relationship, Tina. I don't think Larry'll do anything 'til his mother passes. He's not just under her thumb, he's locked tight in her fist. And there's little sign of her grip easing.'

She gave a deep sigh. 'I know all that, Scobie. And the old biddy could live another ten or twenty years, even if she is almost eighty. But I'm thirty-seven next birthday and there isn't a queue of fellas to my door. It mightn't be an ideal relationship but at least it is a relationship. And Larry's all right when he's away from the old hag. And I know if she signed over the farm to him tomorrow, he'd marry me straight away.' She gave a little laugh. 'But there's little chance of that. Just have to keep praying for a heart attack, won't I! Or else, for one of her bulls to do me a favour. But I think they're even afraid of her as well.'

'Land,' Gerry said. 'It has an awful lot to answer for in this country. In a lot of cases, it grows nothing but misery.'

'You're right there, Scobie. You want more tea?'

He shook his head. 'No thanks. I'm good.'

She gave another deep sigh and walked back behind the counter.

Gerry finished of the last of his food and then drained the last of the tea. He pushed back his chair a bit and smacked his stomach with both hands. The complaint had been satisfactorily dealt with.

He walked back up to the counter and handed Tina a tenner. 'That was lovely, Tina. Keep the change.'

'Thanks, Scobie,' she said. 'See you soon.'

He walked to the door. Two of the builders were still sitting at the table, newspapers spread out on the table in front of them. As he passed, he could see that both papers were open at the racing pages. Men after his own heart. He could see the other two outside, lounging against the wall, cigarettes in their hands. The two school runners were still sipping their coffee, heads close together, probably talking about Syl Carpenter and what they would like to do to him.

He went out and headed back towards the station.

*****

CHAPTER 8

The ballroom in the Cloisters had a good crowd in it when Gerry arrived a few minutes before three o'clock. He recognised most of them. There was a row of empty seats on a raised platform with a microphone stand to the front. Close beside, were two long tables covered with bottles of red and white wine, bottles of mineral water, a coffee and tea dispenser, plates of savouries and glasses, cups and saucers and small plates. Four hotel staff stood behind the tables, but they stood with their hands behind their backs, their stance telling people that they were not ready to serve anything yet. The odd person who didn't get this subliminal message, were given a shake of the head when they requested a glass of wine. Nothing would be served until the guests had arrived and the speeches were over.

He smiled when he saw Andrew Hogan. Handy Andy! You really didn't know people, did you. The chairman of the council, Tim Delaney was there, dressed in a smart blue suit with a snow-white shirt and a tie which featured a big statue of liberty in the centre. His wife was beside him, dressed in a long sequinned blue gown which was, in Scobie's opinion, much too formal for the occasion. He saw other members of the council with their wives, none of whom were as formally dressed as Alice Delaney, and some of the more prominent business men including Phillip Tattinger, head man at the American Creufield Engineering Company, one of Kilbracken's biggest employers. They too were accompanied by their partners. Father O'Mahoney was chatting to Doctor Mallory and he saw Rachel Kelly the hairdresser, talking to one of the councillor's wives. He did a double take when he saw his landlady, Ms. Timoney, standing alone on one side of the room. He walked over to her. 'Didn't think this would be your cup of tea, Ms. Timoney.'

She gave him a little smile. 'Normally it wouldn't, detective sergeant. But I was told that there may be some travelling over and back by some of the film crowd and as you say, that is my cup of tea.' She glanced around the room, her gaze stopping on Rachel Kelly. 'I see that creature you had the misfortune to dally with once, is here,' her voice dripping with disdain.

Gerry felt his face blush. He had shifted her one night in Aces casino when he had been as full as a bingo bus. And if that wasn't bad enough, they had run in to Ms. Timoney as they were leaving his flat the next morning and the two women had exchanged sharp words. Not one of his most pleasant recollections by any means. He moved to change the topic of conversation. 'You a moviegoer, Ms. Timoney?'

'Definitely not, detective sergeant. Films nowadays are so crude. They all seem now to be just full of bad language, nudity and sex. Not like in the old days when there was honest to God decency. Films like 'It's A Wonderful Life' and 'How Green Was My Valley and 'White Christmas.' Good wholesome entertainment.'

Gerry was sorry he had asked. She looked like she was ready to go on one of her moralistic rants. He felt a surge of relief when Father O'Mahoney came over to them. 'Ms. Timoney. Scobie. Quite a gathering, don't you think?'

'A bit of a Kilbracken who's who all right,' Gerry said. 'What brings . . .' He was interrupted by a loud piercing noise from the microphone.

Tim Delaney winced as the microphone in his hand emitted the sharp piercing noise. He waved it around and breathed a sigh of relief when the ear-splitting sound faded. He put it up to his mouth again. 'Ladies and gentlemen. If I could have your attention please. The minister has just arrived, so we will be getting proceedings under way in the next few minutes.' He looked over to the door as Risteard O'Duinn came in, another man close behind him. He raised the microphone again. 'Ladies and gentlemen. Our minister for the arts, Mr. Risteard O'Duinn.' He put the microphone under his arm to lead the applause.

In a small room off the main ballroom, Sam Brookman, Harold Zwimmer, Faye Knight, Syl Carpenter, Sabrina Metcalfe, Harriet Taylor, Jerome Scott and Harvey Rockwell stood around. Standing a bit apart from them and looking very nervous was Sean Dolan, the Kilbracken town clerk. He was to lead out the Hollywood guests when he heard Tim Delaney start the introductions. He sneaked another covert look at Sabrina Metcalfe and he felt the shiver run up his spine again. God, she was beautiful. And so sexy. Dressed in a body hugging gold pants which accentuated all of her delicious curves and a pale-yellow blouse which was open half way down her front showing a beautifully tanned and unblemished cleavage between two perfectly formed breasts with the nipples clearly visible through the flimsy material. Her auburn hair, which was normally long and wavy in the films and photographs he had seen, was now cut short and framed around her face but it didn't detract one iota from her striking looks. It actually made her even more sensuous looking. Her generous lips were painted a bright red which probably on anybody else, would have looked cheap and garish but on her, it just looked right. And that little beauty spot on her cheek. Such a small thing but it just seemed to complete her. Like a full stop at the end of a sentence. He blushed and quickly averted his eyes as she caught his examination.

Sabrina paid no attention to the middle-aged man's perusal of her body. She was well used to it. She looked at Harold Zwimmer. 'Harold darling. Is it going to be much longer before this circus starts? We've been here a while now.'

The producer gave her his best smile. 'Should be soon now, Sabrina.' He looked at his watch and then over at Dolan. 'We gonna be much longer, pal?'

Dolan blushed again. He could feel all their eyes on him. He was just about to mutter some platitude when he heard the screech of the microphone and then Tim Delaney's voice. He breathed a sigh of relief. 'They're just about to get under way, Mr. Zwimmer.'

Out in the ballroom, Tim Delaney stood waiting as O'Duinn made his way towards the stage, stopping occasionally to shake hands and exchange pleasantries with some of the guests. When he got to the stage, his shook hands with the chairman. 'Well, Tim. Let's get this show on the road.'

Delaney raised the microphone. 'Mr. Minister, ladies and gentlemen. As chairman of Kilbracken urban district council, I would like to welcome you all here today to what is a most auspicious and exciting occasion.' He beamed around the room. 'For the next few months, Kilbracken will be our very own Tinseltown.' He waited for the burst of applause acknowledging this piece of wit and when it didn't come, he quickly continued. 'I'm not going to keep you waiting any longer. Ladies and gentlemen, please put your hands together and give a hearty *cead mile failte* to our guests from Hollywood, Mr. Sam Brookman, director, Mr. Harold Zwimmer, producer, Mr. Syl Carpenter, the beautiful and talented Miss Sabrina Metcalfe, Mr. Harvey Rockwell, Miss Harriet Taylor and Mr. Jerome Scott.'

Gerry clapped along with the main body in the room as the Hollywood group came out of the room and were directed up onto the stage. O'Duinn shook hands with each. When they were all seated, he took the microphone from Tim Delaney who sat down next to Harvey Rockwell. He waved a hand at the seated group. 'Once more, ladies and gentlemen. For our Hollywood guests.'

There was another round of applause. He raised the microphone again. 'As minister for the arts, and a great fan of Hollywood movies, it is a particularly satisfying for me personally to be the government's representative here today and to be the one to announce the name of the film these giants of the movie industry have come to make in our country and your town.' He gave a smug grin. 'It is going to be a swashbuckling adventure entitled 'The Arrow of Justice.' And as you all know by now, the male lead will be Mr. Syl Carpenter and the female lead will be the beautiful Miss Sabrina Metcalfe.' He turned and gave a little bow to the actress. She gave him a slight nod in return. He turned back to the main crowd. 'Mr. Harold Zwimmer is the producer and the director is Mr. Sam Brookman and both are men highly respected in the film world. Miss Taylor, Mr. Scott and Mr. Rockwell are the main supporting actors.' He turned around to the seated group and clapped his hands, the sound amplified by the microphone. The assembled crowd applauded again. When it had died down, he said. 'Some of our own Irish actors will also be involved as will members of the defence forces and of course, quite possibly some locals here as extras. Now as I'm sure you can imagine and appreciate, our guests here are still a little bit jet lagged after the long trip from Hollywood. There'll be no speeches from them but they will stay with us for a short while and mingle.' He held up his hands. 'But please. Don't be asking for autographs or photographs. We're just going to have the official photograph and that is all.' He returned the microphone to the stand and everyone grimaced as another piercing sound cut through the air before fading again.

Gerry turned to Father O'Mahoney and Ms. Timoney. 'Can I get either of you a glass of wine? They've started serving now.'

Ms. Timoney shook her head. 'It's a bit early in the day, isn't it, detective sergeant? Anyways, I'm just going to give a few of my cards to the producer fellow and then I'm back to work.'

The two men watched her walk over towards the group who were now standing at one of the tables, wine glasses in their hands.

'How about you, Father?'

'I'm as partial to a nice glass of red as the next man, Scobie,' the priest replied.

Gerry quickly walked over to one of the tables and was back a minute later with two glasses of red wine. He handed one to the priest and both men took a sip.

Father O'Mahoney held up his glass. '*Vinu bellum iucunumque est, sed animo corporeque caret.*'

Gerry grinned at him. 'Now, Father. You know I never got past *et* *cum spiritu tu*o so you'll have to explain that one.'

The priest took another sip. 'It's a nice little wine but it lacks character and depth.'

Gerry nodded. 'You're right there, Father. Typical council plonk. They serve the same for every official do. Whoever buys it obviously isn't a wine drinker.'

They both took another drink, Gerry's draining his glass. He looked at the priest. 'Chance another, Father?'

He shook his head. 'Not for me, Scobie. I've a few calls at the hospital to make. Wouldn't do to be breathing alcoholic fumes all over them.' He grinned. 'Why don't you get yourself another glass. I'm sure you could manage a few more.'

Gerry returned the grin. 'Just might do that, Father. Give the auld blood a bit of a flush out.'

The priest laughed. 'I'd say if they bottled your blood, Scobie, it would be at least forty per cent proof.' He finished off his own drink and left down the glass. 'That's me done. I'll see you around.'

'See you, Father,' Gerry said.

He walked back over to the table and got another glass of wine. He turned as he felt a tap on his arm. Rachel Kelly stood smiling at him, a glass of white in her hand. 'Hiya, Scobie. Long time, no see. How have you been keeping?'

Gerry gave a slight shrug of the shoulders. 'Hangin' in there, Rachel.'

She edged a bit closer to him. He could smell her perfume. 'We had a good night that night, didn't we? Thought you might have given me a shout afterwards.' She laughed. 'You know a girl doesn't like to be blown out after just one night. Kinda gives you a complex.'

Gerry mentally winced and cursed himself again for getting so drunk that night. He couldn't remember who had shifted whom. Rachel Kelly had a reputation for latching on to anything in pants and even if it was her who had moved in on him, he had let her. And now here she was again. She was almost on top of him. He stepped back a bit. 'If I'm to be totally honest, Rachel, I don't remember too much.'

The smile which she probably had hoped was seductive, quickly disappeared. 'God, you really know how to make a girl feel good, don't you, Scobie! Fuck you.' She turned on her heel and walked off.

Gerry let out a long breath. He knew he had been a heel but feck it. The only way to get through to the Rachel Kellys of this world was with a hammer. They could be like limpets and if you didn't knock them off straight away, they could be very difficult to shift. Thank God he had only had two glasses of wine and not a skinful. That's what had got him into trouble the last time.

He grinned as a large body loomed up in front of him. Moby Dick had arrived.

Dick Larkin held the wine glass in his hand, his big fist completely covering the body of the glass, the stem only visible underneath. He was wearing an ill-fitting grey suit with the cavernous pants held up by tartan coloured braces, a blue shirt whose buttons were at bursting point and a tie which was loosely knotted around the fat neck. He was sweating profusely, and his face was flushed a deep red. He looked at Gerry. 'What are you doing here, Tierney?'

Gerry smiled at him, knowing that alone would annoy the other man. 'I'm your official liaison from the Garda Siochana, Moby. You come through me with any enquiries or requests.'

Larkin snorted. 'Then we'll have fuck all enquiries or requests. I'm not going cap in hand to you for anything. I don't like you, Tierney. Never have. And now that I'm out of the force, I don't have to put up with any of your shit anymore.'

Gerry took a sip of his wine. 'Security advisor. Must say I'm impressed, Moby. Hobnobbing with the Hollywood set.' He leaned in a bit closer and dropped his voice to a conspiratorial whisper. 'Heard through the grapevine, they might even be considering you for a part in the film.'

Larkin's eyes widened. 'What'd ya hear?'

Gerry looked around him as if checking to make sure they weren't being overheard. 'Well. apparently, there's a scene involving Miss Metcalfe that requires the presence of a man of – how will I put it – considerable physical stature. Yeah, that's it, considerable physical stature. And none of the Yankee crew have that.'

Larkin's voice was low and hoarse. 'What's the scene?'

Gerry looked around him again. 'Got this from the producer fella a while ago. Just before you came in. Asked me if I knew anybody who might fit the part. I told him about you and Boss O' Connor. But the fact that you're already employed by them as a security advisor, well, that might just be in your favour.'

Dick Larkin licked his lips. 'But what's the scene?'

'Well from the little he told me, apparently Miss Metcalfe is captured by a band of outlaws and back in their camp, they strip the clothes off her and are queuing up to ravage her. But the guy who looks after their camp is a big kindly giant who steps in to protect her. I don't know the full details but that's the gist of it from what I've heard.'

Larkin stood back and looked hard at him. 'You're takin' the piss, aren't you, Tierney? Why would they be askin' you?'

Gerry shrugged his shoulders. 'Probably because I'm a cop and they think I know everybody. Tim Delaney introduced me to him.'

He tried to keep a straight face as he saw Moby lick his lips, his beady eyes squinting as if he was trying to picture the scene. He still had a doubtful look on his moon face but there was also an underlay of hope. 'And you mentioned me and Boss O'Connor?'

'I did,' Gerry said. 'Personally I couldn't give a fish's tit which of ye they give the part to. Just said I'd mention it for old times' sake.'

They both looked over to where Harold Zwimmer was in conversation with Tim Delaney. Gerry lifted his arm and pointed a few times to Moby beside him.

Delaney waved a hand and made some comment to Zwimmer who nodded in reply. Moby saw the nod and assumed it was an acknowledgement of Scobie pointing him out. He waved over himself, a wide grin splitting his face.

Gerry left down his glass. 'Well that's me done here, Moby. I'll probably see you around.' Larkin was now looking at Sabrina Metcalfe, his mouth open like a love-struck teenager. He didn't even break the look to see Gerry as he started to walk away.

'Yeah, okay. I'll see ya.'

At the door, Gerry turned around and couldn't stop himself laughing when he saw Moby heading over to Delaney and the producer. He would have loved to hang around to hear the exchange, but he thought it wiser to be gone. He was still whistling ten minutes later as he opened the door into McCluskey's.

Macker looked at him. 'Someone's in a good mood. You win the lotto or what?

'Nothing like that,' Gerry said as he sat up on a high stool. 'Just having a whale of a time. Now fill us a pint.'

*****

47

CHAPTER 9

He was on his second pint when the door of the bar burst open and Dick Larkin lurched in. His heavy jowls were beetroot red, the two eyes in his head bulging and wild looking. Macker gave him a puzzled look and then looked at Gerry.

'What's up with Moby?'

Gerry didn't get a chance to answer as Larkin's large body loomed in front of him. 'You miserable fucker, Tierney. I've a good mind to pull you off that stool and give you the thrashing you deserve.'

Macker raised a hand. 'There'll be none of that here, Larkin. What's bugging you anyways? What's Scobie done?'

Gerry swung nonchalantly around on the stool. 'I take it you didn't get the part so, Moby?'

Macker looked from one to the other. 'What part?'

'What fuckin' part is right,' Larkin shouted. He pointed at Gerry. 'This fucker told me he told the producer on that film that's being made here, that I was right for a part they were looking for someone well-built for.' He turned back to Scobie, his nose only inches away from Gerry's, spittle flecking his double chin. 'But it was all a wind up wasn't it? Just another of your sick fuckin' jokes. Makin' me make a gobshite of myself in front of the producer.'

Gerry picked up his pint and took a pull and then left it down again. He looked calmly at Larkin. 'Guess I must have got it wrong so. I have to confess, I wasn't talking to the producer and he didn't ask me if I knew any big people. And I did make up that scene with Sabrina Metcalfe. But I can honestly say, I did overhear him saying to Tim Delaney that he was looking for a moron from Limerick. And sure isn't that what you are?' And then he smacked his forehead with the heel of his hand, as if a sudden revelation had hit him. 'Oh God! Now that I think about it, he was talking to Delaney about his Irish ancestry. I think now in hindsight, he might have said, a Moran from Limerick.'

Larkin's eyes looked as if they would burst from his head like balls from a canon. He was clenching and unclenching his fists, his teeth audibly grinding.

Gerry sat calmly on his stool. He knew the other man long enough to know he would never get physical. The only weapon he had was bluster. It had often worked with petty criminals in the past who would be overawed by the bulky body towering over them but to those who knew him, he was just a mountain of lard with no backbone.

He glared at Gerry. 'I'll get you for this, Tierney. You can take that to the bank. Sooner or later, I'll get you for this.' He turned on his heel and banged out through the door.

Macker stood looking at the door and then slowly turned back to Gerry. 'What the hell was all that about, Scobie? Did you really set Moby up like he said?'

Gerry took another pull from his pint. 'Can't tell you a lie, Macker. The big bollocks annoyed me in the hotel. Full of his own importance. Just thought I'd have a bit of fun and take him down a peg or two.'

The bar owner laughed. 'By the sound of it, you took him down a whole bloody clothes line. He was really pissed.'

Gerry finished the last of his pint and pushed across the empty glass. 'Feck him. He's just a big feckin' boil on the arse of society. Now – stick another pint in there like a good man.'

McCluskey took the glass and left it aside. He took up a fresh one and put it under the tap and began filling it. He looked over at Gerry. 'Was your woman Sabrina Metcalfe there?'

Gerry grinned. 'That she was, Macker.'

The bar owner left down the swirling pint to allow it to settle. 'Is she as good looking in the flesh as she is on the screen or in the magazines?'

Gerry pursed his lips, pretending to be mulling over the question. 'Well let me put it this way, Macker.' He nodded to the still settling pint. 'That's her in the magazines. And when that's settled and topped off, that's her in the flesh.'

McCluskey laughed. 'I'm sure she would be tickled pink to hear herself compared to a pint of Guinness. Even if it is one of mine.'

Gerry grinned back at him as he slid off the stool. 'And sure what better comparison to make! Aren't you the king of pint pullers? At least, that's what you tell us. Now, I'm going to check the auld plumbing. Have Miss Metcalfe finished off when I come back.'

He strode off to the toilets.

The pint was sitting on the counter when he came back but now there was a small group of new arrivals sitting at one of the tables. He groaned inwardly when he saw Tim Delaney and Andrew Horan. He recognised a couple of the faces he had seen in the Cloisters earlier.

49

Delaney gave him a beaming smile. 'Come over and join us, detective sergeant. Meet some of our American guests from Hollywood.'

Gerry walked over and Delaney stood up. 'You know Councillor Horan, don't you?' He didn't wait for Gerry to confirm this. 'This young lady here is Miss Faye Knight, personal assistant to Mr. Brookman the director and Mr. Zwimmer the producer. This other good looking lady is Miss Ruby Lipman. She's the person responsible for all the beautiful costumes that will be seen in the film. And these two fine looking gentlemen here on my right here are Jerome Scott and Harvey Rockwell who are both starring in the picture along with Miss Metcalfe and Mr. Carpenter.' He gave a little laugh. 'We're just showing them a little bit of local culture.'

Gerry acknowledged them all with a nod and a 'nice to meet you all' and then his eyes were drawn back to Faye Knight. She was a very good-looking woman, probably mid to late twenties, with light chocolate coloured skin and large brown eyes. Her black hair was short and when she stood up, he estimated her height at around 5 feet 10. She gave him a white toothed smile. 'Nice to meet you......detective sergeant, is it?' The voice low and husky. For some reason, he immediately thought of melting chocolate. He gave her one of his best smiles. 'Gerry. Gerry Tierney. But my friends call me Scobie.'

Ruby Lipman remained seated but extended her hand. He estimated her age to be mid to late forties. Around 5 feet 6 but with a good layer of padding on her bones. She had a head of wild blonde hair, but he could see the black roots peeping through. Her face was heavily made up with her over large lips painted in a bright orange lipstick. She also gave him a wide smile as she stuck out her hand. 'So nice to meet you, Scobie Tierney.' But no melting chocolate thought jumped into his head again. Her voice was deep and masculine sounding. He wondered briefly if she was possibly a transvestite or a transsexual. These Hollywood crowd were all sorts. He shook the extended hand. 'And nice to meet you too, Miss Lipman.'

She held his hand a bit longer than just a handshake. 'It's Ruby. Call me Ruby.'

'Okay, Ruby,' he said. He managed to extricate his hand from hers.

The two men nodded to him. Jerome Scott was probably early twenties and although he remained seated, Gerry could see that he was probably a good four to five inches above the six-foot mark. He had an athlete's body and the looks of a young Harry Belafonte. Harvey Rockwell was the polar opposite. Mid-thirties, white, short and fat with a balding head, red beard and eyes which almost met over his nose. It was he who spoke. 'Ain't some of you guys going to put up some drinks here? Isn't that what we came in for?'

Delaney looked at Horan who didn't budge and then looked at Gerry. 'This is your local I believe, Tierney. Perhaps you might do the honours.'

Gerry smiled at him. 'Of course, councillor. No bother at all.'

He turned to the bar where McCluskey stood. 'Hey, Macker. Can you come over here and take an order from Councillor Delaney here? He wants to get in a round for his guests. And I'll have a large jemmy.'

He could see Delaney grind his teeth. He nodded to the group again. 'Nice to have met you all. Hope you enjoy your stay in Kilbracken.'

He walked back to the bar and picked up his pint and took a deep draught which dropped it down over a third. He glanced back at the group who were giving their orders to McCluskey. Delaney caught his eye and gave him a thunderous look. He lifted his pint in acknowledgement and took another deep pull. 'And feck you and the horse you rode in on, Mr. Lord Mayor. Ye want to get up a lot earlier in the morning to catch me out like that.'

McCluskey came back behind the bar and began filling two glasses of Guinness. He grinned at Gerry. 'Delaney said that he was only buying for the group at the table. That you weren't included.'

Gerry sniggered. 'Feckin' knew well, the miserable auld bollocks. Only said that to annoy the git anyways. Sure fill us a large one anyways. I'll pay for it myself later when old Scrooge isn't looking.'

McCluskey grinned again. 'He's some miserable auld shite all right. The two buckos asked for pints, but he suggested glasses. Just in case they didn't like it. And the two women asked for large gins, but he whispered to me to give them singles and fill them up with tonic.'

'And what about Handy Andy?' Gerry asked.

It was McCluskey's turn to snigger. 'That fucker! He asked for a whiskey first but changed it to a glass of beer after Delaney growled at him. And he's still sitting there with one hand in his pocket.'

Gerry laughed. 'And it's not his loose change he's playing with, the bollocks.'

McCluskey took up a glass and filled a double shot from the

Jameson optic and slid it across to Gerry. He picked it up and then looked over to the table. He waited until he saw Delaney look over and then he lifted it in salute and then took a pull. He almost spluttered the drink from his mouth as he saw Delaney's mouth drop open and then clamp shut as he gave an extremely dirty look at McCluskey. McCluskey caught the look as well. 'God that was so worth it, Scobie. Just to see the look on his face. That fecker is so tight, you wouldn't get a caraway seed up his arse with a sledgehammer. That whiskeys on the house.'

The bar owner quickly filled the other drinks and then topped off the two glasses of Guinness and put the lot on a tray. He totted them up on the till and tore off the receipt and put it on the tray as well. Gerry watched as he carried the tray over to the table and began to set the drinks down in front of the small group. He grinned when he saw Delaney grab the receipt from the tray and begin to go through it and then look up, a somewhat surprised look on his face.

When he looked over at Gerry, he took up the glass of whiskey and positioned it in his hand so that his index and middle finger formed a V to the front of the glass. He then raised it again in salute. Delaney quickly looked away.

Gerry tossed off the last of the whiskey and then finished off the pint as well. As McCluskey came back, he slid off the stool.

'You away, Scobie?'

'Yeah,' Gerry said. 'Probably grab an auld takeaway from Luigi's and then home.'

'You be in later?'

'Probably not,' Gerry said. 'Might just surprise myself and have an early night.'

He walked to the door and as he passed the group at the table, Ruby Lipman reached out and tapped him on the behind. 'Leaving so soon, Scobie Tierney?'

He turned around. 'Yeah. Enjoy the rest of your evening.'

She pouted at him. 'That's a pity. Maybe we'll see you again?'

He split his look between her and Faye Knight. 'Well Kilbracken is no Los Angeles, so it's quite possible.'

Faye Knight sat with a small enigmatic smile on her lips but said nothing. Lipman gave him the full wattage. 'Well that would be nice, Scobie.' He gave her a weak grin and went out the door.

*****

CHAPTER 10

They were back in O'Driscoll's house, all sitting around the formica topped table in the kitchen. A tray of German beer sat in the middle, the plastic cover ripped off and half the contents now divided amongst them. Ratser Whelan was already half way through his can although O'Driscoll and Corbett hadn't opened theirs yet. O'Driscoll prised a nail under the steel tab and then worked a finger under and peeled it off. He took a swig and then wiped his mouth. 'Okay Corby. What did you find out from Lugser?'

Corbett fiddled with his can but didn't open it. 'His step uncle has a hidden cellar all right. He's never seen it himself mind you, but it's definitely there. He knows that. He remembers the auld fella telling him all about it at a wedding a while back. There's a trap door in one of the cowsheds under one of the milking stalls. You have to remove a slatted pallet to get at it.' He grinned. 'The provos he hid were apparently less than happy. There was cow shite everywhere. The real runny stuff. And the smell was rank. And there's a great big pile of silage right beside the shed wall so you could never get away from the smell. If the cops had known that, they could have just sat around and waited 'til they smelt them. They must have stank like skunks by the time they left.'

Ratser took another swig from his can followed by a deep pull on his cigarette. 'Fuck sake! Sounds like a right shithole.'

Leery O'Leary looked at O'Driscoll. 'You should feel at home so, Ratser. When was the last time you had a shower or a bath?'

'And you can fuck off too, ya cross eyed git,' Ratser said.

O'Driscoll banged his can off the table. 'Shut the fuck up, the two of ye.' He looked over at Corbett. 'Anything else? Is the old man still living on his own?'

Corbett took a swig. 'And that's the next bit of good news. The auld fella had a stroke a few days ago. He's in hospital and when he gets out, he goes to a nursing home.'

'And this place is out in the sticks?' O'Driscoll said.

Corbett nodded. 'According to Lugser, the nearest house to it is about a half mile away.'

'So we mightn't have to go into the shithole at all so,' Ratser said.

'He must have stock,' O'Driscoll said. 'Who looks after them?'

'Neighbour took them over to his place,' Corbett said. 'He only had a couple of cattle.'

Ratser looked hopefully at O'Driscoll. 'So if the place is deserted, we can stay in the house, can't we?'

'We use the cellar,' O'Driscoll said. 'We can't afford any chances.'

When Ratser said nothing, he looked over at Fatty McGivney. 'So Fatty. What's the story on this film?'

McGivney stopped his digital probing of his nose. 'The Hollywood crowd arrived yesterday. The big shots are staying in the Cloisters hotel in Kilbracken. According to the paper, they're starting shooting tomorrow with a lot of the action taking place in some woods outside the town. I checked the area on Google and this woods is about four miles from the town. We should be able to grab her going or coming.' He tossed off the last of his can, squeezed it into a lopsided hourglass shape and then reached out and grabbed a fresh one. He expertly popped the tab and gurgled down half the contents.

O'Leary looked at him.

'So, boss. When are we moving?'

O'Driscoll stood up. 'Tomorrow. We drive down to this farm and suss out the cellar and this woods. See how near they are to each other and what the roads are like. We bring enough provisions for about five days. I don't want any of us going into the town. We stay in the cellar before and after the snatch. With a bit of luck, we can grab her in the next day or so and hopefully, have traded her within another couple. Once the ransom's been paid, we head straight back to Dublin and when we're back, we tell one of the papers where she is.'

'The van?' O'Leary asked. 'Where we gonna hide that?'

O'Driscoll looked at Corbett who shrugged his shoulders. 'It's a fuckin' farm. Sure there has to be plenty of places to hide it.'

O'Driscoll stroked his chin. 'Let me think on that one. You give Lugser the new phone?'

Corbett nodded. 'Yeah. Slipped it to him when the screws weren't looking. He texted me later to say he had it back in his cell.'

'And he knows what to do?' Corbett nodded again.

'Yeah. I text him when we have your woman and he makes the call to the newspaper about an hour later with the ransom demand.'

'Good,' O'Driscoll said. 'They'll be checking to see what area the call came from and that should focus their attention in Dublin.'

McGivney laughed. 'About time we used them bloody masts to

our benefit.'

Ratser lit another cigarette from the stub of the one he had eked the last pull from. 'And have you figured out how we collect the ransom? If we're in this shithole in the arsehole of nowhere and want the cops to think we're in Dublin, how are we going to organise that?'

O'Driscoll grinned. 'We sub-contract the pick up.'

'To who?' O'Leary asked.

'Spence,' O'Driscoll said.

They all looked incredulously at him. Even one of O'Leary's eyes managed to focus on him.

'Spence?' McGivney shouted. 'That fucking pyscho! Are you mad in the head or what!'

Ratser brushed the fallen ash off the table with his sleeve. 'Ye can't trust that bastard,' he said as he sucked in another lungful of smoke. 'He's likely to collect and then tell us all to fuck off. He'll have the loot and we'll be left with just the cowshite.'

O'Driscoll grinned. 'Tell them, Corby.'

Danny Corbett took a fresh can from the pack and pulled off the tab. 'We owe Spence a hundred and fifty thou for the stuff Lugser got caught with. He gets another hundred k for doing the pick up. If he doesn't cough up the rest to us, we threaten to rat him out to the cops.'

'Ah for fuck sake!' McGivney shouted. 'Rat him out how?'

O'Driscoll looked at Corbett and nodded.

Corbett took a small recorder from his pocket and held it up. With all bar two of the eyes in the room focussed on it, he pressed the play button. It was Spence's voice which they all knew, the heavy Northern twang very much in evidence. 'And I make all the arrangements for the ransom pick up, give the details to your guy and he makes the call to the paper?'

'That's right, Mr. Spence.'

None of them recognised O'Driscoll's disguised voice.

'Then I make the pick-up and call you to release the Metcalfe broad.'

'Right again, Mr. Spence.'

'And I take out my share and give ye the rest to divvy up?'

'Yes. That's the arrangement. We're all working for you on this one, Mr. Spence. It's your show.'

There was a laugh. 'Yeah. My show all right. What the fuck is up

55

with you anyways? You sound like you swallowed a consumptive fuckin' frog!'

'Throat infection. Raw as a bear's arse.'

Corbett hit the stop button. Ratser looked at O'Driscoll, a doubtful look on his face. 'I don't know, boss. Threatening that fucker could send him ballistic. He'd be after us all.'

O'Driscoll smiled again. 'For once I have to agree with you, Ratser. And we probably won't have to. If he starts to bitch, we'll offer to double his cut. That would be half a mill for him. I think he'll take it. He's a business man. The recording is only a last resort.'

'So what'll be left for us?' McGivney asked.

'We'll be asking for two million. That should be nothing to this film crowd. That'll leave a million and a half between the six of us.'

Ratser's face took on a sly look. 'You're not giving Lugser the same as us, are you? He's doing fuck all except making a couple of poxy phone calls. And if the dozy git hadn't got caught in the first place, we wouldn't have to be doing this at all.'

'Lugser's getting fifty. We split the rest,' O'Driscoll said.

'What about the pick up?' O'Leary asked. 'Have you sorted that out with Spence?'

'That's his responsibility. He'll organise that. Lugser will ring him before ringing in the ransom demand and he'll tell him where and how the drop is to be made.'

'It has to be a clean pick up,' O'Leary said. 'I'm sure the cops aren't going to let two million big ones waltz off without them trying to keep tabs on it.'

'Spence will handle it,' O'Driscoll said. 'With his operation, I'm sure he'll cover all possibilities. It's not the first time he's handled ransom pick-ups. We all know that.'

Corbett nodded. 'Yeah, you're right there. Sure wasn't it him who started the tiger kidnaps. Perfected it to a fine art until every Tom, Dick and Harry got in on the act and fucked it up. If anyone can organise a clean pick up, it's Spence.'

'Right,' O'Driscoll said. 'Let's get down to the nitty gritty.'

*****

CHAPTER 11

Shooting began on the Monday morning at six o'clock, but Sabrina wasn't required until later that day. She lay in the bed, luxuriating in the softness of the deep mattress and pillows. She had to admit, the bed was extremely comfortable and overall, while it wasn't a suite, the room was big and spacious. A long way from the small cramped box room she had grown up in back in Bixby, Oklahoma with its narrow steel bed with the broken springs and the wafer-thin mattress and patchwork quilt which was old, worn and frayed. The house itself was more of a shack with only two bedrooms, a living room, small kitchenette and even smaller bathroom. The living room boasted a battered old three-piece suite, a low timber coffee table which was badly marked with cigarette burns, a small black and white television set with rabbit ears and a cabinet on which one of the doors hung loose. She had hated that house and by extension, had resented her mother for being the sad case she was that couldn't provide better.

But that past life was dead to her now. Mary Harte was dead, and her mother was equally locked away in the past. She had severed all ties with Bixby after getting away from it, and with her mother and the few friends she had had, most of whom were probably in jail now. And she probably would be too if Imogen Meyers hadn't chanced to stop for coffee across the road from Brambles Superstore. She brought up the image of the older woman the last time she had seen her. It had been the day she had told her she was leaving. Their parting had been quite acrimonius, with Meyers accusing her of being an ungrateful bitch who had just used her to further her career and as soon as she had established that – and it was Meyers who had created it all for her – she was dumping her like a spent battery. She who had spent a lot of money on grooming her in every way -physically, socially and theatrically – to turn her into the actress and screen icon she now was. She could still see the angry face, the lips drawn in a sneering line as the bitter word were hurled at her. And she knew that everything Meyers had said was true. She had deliberately used her to further her career. But the woman had used her too. Used her to satisfy her sexual lust for young females. It hadn't bothered her too much. Meyers had been surprisingly tender in her lovemaking for such an outwardly butch woman and while Sabrina hadn't been overly fond of the attention, it had just been a routine chore for her. Something to put up with for the time being. A means to an end. After her first few successes on the screen, she had contacted Marty Klugman and when he had agreed to become her agent, she had quickly ditched Meyers.

She lazily reached over an arm when the phone beside the bed rang. Her watch showed eleven o'clock. It was Boardman ringing from the set. 'Sabrina darling. We will need you here in ninety minutes. The car will be outside for you in an hour. Is that okay?'

She was reluctant to leave the warm confines of the bed but at least she had had a rest. Carpenter and the others had been on set in the woods since seven. 'Of course, Sam. I've been up for a while now. Going over the script.'

'That's my girl,' Boardman said. 'See you soon.'

When he rung off, she dialled down to reception. 'This is Sabrina Metcalfe. I would like some breakfast in my room please. A bowl of muesli with skimmed milk, two very lightly grilled pieces of bacon with the rind cut off, some freshly squeezed orange juice – make sure it is not from a carton – a single slice of brown toast with a very light coating of butter and a pot of Japanese green leaf tea.'

On the reception desk, Lelia Browne made a face at the phone. Breakfast was supposed to finish at ten. And here was Miss High and Mighty looking for a special over an hour later. But she knew her place. 'Of course, Miss Metcalfe. I will get the kitchen onto it straight away.'

She rang through to the kitchen where her fiancée was one of the chefs. They were only engaged for three months and the hotel allowed them work the same shifts. 'Peter. Your wet dream fantasy up on the fourth floor is looking for her breakfast. Muesli with skimmed milk, two half raw rashers without the rind, juice from an orange and not a carton, a slice of brown toast with feck all butter and a pot of Japanese green leaf tea, whatever the hell that is. Okay?'

'No problem, Lelia,' her husband to be replied in his lilting Kerry accent. 'And just to let you know, you're my wet dream fantasy and not the Hollywood Barbie doll. And for your information, green leaf tea is made from the Camellia sinensis plant and in Japan, the plant is steamed instead of pan fired. Gives the tea a leafier taste. So there's a little bit of useless information for you.'

She laughed. 'Well thanks for the compliment and the tea education. And just to return the compliment, I wouldn't crawl over you to get to your man Syl Carpenter either. Give me a bit of Kerry rough over Hollywood muscle any day. And as for your Japanese green tea – well, you can stick that where the sun don't shine. I'll stick with the cup of Barry's'.'

Peter Behan laughed. Lelia had made quite a journey from being the painfully shy girl he had met three years ago to a now much more confident and open person with a sparkling personality and great sense of humour. He again felt the surge of happiness that he had stuck with his courtship of her in the early days despite her best efforts to put him off. But he had persisted and as his considerate attentiveness peeled back the protective cocoon her shyness and lack of confidence had wrapped around her, he uncovered a person of great sensitivity, depth and character. They still had not had sex together and he knew that the first time would be on their wedding night. And he had come to accept that. Despite her burgeoning confidence, she still held on to her values, old fashioned and all as others thought they were. It actually endeared her more to him. And despite this unwillingness to go the whole way, she was a passionate woman who enjoyed exploring all the other aspects of their relationship. The engagement ring had loosened her bra, but she had made it quite clear that no other piece of clothing would be removed until the gold band was on her finger. It frustrated him at times but he loved and respected her too much to make an issue of it. He smiled again to himself and then set about getting the breakfast ready.

Upstairs in her room, Sabrina had a quick shower and dried herself with one of the four big white fluffy towels which were neatly stacked on the ledge beside the bath. She strode naked out into the bedroom and stood in front of the long mirror and examined her body. She was tanned all over from her hours of sunbathing naked beside the pool. She hated to see women with white strips across their breasts or buttocks where the bikini lines were. To her they looked quite ridiculous. She wondered was Syl Carpenter tanned all over or would he have the white triangle a lot of men had. Somehow, on men with muscular physiques, it didn't look too bad but on others, it looked quite comical. But Richard was another case altogether. As someone who disliked the sun and never sat out unless covered all over, he was pasty looking from neck to toe. But he more often than not, never bothered with any protection on his face, his dislike for oils and creams stronger than his aversion to the sun. And so when naked in their bedroom, he reminded her of a matchstick. A long thin white body with a big red head. Not for the first time, she wondered why she was still married to him. Was getting a title that important to her? Wasn't she the current queen of Hollywood? But that was a transient title. Sooner or later, some other hot smouldering cutie would dethrone her and then she would be history. Unless of course, she died young. The Marilyn

Monroe's were always remembered and featured at the peak of their success and looks, while other sex sirens who had grown old and wrinkled, were more often than not, shown in – what she herself referred to as – their embalmed look. But properly titled women, no matter how old, had an elegance and regal air about them that transcended age and looks. A wizened Lady Jane would be viewed a lot kindlier than an ordinary wizened plain Jane. People only saw the title. And that was what she wanted for her latter years. And that was why she wouldn't divorce Richard.

She reached for the dressing gown on the bed when she heard the knock on the door. Pulling it on, she cinched the belt around her waist and then walked over and opened the door. A young plump looking waitress smiled at her from behind the trolley. 'Your breakfast, Miss Metcalfe.'

She nodded her in and stood aside as the young woman pushed the trolley into the room and over to the table. She stood waiting as the contents of the trolley were transferred to the table and then the waitress stood back and again, smiled at her. 'Will that be all, Miss Metcalfe?'

'Yes,' she said. And then as an afterthought. 'Thank you.'

The young girl hesitated, one hand on the trolley. Sabrina could see she was working up the courage for what she knew was going to be the question. She didn't wait. She gave an impatient shake of the head, walked over to the sideboard and took up one of the studio publicity shots of her which were stacked in a bundle, grabbed a biro and scrawled her signature across it and then thrust it at the waitress. 'Here. I presume that is what you want.'

Millie McCann took the photo. She had actually been going to ask if she could take a selfie of the two of them, but she was definitely not going to ask now. Miss Metcalfe's manners certainly didn't match her looks. 'Thank you,' she said, dropping the photo onto the trolley. She turned around and wheeled it over to the door, opened it and went out. She glanced down at the photo as she wheeled the trolley down the corridor. It was a colour 8 x 4 of the actress sitting on what looked like a leopard skin mat. She was wearing a tight white satin, almost transparent blouse, shiny silver leggings which looked like they had been put on with a spray can, a thin gold bracelet around each ankle and her feet were bare, their only adornment, a deep plum colour on the toenails. She was laying back, her arms stretched behind her holding her up, the pose stretching the material of the blouse to such an extent that her nipples were clearly evident each side of the deep cleavage. There was just a hint of a smile on her plum coloured lips and she was looking up at the camera, her hooded and heavily made up eyes adding to the smouldering look. Even to Millie, the photograph oozed sex. She signed heavily as she pressed the button to open the lift doors. What she would give to look like that. She pushed the trolley in and pressed the button for the ground floor. As it descended, she looked at herself in the back mirror. She knew she was carrying a lot more weight that she should be and in the black and white hotel uniform, she had to admit, she did look a bit frumpy for a twenty-two year-old. She glanced down at the photo on the trolley again. She would start a new diet. It would be her fifth this year. As the lift arrived at the ground floor and the doors opened, she took up the photograph, ripped it in two and then ripped it again and dropped the four pieces back down on the trolley. All of a sudden, she felt better.

*****

CHAPTER 12

Gerry finished off the last few chips and then binned the vinegar sodden bag into the waste bin near the entrance to the Cloisters Hotel. As he stepped off the footpath to cross in front of the hotel entrance, he had to jump back quickly as a big car swung in and only missed him by inches. He swore under his breath and stood glaring as the car stopped in front of the hotel door.

Sean Donovan got out of the car and groaned when he saw the man approach, a thunderous look on his face. He had been so wired up about having Sabrina Metcalfe in his car again that his mind had been on her and not the road. And now he had almost knocked somebody down. And it had to be Scobie bloody Tierney of all people. Fuck!

Gerry stopped in front of Donovan. 'What kind of a blind bollocks are you, Donovan? You nearly took the feckin' leg off me there.'

Donovan gave him a sheepish look. 'Ah Jeez, I'm sorry, Scobie. Lost my concentration there for a second. I'm really sorry.'

Gerry glared at him. 'Well you could lose your licence now.'

'Ah please, Scobie,' Donovan begged. 'I can't afford to lose this job. Please. Give us another chance. I swear. It'll never happen again.'

Gerry pretended to think about it for another minute. He had no intention of making anything about it, but no harm let the bugger suffer for a little while. Might focus his attention a bit more. Eventually he nodded his head. 'Right. I'll let it slide this time. But next time, keep your feckin' eyes on the road and not up your arse. Where are you off to anyways, lookin' like a prize prick in that uniform?'

Donovan grinned at him, his equilibrium restored now that he had escaped censure. 'I'm chauffeuring Miss Metcalfe out to the film set in Fenner woods.'

He couldn't mask the fawning in his voice.

Gerry gave a grunt. 'So that's what was distracting you. You were probably all over her in your own little mind, weren't you? When you should have been looking where you were going.'

Donovan blushed. 'Well you have to admit, Scobie, she's one fine looking bit of stuff.'

'Listen,' Gerry said. 'If that one had the measles, she wouldn't give the likes of you or me a feckin' spot. Them ones are so far up their own arses, they think they're on a different planet.' He grinned slyly 'Does Dora know about your mental shagging of the Hollywood hotshot? Bet she would have something to say about that.'

Donovan blushed again, this time the red flush rinsing over all his face. If Dora knew what he was thinking, she'd have his guts for garters. He looked to the door hoping the subject of their discussion would appear and end this conversation.

Gerry grinned again. It was so obvious that Donovan had the hots for Sabrina Metcalfe. And he couldn't really blame him. He had seen her himself at the conference the day before and there was no doubt about it, the woman was beautiful and sultry looking and simply oozed sex. He wouldn't mind a cut at her himself. But he wasn't going to go around mooning over her like a pimple faced adolescent. Feck that for a game of snooker! He was about to make another smart arsed comment when the door opened and Sabrina Metcalfe came striding out. Despite it being a reasonably warm day, she was wrapped in a white fur coat with big dark sunglasses, the lenses of which were almost saucer size and concealed a good half of her face. Beneath the hem of the coat which came midway down her calf, her legs were bare and her feet were encased in suede ankle high bootees. A yellow bandana covered her short hair. She stopped at the car, gave Gerry a quick glance and then looked at Donovan. 'Are you my transport?'

Donovan doffed his cap. 'Yes Miss Metcalfe. Remember? I picked you up from the airport. Sean Donovan.'

'Did you?' she said. 'I really don't remember. Must have been the jet lag.' She forced a smile onto her face. 'What did you say your name was again?'

Donovan preened like a peacock. 'Donovan, Miss Metcalfe. Sean Donovan.'

She looked over at Gerry, no real interest in the look. He returned an equally disinterested look. It took her by surprise. She wasn't used to being blanked like this. It was totally alien to her to be treated with such indifference and it annoyed her.

Sean Donovan was still fawning over her. He smiled at her and then nodded over to Gerry, hoping to score brownie points with the detective sergeant by introducing him. 'This here is Detective Sergeant Tierney of the local police.'

She gave an almost imperceptible shrug of the shoulders. A policeman. That explained it. Most of the policemen she knew, thought they were the flesh incarnation of Bruce Willis' on screen macho cop, John McClane. All yippee ki yay tough guys. But all in their own heads. This Irish cop was probably the same. She ignored the introduction and turned to Donovan. 'Can we go now?'

Donovan jumped to open the back door and held it as she slid onto the back seat. When she was settled, he gently pressed it shut and then went around to the driver's side and got in.

Gerry watched as the car went around the small island and headed out the entrance. He had a sardonic smile on his lips. He had met many woman who, like the haughty woman who had just left, were full to the brim of their own self-importance. Women who put themselves up on pedestals and looked down on the rest of the lowly mortals with disdain. Well he wasn't going to be an adoring disciple at the shrine of Miss Metcalfe like Donovan and the rest of them. She could whistle Dixie 'til the cows came home before that would happen.

He turned as the door slid open and Jeremy Clarke came out, a thick binder in his hand. He gave a quick look over to the entrance and then looked at Gerry. 'Miss Metcalfe's car gone?'

Gerry nodded. 'Yup. Just gone.'

The hotel manager held up the binder. 'She left this on the reception desk. I think it's her film script. If she brought it down with her, I'm sure she needs it.' He looked hopefully at Gerry. 'You think you might run it out to her, Scobie? I'm tied up here or I would do it myself.'

Gerry grinned at him. 'Don't tell me you're worshipping at the shrine of Miss Sabrina Metcalfe as well, Jeremy? Is there anybody in this feckin' town who isn't drooling over her like a teething infant? Donovan was almost wetting himself a few minutes ago.'

Clarke laughed. 'I can assure you I have no interest whatsoever in Miss Metcalfe, Scobie. I am merely giving her the same attention I would give any other guest.' He gave Gerry a quizzical look. 'And have you not been smitten yourself, Scobie? You being one of Kilbracken's most eligible bachelors. She is a very striking woman after all.'

'Did you ever hear of a Succubus?' Gerry asked.

'Can't say I have,' Clarke replied. 'Sounds like a Sub 4 sandwich or something.'

'A Succubus is a beautiful and desirable woman from medieval times who was really a demon who seduced men with their beauty and sexuality and left them fecked or dead. I think our Miss Metcalfe is a modern day Succubus.'

'My God, Scobie,' Clarke exclaimed. 'I didn't know you were a student of medieval folklore.'

Gerry laughed. 'Have to confess. Read it on the back of a cornflakes box once when I was on a weekender in Prague. Just liked the name and it stuck in my head ever since.' He held out his hand. 'Here, give it to me. I'll drop it out to the set. Haven't much more to do today anyways.'

Clarke handed over the binder. 'Thanks, Scobie. There's a free lunch in it for you when you come back.'

Gerry shook his head. 'Maybe some other time. Just finished off one of Luigi's cod and chips. That'll keep me going for a few hours.'

Clarke rolled his eyes. 'All that fast food will be the death of you someday, Scobie. I'd hate to see the state of your arteries.'

'Nothing wrong with my arteries,' Gerry said with a grin. 'Sure don't I flush them out most nights with a few pints of Arthur G and a couple of Jemmies.'

Clarke laughed. 'You're incorrigible, Scobie. Thanks for doing this.'

Gerry took the binder and strolled back to his flat where his car was parked.

Twenty minutes later, he was stopped at a barrier across the road leading into the woods. Two men in black windcheaters with the name ARMOUR SECURITY emblazoned in bright yellow letters across their backs approached him. He rolled down the window and waited.

'Sorry mate,' one of them said in a strong Dublin accent. 'This place is off limits for the next few weeks.'

Gerry held up the binder. 'Have to deliver this to Miss Metcalfe. She left it behind her in the hotel.'

The man turned to his co-worker, a wide grin on his face. 'Jesus, Arty. These red arse culchies will try anything to get to see your woman Metcalfe.' He turned back to Gerry, the grin gone from his face. 'I've just told you can't go through so fuck off out of here before we have to give you a bit of physical encouragement.'

Gerry switched off the engine and opened the door and got out. The two men shared a sneering look.

The second man looked at Gerry and then at the other man. 'Looks like they're so fucking thick down here, Willie, they don't understand plain fucking English.'

His companion clenched one hand over the other and loudly

cracked his knuckles. 'Looks that way, Arty. Guess I'll just have to explain things to him in a different language.'

Gerry stood still as the guy called Willie slowly walked over to him. When he was just a foot away, he held up the binder. 'Look lads. You can see it's the film script. She honestly did leave it behind her in the hotel.'

Willie stuck his face out until they were almost nose to nose. 'I don't care if it's the fucking Book of Kells or her last will and fucking testament. You and it aren't going any further. Now push off or I'll make you.'

Gerry looked at him. 'Are you threatening me?'

'You're damn fucking right I'm threatening you.'

'I could report you to your superiors for this,' Gerry said.

The two men shared another look and both laughed and then Willie said. 'It'd be very hard report anything with no fucking teeth.'

Gerry reached into his pocket and took out his wallet and extracted his ID card and held it up. 'Or I could just arrest you for threatening a police officer.'

The look shared this time by the two had little bravado in it. It was Arty who spoke. 'Ah Jaysus, officer. We didn't know you were a cop.'

Gerry threw him a withering look. 'So it's all right to abuse everybody else, is that it?'

Neither said a word, their eyes downcast.

Gerry stuck the card back into the wallet and put it away. He looked from one to the other. 'I strongly suggest the two of you brush up on your manners and be a lot more civil to anybody you stop here. I'll be keeping an ear out for any complaints.'

He got back into the car and started the engine and began to drive forward. The two rushed back and quickly pulled the barrier from across the road. He saw them standing looking after him in his rear mirror as he drove into the woods.

A few hundred metres into the woods, he came to a clearing where there were four forty foot containers, an array of camera equipment and large industrial spotlights, six luxurious looking trailers, four portaloos, a general assortment of chairs, and tables and a long catering truck which had a large awning in front and two men in chef whites behind the counter. There was nobody else visible.

He pulled up near the catering truck and got out and walked over.

'I'm looking for Miss Metcalfe,' he said.

'Not here,' one of the chefs said. 'They're all up in Fenner House shooting some indoor scenes. Won't be back for a few hours at least.'

Gerry knew Fenner House. It was an old period residence on a large forty acre estate adjoining the woods, currently owned and very infrequently occupied by William Hilliard the Third, a forty something year old American from Buffalo, New York, a self-made millionaire in the high tech industry. Gerry had met him once and hadn't liked him. He had asked for a senior officer to call to deal with some fishermen who were fishing for salmon in the Fenner river, most of which ran through the estate except for a hundred metre stretch which curved just outside the estate's boundaries. Despite this, Hilliard claimed the whole river was his and he owned all the fishing rights. Gerry had politely informed him that the part of the river the fishermen were fishing, was not in the estate and therefore the salmon in it, were open to anybody with the proper fishing licence which the two men had. He had then casually asked if he himself had a fishing licence. The American had become quite aggressive and eventually told Gerry to fuck off back to the boghole he'd come from. As he now drove up the long driveway towards the house, he just hoped Buffalo feckin' Bill the turd wouldn't be there.

*****

CHAPTER 13

There were two more security men manning the gateway into the big house. Gerry didn't bother explaining about the film script – he wasn't going to risk another Willie and Arty performance. He flashed his ID card which got him waved straight in.

He drove over to the side of the big house where there was a luxury coach, a forty foot curtain sider and two limousine cars parked, one of which looked like the car Sean Donovan was driving. There was also a banged up Renault which he immediately recognised as Moby Dick's. Donovan was leaning against the side of the bus talking to another man wearing the same chauffeur's outfit and a guy in overalls, probably the truck driver. All three were smoking. He could see the bus driver in the front of the bus, his feet up on the dash, his eyes closed. He pulled in beside Donovan's car, killed the engine and got out. Donovan gave him a surprised look. 'Scobie! What are you doing here?'

Gerry grinned at him. 'Just drove the same route as you to check there were no body parts on the road.'

Donovan gave a quick sheepish glance at the other two. 'Just a little private joke between the detective sergeant and myself.' He looked back at Gerry. 'Seriously though. What are you doing here?'

'Your passenger left her script in the hotel. They asked me to run it out to her.'

Donovan licked his lips. 'Sure you can give it to me. I'll see that she gets it. You probably have a lot of other things to be doing.'

Gerry grinned. He could see the hopeful look on the other man's face. Probably wondering already, what show of gratitude Sabrina Metcalfe would bestow on him for this little service if he got to deliver it to her. He shook his head. 'Arra you're all right. I've nothing else on so I'm in no hurry.' He nodded to the house. 'She in there?'

Donovan made another effort. 'I don't think they'll let you in, Scobie. You have to be accredited for the set. I'll do it for you.'

Gerry shrugged his shoulders. 'Well I got this far, didn't I? And I have to see Dick Larkin anyways. As the official Garda liaison officer, I have to keep in touch with the film's security advisor. Even if it is Moby feckin' Dick.' He didn't wait for Donovan to speak again, striding quickly off towards the house. He took the twelve steps up to the large open door, two at a time. He stopped at the entrance to the hallway at the end of which, two double doors stood open giving a clear view into one of the house's main rooms. It was cavernous in size, almost the size of a ballroom. And it was a hive of frenetic activity. There had to be at least thirty people milling around. And that was only what he could see in the vicinity of the doorway. He started over but stopped when a large presence loomed in front of him.

'What the hell are you doing here, Tierney?' Dick Larkin asked.

Gerry grinned at him. 'I'm investigating the disappearance of reason and sanity from the male population of Kilbracken since this movie crowd came to town. Or, to be more sepcific, since Miss Metcalfe came to town.'

Larkin glowered at him. 'Spare us more of your smart arse codology, will ye? You're about as funny as a boil on me arse.'

Gerry grinned again. 'A boil on your big arse, Moby, would be like a pimple on a rhinoceros. If you asked a doctor to lance it, it could take him an hour to track it down on that sea of mottled flesh you keep under that tent of a trousers of yours.'

Larkin's face flushed even redder. 'If you've no offical business here, Tierney, I suggest you take your smart alecky comments, stick them up your arse and fuck off out of here.'

Gerry held up the script. 'This is Miss Metcalfe's script. I'm just here to return it to her.'

Larking held out a pudgy hand. 'Give it to me. I'll take it.'

Gerry pulled it away. 'Sorry, Moby. No can do. This is property recovered by the police and as such, it is our responsibility to hand it over to the official owner. You of all people should know that. You were sort of a policeman once, weren't you? Even if you were the proverbial waste of feckin' space.'

Larkin struggled for a quick retort and was still trying to come up with his own put down when Faye Knight walked over. She gave Gerry a wide smile. 'Mr. Tierney. To what do we owe the pleasure?'

Gerry held up the script again. 'Miss Metcalfe left this behind her at the hotel. The manager asked if I would deliver it to her.'

'That's very good of you, Mr. Tierney,' she said. 'Unfortunately, she's in the middle of some scenes now so I'm afraid you won't be able to hand it over to her in person.'

Gerry shrugged his shoulders. 'Don't bother me, Miss Knight.' He held it out. 'Maybe you would see that she gets it.'

She gave him a slightly bemused look as she took it from him.

'Are you not a little disappointed that you can't hand it over to her yourself? That you're not going to have the opportunity to receive the gratitude of the sexiest woman in Hollywood?'

Gerry gave a little laugh. 'Well I'm not going to rush home and slash me wrists, if that's what you mean. And I did meet her earlier today, outside the hotel. Sure she's only another woman.'

The bemused smile widened. 'I don't think our Sabrina would be too enamoured to be referred to as just another woman. She is after all, regarded as the queen of Hollywood.'

Gerry gave her his own bemused look. 'And from what I've seen of her, she certainly believes it herself. A bit too big a member of her own fan club for my liking.'

'You don't like confident, self-assured women?'

'I've nothing against confidence and self-assurance,' Gerry said. 'But when they morph into overinflated ego and self idolatry, well that's a different story. And I think the queen of Hollywood as you call her, is so pumped up with her own self-importance and high opinion of herself, it's a wonder she hasn't floated away like a helium balloon.'

Faye Knight laughed and he liked its sound. He was enjoying their conversation despite the presence of Moby Dick who stood looking at the two of them, a slightly sneering look on his face. It was then Moby decided to put in his two halfpence worth. 'That's rich, coming from you, Scobie. Surely you think you're the greatest thing to happen to the Garda Siochana since Adam was in fig leaves. You're in no position to criticise Miss Metcalfe. You've a bigger head than anybody.'

Gerry turned to him. 'Maybe you're right, Moby. I'm probably not half as good a cop as I think I am. But then, I used to measure myself against you and seeing as you were such a feckin' cloth head, I suppose I could have looked better than I really am.'

Larkin visibly bristled, his small eyes shrinking to pin points. 'Fuck you, Tierney.' He looked at the woman. 'I apologise for my language Miss Knight but Tierney here was always jealous of me. He only got promoted over me because he licked up to the superintendent.'

Faye Knight held up her hands in a sign of appeasement. 'Please, gentlemen. Why don't we call a truce? I am sure you were a very professional officer, Mr. Larkin and Detective Sergeant Tierney is also a very capable policeman.'

She had to smile when both men just gave each other a contemptuous look. Further argument between the two was cut short when Harold Zwimmer came out from the big room and came over to them. He nodded to the two men and then spoke to Faye. 'They're wrapping up inside. I need you to get a copy of the script and go through Sabrina's lines and highlight them for her. She seems to have mislaid her own copy.'

Faye held up the script in her hand. 'Have it here. She left it at the hotel.' She indicated Gerry with a flick of the head. 'Detective Sergeant Tierney here was kind enough to bring it out.'

Zwimmer looked at Gerry as he took the script from his assistant. 'That was very good of you, sir. A detective sergeant? You probably know our local security advisor Mr. Larkin here so, he being an ex-policeman.'

Gerry grinned. 'Oh I know him all right. We were just renewing acquaintances.' He could see the smile crease Faye Knight's lips.

Zwimmer looked at him and then at Dick Larkin. 'Well you two gentlemen might just be able to help us out with something. We will be looking for some large dogs for a few scenes. You know anybody local who could help us out with that? Somebody with well trained dogs?'

Larkin spoke quickly, ensuring he got in before Gerry. 'There's a settled traveller in town. Has two big dogs. I can have a word with him.'

Zwimmer gave him a puzzled look. 'What do you mean settled traveller? You mean he's a retired salesman?'

Larkin gave a snort. 'This guy was never a salesman. More of a con man if you ask me. But he does have two big dogs.'

'What kind of dogs are they?' Zwimmer asked.

Gerry said nothing. He knew Moby Dick wouldn't have an idea what breed they were. As with everything else, he never bothered his fat arse with details. He would know two kinds of dogs. Big and small.

Zwimmer stood waiting.

'They're em...they're big...big dogs. Same size as them little horses you see in circuses.'

'But what breed are they?' Zwimmer asked.

Gerry could see the sheen of sweat on Moby's forehead.

'Breed? Likely half breed mongrels knowing Doyle. They could be a cross of anything.' He chewed on his lip. 'Maybe best leave them. They're probably as wild as the owner. And that's saying something.'

Zwimmer shook his head. 'Pity. Means we will have to go to Dublin or London now.'

'They're Japanese Akitas,' Gerry said. 'But Doyle has them trained to the last. You hire him as well, his dogs will do anything you want.'

'Great,' the American said. 'They would be perfect. How do we go about hiring this guy and his dogs?'

Larkin jumped in first again. 'I can arrange it. I know Boss Doyle.'

Zwimmer gave him a dismissive look. 'But you didn't know what kind of dogs he had. And you seem to have a very low opinion of the guy himself.' He turned to Gerry. 'Maybe you, sir, would have a word with this Mister Doyle. I can have Faye here type up a contract and then the two of you could arrange to meet with him and nail things down. We would only require the dogs for an odd day here and there.'

'No problem,' Gerry said. 'I'd be delighted to help. But I wouldn't bother typing up a contract. Boss does everything with a handshake. That's the only contract he uses.'

Zwimmer gave a little laugh. 'Well that certainly will be a first for us. Normally in Hollywood, they're stabbing you in the back while they're shaking your hand.'

They all turned as Sam Brookman came over.

Zwimmer introduced him to Gerry. 'This here is Detective Sergeant Tierney. He very kindly brought out the script Sabrina left back at the hotel. And now he is going to organise a local man who has two Japanese Akitas which we can use for the chase scenes.'

Brookman extended his hand. 'That's damn good of you, officer.' He shook Gerry's hand and then turned to Zwimmer. 'We've got a conference call in twenty minutes with Enrico.'

Zimmer nodded. He extended his hand to Gerry. 'Thanks again for your help, sir. I'll leave you to arrange things with Faye here. She knows the schedule and when the dogs will be needed.'

The two walked off, heading back to the main room. They stopped just outside the double doors when Sabrina Metcalfe came out. There was a short conversation and then the actress came over to the other three. She was dressed in a tight fitting pants and top, deep green in colour and obviously designed to replicate the outfit worn by Robin Hood. But unlike that famous Sherwood Forrest resident, her outfit was made from smooth velvet and not deer skin as was probably the original Robin Hood's. She ignored Faye Knight and Dick Larkin and focussed her smouldering look on Gerry, her wide smile attesting to a much improved frame of mind from that morning. 'So – we meet again, detective sergeant. Our paths are destined to cross it seems. And Harold tells me you found my script and came all the way out here to return it. That was most generous of you.'

Gerry grinned. From the corner of his eye he could see Moby Dick looking on, a big moronic smile on his moon face. He was obviously hoping that the actress would shortly include him in the conversation. Like a dog waiting hopefully for someone to throw him a bone. He could also see that Faye Knight had a slight sardonic smile on her lips, a smile which seemed to say 'I've seen it all before'. He looked back at the actress. 'It was no big deal. You left it on the reception counter. If there's anybody to thank, it's Jeremy Clarke at the hotel. He asked me to drop it out.'

She put a hand on his arm. 'You are too modest... Scobie, isn't it?' She arched a perfectly shaped eyebrow. 'What a cute name.'

Gerry had to grin again when he saw Faye Knight roll her eyes. Moby's smile had slipped and he was now glaring at Gerry, resentment reflected in the squinting eyes.

'You will have to let me repay you in some way,' Sabrina Metcalfe said, her hand still resting on his arm. Her smile morphed into a slight pout, one which looked out from magazines, billboards and cinema posters all over the world and which caused elevated testosterone levels in both young and old males of all nationalities on seven continents. And he had to admit, he too could now feel a sexual stimulation. It was more mental than physical but he knew that the transition from one to the other was something she could engender anytime she wanted. And he knew she knew it too. He could see it in her eyes. She was playing with him. He was saved from making a decision as to his next move when Syl Carpenter came striding over. Sabrina Metcalfe's hand dropped from his arm.

'You ready to go, Sabrina?' the big man asked. 'Sam wants us back in the woods for one more scene before we wrap up for the day.'

She broke eye contact with Gerry and turned. 'Of course, Syl darling.' She threaded her arm through his and with an all-inclusive smile to the others, allowed herself to be escorted towards the door.

When they had gone out, Moby Dick grunted. 'Better get myself back as well. Make sure everything is okay there.'

Gerry and Faye watched him lumber away and then she turned to Gerry. 'Think you had a lucky escape there, Scobie. You were getting the full head on Sabrina Metcalfe treatment.' She gave a little laugh. 'But then again, maybe you don't look on it as a lucky escape. Probably disappointed Carpenter came over and interrupted her little seduction scene.' Did he notice just the teeniest hint of jealousy in the remark?

He hoped so.

He grinned at her. 'Don't you worry about me, Miss Knight. I've been around the block a good few times in my day. Fluttering eyelashes and simmering looks don't cut any ice with me unless I want them to. And I'd say, that one is as shallow as a saucer.'

Knight laughed. 'Well obviously I can't jeopardise my job by making any disparaging remarks about Miss Metcalfe. But I will say this. You are a very astute student of people, Detective Sergeant Scobie Tierney of the Irish police.'

Gerry grinned again. 'Well in that case Miss Faye Knight of Hollywood, California, how about you let me take you out and let me show you just how astute I can be.'

'And pray, what does 'out' mean in a place like Kilbracken?' she asked, a mischievous smile on her lips.

Gerry made a face. 'Well we mightn't have a Beverly Hills Polo Lounge or a Cecconi's but we do have one or two restaurants where you're guaranteed to leave with your stomach lining intact. And after that, there's always Mackers for a drink.'

She looked closely at him. 'You've been to Los Angeles?'

He nodded. 'Yes. I have.' He didn't add any more.

She knew there was more to be told but she didn't press him. 'Well I would be delighted to accept, thank you.'

'How's tonight?'

'Tonight would be fine,' she said. 'Now, I better get out to the bus or they will go without me.'

'Pick you up at the hotel at around eight. Would that be okay?' Gerry said

'Eight is fine. I'll see you then.'

He watched as she walked away and out the front door.

When he himself got to the door, the bus was pulling away. He could see her sitting up at the front. He made his way to his car and was soon driving back to town.

*****

CHAPTER 14

It was after eleven o'clock at night when Danny Corbett drove the white Ford van into the yard and pulled up in front of the old farmhouse. It was a clear night with a full moon so visibility was quite good. As soon as he killed the engine, Ratser Whelan slid across the side door and jumped out. He was quickly followed by Leery O'Leary and Fatty McGivney. All three began to vigorously rub their backsides. Corbett got out from the driver's side and Billy O'Driscoll hopped out from the passenger seat, a large flashlight in his hand. Ratser glared at Corbett. 'Ye must have hit every fuckin' pothole between here and Dublin. We were bouncing' around in the back there like the fuckin' balls in the lotto machine. Leary's eyes are almost straight in his head after all that rattling' around.'

Corbett grinned a yellow toothed smile. 'Don't blame me, mate. I didn't fuck up the roads. And Billy insisted we use the back roads.'

Ratser gave another deep rub to his behind. 'Well ye could have slowed down when ye were goin' over them. I think ye deliberately speeded up when you saw one. I don't know how many bloody times I whacked me head off the roof.'

O'Driscoll waved a hand. 'Cut your whining, Ratser. Let's find this hidden cellar and get sorted. Then Danny can take the van and head off.'

'Why don't we just park it in one of the sheds?' O'Leary asked.

O'Driscoll gave him a dismissive look. 'Were you paying any attention when we went through all this the other night? We don't want anything around here that we can't hide in the cellar with us. We can't be too careful. This place has to look deserted if anybody comes around. And Mandrake himself and a roomful of magicians wouldn't be able to get the van into the cellar.'

'How come he gets to stay somewhere decent while we're all going to be under this big heap of shit? Why's he not coming back after he stashes the van? We should all stick together.' Fatty McGivney said.

O'Driscoll shook his head in exasperation. 'For fuck sake! Is there even one fuckin' brain cell between the bloody lot of you. So we all go down into the cellar. What then? Who puts the slatted pallet back over the trapdoor to hide it again? And someone has to check out the roads and Metcalfe's travel arrangements.'

'Oh yeah,' McGivney said. 'I never thought of that.'

'No, you fuckin' didn't,' O'Driscoll said. 'And for your information, Corby will be sleeping in the van. Now, let's find the bloody thing and get our stuff into it.'

Corbett headed over to a shed near the back of the yard. 'It's in here according to Lugser.' The others followed.

The shed was about thirty foot long by fifteen foot wide with one side divided into four stalls by concrete walls about three foot high. The front of the stalls were open and each had a full width timber slatted pallet over the concrete flooring. A mixture of runny cowshite and water formed a slimy covering over the concrete and was just visible through the tight timber slats. But even if it hadn't been visible, its presence was strongly advertised by the overpowering stench. An old cart stood along the other wall, the type pulled by a horse or donkey before tractors took over. It was a solid piece, its spoked wheels still intact and still with the steel hoops around them. Its shafts rested on two concrete blocks.

'Ah for fuck sake!' O'Leary said as he pinched his nose. 'This place stinks.'

'Get used to it,' O'Driscoll said.

Corbett was standing at the end stall on the left hand side of the shed. 'It's in this one Lugser said.'

They all walked over. The long slatted pallet covered most of the floor. It was heavily stained with dried cowshite but the slimy brown film visible underneath was more liquid than solid.

O'Driscoll nodded to the pallet. 'Lift it up and let's see what we've got.'

Nobody moved.

He glared at Whelan. 'You, Ratser. Lift it up.'

Ratser gave him a disgusted look but he knew by the look on O'Driscoll's face that arguing why he was being given the honour would only incense the other man further. Grimacing, he gripped the edge of the pallet and lifted it up and stood it on its edge. He cursed loudly when some of the brown slime dripped onto his jeans. But they could all see the steel cover just about visible under the slime. It was about four foot square with an indented handle in which the slime was pooled. O'Driscoll nodded to Ratser. 'Go ahead, Ratser.'

He stooped down and tentatively edged his hand into the small recess, his face twisting in disgust as the brown slime covered his gloved fingers. They were all wearing two pairs of surgical gloves, another of O'Driscoll's rules. Trying hard not to retch from what was now an overpowering stench, he levered the cover up and let it fall back against the standing pallet and then quickly jumped back as the slime rolled down the cover.

They all leaned over to have a look, their noses wrinkling as the noxious smell seemed to intensify with the lifting of the cover. They could see timber steps going down. They looked like and probably were, an old staircase which had been cut to suit and then just dropped down into the hole. They too were heavily stained with the brown markings of cow excrement, the newest addition from the raised cover glistening fresh on the top step. Ratser was holding his stained and dripping hand out as if it was a leprous appendage, despite the fact that he was wearing gloves.

Nobody made a move to descend down the steps. O'Driscoll looked from one to the other and then said, 'Arra fuck it. Come on.' He turned on the big flashlight and started down. Corbett followed close behind with O'Leary and McGivney following and Ratser bringing up the rear.

The steps led down to a short tunnel and then a rectangular room which was about fifteen foot square and a little under seven foot high. Just inside the entrance, there was a light switch on the wall. O'Driscoll hit the switch and the room lit up but not overly bright. It was obvious that the bulb in the light was a low wattage.

There was a small table in the middle with four plastic garden chairs around it. The top of the table was badly marked with cigarette burns and a large ashtray sat in the middle, overflowing with grey ash and squashed butts. There were three chipped and badly stained cups, two plastic plates, some crumpled crisp bags and a well-thumbed girlie magazine which featured a big bare breasted woman on its cover. She was wearing a wide smile but her three middle teeth had been blacked out by biro.

There was a wooden bench along one wall and two bunk beds along the opposite one, both covered with old brown coloured blankets which were badly mildewed. Some of the edges bore the obvious signs of rodent nibbling. The only other thing in the room was a large galvanised bucket which on examination, was half full of dried human excrement. Near the top of one wall, there was a space where it looked like two blocks had been removed to give access to the wall cavity which was empty of any insulation.

Fatty McGovern cast a disgusted look around the room. He looked at O'Driscoll. 'You can't be fuckin' serious! We'll be fuckin' dead after a few hours in this shit hole, never mind a few days. I'm suffocating' as it is.'

O'Driscoll ignored him. He turned to Corbett. 'You and Leery go back to the van and bring down the stuff.'

When the two went back into the tunnel, he walked over and put a hand into the wall aperture. He felt a very slight movement of air. He withdrew his hand and turned to Ratser. 'Find a shovel or fork or something with a long handle and then stick it up through here. See if anything is stuck up there. And you...,' he said turning to Fatty. '...you go outside and look for a vent or an opening on the outside wall. It's the same side as that heap of shit outside so it might be blocked. If it is, clear a space around it.'

Ratser headed up the stairs and when Fatty went to follow, O'Driscoll called him back. He pointed to the bucket of excrement. 'Take that outside with you and dump it and then rinse out the bucket and bring it back.'

Fatty gingerly picked up the bucket and held it at arms length. He gave it a quick look. 'Jeez! There's mushrooms or some other fuckin' fungus growin' in it.'

O'Driscoll laughed. 'Well sure if you want to go look for a few eggs up top, you can make yourself a mushroom omelette later.'

As he went out, Corbett and O'Leary came down, both carrying large boxes. Ratser was close behind with a two pronged pitchfork in his hand. He walked over to the wall and pushed it into the rectangular aperture and hefted it up and down a few times.

Fatty's voice came floating down. 'For fuck sake! Will ya pull out that fuckin' fork. Ye nearly took the two eyes out of me bleedin' head.'

Ratser quickly pulled the fork down and pulled it out.

'Just one more left,' Corbett said, after they had left the two boxes down on one of the bunks. 'I'll get it and then I'll head off when Fatty comes back.' He looked at O'Driscoll. 'So I do a recce of the area in the morning?'

O'Driscoll nodded. 'Yeah. But go to the hotel first and go early. We need to know what time she leaves for the woods. We'll just have to assume it's much the same time every day.'

Fatty came back down the steps, the empty bucket dripping water but empty of its fetid contents. He left it down with a bang and then looked over at Ratser. 'What the fuck were you wriggling that fork around for?'

Whad'ya mean?' Ratser said.

'There's no capping on the wall. There was only a plank across the top to stop the shite falling in and I took it off. When I looked down to make sure it was clear, that fuckin' fork nearly skewered me in the head.' He looked down at his muck covered boots. 'And I had to climb up a mountain of shite to get at it.'

'Right,' Corbett said. 'I'll head now. I'll be back sometime in the morning.'

They all watched as he went into the tunnel and when he had disappeared, Ratser looked at O'Driscoll. 'Do we really have to stay down here? Why can't we stay in the house until we grab your woman?'

'Two reasons,' O'Driscoll said. 'There's always the chance somebody will come around and then who would cover the trapdoor after we've all scuttled back down here? And secondly, we would have to break into the house and that could be a problem for us later on. When we leave here, there has to be no clue that we were ever here. So, we stay down here and you'll just have to make the best of it. There's some scented candles in one of them boxes. Take them out and light them. That should help with the smell.'

Ratser and Fatty both rifled through two of the boxes.

'Have 'em,' Fatty said.

He pulled out a plastic bag and quickly tore it open and took out three of the six stubby candles it contained and handed them to Ratser. 'Stick them around the place and light them fuckin' quick.' He grabbed the other three himself.

Ratser looked at the candles in his hand, examining the label on each. 'All lavender and honeysuckle. Don't think that'll be much of a match for undiluted cow shite. Are yours the same?'

Fatty snorted. 'Just light the fuckin' things will ya!' He set his own three down on the table and took out his lighter and lit them.

Ratser put his down on the bench and soon they too were flickering. He inhaled a deep breath and then laughed. 'I'll have to get on to some of them perfume crowds. Tell them about this new scent we've just invented. Lavender, honeysuckle and cowshite. They could call it Lahoncoshi. Could be popular with all them culchies who have moved to the cities. Remind them a little bit of the shitty farms they came from.'

O'Driscoll pointed to the plastic bag which Fatty had thrown on the floor. 'Pick that up and put it in the box. We don't leave anything behind us.'

'Is that all the candles we have?' Leery asked.

O'Driscoll shook his head. 'There's another six. Probably in the other box. But that's enough lit for now. We have to spare them.'

He walked back over to the wall and put his hand in the aperture again. 'There's a good flow of air now.'

Fatty sniffed. 'Yeah. And it's now bringing in the stink from outside even more. It's no fuckin' contest, is it? Six poxy candles against a couple of tons of cowshite.'

O'Driscoll glowered at him. 'Well you keep that arse of yours clamped tight. We don't want some of your infamous stink bombs adding to the problem.' He looked at the other two. 'Now. Let's get the rest of the stuff out of these boxes.

*****

CHAPTER 15

Gerry arrived at the Cloisters a few minutes before eight. There were a few people sitting around in the reception area but Faye Knight wasn't one of them. He walked over to the desk where Eileen Hardiman, one of the receptionists, was finishing off a phone call. She put down the phone and smiled at him. 'Well Scobie. To what do we owe the honour of your presence here tonight?'

He grinned at her. Eileen was another of the many women he had dated fleetingly since coming to Kilbracken. Of medium height, she had long curly black hair and though she leaned a little to the plump side, she was still very attractive looking with a ready smile and a warm personality. She was in her early thirties and was now in a stable relationship with Artie Connell, a mechanic in Diskin's garage. 'Well seeing as you're unavailable any more, I thought I'd try second best and give one of these Hollywood crowd a shot.'

She laughed. 'You had your chance, Scobie. It wasn't me who said we should – how did you put it? – not cramp each other's style. Wasn't that it? And that was after only three dates. You cramp easily, don't you, Scobie?'

He grinned again. 'What can I say, Eileen? When I'm a wizened old man sitting stooped in my little room in the Sunset Valley nursing home, my Zimmer frame at the end of the bed and my teeth in the glass of water on the bedside locker, I'll look back on that statement and then I'll ring the bell and when the nurse comes in, I'll ask her to give me a good kick in the arse for being so stupid.'

'And then you'll probably straighten up, grab her and throw her on the bed and ravage her,' Eileen said, her face creased in a wide smile.

It was Gerry's turn to laugh. 'Have you ever seen the size of the nurses in Sunset Valley, Eileen? You would need a ten ton forklift to pick some of them up.' He shook his head, a smile still playing on his lips. 'No. When I'm that age, if I ever get there., the only things I'll be thinking about are the three hots. A hot meal, a hot whiskey and a hot water bottle. I'll leave the hot nurses to the younger generation. And the chances are, my liver will have given out long before then anyways.'

Eileen looked over to the elevator as the bell pinged and the doors slid open. She looked at Gerry. 'I think your date has just come down. Miss Faye Knight no less. I'm impressed, Scobie.?'

Gerry looked over as the American woman walked over towards him. She was wearing a cream coloured dress which beautifully set off the silken colour of her brown skin and the two perfectly shaped breasts. She wore red high heeled shoes but despite the height of the heel, her walk was steady and well balanced. Her short black hair was framed around her face which bore little make up apart from a light red coloured lipstick on the generous lips. There was a single strand of white pearls around her slender neck and a small diamond stud in each ear. She carried a small beige coloured clutch bag in her hand and when she got nearer, he could see the bright red nail varnish on the perfectly shaped nails at the end of the long tapered fingers. He felt the blood race in his veins as she stopped in front of him and he got the strong smell of the scent she was wearing. He was tempted to close his eyes and inhale it as deep into his lungs as he could. Instead, he kept his eyes open, took a short breath and smiled. 'You're looking particularly lovely, Miss Knight, if you don't mind me saying,' he said, ignoring Eileen who stood with a wry smile on her face.

Faye Knight gave a little curtsy. 'Why thank you, Scobie. But please. Faye is my name. Miss Knight makes me feel like an old spinster school teacher or librarian or something like that.'

'Faye, it is so,' Gerry said taking her arm. He glanced at Eileen who still stood behind the desk, the smile wider now. 'We'll see you, Eileen.'

'Have a good night,' the receptionist said. 'Do you want me to call a taxi for you?'

Gerry shook his head. 'No thanks, Eileen. I have Timmy O'Shea waiting outside.'

'Going out of town so,' Eileen said. 'Somewhere nice I hope.'

Gerry decided to play along with her for another while. 'I'm taking Faye to The Eden.'

Eileen gave him a grin and then looked at the other woman. 'Oh you'll enjoy The Eden, Miss Knight. They do a lovely hot meal and they make the nicest hot whiskey.' She cast a sideways glance at Gerry.

He steered Faye away from the desk before Eileen could think up some reference to a hot water bottle. 'See you, Eileen.'

Her 'Have fun' reply followed them out the door where Timmy O'Shea stood leaning up against his Renault Fluence with the taxi sign on the roof. He quickly flicked the cigarette he was smoking to the ground and opened the back door. Gerry helped Faye in and slid in after her, ignoring the knowing wink from O'Shea.

The driver closed the door and climbed into the driver's seat. He looked at both in the rear view mirror. 'The Eden so,' he said as he hit the starter and eased the car away from the door of the hotel.

Gerry sat back in the seat and felt another hot rush as Faye snuggled in close beside him, her arm linking into his. Her scent invaded his senses again and this time, he briefly closed his eyes and luxuriated in it. When he opened them again, he caught O'Shea's eyes in the mirror. He could see the amusement in them.

Timmy O'Shea was sixty two years of age, happily married to his wife Angela for thirty nine years, a partnership which had yielded three daughters and two sons, all now married themselves and spread all around the world. They had grandchildren in Australia, Dubai, London and Brussels whom they seldom saw except on skype but they also had two grandsons in Cork whom they saw a lot more regularly in the flesh. Timmy had been one of the first locals Gerry had met when he arrived in Kilbracken and the two had become good friends over the years.

'So,' Timmy said as he sped out of the town. 'Are you not going to introduce me to this lovely lady, Scobie?'

Gerry caught the twinkling eyes in the mirror.

'Faye,' he said. 'The back of that old grey head in front of us belongs to Timmy O'Shea, the nosiest taxi driver in the whole of Ireland. And you,' he said to the two eyes again reflected in the mirror. 'This is Faye Knight, assistant to the producer and director of the film being shot here.'

O'Shea slowed down and half turned his head so that he just got her in his peripheral vision. 'Very nice to make your acquaintance, Miss Faye Knight, assistant to the producer and director of that film. With a position like that, I'm sure you must be a very intelligent and highly educated woman. So what are you doing out with this reprobate of a Keystone cop, if you don't mind me asking?'

The laugh was light and tingling. 'And very nice to meet you, Mr. O'Shea. As for what I am doing out with Scobie, well, he was gentleman enough to ask and as a very intelligent and highly educated woman, it would have been very bad manners to refuse. Especially as I am a guest in your town and in your country. And I have to say, Scobie has been very kind and courteous in the very short time I have known him.' She squeezed Gerry's arm. 'Do you have a different opinion of my escort for the night, Mr. O'Shea? Should I be running for the hills?'

His laugh was deep and hearty. 'It's running to the loo you'll be if you go drinking with him. Scobie has a penchant for Guinness and

Jameson whiskey which a lot of us have discovered much to the regret of our kidneys.'

She laughed again. 'Well you know us Hollywood crowd, Mr. O'Shea. Sure don't we live in constant debauchery. Isn't that what all the papers and magazines say?'

O'Shea squinted as the headlights of a car behind filled his mirror and the loud sound of a car horn interrupted their banter. The driver behind was constantly flashing his lights and the intermittent sound of the horn grated on all their ears.

'So what else did Santy give you for Christmas,' O'Shea shouted as the road widened and the other car pulled out and swiftly accelerated past. 'If I catch up with you, I'll shove that bloody horn up your arse.'

He half turned again. 'My apologies, Miss Knight, for my rather crude vernacular but idiots like that get on my goat big time.'

'No need to apologise, Mr. O'Shea. I drive in Los Angeles. I am well used to both that behaviour and sentiments like that. I've expressed them quite often myself.'

'Did you catch the licence number?' Gerry asked.

'Didn't need to,' O'Shea replied. 'That was one of Sweeney's limos.' He turned in the seat. 'They have the contract for your film.'

Faye nodded. 'Yes. We have a contract with them for three limousines and a bus.'

'Probably some of your colleagues going to The Eden as well,' O'Shea said. 'Hotel probably recommended it.'

Gerry winced. He had hoped none of the others would be there. He just hoped it wasn't Ruby Lipman. If she was there, HE could be on the menu.

They drove in silence for the next five minutes and then O'Shea pulled into the big car park in front of the single storey building which was all lit up. Gerry judged by the number of cars that the restaurant was fairly full. But he had booked a table and he knew Bill Watson, the owner chef.

When the car stopped, he opened his door and got out. Timmy O'Shea was already opening the other door for Faye. Gerry came around. 'What do I owe you, Timmy?'

'Fifteen will cover it, Scobie.'

Gerry handed him a twenty and then took Faye's arm. 'I'll ring you when we're ready for home,' he said. 'Be about two hours.'

O'Shea grinned at them. 'Have fun, children. I'm just going over to see who was driving Sweeney's limo. Give him a few lessons on the rules of the road. I'll see you both later.'

Gerry guided Faye up the four steps to the restaurant and when he pushed open the door, he immediately got the loud hum of conversation. As the full car park had suggested, the place was crowded.

Harriet Taylor, Harvey Rockwell, Jerome Scott and Ruby Lipman were standing in a little group at the reception counter. They turned as Gerry and Faye came in.

'Faye. Scobie,' Ruby Lipman said, a surprised – and Gerry thought – somewhat annoyed look on her face. 'Didn't know you two were hanging out together.'

'Just a little thank you to Scobie for bringing out Sabrina's script today,' Faye said, squeezing Gerry's arm at the same time.

'Oh, right,' the other woman said. 'Would you like to join us? The place is full but they're organising a table for us.' She gave a little smirk. 'It's not often they get Hollywood people in this place.'

Before they could reply, Elsie Watson came over. She addressed the small group. 'We will have your table ready in about five minutes. I'm afraid it's not the best positioned but as I'm sure you will understand, we are doing our best to accommodate you.'

'Could you squeeze room for another two?' Lipman asked, indicating Gerry and Faye with a nod of her head.

Elsie Watson smiled a wide smile. 'Hello, Scobie. Good to see you again.'

'How's it going, Elsie?' Gerry said. 'Although looking around, that's a stupid question, isn't it? Bill must be flat out in there. Tell him he better not be sweating into my feckin' soup.'

Watson gave a quick glance around the full restaurant. 'Yes. Business is very good, thank God.' She looked back at Gerry, a pretend insulted look on her face. 'And I'll have you know, Scobie Tierney, my husband does not sweat into anybody's food. This is a high class establishment with the highest of standards. It isn't Luigi's chipper, which I know you are more familiar with.'

The others nervously watched this little exchange, glancing from Elsie to Gerry, unsure how to take it. It was only when the two started laughing that they understood the two were only having a laugh and relaxed. 'Come on,' Elsie said. 'Let me show you to your table.'

'You booked?' Ruby Lipman said as Gerry and Faye squeezed by.

'Scobie did,' Faye replied.

The four stood watching as Elsie led them to a table beside one of the big bay windows and held out a chair for Faye. After she had handed them a menu each, she came back to the others. 'If you follow me, your table should be ready now.'

She led them through the restaurant where Taylor, Scott and Rockwell attracted a lot of looks and whispered asides.

The table was located behind a pillar right beside the swing door into the kitchen.

Ruby Lipman grimaced and then turned to Elsie. 'Is this the best you can do? It's kind of cramped, isn't it?'

'I'm afraid it is the best we can do. As you can see, we are totally full and we are only obliging you by sticking in this table. We didn't want to disappoint you.'

'It's fine, thank you,' Jerome Scott said as he sat down on one of the chairs the far side of the table. 'We appreciate you making the effort for us.'

Harriet Taylor nodded and smiled at her as she took the chair opposite him. 'Yes. We do appreciate it.'

Rockwell took the chair beside Scott which left the one nearest the kitchen door for Ruby. She reluctantly sat down.

Elsie handed each of them a menu. 'The waitress will be along shortly to take your order. Bon appetite.'

She had only walked away when the kitchen door was opened by one of the waitresses with a laden tray in her hand. It swung back and hit off the back of Ruby Lipman's chair.

Oh I'm terribly sorry,' the waitress said, giving them all a nervous look before moving on with the tray.

Ruby Lipman glowered after her and then quickly shuffled her chair forward when the kitchen door swung open again, coming to within an inch of hitting off her chair again. She splayed her hands indicating the now absence of any space between her stomach and the table. 'I can't even breathe now,' she said.

Scott grinned at her. 'Well you'll just have to suck it up, Ruby.'

Opposite him, Harvey Rockwell laughed, patting his own ample stomach which had a few inches to spare between it and the edge of the table because of the more generous space on their side of the table.

'Or maybe, suck it in.'

Lipman glowered at him. 'Are you saying I'm fat?'

Rockwell grinned at her. 'Well you have to admit, Ruby, you're carrying a lot more surplus than Harriet here or Faye. Or even Jerome. I won't include myself in the comparison for obvious reasons.'

She had a fiery retort on the tip of her tongue but bit it off when the waitress appeared.

'Are you ready to order?'

The other three quickly put in their orders while she scanned the menu.

'I'll have the deep fried Brie for starter and then I'll have the pan seared Venison,' she said, holding out the menu to the waitress.

'Harriet Taylor looked up from the wine list she was perusing. 'White or red?'

'Red for me,' Harvey Rockwell said.

'And me,' Jerome Scott added.

Taylor looked at Ruby. 'Ruby?'

'What are you having yourself?'

'I'll go with red too,' the young actress replied.

Lipman gave a little snigger. 'I'll go with white so. A Sauvignon Blanc.'

The order was put in for two bottles of red and one of white.

When the waitress had left, Harriet Taylor looked over to the table where Gerry and Faye were deep in conversation. 'I think there's more than a thank-you dinner going on over there, if you ask me. They look very cosy together.'

Ruby Lipman gave a derisory snort. 'From what I've heard of that Irish cop, he fancies himself more than a little bit.'

'Who told you that?' Scott asked, nonchalantly nibbling one of the tapered bread sticks.

'That Irish local security advisor, Larkin. He was in the police force with Tierney before he retired. Says Tierney thinks he's Colombo and Casanova all rolled into one.'

'I don't know about him being Colombo but I wouldn't kick him out of the bed,' Taylor said.

Scott glanced over at the other table, a dreamy look in his eyes. 'No. You're right there, Harriet. I wouldn't kick him out either.'

Rockwell gave a little laugh. 'Don't think he's one of your lot, Jerome. Not the way he's looking at Faye anyways. He doesn't look like he's gay.'

Scott pursed his lips. 'Appearances aren't everything you know, Harvey. My lot, as you so crassly put it, don't all go around with a gay sticker on their forehead. And as you well know, some of the most macho men in Hollywood are closet queens.'

Their conversation was interrupted by the arrival of the wine and they all sat quietly as the young waiter poured it out. He was rewarded with a polite 'thank you' from Harriet Taylor accompanied by a smile, a grunt from Harvey Rockwell but Jerome Scott gave him a glittering smile and patted his hand. 'Thank you so much, darling.'

The young lad blushed a deep red but didn't instantly pull his hand away. He gave Scott another shy smile and then went back to the bar.

Ruby Lipman picked up her glass. 'The copper mightn't scratch with the same foot as you, Harvey, but that young waiter guy might be worth a bit more of your attention.'

Scott looked over to the bar and smiled again. 'Yes. I might just look for a bit of room service later on.'

*****

CHAPTER 16

At the other table, Faye Knight took a sip of her glass of red wine. She held the glass in both hands and peered over the rim at Gerry. 'So, Detective Sergeant Scobie Tierney of the Irish police, what's your story?'

Gerry took a slug of his own wine. He would have preferred a pint of Guinness or a Jameson whiskey but the restaurant only served wine. He had often taken issue with Bill Watson over the fact that, despite the restaurant having no problem in getting a full licence, the chef owner was quite happy to operate with just a wine licence. He felt it maintained the restaurant's class and serving spirits or pints would somehow lower the tone of the place. Gerry had told him he was only a feckin' snob.

He took another deep pull from the glass and then topped it up from the bottle beside him. 'No major story to tell really. Thirty four years of age, a copper for sixteen of them. Served in a few places around the country before coming here to Kilbracken eight years ago after getting promoted. Never married and no children that I know of.'

Faye smiled at him. 'Such an in depth history. I'm really impressed, Scobie. Must have taken all of ten seconds.'

Gerry laughed. 'We're not all Jekyll and Hyde's you know. Some of us are just what we appear to be.'

She left down her glass. 'So Scobie Tierney just materialised, became a cop and came to Kilbracken. That's it?'

Gerry picked up the bottle to add a drop to her glass. And that was all that was literally left in it. He caught a waiter's attention and waved the empty bottle and when he got an acknowledging nod of the head, he left it down again. 'Born in a place called Tuam in Galway. Parents now both dead. Have one sister married in Australia with three kids I've seen once. What else can I tell you? I love being a cop. Have some good friends in the force whom I hang out with whenever they can get away from their wives and a few others who are not coppers. That's me in a nutshell.'

He saw the waiter approaching with the new bottle of wine so he quickly lifted his glass and swallowed down what was left. They both stayed silent as their glasses were replenished. Their starters arrived immediately after, the waitress placing the goat's cheese with pears and hickory in front of Faye, and the black pudding in front of Gerry.

Faye nodded to the large plate in front of him in which the two fat rings of black pudding sat on top of a thin sliver of toasted bread in the middle of the plate. 'I've never seen that before. What is it made from?'

Gerry grinned as he took up the fork and cut off a wedge of the pudding. 'Pig's blood,' he said before popping the contents of the fork into his mouth.

'Oh my God!' Faye said. 'Are you serious?'

Gerry grinned again. 'Cross me heart and hope to grow a snout and trotters if I'm lying. It really is made from pig's blood. You should try a bit.'

She violently shook her head. 'I don't eat anything animal. And that sounds absolutely disgusting to me.'

'Arra not at all,' he said. 'We even eat it raw here. Nothing nicer than a few wedges of black pudding and a creamy pint of Guinness. Better than all your fancy auld stuff.'

She smiled. 'Well that is something we will never agree on.'

'So,' he said. 'Now that I've given you my history, what's yours?'

'Nothing special about mine either,' she said as she nibbled on a piece of cheese. 'I'm twenty four years of age, born in Sacramento. Graduated with a degree in business administration from the California State University. Started work for one of the smaller studios in Hollywood and just two years ago, was asked by Harold Zwimmer if I would go work for Global Pictures.' She finished off the rest of the cheese and the last slice of pear. 'My parents are still alive and I have two older brothers and a younger sister. Zach is with the Marine Corps and Gary is a dentist. Ella is still in High School. And that is me in a nutshell.'

He took another mouthful of wine. 'And is there no special somebody back in Hollywood or Sacramento?'

She said nothing as the waitress came over. 'Finished?'

They both nodded and she quickly removed the two plates.

Gerry took up the bottle and went to top up her glass but she placed a hand over it. 'Not for me, Scobie. I'm not a big drinker and if I have any more, I'll be like a wet rag all of tomorrow.'

He tipped the bottle into his own now nearly empty glass. 'Guess I'll just have to finish it myself so.' He examined the label. 'Wouldn't want the people at Chateau Du Movinaise to think we didn't appreciate all their hard work.'

The waitress came back and left the two large plates down in front of them.

Faye gave a surprised look when she saw the steel cover over Gerry's plate. There was none on her own. 'Have you got something special?'

Gerry laughed. 'That's just Bill. He always puts a cover on mine.' He gave hers a quick glance. 'What did you say that was?'

'Grilled aubergines with spicy chickpeas and walnut sauce.'

He made a face. 'Feck sake! Don't know how anybody can eat stuff like that with ne'er a bit of meat in it.'

She looked suspiciously at his now uncovered plate. 'And pray what is that? Looks like a lump of charcoal or something?'

He laughed. 'Charcoal me arse. It's a steak. Well done.'

'But it's incinerated.' she said.

He laughed again. 'Just how I like it. My all-time favourite meal. Well done fillet, French fried onions, mushrooms and chips. You can't whack it.'

'I couldn't eat it,' she said. 'Never mind whack it, whatever that means.' She began eating her own meal.

Gerry took up the steak knife and cut through the steak, the blade immediately staining with black powdery flecks. He added a mushroom to the lump of meat on the fork, a full onion ring and then stabbed the lot into the pile of chips, spearing three. The large ensemble was then stuffed into his mouth.

'So? You never answered my question about a special person back in the states. Is there somebody back there staring at your picture and pining away? Counting the days until you return.'

He expected her to laugh but her face remained serious. 'There is and there isn't,' she said, her voice low and with a very slight tremble in it.

He paused in his masticating of the dry meat. 'Ah God, I'm sorry, Faye. I didn't mean to be flippant. Do you want to talk about it?'

She took a sip of her wine. 'His name is David. We were engaged for a year. He broke it off two months ago.'

'I'm really sorry, Faye,' Gerry said. 'I just can't imagine anybody doing that. He must have a hole in his head.'

The tears flecked her eyes. 'No. Not a hole. A tumour.'

Gerry winced. He could see she was hurting now, whatever memories she had, obviously being very painful. He mentally cursed himself. Trust him to winkle out the one subject she probably didn't want to be brought up. He reached over and stroked her hand. 'I'm really sorry, Faye. I'm an idiot for bringing it up.'

She gave him a sad look. 'You weren't to know, Scobie. It's just one of those things.' She stifled a sob. 'I wanted to stay with him. Be with him while he goes through his treatment. But he said it wouldn't be fair to me. He couldn't allow that. I pleaded with him but his mind was made up. He told me I had to respect his wishes. He is on an intensive course of chemotherapy. They're hoping it will reduce the tumour so they can operate. He said that if they do get to operate and it's a success, well then we can look at getting back together. He moved back in with his parents and I keep in touch with them.' She wiped her eyes and gave him a weak smile. 'And that's it.'

They both went silent and for the next few minutes, both picked at their food, their appetites now blunted by the recollection. Eventually she put down her fork and forced a stronger smile onto her face. 'So now, we didn't hear anything about you. There has to be, or has been, someone special in your life.'

He left his own knife and fork aside, his meal only half eaten. He topped up his glass again with the remaining wine, took a deep gulp and then looked at her. 'There was somebody. An American woman.' He smiled. 'And what you might find even stranger, she was from Los Angeles.'

Faye leaned forward, her interest peaked to top level. 'From Los Angeles? Was she over here on holidays or what? How did you meet her?'

Gerry sat back, the memories flooding back as if it was only yesterday instead of over a year ago. Gloria's image floated in front of his eyes and for a moment, he scrunched his own shut as the image brought the deep feeling of loss and sadness back with a vengeance. He had thought he had come to terms with it. But they were both obviously opening up compartments of their lives that they had thought were closed.

It was Faye's turn to reach over and take his hand. 'If you would prefer not talk about it, Scobie, I fully understand.'

He smiled. 'I was over in Los Angeles at an International police convention. That's where I met her. She was an officer with the LAPD. Her name was Gloria. Gloria Ballantyne.' He exhaled loudly. 'It all happened so fast. We both just instantly fell for each other. And in all my life, nothing had ever felt so right. It was as if it was all predestined. We were only together for a week but we shared more love in that week than in all our previous years. At least, it was that way for me. And I think it was for her too.'

'So what happened?' she gently asked.

He closed his eyes again, the circumstances of her death playing in his head like a newsreel. 'She was shot,' he said. He didn't add any further explanation.

He paused and massaged his eyes, the simple innocent action conveying a weariness of life now totally in contrast to the good humour of just a few moments earlier.

Faye said nothing, knowing he was dealing with his memories, just as she had been dealing with hers a few moments earlier. They both needed the few minutes to take the pain of recollection, let it chew at them for the brief few moments and then take it and push it back into the recess of the mind from whence it had briefly escaped.

Gerry physically shook himself and then looked over at Faye. 'I'm sorry.'

She smiled at him. 'What are we like, huh? What say we skip desert and maybe head back to that bar of yours. McCluskey's, isn't it? I might just try one of your famous Jamieson whiskeys.'

Gerry grinned. 'Now that does sound like a right good plan. I'll ring Timmy straight away. But we can have desert while we're waiting for him. The apple crumble and custard here is to die for. You order for me while I go outside and make the call.'

'Make it here,' she said. 'I don't mind.'

He stood up and smiled down at her. 'You mightn't but Bill Watson does. That's another of his sacred rules. I'll be back in a jiffy.'

Fifteen minutes later, they were in the back of the taxi heading back to the town.

'Well? How was your meal?' Timmy O'Shea asked.

'It was very nice,' Faye answered.

O'Shea laughed. 'And I suppose you had the usual cinder block of meat, Scobie? Poor Bill told me he nearly cries every time he sees your plate going out with the cremated steak on it. Refuses to cook it himself. Gets one of the other chefs to do it.' He laughed again. 'I bet he had the cover over it. Doesn't want any the other diners to see it. Thinks it could ruin his reputation.'

Faye laughed. 'It was covered all right. I was wondering why but now I know. Poor Mr. Watson.'

'Poor Mr. Watson me arse,' Gerry said, although he too was laughing. 'If he had his way, me steak would be mooing on the feckin' plate.'

All three were still laughing as they pulled up outside McCluskeys.

*****

CHAPTER 17

Danny Corbett parked the van between two cars to the side of the car park facing the entrance to the Cloisters hotel. He had spotted the security camera the previous morning, but it was fixed over the main entrance door, it's lens pointing straight ahead. He was satisfied the area where he was parked wouldn't come within its range. He had a clear view of the main door. He yawned and then stretched his arms, trying to remove the kinks after a broken night's sleep in the van. He checked his watch. It was just approaching six o'clock. He stretched again. Even the shithole out at the farm would have afforded more comfort than the van. He grinned as he thought of Ratser complaining about the smell. This from a man who had a strong aversion to water and always reeked strongly of stale sweat and whose breath could curdle milk from ten yards. He had learned years ago to always stay downwind of Ratser. Maybe the van wasn't too bad after all.

He saw the bus and the three limos come up the road and swing in front of where he was parked. He sat watching as a group of people came out and got into the bus, joining the others who were already on it. Two men then came out, had a brief conversation with someone in the bus and then got into one of the limos. He continued watching as a big tall man came out and got into another of the big cars. The bus pulled away and the two limos followed. He hunkered down in the seat as they drove past.

It was five minutes later when he saw her come out. He clicked his tongue in admiration. Even at that hour of the morning, she was beautiful looking. She was wearing a yellow jacket over a pale blue blouse with tight blue leggings and short cowboy style boots. She had a blouse matching scarf knotted around her neck and even from the distance of twenty odd metres, he could see that her face was beautifully made up. A satchel type bag was slung over her shoulder. She stood waiting as the last limo edged forward and the driver hopped out and opened the back door. A minute later, the limo passed his van. He allowed it to go out and get about a hundred metres ahead and then he slowly pulled out and followed it. They drove out of town and were soon on the narrow road which he knew, led to the woods. He had checked it out the day before. He grinned as he followed the limo ahead. There was no other traffic on the road. It was obviously too early for the good folk of Kilbracken to be up and about.

And that was just fine. All they would need with a bit of luck, was five minutes or less. Stop the car, grab her and the driver, into the van and away. Of course, they would have to incapacitate … he liked that word … incapacitate the driver before driving the van out of concealment. They couldn't let it be seen. And they would be wearing balaclavas and boiler suits. Nothing to identify them in any way. And getting the limo to stop would be easy too. There was an unmanned railway crossing with a derelict hut about a mile from the woods, which, by the unkept look of it now, hadn't been used in a long time. All they had to do was open the gate across the road once they knew she was on the way. O'Driscoll had worked it all out after he had given him the lowdown on the road between the town and the woods.

He followed the car across the crossing and when he saw the woods in the distance with the security barrier in front, he slowed down and pulled into the side of the road. He could see the two security men waving the limo past them. He did a U-turn on the road and headed back to the farm.

He parked the van down a narrow laneway about a hundred metres from the farm. It was rutted and overgrown and obviously never used. They had considered hiding the van there after the snatch but O'Driscoll had decided against it. It would be too close to their hidden lair and if it was discovered, it could attract a lot of police activity around the farm. He would drive the van to Kilkenny city and park it in a supermarket carpark. He would stay in Kilkenny until he got the call from O'Driscoll to come and pick them up after the ransom had been collected by Spence's people. There was an old abandoned shed about a mile from the farm and once they got the word that the money was secured, the actress and the driver would be brought there and tied up. When they were safely back in Dublin, an anonymous phone call to one of the newspapers would tell where they were. He had asked O'Driscoll why they just didn't leave them tied up in the cellar and not risk having to bring them to the old shed. He grinned to himself. That was why O'Driscoll was the leader. Up there for thinking, down there for dancing. He would never have thought of it. If they were found in the cellar, the cops might just be able to link Lugser to it through his step uncle and it wouldn't require a giant leap for the buggers to track back his own visit to him in prison shortly before the kidnapping. And that could make them all, as they say in Hollywood movies, people of interest. He had to hand it to O'Driscoll. He was on top of everything.

He went into the shed and went over to the end stall and lifted the slatted pallet and left it standing on its edge. He opened the trap door and went down, letting it close over his head and shifting quickly to dodge the fall of some of the viscous brown covering.

O'Driscoll and Leery were sitting at the table. Ratser and Fatty were sprawled on the bunks. Fatty had his eyes closed but Ratser was working a finger deep up one nostril. There were six scented stubby candles lighting on the table. The smell in the room was quite pungent and cloying, the scent from the candles mixing with that of the cow excrement and silage and the combination was quite sickening. He breathed in short breaths, spacing them out as much as he could.

'All go okay?' O'Driscoll asked.

He nodded. 'Yeah. They all leave shortly after six, the bus first, then the limos. She was the last to leave again.'

'Good,' O'Driscoll said. 'Hopefully it will be the same tomorrow.'

Ratser pushed his finger deeper up his nose. The two pairs of gloves were making it difficult for him to get any traction. He wriggled it around and then gave a satisfied grunt as he pulled it out, a dried bogie stuck to the top. He held it in front of his face, examining it as if it was some new interesting discovery and then flicked it to the ground. 'We gonna do it tomorrow so?'

O'Driscoll didn't answer, just sat there staring at him.

Ratser gave him a puzzled look. 'What?'

'How many times have I told you about not leaving anything lying around? We don't leave anything. Not a scrap. When we leave here, it has to be as if we were never here.'

'So?' Ratser said. 'We're all throwing everything into the black bag, aren't we?'

O'Driscoll glared at him. 'And what have you just flicked to the floor?'

Ratser gave him an incredulous look. 'Ah for fuck sake! You're not serious, are you?'

O'Driscoll stood up. 'Yes I am fucking serious. The cops can extract DNA from anything. Even from one of your disgusting dried snots. Now you get down on your hands and knees and find that fucking thing and bag it.'

Corbett laughed. 'And don't expect any of us to help, you snotty bastard.'

Ratser threw him a dirty look but got off the bunk and down onto his hands and knees and began scouring the floor. He gingerly picked up the contentious piece of nasal product and stood up. He walked over and picked up the black refuse bag and with great deliberation, brushed the offending matter into the bag. He looked over at the others. 'Well? Everybody happy now?'

O'Driscoll ignored the caustic remark. 'Right. Let's go through things for the final time.'

They all gathered around the table.

He looked at Corbett. 'You be here at half five in the morning and pick us all up. You drop us at the railway crossing and then you go to the hotel. You ring me as soon as she's moving and you follow.' He looked at Ratser. 'The driver is yours and Fatty's. You grab him as soon as the car stops. Me and Leery will grab Metcalfe. Corby stays with the van.'

'What do we do with him then?' Ratser asked.

'He comes with us. Leery takes the car and drives it back to Dublin to Spence's yard in Lucan. They'll look after it there. Then he goes home and waits.'

Leery gave him a worried look. 'I'll never make Dublin. Sure once they miss her on the set, they'll be out looking for the car.'

'We take his phone and send a text back to his base saying Miss Metcalfe has suddenly decided she's taking the day off and has asked to be driven to Dublin for some shopping. According to what Fatty read on the internet, she's done this on other films. Does it quite often in fact. The film crowd will probably ring the limousine company when she fails to show up. With all the to-ing and fro-ing, that should give you plenty of time to make Lucan and Spence's yard. The car will be in a crusher before anybody's the wiser. We take her and the driver back to the cellar. We give you enough time to get back to Lucan with the car and then we make the call to Spence. He'll contact Lugser with all the details and then Lugser will make the ransom call. With a bit of luck, we will be back in Dublin within a day or two with Spence off our backs and a good few quid to divvy up between us.' He looked around them. 'Everybody okay with everything?'

Leery still looked a bit doubtful. 'What if anybody sees me driving the limo?'

Corbett shook his head. 'They won't. It's got tinted windows. Nobody can see in.'

O'Driscoll nodded. 'So you just drive it nice and easy. No speeding to get back quick. You drive into Spence's yard, leave the keys in it and then head off home. Believe me, you've got the handiest job.'

'Yeah,' Fatty said. 'And you don't have to spend another fuckin' minute down this stinkin' shithole. While we're back polluting' our already fucked up lungs, you'll be having a nice morning drive in a big fancy limousine and then you'll probably go off and have a few pints.'

Leery felt better. He grinned at Fatty. 'Ah you're makin' me feel sorry for ya now. The tears are runnin' down me fuckin' legs.'

Fatty glowered at him. 'Fuck off ya gimp-eyed git.'

O'Driscoll banged a fist down on the table. 'Cut the crap, ye two. Let's all just concentrate on the couple of days ahead. We get this done, then ye can slag each other off 'til the cows come home as far as the rest of us are concerned. But until then...' He mimicked pulling a zip across his lips. 'Keep it shut.' He turned to Corbett. 'You bring your boiler suit and balaclava with you. They're over there in the box that's still taped. I know Metcalfe and the driver won't see you, but we leave nothing to chance.'

Corbett nodded and stood up and went over and ripped the masking tape off the box. He took out one of the folded boiler suits, checked the size on the tag and satisfied that it would fit, rooted back in the box and then looked up. 'I don't fuckin' believe it,' he said.

O'Driscoll looked at him. 'What?'

Corbett reached into the box and pulled out a rubber Donald Duck mask and held it up. 'There's no balaclavas. Only a heap of these.'

O'Driscoll's eyes widened and he glared over at Fatty. 'I told you to get balaclavas. What the fuck are these?'

Fatty shrugged his shoulders. 'Couldn't find any so I got masks instead. What's the difference? Once our faces are covered, isn't that all that matters?'

Corbett waved the mask in his hand. 'And how the fuck are we supposed to talk in these with these big fuckin' beaks sticking' out and no opening for our mouths? Answer me that one, genius.'

O'Driscoll rolled his eyes. 'For fuck sake, Fatty! Can you do anything right?'

He took the mask from Corbett and thrust it at Fatty. 'You take this, and the other ones and you cut off these fuckin' beaks and leave a small slit for our mouths. Do you think you can manage that?'

Fatty took the mask from his hand without a word.

'Right,' Corbett said. 'I'll head back into Kilkenny now and all going to plan, I'll see you all at five thirty in the morning.'

'We'll be ready,' O'Driscoll said. He too stood up and walked over to one of the other boxes and took out a bundle of plastic ties and two small hessian sacks. 'Here. Stick these in the van. We'll need them tomorrow morning.'

Corbett took them from him grinning. 'Yer woman isn't going to like having one of these stuck over her head.'

Ratser laughed. 'Yeah. Might toss her hair a bit.'

Leery took up the battered pack of cards from the table. 'Anybody for a bit of poker? It's going to be another long fuckin' day.'

Ratser shrugged his shoulders. 'Might as well. Damn all else to do.'

'I'll leave ye to it,' Corbett said.

O'Driscoll watched him leave and then sat down at the table. 'Right, Leery. Deal 'em out and make sure they're all off the top.'

*****

CHAPTER 18

Danny Corbett lifted the cover and stood back as the blast of hot fetid air which rushed out, caught in his throat and made him gag slightly. O'Driscoll's head appeared through the opening. When he was out of the cellar, Ratser, Leery and Fatty quickly followed. When they were all standing in the main part of the shed, he dropped down the cover and then the slatted pallet. Ratser and Fatty rushed to the shed door and began to take in great big gulps of fresh air.

"Fuck sake,' Rasher said. 'Down there is worse than the Dublin sewers. Me fuckin' eyes are stingin' the head off me.'

Fatty took another great big gulp of air. 'I've been in some shitholes in me time but that literally is the worst ever. I'd say me lungs are shit lined at this stage.'

Leery grinned. 'Pussies. That's what the two of ye are.'

Ratser glared at him. 'Your fuckin' nose must be as fucked up as your eyes if that stink doesn't affect you.'

'That's enough,' O'Driscoll said. 'With a bit of luck, all we'll be smelling in a couple of day's time is money, money, money. So, cut the complaining' and let's get crackin"

They all went out and got into the van, O'Driscoll and Corbett into the front with the other three in the back. All wore blue boiler suits and disposable gloves and each carried a Donald Duck rubber mask which now had a slashed gash where the beaks had been.

Corbett started the engine and drove out of the yard.

Fifteen minutes later, he was parked outside the dilapidated hut at the old railway crossing. He sat with his elbow out the window as the others got out.

'Right,' O'Driscoll said. 'You get to the hotel and as soon as they start leaving, you ring me each time. Hopefully, she'll be last as before. Once you've confirmed that, we'll pull across the gate when the others have gone on.'

Corbett nodded. 'Will do. I'll hang a few hundred metres behind.'

O'Driscoll watched as he drove away and then nodded to the other three. 'Right. Into the hut and keep your heads down. With a bit of luck, we'll be back in the cellar with Metcalfe and the driver within the hour.'

Ratser made a face. 'I don't call going back to that shithole, a bit of luck.'

Corbett reached the hotel and parked in the same spot to the side, again ensuring he was out of camera range. He checked his watch. It was just approaching 6.15 so he had – assuming they stuck to the same timetable – fifteen minutes or so before the bus and limos would arrive. He took out his packet of cigarettes and lit one. He drew the smoke deep into his lungs and savoured the nicotine rush before blowing it out in a series of rings. He was quite expert at that. He cracked open his window to allow the smoke wisp out through the narrow gap. He just hoped everything went to plan. His share would be about a hundred and eighty thousand. He had never seen the colour of that kind of money. He lay back and mentally began to spend it. A holiday abroad would be first on the agenda. O'Driscoll was only going to give them a small sum initially. He didn't want any of them blowing big money and attracting attention immediately after the kidnapping which was what Ratser and Fatty were likely to do. They would all just get a couple of grand and O'Driscoll would stash the rest until he decided things had cooled down sufficiently and even then, he would drip feed them their share. The other three didn't know this yet and he grinned as he thought what their reaction would be. He had no problem with it and he knew Leery would be okay with it too but Ratser and Fatty would bitch big time. Particularly Ratser. He finished the last of the cigarette and pushed the butt out the window. He gave a wry grin and then opened the door and leaned down and retrieved the butt. As O'Driscoll said, you just can't be too careful. He crushed it into the ashtray.

He hunkered down as the bus drove in followed by the three limos.

As before, there were already people on the bus – probably those who were staying in the hotel in Kilkenny. He watched as others came out of the hotel and got on board. A few minutes later, the bus pulled away. He sat watching as the big man came out and got into the front of one of the limos. Two more men came out and after a brief word with the other man through the open window, got into one of the other limos. Both cars started up and drove away.

He took out his phone, scrolled up O'Driscoll's name and pressed. 'Yeah?'

'Bus left a few minutes ago and the other two limos are just behind. The package still hasn't come out.'

'Good,' O'Driscoll's voice reflecting the satisfaction he was obviously feeling. 'Ring as soon as she pulls away.'

He ended the call and sat back waiting, his focus on the front door of the hotel in front of which the third limo was parked, the driver outside and sitting on the bonnet. When he saw the driver jump up, he knew she was coming.

Sean Donovan gave her the best smile he could conjure up as he opened the back door of the limo. 'Good morning, Miss Metcalfe. Hope you had a good night and slept well.'

Sabrina Metcalfe stopped at the door. She was wearing bright canary yellow leggings, a powder blue loose-fitting blouse which still could not conceal her firm breasts and short blue suede ankle boots. A large holdall bag was slung over her shoulder. He noticed she had little make up on except for a light application of pink lipstick but even this natural look in no way detracted from her sexiness. And she was wearing a strong musky scent which had his heart accelerating way above its normal rhythm. He inhaled it as discreetly as he could.

'Thank you,' she said. 'I'm terribly sorry. I've forgotten your name again.'

'Donovan, Miss Metcalfe. Sean Donovan.'

'Oh yes. Mr. Donovan.' She left it at that. What kind of a night she had and how she had slept were none of his business. She slid onto the back seat, a thin satisfied smile forming on her lips as she recalled the previous night. She had declined an offer to join the others for the trip out to the restaurant which the hotel receptionist had recommended and dined alone in her room. Richard had phoned while she was eating to tell her that he had just had a phone call from England telling him that his father had taken a turn and was seriously ill. He was taking the first flight he could get to go there. She had voiced sympathy at the news of the old man's heart attack but had felt nothing but a satisfaction which had bordered on elation. Maybe this was the time the crusty old git would finally shuffle off and leave the title to Richard. She had rung room service for a bottle of Dom Perignon champagne to be brought up and when she had answered the knock on the door a few minutes later, Syl Carpenter had stood with a bottle of Cristal champagne in his hand and a large smile on his handsome face. He had met the waiter coming up and taken it from him. He had passed on the hotel's apology that they had no Don Perignon and the hope that the Cristal would be acceptable. And of course, she had invited him in. Thirty minutes and a half bottle of champagne each later, they were naked on the big bed, each marvelling in the exquisiteness of the body they were feverishly exploring with hands and tongues. Even now, the memory of the hardness of his toned body sent a warm shiver of pleasure coursing down her spine. Compared to Richard, it was like comparing granite to putty. But despite this muscled hardness – she had expected him to be rough and macho – he had been an extremely considerate and gentle lover, easing them both into an almost languid rhythm which had left her gasping and groaning with intense pleasure. He had brought her to sexual heights she had never before experienced or thought possible. Their love making had lasted well over the half hour and her final groan of pleasure had come from the very tips of her toes. Even now the next morning, she felt as if she was still glowing all over.

Sean Donovan sneaked a look in the rear-view mirror at his back seat passenger as he put the car in gear. She was smiling to herself with her eyes closed, as if enjoying some little secret only she was privy to. His breath caught in his throat as her hand briefly slid between her legs and gave herself a little rub. She opened her eyes and caught his look and her smile widened. She really felt good this morning. He had to wrench on the wheel to avoid hitting the pillar. He quickly concentrated on the road in front of him.

He spoke back over his shoulder. 'Would you like me to put on some music?'

The reply was low and purring. 'That would be nice.'

He flipped open the glove compartment and took out the one CD it contained, The Righteous Brothers Greatest Hits, one of his all-time favourites. He slid it into the player and soon the car was filled with Bill Medley's and Bobby Hatfield's soaring rendition of 'You've Lost That Loving Feeling'.

In the back seat, Sabrina allowed the music to take her over, luxuriating in the almost sensual acoustic coupling of Hatfield's tenor voice with Medley's deep bass.

Up front, Sean Donovan too allowed the music fire his imagination and in his mind's eye, he was exploring the naked body of his back-seat passenger. He sneaked a quick glance in the rear-view mirror. The subject of his thoughts was lying back, her eyes closed, her head slightly swaying to the music.

Reluctantly drawing his eyes back to the road, they widened in surprise when he saw the gate at the old railway crossing pulled across the road in front. The crossing hadn't been used in years. Probably some kids acting the maggot. He slowed down and pulled up in front of it. He turned and looked back at her. 'Won't be a tic, Miss Metcalfe. Some idiot has pulled the gate across the road.'

Sabrina merely nodded, her thoughts still centred on Syl Carpenter. Everything she had heard about him was true. She now knew that for definite.

She snuggled back in the now stopped car and closed her eyes again, allowing the memories of their love making to take over again.

Sean Donovan cursed as a splinter from the rotten gate post he was pulling on sleeved in under the skin of his thumb. That was all he feckin' needed! He was gingerly examining the invaded digit when the coarse bag was pulled over his head and a vicious kick to the back of his legs sent him sprawling to the ground. A heavy body landed on top of him and pinned him on the road. His hands were roughly pulled together behind his back and he winced as plastic ties were cinched tight over his wrists. He started to shout but the body on top shifted position until it was lying across his head. He struggled for breath as the heavy weight pressed his face onto the hard asphalt, forcing the rough sack to clog his mouth and nostrils. He arched his back and kicked his legs but there was no easing of the pressure on his face and panic hit him as his oxygen starved lungs began to burn. But the pain from his burning lungs suddenly took second place as a vice like grip suddenly clamped itself over his heart and squeezed until he felt it would burst like a rotten tomato. He felt the tears roll down his cheeks as the crushing pain jolted his body like an electric shock and when the black cloud started to descend, he welcomed and embraced it for the relief it brought.

Fatty felt the body suddenly go limp under him. He looked at Ratser who was on one knee beside them and nodded. The driver had obviously decided that there was no point in struggling any more. Together, they hefted the body up and carried it over to the van where O'Driscoll and Leery were already pushing a struggling Sabrina Metcalfe in through the back door. She too had a sack over her head and her wrists tied with plastic ties. The sack had a piece of string tied around it at mouth level pulling the coarse sacking tight into her mouth and effectively reducing her cries to a low muffled mewling. They hefted the driver in through the door and jumped in after him. Leery stood at the open back door, leaning into the van. He reached in and went through the driver's pockets until he found the mobile phone. He looked at the still figure. Why hadn't he moved or made a noise while he was searching him? He prodded the body with his hand and when there was no response, he put his ear to the chest. He then lifted the cinched hands and felt for a pulse. He looked at the other two who were now sitting on the floor, their backs to the panel which separated the driver's cabin. 'For fuck sake! What did ye do?'

When they gave him a puzzled look, he indicated with his head for them to get out of the van. When they were outside, he closed the door. 'That fella's brown bread.'

Ratser threw a worried look at Fatty. 'He can't be. I didn't hit him. Did you?'

Fatty shook his head. 'No. Maybe he's just fainted.'

Leery snorted. 'He's fuckin' dead I'm tellin' ya.'

Ratser shot a fearful look at Fatty. 'I only tied his wrists. You were lying on his head.'

Fatty's face visibly paled. 'I only did that to stop him shouting. That wouldn't have killed him. He must have had a dodgy ticker or something. How the fuck was I supposed to know that?' He looked again at Leery. 'Are you sure he's dead?'

Leery opened the door. 'Check for yourself.'

Fatty leaned in and felt for a pulse. He dropped the limp wrist and slowly closed the door again and looked over at Ratser, a shocked look on his face. 'He's fuckin' dead all right. What do we do now?'

They were all wondering how O'Driscoll would react to this unforeseen development.

'We have to tell him,' Leery said.

'He'll go fuckin' ballistic,' Ratser said.

Leery shrugged his shoulders. 'Well unless you can give the stiff the kiss of life and do a Lazarus on him, we don't have much choice, do we?'

He didn't wait for a reply, stepping around from the back of the van and going up to the front passenger window where O'Driscoll sat talking to Corbett. 'You ready for off?' O'Driscoll asked.

Leery managed to focus one eye on him. 'We got a problem, boss.' He nodded to the back of the van. 'Can you come out for a minute?' O'Driscoll gave him a puzzled look but opened the door and got out. He followed Leery around to the side of the van. Ratser and Fatty stood at the back, their eyes down.

Leery managed to keep the eye focussed on him. 'The driver's dead. I've checked.'

O'Driscoll's eyes widened in disbelief. 'He's what?'

'Dead,' Leery said again. 'Must have had a heart attack. You can check for yourself.'

O'Driscoll slid open the side door and leaned in and felt for a pulse as Fatty had done a minute earlier. He jerked back and slammed across the door.

Ratser couldn't stop himself when he saw the angry face swing around to them. 'It was Fatty. He lay on his head. He must have been smothering' him and that's what gave him the heart attack.'

Fatty glowered at him. 'It wasn't my fault.'

O'Driscoll glared at him. This catapulted them into a whole new ball game. Even if it was an accident, they were now guilty of manslaughter as well as kidnapping. He needed time to think. He looked at Leery. 'Did you get his phone?'

Leery took it out and handed it to O'Driscoll who quickly scrolled through the list of contacts. 'It's there. Under, office.'

He handed it back to Leery. 'You get going. Keep to the speed limits. In about fifteen minutes, pull in and send a text saying that Miss Metcalfe has changed her mind about working today and has asked to be driven to Dublin for some shopping. Leave it at that. If it rings back, don't answer it. Then get on to Lucan and text me when you've delivered the car. Leave the phone in it. And then go home and stay low.' He glared at the other two. 'Get in.'

Leery quickly walked over, picked up the driver's hat from the road and got into the Merc. He was glad to be getting away. Once he got the car to Spence's yard, he was finished. And it couldn't come a moment too soon for him. He now had a bad feeling about the whole thing. He stuck the chauffeur's cap on his head and put on his own dark sunglasses and drove off.

Corbett glanced over at O'Driscoll as he climbed back into the passenger seat. He started up the van and drove off. 'What was all that about?'

O'Driscoll exhaled deeply though his nose. 'The bloody driver has only gone and snuffed it. Fucking heart attack.'

Corbett stared at him. 'Oh sweet Mother of Divine! He's dead?'

O'Driscoll nodded. 'Dead as a bleedin' dodo. Ratser and Fatty must have gone too hard on him. I'll fuckin' swing for those two.'

'So what do we do now?' Corbett asked.

'What can we do only keep going,' O'Driscoll replied.

'We can't give up now. We stick to the plan,' he added. They drove on in silence and when they drove into the farmyard, O'Driscoll hopped out and slid across the side door. 'Get yer woman.' He nodded at the driver's body, '… and that, into you know where. And remember, not a word about where we are or who we are. No names at any time. Right? And don't forget her bag.'

The two heads nodded, Ratser already slinging the bag around his neck. He walked ahead into the shed as Ratser jumped out and when Fatty slid Sabrina Metcalfe out to the door, Ratser hefted her across his shoulder like a sack of spuds. Fatty hopped out and Corbett helped him lift the driver's body and the small procession made its way into the shed where O'Driscoll was standing with the trapdoor open. He stood to one side as Ratser first went down with his load and then Fatty slid the driver's body down when Ratser came back. When they had disappeared, he turned to Corbett. 'Right. You know what to do. With a bit of luck, this will all be over in a day or two.'

Corbett nodded and when O'Driscoll disappeared down the stairs, he closed the cover and replaced the slatted pallet. He then went out and got into the van and drove away.

*****

CHAPTER 19

Gerry whistled as he stepped out of the shower and reached for the towel. He was feeling damn good in himself. They had gone into McCluskey's after coming back from the restaurant and it had been virtually empty and that had suited the two of them just fine. While Faye had only had two sparkling waters, he himself had managed four whiskeys and he had greatly enjoyed the hour plus she had stayed with him. They had both agreed to park their sad stories for the rest of the night and their conversation had been light and amusing and centred around favourite films, Irish drink and Faye's father's belief that his family had Irish ancestry from way back. When Gerry had jokingly said that maybe they were related to the Knights of Columbanus, she had been genuinely impressed and had said she would ask her father if there was any mention of a place called Columbanus in his family history. She had feigned anger when Gerry had mischievously explained that the Knights of Columbanus wasn't a place in Ireland but a Catholic lay person's organisation dedicated to the promotion of Christian values and ideals.

He had walked her back to the hotel, both holding hands like two teenagers. When he had offered to see her up to her room, she had given him a wide smile and declined his offer. But she hadn't done it in a dismissive manner. She had cited an early morning start the next morning but had then said that maybe if he asked her out again the next night, which was a Friday night, she wouldn't have to worry about an early start the next day. He had immediately confirmed the date. She had then kissed him lightly on the lips and he now licked his own, recalling the sweet taste of her lipstick and the fullness of her lips. The kiss had been full of promise.

He walked over and examined his naked body in the full-length mirror on the wardrobe door. He grimaced as he noticed the beginning of a slight stomach bulge. He would have to cut back on the drink and particularly fast food. He sucked it in and re-examined himself as he held his breath. Yeah – that was much better. He would cut back and maybe visit the gym a bit more often.

He pulled on a clean pair of boxers and then his shirt, pants, socks and shoes. He ran a quick comb through his damp hair. He had shaven before the shower. Out in the living room, he grabbed his jacket from the back of the chair and after checking that he had his wallet, threw a final glance around the room and then went down the stairs and out the door.

He decided to walk to the station as part of his new resolution to lose a bit of weight. He slowed down as he approached Supermacs. As if on cue, his stomach rumbled. He stopped at the door. Feck it! Delaying another day wouldn't kill him. He could start the diet tomorrow. He pushed open the door and walked in.

Tina Dolan was leaving a tray of food down in front of a young couple and two children. Two women sat at another table, cardboard cups of either tea or coffee in front of them. They were in animated conversation. An elderly man whom Gerry recognised as Tom 'Tombstone' O'Neill, a retired grave digger, sat at another table, the full breakfast in front of him and a newspaper propped up against the large sugar container. He looked up as Gerry came in and nodded. 'How's it going, Scobie? Here for one of your five a day?'

Gerry grinned. 'Same as you, Tombstone. Need to put in a bit of foundation for the day.'

The older man laughed. 'Yer right there. I couldn't function without a bit of John Travolta and Olivia Newton John. Even if the doc did tell me to avoid them.'

He laughed again when he saw Gerry's puzzled look. 'Ah Jeez, you're fierce slow, Scobie. Grease. Remember? The film?' He stabbed a shiny sausage with his fork. 'Ye can't have a good fry-up without grease.' He chuckled as he held it up and began to sing in a passable baritone voice, 'You're the one that I want, oo, oo, oo.'

Gerry grinned and finished off the line in his own much less melodious voice. 'The one I need. Oh yes indeed.'

Tina Dolan came over to the table. 'Are you two trying to drive out the few customers we have? I don't know which of you is worse. I've heard better singing from the rear end of a constipated bull.'

'Well that's us put in our place, Scobie,' Tombstone said.

'Aye,' Gerry said. 'I think we'll have to cancel our application to X Factor so.'

The waitress rolled her eyes. 'X Factor? The feckin' bull would have a better chance than you two. And I mean you two gobshites and not Bono and the lads. Now – what do you want, Scobie? The usual is it? Full Irish with an extra egg.'

Gerry nodded. 'Yes please, Tina. And sure stick on an extra sausage and rasher as well. I'm starting a diet tomorrow so you'll be seeing a lot less of me. Might as well go out with a bang.' He gave a little laugh. 'Or should I say, with a banger.'

She gave an ironic laugh. 'You? A diet? I'd say you'll last about two or three days and then you'll be back in here stuffing your face again.' She walked away and headed back behind the counter.

Tombstone grinned up at him. 'Think she's right, Scobie. Can't see you lasting too long on rabbit food. And sure what's wrong with you, anyways? You don't have much of a gut.' He patted his own ample girth. 'Not like me, anyways.'

Gerry made a face. 'It's coming though. Was able to get a good grip each side this morning.'

The old man laughed. 'Sure they're only love handles, Scobie. Give the women something to hold on to while you're........you know ... doing the business.'

Gerry laughed. 'Maybe you're right. But sure I'll give it a try anyways. At least then I can tell myself I tried. Have to confess though. The thought of eating nothing but all that auld green shite is already bringing me out in hives.'

He looked over as Boss O'Connor came out of the toilet and sat down at one of the tables. 'There's a man I want to see,' he said. 'I'll see you around, Tombstone.'

'See you, Scobie. Good luck with the diet.'

Gerry walked over and stood in front of the table.

Boss O'Connor paused in his mouth mangling of a mixture of egg, sausage, rasher and black pudding. 'How's she cutting, boss?'

Gerry pulled out a chair and sat down. 'Going fine, Boss. Don't often see you in here. You been a bad boy at home or what?'

Boss gulped down the mouthful of food and laughed. 'Arra nuttin' like that, boss. The queen's gone over to her sister in England for a visit so I have to fodder for meself for the next couple of days. And you know what they say, boss. The auld breakfast is the most important bit of grub of the day.'

Gerry nodded. 'Can't argue with you there, Boss. Glad I bumped into you though. You know that picture that's being made here?'

Boss paused in his mangling of another melange of food. 'Up in the woods?' He nodded. 'Yeah. Pain in the arse if you ask me. Can't get to run the dogs up there in the mornings. Fuckers won't let me in. A couple of smart arse security guys blocking the way. I'm still tryin' to decide whether I'll go back up this mornin'. There's nowhere else as good for the auld dogs to open up. And if I decide to, a couple of poofters in yellow jackets aren't going to stop me.'

Gerry grinned. The security guys had been lucky so far. It would take a platoon of Irish rangers to stop Boss O'Connor and his dogs if he was set on running them in the woods. He'd swat a couple of security men aside like flies.

He leaned over a bit to the other man who was wiping a piece of toast over the now empty plate, mopping up the last of the egg yokes and grease. 'How would you like to run the dogs in the woods and get paid for it?'

Boss looked up, puzzlement on his face. 'What are you talkin' about, boss? Whad'ya mean, get paid?'

Gerry grinned again. 'Was talking to the producer fella the other day. Seems they need a few dogs for some of the film. I suggested they contact you.'

A wide grin spread across the beefy face. 'Fuck sake, boss! Are ye serious? That'd be great.'

Gerry nodded. 'I'm meeting the producer's assistant tonight, a young lady called Miss Knight. If you meet us in McCluskey's, she can have the contract with her for you to sign.'

O'Connor laughed. 'Contract me arse. I don't bother with contracts or any of that auld paper stuff, unless it's to wipe me arse. Once we agree a price, I'll spit on me hand and she can shake it. Deal done then.'

Gerry had to laugh. He could only imagine Faye's reaction to being offered a spit on a shovel of a hand from Boss. 'Sure we will sort it out some way, Boss. Around nine? That be okay with you?'

Boss stood up. 'Sound as a bell, boss. I'll see yis then.' He turned to walk away and then turned back. 'And thanks, boss. There's not too many would have done that for me. I won't forget it.'

Gerry waved a dismissive hand. 'No bother, Boss. See you tonight.'

Tina Dolan came down, a tray in her hands. She balanced it on her hip as she took off the large plate and left it down on the table in front of him. The small teapot and plate of toast followed. She then took up Boss' empty plate and cup and put them on the tray.

Gerry licked his lips as he looked at the plate of food. There were two fried eggs, four rashers, four sausages, three discs of black and white pudding, a scoop of beans and two halves of a fried tomato. A smaller plate had four slices of toast with four tabs of butter on top.

Tina Dolan smiled when she saw this reaction. She would bet a penny to a pound, he'd be back in a few days. There was no way he would stick to a diet.

Gerry took up one of the butters and took the paper off. He looked up at Tina who was still standing with a knowing grin on her face. 'What?' he said.

Her grin widened. 'Nothing. Just enjoying watching a condemned man eat his last decent meal.'

Gerry laughed. 'Arra feck off, Tina. I'll last a few days anyways with this inside me. Sure there's enough here to keep me going for a week.' He spread the butter on one of the slices of toast. 'How are things going with you and mammy's boy? Any sign of him breaking away from the apron strings?'

She snorted. 'There's as much chance of that as you staying on your diet.'

She sat down in the chair Boss had vacated. 'I've a good mind to tell him he has to choose. Me or her. What do you think?'

Gerry stopped with a forked sausage half way to his mouth. 'Don't know if that would be a good idea, Tina. As you well know, the Irish mammy – and I'm not just talking about Larry's mother – holds a certain position with their sons. There's not too many sons around who would deliberately cut them out of their lives, even for their girlfriends. And as you have said yourself, Mrs. Ward still owns the farm. Larry would be walking away from that as well.' He bit off half the sausage. Tina said nothing, her dejected face reflecting her grudging agreement with everything Gerry had said.

He took a mouthful of tea. 'You have to be cute and play the old bat at her own game.'

'And how do I do that?'

Gerry chewed on another mouthful of sausage. 'What do you know about Mrs. Ward?'

Tina's lip curled up into a sneer. 'Well I know she's a crusty old bitch who henpecked her husband into an early grave, keeps Larry on a tight leash and doesn't have a good word for anybody, despite all her craw thumping in the church.'

Gerry nodded. 'Yes. She is very much into her religion, isn't she?'

Again Tina's lip curled. 'She's more catholic than the pope, even if she is a bloody hypocrite.'

'So what do you think she would feel about somebody who gave her ... let's say ... maybe a bible with a little dedication in it personally signed by the pope? I would imagine that person would be very favourably looked upon.'

A glimmer of hope dawned on her face. 'I know you got some stuff from the pope that time you sorted out that thing in Rome but didn't you give the bible to Ms. Timoney? She was flashing it around for weeks afterwards. Larry told me his mother was furiously jealous. You didn't get a second one, did you?'

Gerry shook his head. 'No. Only got the one. But I'm sure if I asked the good padre from Athlone who's the pope's personal secretary, he would oblige me again. He did tell me if there was anything he could do for me again, all I had to do was ask.'

Tina grasped his hand. 'Would you, Scobie? Would you do that? God, if I presented something like that to her, I'd say she'd nearly marry me herself.'

'Leave it with me,' Gerry said as he focussed his attention back to the plate of food. 'I'll see what I can do.'

Tina stood up. 'You do this for me Scobie Tierney and you can forget about that diet of yours. There'll be a free breakfast for you here every day as long as I work here.'

Gerry sighed as she walked away. That was one offer he would find very hard to refuse.

*****

CHAPTER 20

Sam Brookman was struggling to control his anger. 'It's just not good enough. She just can't swan off whenever the mood takes her. Our whole schedule for today is screwed up now.'

Harold Zwimmer rubbed a tired hand across his forehead. 'Can we not shoot around her scenes today?'

Brookman chewed on his lip. 'I suppose we can. But it's going to take us an hour or two to rejig things. And we wouldn't know anything if the driver hadn't texted his base to tell them and they rang Faye. Not even the courtesy of a phone call from Sabrina herself.'

Syl Carpenter came striding over. 'Just heard the news from Faye.' He made a face. 'Sabrina's suddenly decided to go shopping in Dublin. That's a bit of a liberty, isn't it? Considering we had some major scenes to do today and we were all getting a free day off tomorrow anyways.'

'It's unprofessional, that's what it is,' Brookman said. 'And I'll bloody tell her that when she deigns to come back. And Enrico is not going to be happy either.' He looked at Zwimmer. 'Maybe it would be best if we kept this to ourselves. No point upsetting the big man back home. What do you think?'

Zwimmer scratched his chin. 'Maybe you're right. Once we don't lose too much shooting time, it shouldn't be a big deal. Faye'll be all right.' He looked at Carpenter. 'That okay with you, Syl? We keep this between the four of us?'

The actor shrugged his big shoulders. 'Fine by me. You're the producer and director. It's your decision. Once I still get the day off tomorrow. I've made plans to do a bit of fishing with that guy Larkin.' He gave a wry grin. 'I just hope he doesn't sink the boat.'

'Tomorrow's still free,' Brookman said. 'Even if we wanted to do some shooting, we can't. Union rules. Crew have to get the day off.' He slapped his thigh. 'Right. That's it so. We'll say Sabrina was feeling a bit under the weather so we decided to change the shoot around a bit. That okay with you two?' The other two men nodded.

The director grabbed Carpenter's arm. 'Right, Syl. We can shoot the love scene with you and Harriet and then the fight scene with Jerome.' He looked over at Zwimmer. 'Will you fill in Faye and get her to round the others up. I'll talk to the crew.'

Zwimmer watched as the two strode off. He had to agree with

Brookman. Sabrina's conduct was very unprofessional. No matter how big a star you were, there had to be some ground rules. He waited as he saw Faye come out of one of the trailers which was used as the onsite office.

'So?' she said. 'What's the decision?'

'We shoot around her scenes. Can you tell Harriet and Jerome to get ready?'

He put out a restraining hand as she went to walk away. 'The official story is, she's feeling a bit under the weather and we've given her a bit of time off. And we're not going to say anything to Enrico either.'

She nodded. 'Right. Just as well not to say anything to the others about her sudden urge to go shopping. It doesn't really concern them and I don't think they would be too bothered anyways. They all know she's a bit of a prima donna. And I think Enrico has enough on his plate by the sound of things. I presume you told Syl what the story's to be?'

'He's clued in and on board,' Zwimmer said. 'You've tried Sabrina's phone?'

'A few times,' she said. 'Just keeps going to voicemail. I've left a message.'

'Did you ring the limousine crowd?'

She nodded. 'They've tried the driver's phone a few times as well. He's not answering either.'

Zwimmer grunted. 'Probably under instructions not to from Sabrina.' He shook his head. 'Can you imagine what she'll be like if her husband gets that family title? There'll be no putting up with her then.'

Faye laughed. 'Lady Sabrina Tremayne. You have to admit though, it does have a nice ring to it.'

Zwimmer rolled his eyes. 'Well God preserve us all when she's called that. We will all be expected to bend the knee to her then. Even Enrico.'

Faye's expression turned serious. 'Is the studio in trouble, Harold? Mr. di Angelo seemed a bit anxious at the meeting before we left. I got the impression things were a bit iffy. He and Mr. Goldstein....I don't know.......just seemed a bit nervous when they were talking about costs and time schedules.'

The producer pursed his lips. His voice lowered to a conspiratorial tone. 'It's a bit exposed at the moment all right. A few of the recent productions aren't going too well at the box office and unless things pick up, they could prove very costly for the studio. And now with this shoot going on here and the other two back in the States, money is very tight.' He gave a resigned shrug of the shoulders. 'I'm not saying the studio is in trouble but it will have to walk an extremely tight rope for the next six months or so.'

'Do you mind if I ask you something else?' Faye asked. 'You don't have to answer me if you don't want to.'

Zwimmer nodded. 'I think we've known each other long enough for you to be able to ask me anything. Don't you, Faye?'

She took a deep breath. 'Is Mr. di Angelo connected. You know … to the Mafia.'

She expected the producer to laugh but when he didn't, she looked intently at him.

Swimmer's face remained serious. 'Enrico is a complex man, Faye. I know there have been rumours about his connection to certain people who … how shall I put it … are of interest to the authorities. And it is quite possible he has some friends of dubious character but is he himself a mafia member? No. I don't believe he is. He would be in much the same position as Sinatra was. Why do you ask?'

Faye bit her bottom lip. 'It was just something my father said to me recently.'

'And what was that?' Zwimmer asked.

'A friend of his, Joe Tramello, an agent with the FBI, told him that I should consider my position with the studio. That they were looking closely at its financing and at Mr. di Angelo.'

'Well, that is interesting,' Zwimmer said. 'I wouldn't say anything about this to anybody else, Faye. As you know, there are ears everywhere in this industry. But maybe, we should both review our situations in light of that little piece of information. If your father hears anything else from his friend, maybe you would tell me.'

Faye nodded and was about to voice her assent when her phone rang.

'I'll see you later,' Zwimmer said softly and then walked away.

Faye pressed the answer button and when she heard 'How's my favourite Knight of Columbanus', she smiled.

'If it isn't my favourite Irish policeman. I'm fine, Scobie. And you?'

'Full of the joys of life and the Irish breakfast from Supermac's.'

She laughed. 'Well there can't be too much room for anything else so.'

'There's always room for you, Faye me darlin'. You still okay for tonight?'

'Yes, Scobie. And free all day tomorrow.'

She laughed again when she heard the little whoop. 'Brilliant. What say I pick you up at the hotel around seven. There's a funfair in town. You like funfairs, Faye? The big wheel, waltzers, bumpers and all that stuff?'

'Will they have candyfloss?'

'If they haven't, I'll make it meself for you.'

'With an offer like that, how can I say no.'

'Great,' Scobie said. 'See you at seven.'

She didn't know why she said it before he hung up. 'Scobie. That chauffeur fellow who is driving Sabrina Metcalfe. Is he … you know … reliable?'

'Sean Donovan? He's all right as far as I know. Why are you asking?'

She was beginning to feel foolish but continued. 'He texted his base to say Sabrina had decided to go shopping in Dublin this morning instead of going out to the set. I know Sabrina has done that before but normally she rings herself. And she's not answering her phone and neither is he. I just have this uneasy feeling. She had some major scenes this morning and it just seems a little strange that she would suddenly decide to abandon everything and take off shopping. She would have known all the work that went into the set up.'

'From the little I've seen of Miss Metcalfe, I'd say she's a woman who makes up her own mind. But sure I'll pop into the taxi office and see if Donovan has been in touch with them since and if he hasn't, I'll check with his wife. 'He gave a little laugh. 'Although I don't think Seamy boy would want her to know he's off on his own with one of the sexiest women in the world.'

'Maybe I'm just being foolish,' Faye said. She lightened her voice. 'So! The funfair tonight. What should I wear? It's been years since I've been at one.'

'Leave that up to yourself. Once it's comfortable. You'd look good in a sack anyways.'

She laughed. 'Well I'll check my wardrobe and see if I have a sack that fits. See you at seven.'

Ruby Lipman came over to her as she put her phone away. 'So the queen is feeling a bit under the weather and she gets to have the day off.' She gave a sneering snort. 'Wasn't feeling that great myself this morning but I don't get the day off like Miss High and Mighty.'

Faye grinned at her. 'Well you have to admit, Ruby, your condition is down to too much wine from last night. I don't think that constitutes grounds for time off in Sam's eyes.'

Lipman laughed. 'God, I had a right skilful all right. I had a full bottle of white and then I had three of those Irish coffees afterwards. And if that wasn't bad enough, the restaurant gave us all a thing called Baileys. A beautiful creamy liquor. And Jerome and Harvey didn't like it so I drank theirs as well.'

Faye made a face. 'God, Ruby. How the hell did you even get out of the bed this morning. I wouldn't be able to function for a week if I drank that much'.

The other woman gave her a sly smile. 'And whose bed did you get out of? Yourself and that Irish cop seemed to be very cosy last night.'

'He's nice, isn't he?'

'Wouldn't crawl over him to get at Harvey, that's for sure. You seeing him again?'

Faye nodded, a smile on her face. 'This evening. We're going to a funfair of all things.'

'And after?'

Faye smiled again. 'That remains to be seen.'

*****

CHAPTER 21

Sabrina felt as if she was suffocating, her breath bouncing back on her face in the hot confines of the clinging sack which was still over her head. At least they had untied the string from around her mouth, although her hands were now tied to the sides of the chair in which they had pushed her. But it wasn't just the heat. The smell of wherever she was, was quite sickening. She swallowed hard as another gourd of hot bile rose up her throat. She was still having great difficulty taking in the events of the last thirty minutes or so. One minute she had been dreamily reliving her night of passion with Syl, the next she was being roughly bustled into a van with her hands tied and a filthy sack over her head. She had bounced around on the floor of the van for about fifteen minutes and then when it stopped, she had been hoisted onto somebody's shoulder like a bag of potatoes and carried to wherever she now sat. Nobody had said a word during that time. And what had happened to the driver? She hadn't heard a peep out of him since he got out of the car to pull back the gate.

She heard them moving around. 'Please. Please let me go. I'll give you whatever you want.' She knew her voice was high pitched and whining, totally unlike the honeyed sexiness of her screen voice, but under the circumstances, it was the best she could do.

The answer was short and rough. 'Lady, you've just to do two things. Sit quietly and shut the fuck up.'

Ratser grinned at O'Driscoll's response to the woman's plea. 'Yeah,' he said to the covered head, 'keep quiet or else you'll be takin' the main part in The Big Sleep.' He looked around to see if any of the others had gotten this -in his opinion – smart quip about one of his favourite movies starring one of his favourite actors, Robert Mitchum. He had seen it three times, once in the cinema and twice on television although the second time on television, it had been the original version with Humphrey Bogart. He had still preferred the Mitchum version. The only response he got was a contemptuous look from O'Driscoll.

O'Driscoll pulled Danny Corbett over to the tunnel, out of earshot of the others 'You take off and head back into Kilkenny. As soon as Leery texts to say that the car's been looked after by Spence's crowd, I'll ring you. You can text Lugser then and he can make the call a few hours after that. Spence should have given him all the pick up details by now. This whole thing could be over in a couple of days.'

Corbett turned to look back to where the lifeless body lay on one of the bunk beds, the sack now removed from the dead man's head. He was still having difficulty taking in the man's death. He turned back to O'Driscoll. 'Jesus, Billy. What are we going to do about the driver? This whole thing is really fucked up now.'

O'Driscoll exhaled heavily. 'Nothing we can do. We just have to stick to the plan. I'm sure when they find them, they'll do a post mortem on his body and they'll see it was a heart attack.'

'It'll still be manslaughter,' Corbett said.

'Only if we're caught. And what choice have we anyways? We have to see it out. There's nothing else we can do.'

Ratser and Fatty heard the whispered voices in the tunnel. They both knew full well what was being discussed. Neither of them was too upset because the driver had had a heart attack and died. But the fact that O'Driscoll was blaming them, that did bother them. And it bothered Ratser more because as far as he was concerned, it was Fatty who had caused it. But they were both getting blamed. And that was unfair. He had only held the man's legs. It was Fatty who had sat on his head and probably smothered the poor bastard.

Fatty knew he had wilted a bit under the glance from O'Driscoll earlier, but it had also annoyed him, although he had been careful not to show it. It wasn't his fault the driver had had a dodgy ticker. Bugger could have popped his clogs at any time. But they were all blaming him for it. Even Ratser who had been holding the man as well, was saying it was his fault. Well they could all blame him as much as they wanted. It didn't change a thing. They were all in it together.

They both watched as O'Driscoll came back after Corbett had left. That meant things were back on track. The quicker this whole thing was over, the better. The driver's death was unfortunate but hey, shit happens.

They all turned as the woman's strained voice came through the sack. 'Please. Whoever you are. I can't breathe properly.'

O'Driscoll walked over and stood behind her. He reached down and gripped the bottom of the sack. Carefully, he began to fold it into pleats until it had cleared her mouth and nose. He held it then and nodded to Ratser. 'Get the roll of masking tape from the box over there.'

Ratser went over and got the tape. He came over and extended it to O'Driscoll who was still holding the folded sack over the woman's upper face. O'Driscoll angrily shook his head.

'How the hell can I do it? Hurry up for fuck sake.'

Ratser began to pick at the tape with a nail, trying to get a start on the roll. He couldn't even find the start of the tape. He wished now he didn't bite his nails down to the stumps they now were.

O'Driscoll glowered at him. 'Will you hurry up, for fuck sake. I can't stand here all day.'

He tried picking with two stubby fingers, his hands now getting sweaty and making things even more difficult. He threw a helpless look at O'Driscoll. 'Bloody tape is welded to itself.'

He picked furiously at it but all he was managing to do now was cover it in a sheen of sweat. It was suddenly pulled from his hand.

'For fuck sake!' Fatty said giving him an exasperated look as he grabbed it from him. He probed the roll with a large dirty finger nail and grunted with satisfaction as he prised up a corner of the tape and then pulled gently and extended a long strip. He quickly pressed the end over the folded sack and as O'Driscoll moved his hands in unison with his, wound the tape around the sack a few times until it was tight over the top half of the woman's head. He leaned down and bit off the tape and pressed down the end. The taped sack now looked like a turban which had slipped down over her eyes. He gave his handiwork a satisfied look and Ratser a sneering one and then lobbed the roll into the box with a shot Michael Jordan would have been proud of.

Sabrina gulped in a few mouthfuls of air. The smell was even worse now that her mouth and nose were free, but at least there was no confined suffocating heat which had made her feel her head was in an oven. She was about to say thanks but stopped herself. Why the hell should she thank them? They had kidnapped her. And manhandled her. And now here she was, tied to a chair sitting in some place that smelled like a shithouse and with her eyes covered by a dirty sack. No. Thanking them would be the last thing she would do. It had to be a ransom job. There was no other explanation. She just hoped that the studio and Richard would get their act together quickly and get her out. Her lips were very dry and a few licks from her equally dry tongue did nothing to moisten them. She lifted her head. 'Please. Could I get a drink?'

O'Driscoll nodded to Ratser who went over to the table and got one of the cans of coke from the half full twelve pack. He popped the tab and walked back over. Gripping the woman under the chin, he tilted her head slightly and put the can to her lips, tilting it as well. Fizzy coke dribbled down her chin as she gulped thirstily from the steady flow. She had to keep gulping as the can was tilted further and more of the coke ran down her chin and onto her top but then suddenly it was empty. She would have much preferred water but at least it had gotten rid of the dryness. Again, she stopped herself from saying thanks.

Ratser squeezed the empty can and flung it into the corner but a glaring look from O'Driscoll sent him scurrying after it. He retrieved it from the floor and put it into the big bag in which they were putting all waste.

O'Driscoll pulled up a chair in front of the actress and sat down. He kept his voice low. 'Just so we understand each other, Miss Metcalfe. You will be held here until your studio or your husband pays for your release. It would be best for all of us if you just sit quietly until the deal is done. Hopefully, assuming the studio and your husband value you as a leading star and a wife, this will all be over in a matter of days. I only expect you to speak when you are hungry or thirsty or need to go to the toilet.' He gave a little laugh. 'Unfortunately, we only have a bucket for the latter and you will have to just take my word that none of us will look. Is all that clear?'

Sabrina nodded her head. She knew in her heart that there would be no privacy if she did have to use the bucket but the fact that she herself wouldn't be able to see them looking at her, well that itself was some comfort, albeit, a very small one. But she would hold out a long as she could. If at all possible, nobody was going to see her squatting over a bucket. She would drink sparingly – only when she absolutely had to – and eat even less. She wondered again about the driver. Why wasn't he saying something? There hadn't been a peep out of him since the abduction. Was he even here with them or had they put him somewhere else? But that was unlikely. Why would they be splitting them up? It made no sense. She thought about Richard. What would be his reaction when he heard? She knew he didn't have the kind of money these people were probably looking for. They probably wouldn't even have it between them. Sure, she was a big earner but she was an equally big spender. Neither of them ever countenanced a rainy day. But it was certainly raining now! And Richard's family in England? If what Richard had told her was true, there was no big pot of cash there either. Like with a lot of the gentry in England, the maintenance of the stately home – which in a lot of cases were old crumbling edifices – ravenously ate up a lot of the old money these relics of a different age lived on and this was true of Richard's father. She wondered was the old man still alive or had he died since. She gave a little laugh to herself. Maybe she was already Lady Tremayne. How ironic would that be? A lady of the realm sitting with a dirty sack over her head, her hands tied to a chair in the middle of a foul-smelling room, with a bucket for a toilet. That would certainly make her stand out in Burke's Peerage.

It would have to be the studio. But would they pay up? She was, after all, only an actress. Not family to any of the studio bosses. How would Enrico di Angelo react? He was a hard-headed business man, not prone to sentimentality of any type. The only thing which would work in her favour was the publicity. She was, after all, the queen of Hollywood. The public – her public – would expect the studio to do all they could to effect her release. It would be extremely bad for their image if they did not at least, be seen to be doing everything they could. But how long would these negotiations take? Knowing di Angelo, he would drag it out to the last, trying to save every cent he could. He would be hoping that the police would find her before he had to part with any money. She knew nothing about the Irish police or how good they were at this sort of thing. The image of the policeman Donovan had introduced her to, came into her head. What's this his name was? Something weird. Sounded like a bad rash or something. Scobie – that was it. Scobie Tierney. She addressed the image in her head. 'How good are you, Scobie Tierney? Will you be able to find me?'

She grimaced as she felt the pressure start to build on her bladder. That was all she needed now. She should have gone in the hotel earlier. She clenched her buttocks but she knew nature was going to prevail. There was no point prolonging the discomfort and risk wetting herself. And to hell with them. Let them see her squat if they were perverted enough to want to. 'I need to relieve myself,' she said.

Ratser grinned over at Fatty and then looked at O'Driscoll and when he just nodded, he went over and began untying the woman's hands from the arms of the chairs. He jerked her up to a standing position and then steered her over to where Fatty had moved the bucket out from the wall, making sure to use only his foot.

Ratser tapped her lower leg with his foot. 'Spread your legs.' He grinned over at Fatty. Who would ever have believed he would be telling the sexiest actress in the world to spread her legs. When she widened her stance, he edged the bucket under her with his foot. 'It's right under you.'

Fatty stood watching, a lascivious look on his face as the woman peeled down her leggings to her knees. He took a sharp intake of breath when he saw the small diamond shaped thong, barely big enough to cover what it was supposed to.

He held his breath as she squatted down gingerly until her bottom touched the rim of the bucket. He sneaked a quick look at Ratser. He too stood transfixed, his dilated eyes firmly fixed on the woman and the bucket.

Sabrina could feel their eyes on her. She gripped the front of her leggings and pulled them partially up until they concealed her front and then quickly pulled the thong to one side and sat down on the bucket. She held the leggings in front of her with one hand and the thong with the other, blocking off their view. The stream of urine noisily hit the bucket – it must have been empty – but she didn't care about that. They could have all the sound effects they liked but at least, she was fairly sure she had deprived them of the main visuals. When she was finished, she let the thong slide back and then half stood up and quickly pulled her leggings back up fully. She allowed herself to be guided back to the chair and sat down. Her hands were once again tied to the chair's arms. The sack over her eyes spared her the sight of the two men peering into the bucket, as if they were carefully examining some wonderous newfound specimen of something or other instead of approximately two inches of still steaming pee. She couldn't stop a smile creasing her lips when she heard the same voice which had listed out the rules of her captivity to her a while ago shout, 'For fuck sake! Will ye take your heads out of that fuckin' bucket, ye pair of fuckin' pissheads!'

Sabrina smiled again. She would give him that one. Pissheads indeed.

*****

CHAPTER 22

Leery watched as the large crane with the big circular magnet hoisted the limousine high in the air and swung it around over the crusher machine. He stood transfixed as it was lowered between the two massive jaws and the magnet disconnected. The car dropped the couple of feet into the gaping maw. The machine growled to life and slowly the two jaws started to come together, crumbling the big car as if it was made of cardboard. He watched as the window glass shattered and the car body folded and contracted like a crushed beer can. The big jaws then opened partially and then two hydraulic rams compressed the flattened car into a square block of metal. The magnet then swung back and lifted out the block and swung it around where it was dropped into a pile of other compressed blocks.

One of the yard workers came over, a grin on his face. 'Cops will have a hard time tracking down that baby now, eh?'

Leery didn't reply. All he wanted to do now was get the hell back to his own neck of the woods and have a drink. He walked out of the yard and stopped outside the gate and took his own mobile from his pocket. The driver's phone was now part of the square block of steel along with the hat which he had left on the seat with the phone. He brought up O'Driscoll's name and tapped on it. It was answered almost immediately.

'It's done,' he said.

'Good. I'll be in touch. And remember, stay low.' The phone went dead in his hands.

He walked the hundred yards to the empty bus stop and slouched against the shelter frame. He wiped a hand across his forehead. He was sweating but he knew it was nervous sweat and not from the short walk. Should he have told O'Driscoll? For the fourth or fifth time since it had happened, he reasoned himself into believing it hadn't mattered and there was no point telling anybody. It had only been a routine checkpoint after all. The guards had only been checking tax and insurance and the limo had been fully compliant with the appropriate discs on the windscreen. Sure he had had to let down his window but he had been wearing the hat and the sunglasses so he really couldn't be described in the future by the young female guard who had approached him. She had merely given him a quick glance, examined the discs on the windscreen and then waved him on.

What was the point telling anybody about that?

He stood up straight as the bus came around the corner and pulled up. He waited as an elderly woman, bent in two with a fully laden pull along shopping trolley, stopped in the open doorway. She looked at Leery, an appeal for help on her face. He didn't move. A male passenger sitting in the front seat, hopped up and after giving Leery a disgusted look, jumped down, took the trolley from the old woman and left it on the footpath and then took her hand as she gingerly stepped down. Leery didn't even wait for the handover. He brushed past the two and jumped up and dropped four 2-Euro coins into the tray. The driver gave him a dirty look and then took the four coins and punched out a ticket. Leery peeled it off the machine and then stood, waiting for his change. When there was none forthcoming, he looked at the driver but he knew by the look he got back, no change was going to come. He thought briefly of making an issue of it but it was only seventy cents. Fuck it. When their little venture was over, he could buy the fuckin' bus. He went down the back and sat down. The good Samaritan got back on and after throwing another baleful look down at Leery, retook his seat at the front. He exchanged a few words with the driver which Leery knew were probably about him but he wasn't bothered. He was still thinking about the Garda checkpoint. The young guard had stooped down and looked into the car but it had only been a cursory look. No – there was nothing to worry about. Chances were, she wouldn't even remember checking the limo. God knows how many cars she had stopped. It was an extremely busy road. He sat back, his mind now moving on to the prospect of having a sum of life changing money in the very near future, all things going according to plan. The driver's death was an unforeseen complication but there was nothing they could do about that now. They had been going to hold him with the actress anyways so the fact that he was now dead, well it didn't really alter things.

Forty minutes later, he pushed through the door of The Horse's Head pub. It wasn't his regular haunt – that was The City Arms back near his flat – but he occasionally had a pint or two in it now and again. He hopped up on a bar stool and when the barman came over, he ordered a pint of lager. When it was left down in front of him, he handed over a tenner and then took up the cold glass and took a deep pull which brought the frothy top almost half way down. He licked his lips. God that was good. The barman left his change down on the counter in front of him. 'Bloody hell, you were thirsty.'

Leery ignored the comment.

The barman shrugged his shoulders and walked away to serve another customer.

He took another pull from the pint. He grinned to himself as he thought of Ratser and Fatty still stuck in the shithole. Maybe he should take a selfie of himself with the pint and text it on to Ratser. That would really get up his nose. He finished off the pint and tapped the counter with the empty glass. When the barman looked over, he waved it at him. The barman nodded and a few minutes later, put a fresh pint down in front of him. Leery paid without speaking. When the barman had gone off again, he took out his phone and pressed on the camera ikon. He then picked up the full pint, put a wicked grin on his face, held the phone in front and took the picture. He took a mouthful from the pint and then examined the picture. Apart from the screwed stare of his eyes, it was a good picture, clear and well defined with the pint looking particularly appetising. He grinned to himself, tapped on message, scrolled through his list of contacts, brought up Ratser's number, added the photo as an attachment and then paused. What comment would he put? He thought for a few moments and then he began to type – 'greetings from me in the Horse's Head to you in the cow's hole'. He grinned again and pressed send.

Ratser took out his phone after hearing the beep. Who the hell was sending him a message? He went in to his message box. Leery's cross eyed face with the stupid grin peered out at him but it was the frothy pint with what he knew were cold beads of melted frost sticking to the outside that really annoyed the hell out of him. When he read the message underneath the photo, he roared. 'Fuck you, ya cross eyed bollocks!'

Fatty and O'Driscoll both looked over at him.

'What?' O'Driscoll said.

Ratser walked over and trust forward the phone. 'Fucker's takin' the piss big time.' He showed them the image on the screen.

O'Driscoll said nothing for a minute but Fatty exploded. 'That miserable git. I'll fuckin' wring his scrawny neck next time I see him. He didn't have to send that to us. Fucking prick.'

O'Driscoll pursed his lips. That's all they needed now. Leery going off and getting pissed as a newt and then blabbing God knows what to God knows whom. He held out his hand. 'Here, give it to me.'

Ratser passed over the phone and he and Fatty stood watching as O'Driscoll cleared the screen, called up Leery's number from the contacts list and hit the green call sign. It was answered after a half dozen rings. 'Whad'ya think, Ratser? Bet you'd give your back teeth for a pint like that.'

O'Driscoll's voice dripped more ice than the glass had. 'Listen you thunderin' prick, I told you to stay low until all this was over and what's the first thing you do? Go fucking drinking! Now you get your arse out of that pub and back to your pit and stay there until I tell you different, okay?'

He didn't wait for a reply, cutting the call off and thrusting the phone back at Ratser. He glared at him and Fatty. 'Surrounded by gobshites, that's what I am. One bollocks going on the piss and two more here examining it in a bucket as if it was liquid fuckin' gold.' He shook his head in exasperation. 'God give strength. Let's hope the other one is doing what he's supposed to do without joining you gang of clowns.'

Fatty tried to appease him. 'Ah Lugser will, boss. Sure all he has to do is to make the call to the paper and give them Spence's instructions for the ransom pick-up.'

He knew before O'Driscoll's mad look and Ratser's disbelieving one bored into him that he had fucked up. He had mentioned names. He shot a quick look at the woman. Had she heard? He had only used Lugser's nickname but he had used Spence's. He bit deeply on his lip drawing blood.

O'Driscoll couldn't believe what he had heard. Fatty saying Spence's name. A name well known to the police as a major suspect for tiger kidnappings in the past. If the woman could tell them she heard it, they would be all over Spence like a rash. And that was bad news for them all. Spence would have their guts for garters and if he went down, he would make damn sure they all did. He glared at Fatty again but said nothing. He didn't want to compound things by letting the woman know something dramatic had happened. The names might just have passed over her but if he made a big thing of it now, she could just rejig her memory and recall the names, particularly Spence's.

One of the subjects of their conversation was at that moment, in a quandary. He had just received the text from Corbett telling him that the actress had been snatched and that he was to make the call to the paper in a couple of hours. He hadn't been given any other details. He had rung Spence earlier and gotten all the details for the ransom pick up. But now he had a problem. A major one. Just ten minutes earlier, they had all been sent back to their cells and there was a lock down in place and the grapevine had it that there was a search on for mobile phones. He had to get rid before his cell was searched. He estimated he had about twenty minutes before they got to his landing. But if he got rid, he wouldn't be able to make the call to the paper. Did he make it now before disposing of the phone or just dispose of the phone and leave it to one of the others to eventually make the call when they discovered he hadn't?

He weighed up the pros and cons. If he didn't make the call, there would be a lot of confusion. O'Driscoll and Spence would both be wondering why. It would mean that they would have to contact each other to decide what to do and he knew that neither of them wanted that. The agreement was that there would be no contact between them until after the ransom was paid. Corbett had told him that when he had sneaked him the phone. For some reason, they wanted the call traced to the mast which was only fifty or so metres over his head. And if he didn't make the call, they would have no reason to pay him his share. And that was what made the decision for him. He went to the door and listened. They were still on the landing below. He went back to his bunk and retrieved the phone from under the mattress. It was a basic model, no bigger than a ten packet of cigarettes and it was still quite sticky. He allowed himself a grin. Corby had smuggled it in, in his hair of all places. He had a thick head of wavy hair and styled it in sixties fashion, like Elvis Presley and Ricky Nelson. He had shaved out a small area on his head, taped the phone to the bald spot and then combed over and hair sprayed it until it was like wire. The screws hadn't looked twice at his head when they had searched him. But it still was sticky from the tape and the hairspray. He quickly brought up the second number Corby had put on the contact list and hit the call button.

Less than a mile away, Terry Nolan looked around the busy office and when no one else made to answer the ringing phone, she rolled her eyes with annoyance. It was always left to her. But if the call was the makings of a good story, the editor always gave it to someone else. She knew she was only an apprentice but how was she supposed to establish herself if she never got the chance. Her voice reflected her annoyance. 'The Chronicle news desk.'

She had to listen intently to hear the low voice. It was barely a whisper. 'Sabrina Metcalfe the actress, has been kidnapped and that two million must be paid. It is to be brought to the National Stadium on Sunday night next. It is to be left on the floor behind the tiered seating in block N at exactly 9 o'clock. Any sign of police and she dies.'

Terry looked frantically around her, trying to catch somebody's eye. 'Who's calling? How do I know this is true?' The line was dead in her hands.

She slowly replaced the receiver and then stood up and went over to the small office where Larry West, the editor sat behind his desk. She knocked and then entered. He looked up. 'What is it, Terry?'

She cleared her throat. 'Just had a call from someone telling me that Sabrina Metcalfe has been kidnapped and that two million is to be delivered to the National Stadium next Sunday night and left behind the tiered seating in block N at 9 o'clock.'

West pushed the glasses back up on his head. 'Jesus! Just now?'

She nodded. 'Less than a minute ago. I came straight in.'

'She's down in Kilkenny, isn't she? Doing a film down there.'

Nolan nodded. 'Yes. Herself and Sylvester Carpenter are in it. Do you think this is a genuine call?'

West stood up. 'Only one way to find out. Is Rhino around?'

Nolan groaned. David 'Rhino' Brennan was the paper's social and entertainment reporter. Fifty-one years of age, openly Liberace style gay and with a skin thick enough to ignore the myriad of slights and put downs thrown his way over a thirty-year career in journalism. Hence his nickname.

'Haven't seen him,' she said. 'Isn't he in Belfast today and tomorrow covering the royal visit?'

West made a face. 'God, yeah. I'd forgotten. We need to get somebody down there to the film set before the other nationals get wind of it.' He glanced out into the main newsroom and went to stand.

She braced herself. 'I could go.'

He looked hard at her. 'You? Do you not think it's a bit big for you? You really don't have much experience. And aren't you off on holidays tomorrow anyways?'

'We're not flying until late tomorrow night. I could go down straight away. And Mr. Brennan is back tomorrow afternoon so he could go down then.'

West made another of the snap decisions he was famous for. 'Right. Go for it. Go straight to the film set and see what you can find out. And check in with the local police. I'll ring Rhino and he can go straight down from Belfast.' He looked at his watch. 'We'll have to report the call so get yourself sorted. You could be there in a couple of hours.'

She masked her elation as best she could. This was her chance. If she could file something before Rhino got down, it just might be her name under the headline.

Back in Mountjoy jail, Lugser took the sim card out of the phone and popped it into his mouth. He filled a glass of water from the tap and then put it to his mouth and swallowed it down in two gulps. The sim card went down with the second. He then went over to the barred door and flung the phone out as far as he could. It clattered along the corridor and then slid over the edge and fell down to the ground floor. He went back and sat down on his bunk. All he could do now was wait and follow developments on the television. The rest was up to O'Driscoll and Spence. He wondered how long it would take for the sim card to pass through his system. He wasn't looking forward to having to check his shit later on but the card had Spence's call on it giving him all the details for the ransom pick up. Having that might just come in useful some time. He wasn't quite sure how and he would probably never use it but he was a firm believer in never disposing of anything that might prove a bargaining tool at some later date. O'Driscoll did it – Corby had told him about the tape and they had both had a good laugh at it – so what was good for the goose as they say. The rest of them were scared shitless of Spence but he wasn't. Sure what he was; he only was an aging old provo has-been. When he got out, he was going to make a name for himself. The Spences' of this world would soon be making way for younger Turks like him.

*****

CHAPTER 23

Gerry checked himself in the long mirror and was happy enough with the reflection that looked back. He had opted for a pair of brown cords, beige shirt and cream jumper which was loose enough to mask the small gut which had prompted his new resolution to go on a diet. His hair was still a bit damp from the shower and was tending to curl a bit but he made no attempt to try and straighten it. People had told him it gave him a roguish look and sure what was wrong with that? He fancied himself as a bit of a rogue.

He went out into the living room and glanced over at his laptop which was open on the small coffee table. He grinned when he saw he had a message. He went over and opened it up. As he had hoped, it was a quick reply to his one earlier to Monsignor Peter Cunningham in the Vatican. He quickly scanned the short message.

Scobie, good to hear from you and hope all is well. The Holy Father will be happy to accede to your request and the signed bible will be despatched in the next few days. His Holiness sends his best regards to you and asks that his best wishes be also passed on to his good friend, Father O'Mahoney.

God Bless.

Peter.

He grinned as he closed down the lid of the laptop. Tina Dolan's prospects of eventually becoming the new Mrs. Ward were beginning to look a bit better. He grabbed his car keys from the table and headed down the stairs. Miss Timoney was locking the front door of the travel agency when he came out the door. He made a face to himself. She was quite likely to keep him talking for God knows how long. He turned around, a smile now on his face. 'Hello, Miss Timoney.'

She returned his smile. 'Hello, Detective Sergeant Tierney. I must say, you are looking very smart this evening. Going somewhere special?'

'Just up to the funfair that's moved into O'Gorman's field. Thought I might have a look around.'

Her face took on a wistful look. 'Ah, the funfair. God be with the days. I used to love them when I was a girl. The waltzers. The hoopla stalls where you threw the ring and tried to get it over one of the prizes.' She wrinkled her nose. 'Cheap and all as they were. The swinging boats. The roundabouts for the kids. They're called carousels now, aren't they? The big Ferris wheel. But you know what my favourite was?' She didn't wait for an answer. 'It was the dodgem cars. I just loved those.'

Gerry tried to envisage a young Miss Timoney crashing around in the bumpers but the image eluded him. He couldn't even envisage her as a young girl. A terrible thought crossed his mind. Was she hinting at coming along with him?

She was talking again. 'You are hardly going to the funfair on your own,' she said, a questioning look on her lined face.

'Feck it! He knew she would get around to quizzing him on that. But at least she hadn't asked if she could come with him.

'No. I'm going with a friend.'

'A female friend?'

'Yeah.' He just wasn't going to make it easy for her.

'Anybody I know.'

He shook his head. 'I wouldn't think so. She's not local.'

The gimlet eyes narrowed. 'One of that film crowd?'

He sighed with resignation. She was like a Miss Marple. 'Yes. The producer and director's assistant, Faye Knight.' He deliberately looked at his watch. 'And I'm running late. I'll see you, Miss Timoney.'

A small smile ghosted her thin lips. 'Have fun, detective sergeant. But then, you always do, don't you?'

He quickly strode off down the street. He was to meet Faye at the hotel at 6.30 and he was now running five minutes late, thanks to Miss Timoney's trip down memory lane. He passed through the door and was delighted to see her sitting in one of the easy chairs, chatting to the stoutish one whom he remembered was called Ruby Lipman. The one who had suggestively eyed him up in McCluskey's.

They hadn't seen him so he stood at the door looking at them but his attention focussed on Faye. She was wearing a summery yellow dress with a modest rounded neck and which, because she was sitting in the big chair, rode about ten inches up her thighs. Her shapely legs were bare and she wore flat blue runners with the Nike swoosh on them. Her dark hair was full and curly and the only jewellery he could see was a thin gold chain around her neck.

He walked over. "Hello, ladies. You ready, Faye?'

She stood up and pressed a hand across the dress to flatten it down. He was happy to see that it still stopped a good three or four inches above her knees. She picked up a small gold coloured bag with a long chain from the chair and slipped it over her shoulder and then leaned in and gave him a quick peck on the cheek, threading her arm through his.

Ruby Lipman stood up as well. For a woman whose business was costumery, she was dressed like a bag lady with a loose-fitting round neck sweatshirt with an illustration of a big pair of blood red lips and tight psychedelic colour leggings which made her stubby legs look like two lamb shanks stuffed into nylons. She wore monk sandals on her bare feet with her toenails painted a bright red colour which matched the colour of the lips on her sweatshirt and her own wide lips which were now giving Gerry the full wattage. 'If it isn't my favourite Irish policeman,' she said. She too leaned in and gave him a peck on the cheek and then she stood back. He got the strong smell of alcohol mixed in with her perfume. 'Have fun, children. Don't do anything I wouldn't do.'

When she had walked away, Gerry grinned at Faye. 'Well that gives us plenty of scope, I'd say.'

She laughed. 'You're dead right there. Ruby is one of life's true bohemians. She has tried everything at least once. And she likes to be the instigator.' She held his arm tighter. 'Lucky for you, I got to you first. If Ruby had gotten her mitts on you ... well let's just say, the term sucking in and blowing out in bubbles comes to mind.'

An image of the English woman, Edith Harding flashed across his mind. Now there was a woman he had been very glad to let suck him in. He had never had such an intense and sexually charged affair before. Ruby Lipman would have to be at the very top of her game to match her in the bedroom stakes and she certainly fell a long way short in looks as well. He shook his head to dislodge the alluring image of the Englishwoman. That was the past. He turned to Faye. He had missed something she had said. 'Sorry. What did you say?'

'I was asking if we could call to Mr. Donovan's house. See if her husband has been in touch from Dublin. Harold and Stan are still annoyed with Sabrina for swanning off the way she did without a by your leave. I think it only fair to warn her before she runs into them. Not that she's likely to thank me or anything like that. But still ...'

'No problem,' Gerry said as he guided her to the door. 'His house is on the way.' Arm in arm, they walked down the street, Gerry occasionally acknowledging greetings from people they met, some from other men accompanied by envious looks. He groaned when he saw Andy Horan coming towards them. The councillor stood in front of them. 'Hello, Miss Knight. You're looking exceptionally beautiful this evening, if you don't mind me saying.' He nodded to Gerry. 'Detective Sergeant Tierney.'

Gerry was equally as brief. 'Councillor.'

Horan turned to Faye again, a beaming smile on his face. 'And pray tell me, Miss Knight, where is our custodian of the law taking you this evening? Somewhere nice, I hope.'

'We're going to the funfair,' Faye replied, casting a curious look at Gerry as she sensed his antipathy towards the other man.

'The funfair,' Horan said. 'Oh to be young again. Well you will certainly turn some heads, Miss Knight. You look just like a movie star. And that is going well too, I hope?'

Gerry didn't give her time to reply. 'We've got to be going.'

The councillor gave him a resentful look and then smiled at Faye. 'Well I won't hold you up. Enjoy yourselves.' He gave her a little bow.

Gerry took her hand and quickly walked away, tugging her with him. When they were gone a few yards, she stopped. 'That was a bit rude, Scobie. The man was only being polite.'

'He's a creep,' Gerry said. 'Take my word for it.'

She gave him a puzzled look and then glanced back. The other man was standing looking back at them, one hand in his pocket. It looked like he was searching for something in it. When he waved with his free hand, she waved back. He seemed like a nice man to her.

Gerry kept walking and she quickly caught up with him. 'What's wrong with him?'

Gerry stopped. 'You saw him with his hand in his pocket?'

She nodded. 'So what is wrong with that?'

He gave a little snort. 'Well let's just say, he was playing with a concealed weapon and does so every time he meets a good-looking woman, or man for that matter.'

'Oh my God! He seemed like such a gentleman.'

Gerry laughed. 'He's Kilbracken's answer to Saddam Hussein. Handy Andy conceals a weapon of ass destruction, if you'll pardon the pun.'

Faye looked back but the subject of their conversation was no longer to be seen. She looked at Gerry and shook her head.

'First impressions, what? You never know, do you?'

'Forget him,' Gerry said taking her hand again. 'Sean Donovan's house is just up the road.' It was a small row of six terraced bungalows. Donovan's was number four.

Gerry rang the bell and a minute later, Dora Donovan opened the door. She was wearing a big floral-patterned dress which made her look even bigger than her sixteen stone and her bare legs were heavily lined with thick blue varicose veins. She had flip flops on her bare feet which were surprisingly small considering her bulk. She gave Gerry a puzzled look. 'Detective Sergeant Tierney.' Her hand flew to her mouth. 'Oh my God! Has something happened to my Sean?'

Gerry quickly shook his head. 'No, Mrs. Donovan. Nothing like that. It seems Miss Metcalfe got him to take her to Dublin for some shopping instead of going to the set this morning. We're just wondering if he's been in touch with you since. Miss Knight here needs to have a word with Miss Metcalfe.'

The worried look was replaced by one of vexation. 'Shopping? In Dublin? And he didn't tell me. I'll have his guts for garters, the little weasel. He could have gotten me a heap of stuff if I'd known he was going to Dublin.'

'So you haven't heard from him?'

She shook her head. 'Not a dickie bird. He bloody knew well I'd want him to do a bit of shopping for me.'

'Would you mind trying his phone now?' Gerry asked.

She turned without a word and disappeared through a door. She was back a minute later, a mobile to her ear. She held it there for another minute or so and then slowly took it down. 'Not a peep. Bugger must have it turned off. I'll swing for him when he decides to come home.' She gave Gerry a crooked grin. 'Only jokin', officer. It'll just be a tongue lashings'. There'll be no physical violence.'

Gerry thanked her and he and Faye walked away. She stood watching them for a while and then turned and closed the door.

'Don't blame Donovan for not wanting to come home to that,' Gerry said.

Faye was about to say something when her mobile rang in her handbag. She took it out and checked the caller. 'Harold. What's up?'

Gerry watched as her eyes widened and her mouth dropped open. She gave him a frightened look and then spoke into the phone again. 'I'll be right back. Detective Sergeant Tierney is with me. Will I bring him?'

'What is it?' Gerry asked as she put the phone back into her bag.

'An officer from your station called out to the set. He told Harold and Sam that there had been a phone call to a newspaper in Dublin saying that Sabrina has been kidnapped and they are looking for a two million ransom.'

'James Street! Are they sure it's not a hoax?'

She shrugged her shoulders. 'They don't know. Until such time as she shows up, they're treating it as serious. I've got to get back to the hotel. Would you come along? They're meeting with Larkin the liaison guy, and the security people, as well as the limo firm and the local police. 'She gave him a weak smile. 'And that's you, isn't it?'

They quickly made their way back to the Cloisters.

Jeremy Clarke, the hotel manager, met them at the door. 'They're all in the Lilac room, Scobie.' He shook his head. 'God, that poor woman. And Sean Donovan. What's happened to him?'

'Is the lid still on it?' Gerry asked.

The manager nodded. 'Yes. The only people who know are in that room and the film people and your lot have asked that it be kept that way for the moment.' He looked at Faye. 'I'm terribly sorry this has happened, Miss Knight. It's an awful thing. Please God, it will all be resolved successfully soon.'

'I'm sure it will,' Gerry said but as he steered Faye up the stairs to the meeting room, he had his own grave doubts.

*****

CHAPTER 24

There was a loud babble of conversation when they went into the room but it instantly died down as they entered and all heads turned in their direction. Gerry did a quick recce. Freddie Doyle was there with Flann who was the only man in uniform. Both acknowledged him with a nod of the head. From the film crowd, he recognised Brookman, Zwimmer, Carpenter and Ruby Lipman who was still in her bag lady attire. He recognised Peter Sweeney from the limo hire company. There were four other men in a small huddle whom he didn't recognise. He assumed they were from the security company. Moby Dick Larkin stood close to this group but it was obvious from the body language of the other four that they were not inclined to include him in their discussion.

When Zwimmer came over, Gerry left Faye with him and walked over to the Inspector and Flann. 'When did this break?'

'Call was received by the paper about half an hour ago. They contacted their local station and they rang us,' Doyle replied. 'They're working on tracing the call and will let us know. In the meantime, we're to try and keep the lid on it for as long as we can. They're sending down a few guys from headquarters who specialise in things like this.'

Gerry caught Flann rolling his eyes and he had to agree with him. Whenever the city guys showed up, they treated the local officers like mushrooms. Kept them in the dark and fed them a load of shite now and again. He looked at Doyle. 'It's being treated as serious so?'

The senior officer nodded. 'Yes. All efforts to contact either Miss Metcalfe or Mr. Donovan have failed. In light of that...yes...it is being taken as a kidnapping.'

'So what do we know?' Gerry asked.

'Not a lot,' Doyle replied. 'Donovan picked her up at 6.45 which was normal. At 7.15, the limo company got a text, supposedly from Donovan, telling them that Miss. Metcalfe had changed her mind about going to the set and had asked to be driven to Dublin for some shopping. There was nothing more until the newspaper got the call at 11.20 saying that she had been kidnapped and giving details where a two million ransom was to be dropped off.'

'And where's that?'

'National Stadium. Behind a block of tiered seating at 9pm

Sunday night. The caller warned that there were to be no police there.'

'I take it there's a boxing match on that night?' Gerry said.

Doyle nodded. 'National finals. Place will be packed.'

'I'm sure the Dublin boyos will have their lads fairly thick on the ground there, despite the warning in the phone call to keep away.'

'You can sing it,' Flann said. 'But I'm sure whoever's involved, will know that as well so I'd say, they have that covered in some way.'

All three stopped talking when Dick Larkin lumbered over and stood in front of them. He focussed his eyes on Doyle. 'Haven't had the pleasure. You're Inspector Doyle, aren't you? The new man at the station. Dick Larkin. I was a detective in Manor Street for years.' He extended his hand.

Doyle gave him a peremptory nod of the head and then slowly took the proffered hand and shook it. 'Yes, Mr. Larkin, I've heard of you. Superintendent Clancy filled me in on all personnel before coming here.'

Larkin nodded his head in the direction of Zwimmer, Brookman, Carpenter, Lipman and Faye Knight who were all huddled together in a little group. 'Bit of a bummer this. Who'd have thought somebody would snatch your woman.' He looked back at Doyle. "So? What's the plan? How are we going to handle this?'

Gerry snorted. 'What's with this 'we' bit, Moby? Who invited you to the party?'

The big man glared at him. 'I am the security liaison. So that's what I'm doing, liaising.'

'Well you can liaison your big fat arse somewhere else,' Gerry said. 'This is a private police discussion and civilians are not included. And you are a civilian now, aren't you, Moby?' He gave a little snort. 'Not that you were ever much of a policeman when you were in the force.'

Larkin threw a somewhat appealing look at Doyle who chewed on his bottom lip to camouflage the sardonic smile Gerry's last comment had engendered. He didn't mind if Larkin saw it but he didn't want Tierney to see it. From what he had discovered in the short time he was here and had heard from a few of his acquaintances back in headquarters, Tierney was a bit of a smart arse with a reputation for disregarding rules and authority and he didn't like smart arses who did that. He glanced at Gerry and then back at the now red-faced Larkin. Was that embarrassment or anger? Probably a combination of both.

'I appreciate your position, Mr. Larkin. And we shall certainly keep you informed of any developments. But at the moment, nothing has been decided and no plan formulated. My instructions are to wait for the team from Dublin.' He glanced at his watch. 'And they should be here shortly.'

'Thank you, inspector,' Larkin said. He gave Gerry another withering look and then walked away.

Gerry watched him walk back over to the group of security men. 'Feckin' gobshite,' he said. 'A lobotomised gerbil would have more brains.' He turned back to the Doyle. 'What's the story regarding the money? I presume the film crowd are working on it.'

'We haven't really discussed that yet,' the inspector said. 'My instructions were to just get the people in the know assembled here and wait for a Superintendent Maguire and his team from headquarters.' He looked at his watch again. 'I'd say any time now.'

Gerry was about to make another caustic remark when the door opened and three men walked in. They quickly scanned the room and when they spotted Flann's uniform, they came striding over.

One of them, a man in his early fifties, looked from Gerry to Doyle. 'Which one of you is Doyle?'

'I'm Inspector Doyle,' Doyle said.

'I'm Sergeant Flannery,' Flann said, pre-empting the question.

The man nodded and then looked at Gerry. 'And you are?'

'Who's asking?' Gerry said, although he knew full well who it was but the man's imperious manner had already annoyed him.

'My name is Superintendent Pat Maguire. My colleagues are Detective Inspector Larry Fogarty and Detective Sergeant Noel Casey. So I repeat, who are you?'

'Detective Sergeant Gerry Tierney.'

Maguire turned back to Inspector Doyle and then glanced round the room at the other small groups. 'So, these are all the people who know about the kidnapping?'

Doyle nodded. 'Yes. As instructed, we've gathered them all here awaiting your arrival.'

Maguire nodded. 'Right. Well our first priority is to interview everybody in this room. The news is going to break nationally shortly and that will probably initiate the usual clutch of bogus calls and sightings.'

He glanced around the room again.

'Which of them is the main Hollywood guy?'

Doyle nodded over at the film group. 'The small tubby guy is Sam Brookman, the director and the guy on his left talking to the coloured woman is Harold Zwimmer, the producer. You probably recognise Syl Carpenter the actor.'

Maguire studied the group and then addressed his colleague Fogarty. 'Larry, will you ask Brookman and Zwimmer to come over.'

When Fogarty came back accompanied by the two, he quickly introduced the superintendent and the Dublin sergeant to them. He ignored the three local officers.

Maguire addressed them. 'Have you been in touch with your studio back in the States?'

Zwimmer nodded. 'Yes. We spoke to them immediately after we heard. It will take them a while to put together that kind of money. That's assuming, they agree to pay the ransom.'

'You think there might be some doubt over that?' Gerry asked, ignoring the flashed look of annoyance from Maguire.

Zwimmer shared a quick look with Brookman. 'Enrico di Angelo is not a man who does things under pressure from others. Nobody holds a gun to his head, no matter what the circumstances. He will make up his own mind.'

Gerry was about to question this answer but Maguire got in first. 'Well we do not want them to meet this deadline. We need time to investigate so our recommendation is that the studio stall for time. We believe Miss Metcalfe may have been moved to Dublin so that increases considerably the size of the haystack.'

Brookman gave a little grunt. 'That'll be no problem for di Angelo. As Harold says, he's not a man to respond to ultimatums. And even if he was to pay, it would have to be approved by the board first.'

'How about the husband?' Maguire asked. 'Is he likely to come up with the cash?'

The director laughed. 'Tremayne – that's her husband's name – he wouldn't have that kind of dough. I know his family are titled but from what I've heard, there's not much old money behind it. And the old Lord has just died so I'd imagine things are going to be in a bit of a heap there for a while.'

'Good,' Maguire said. 'We will let the Sunday night deadline slip and wait for them to make contact again. In the meantime, we can be checking some leads. Maybe you would convey our instructions to this Mr. di Angelo.'

'And what about Miss Metcalfe?' Doyle asked. 'What happens to her in the interim?'

'She'll be okay,' Maguire said. 'In our experience in these situations, money is the driving factor and they'll make sure she's safe for as long as negotiations are going on. They kill her, they've lost straight away.'

'And what are these leads you have that you are going to check out? From everything I've heard so far, you don't really have anything.' Gerry said.

Maguire gave him a dirty look and then deliberately turned back to the two film men. 'Gentlemen, thank you for your input. If you would contact your people back in the States now and appraise them of our conversation here.'

'Can we leave now so?' Brookman asked.

Maguire nodded. 'You two can. We want a quick word with everybody else. You are both staying here at the hotel, aren't you? We will keep you informed and maybe after you have spoken to your people, you will let us know.'

The two nodded and walked back over to where the other three stood watching.

Maguire turned to Doyle. 'Inspector, we are going to set up in a room here at the hotel. Maybe you would have a word with the manager now and organise that if you don't mind. Once we have established this base, maybe you would assist us by filtering in the rest of the people here for interview.'

Gerry couldn't keep the exasperation out of his voice. 'What's the point of interviewing these people? What do they know? You should be trying to trace Miss Metcalfe's and Sean Donovan's movements from the time they left the hotel this morning. Checking the route. And then you should be trying to trace the limo. See if it was spotted anywhere if she may have been moved to Dublin which I doubt.'

Maguire gave him a cold look. 'When I want your advice, detective sergeant, I will ask for it.' He moved in a bit closer, his voice low and controlled. 'This is my case and I won't stand for any interference from you or anybody else. Understood?'

Gerry stood his ground. 'It might be your case, superintendent, but it's my neck of the woods and you or anybody else isn't going to tell me what to do on my own patch.'

Maguire looked at Inspector Doyle, his expression clearly demanding that the local senior officer control his underling.

Doyle too was feeling annoyed at Gerry's arguing with the Dublin superintendent. That was not the way to do things in his book. Seniority always had to be respected. And this little interchange certainly wasn't reflecting too well on him as the senior officer, despite his short time in Manor Street. These guys were from headquarters, for crying out loud. Where promotions were decided. He didn't want to stay an inspector in this backwater. It was time to show Maguire that he was in control and put Tierney back in his box. Fuck it! He had been warned that he was a handful. He addressed Gerry. 'That's enough, Tierney. Superintendent Maguire is in charge of this investigation and intensified. 'But only when requested. Do you understand, detective … we will do what we can to assist when requested.' His look was at Gerry. Flann could see that Gerry was only a step away from total eruption. His short fuse was perilously close to burning out. He quickly stepped in, afraid that his friend was going to lose his cool altogether and not for the first time, risk blowing his career. He put his hand on Gerry's arm. 'Come on, Scobie. Let's leave them to it.'

Maguire's lip culled into a sneer. 'I think that is good advice, sergeant.' He immediately turned his back on the two and addressed his two colleagues who had watched the interchange between their boss and the local hick with amusement. They had seen it all before. Local guys thinking they knew it all. It wasn't the first time they had seen Maguire slap down a local upstart. 'Right, gentlemen. Let's get this show on the road.' He turned to Doyle. 'The room, inspector? Could you do that now please.'

Doyle quickly left the room while the other three walked over to where the security men and Larkin stood Gerry stood watching them, his lips curled in contempt. 'Feckin' assholes!'

Flann steered him towards the door, half afraid the three Dublin officers had heard the comment which hadn't been in a whisper. When criticising somebody, Scobie didn't do whispers. He breathed a sigh of relief when there was no apparent reaction.

Faye Knight approached them at the door.

'What's happening, Scobie? Harold told us we had to stay to be interviewed. But sure we don't know anything.'

Gerry snorted, making no attempt to lower his voice. 'I know that, Faye. But feckin' Columbo and his two sidekicks over there seem to think you do.'

Again Flann cast a quick look. Had they heard that one? But the three were in a little huddle, Maguire talking to the other two in a low voice.

Gerry was about to say something else when Doyle came back in. He looked directly at Gerry. 'Detective Sergeant, I want you to go back to the station with Sergeant Flannery here. I'm sure you have some other cases that need your attention. I will take over as liaison officer on this.' He didn't wait for a reply, walking straight over to the other three.

Gerry glared after him. 'Feckin' arse licker!'

'Come on,' Flann said, grabbing his arm and pulling him to the door. 'Forget about them'.

Faye Knight nodded. 'Yes, go on, Scobie. I don't want to see you get in trouble. I'll ring you as soon as we are finished here.' She took out her phone. 'Here, stick your mobile number in here.'

Gerry took it off her and quickly entered his number on her contact listing.

'Right,' he said to Flann. 'Let's go. I want to take a run out to the set and see if I can spot anything on the way. See if we can work out where she was abducted. We'll leave the keystone cops to their own devices.'

'Be careful,' Faye said.

Flann grinned at her. 'Scobie, careful? That's like telling a dog with a mallet up his hole to sit down.'

Faye gave a nervous laugh. 'I presume that is a rather descriptive way of telling me that Scobie does his own thing no matter what.'

Flann laughed. 'He mightn't have a mallet up his hole but when he gets an idea in his head, he only know one thing and that's to plough ahead and to hell with everything and everybody else.'

'Feck off,' Gerry said, although he had a grin on his face. 'If we left things to those muppets over there ... well, they couldn't find their own arses even if they had six arms each and eyes in the back of their heads.'

Doyle came striding over followed by the three Dublin officers. He opened the door and pointed to another door just across the corridor. 'It's that one. The Compton Room.' He stood aside and waited as the other three passed and went over and into the room and then he turned to Gerry, Flann and Faye. 'Miss Knight, if you don't mind, Superintendent Maguire will interview you now.'

Faye gave Gerry's arm a squeeze and then walked over and into the room.

Doyle looked at Gerry. 'You're still here, Tierney.'

Gerry made a face. 'That would be a fairly accurate assessment of things, inspector.'

Doyle's face clouded over and he moved in until their noses were almost touching. 'One more smart-mouthed comment from you, Tierney and you'll be directing traffic in the arsehole of Leitrim before you know it. Now I'll tell you just once more, get the hell back to the station.'

Flann grabbed Gerry by the arm. 'Come on, Scobie. Let's go.'

Gerry settled for giving his superior a long heavy-eyed look and then let Flann pull him out.

Outside the hotel, he grinned at Flann. 'James street, I enjoyed that.'

Flann rolled his eyes. 'Some day, Scobie, you'll push it just that little bit too far and you won't have me to pull you away.'

Gerry grinned at him again. 'Well, Flann old pal, as Buddy Holly said, that'll be the day-hay-hay, when I die.'

*****

CHAPTER 25

Gerry left Flann at the station and then got his car and started out towards the woods where the film set was. When he got to the old level crossing, he pulled in to the side and killed the engine. He got out and studied the ground around him. He knew the security check point was only another mile up the road and he guessed that whoever had stopped the car, where he now stood was the most likely spot to do it.

Whoever abducted the actress would have had to find some way to stop her car and the old gate could have been used to do just that. He walked over and closely examined the ground around the old gate and the wooden gate itself. He instantly saw where the ground was freshly disturbed and some fresh much stuck to the bottom of the gate frame post. It was obvious that someone had recently pulled the gate from its long-settled position, the bottom post initially dragging along the ground and scraping up some of the moist muck. It had to be here the abduction happened. He slowly walked along and studied the ground each side of the road but there were no visible clues. Whoever had done it, had made sure that they had left nothing behind. He took out his phone and rang Flann.

'Flann, Scobie. I'm out here at the old railway crossing just past Crotty's bridge. It looks like they used the gate to stop the car.'

'Shit,' Flann said. 'Do you want me to tell Doyle? We better.'

'Tell the luder,' Gerry said. 'There's feck all else to see here but I'm sure he'll want to get the super sleuths from Dublin to go over it. He won't take my word that there's nowt else to see.'

'So what now?' Flann asked. 'What happens next?'

Gerry mulled over the question. If it was his decision, he would already have a large-scale search of the surrounding area under way and a description of the car with every station in the country. But it wasn't his decision. On the contrary, he was being kept well away from it. The Dublin luder and his crew were back in the hotel, interviewing people whom he was sure, didn't have a bull's notion of who had abducted the actress and Donovan. He couldn't be forgotten about just because he was the driver. But it was all a waste of precious time. 'There's not a whole lot we can do on our own,' he said. 'We'll just have to see what supercop decides to do and maybe do the opposite.'

Flann's voice dropped to a whisper. 'Doyle's just come in. Let me have a quick word with him and I'll call you back.'

Gerry leaned back against the gate and waited. It was a few minutes later when his phone rang.

'I told Doyle about the old crossing,' Flann said. 'He's telling Maguire now. Bollocks was a bit pissed off when I told him it was you who had called it in. Apparently, they're now working on the premise that she's been taken to Dublin and are concentrating now on working on some strategy for the ransom handover.'

'What makes them think she's been taken to Dublin?'

'They've traced the ransom call to a mast which is on the roof of Mountjoy prison.'

'Sure that means feck all,' Gerry said. 'A dog with a mallet up its hole would know that.'

'You know that and I know that, but as far as Maguire and his team are concerned, we're a pair of friggin' country bumpkins and they're the brains.' His voice dropped to a whisper. 'And Doyle is licking their arses so hard, his tongue must be cramping. Came in all puffed up with his own self-importance. He and his new best buddies, Superintendent Maguire and his team, were all on the same page now as to the way they should proceed and that is to allow the ransom payment to go ahead but under covert police surveillance. They will track the money and as soon as Miss Metcalfe and Donovan are released, they will then move in.'

Gerry gave a contemptuous snort. It hadn't taken the new inspector long to show his colours. What was it with these temporary guys who took over at Manor Street? They seemed to get one uptight arsehole after another. Doyle was the second since his friend Superintendent Clancy had retired and Gerry knew that sooner rather than later, he would end up in a head to head with him. And the way things were shaping up, it was going to be sooner. 'Well you know what they say about arse lickers Flann, all they end up doing is talking shite and that's what they're all doing now with this plan to track the money. I'm sure whoever is behind this will have thought of that little scenario and planned accordingly. They won't be stupid enough to think that the cops are going to sit back and let them waltz off with a few million euro without trying to keep tabs on it and whoever picks it up.'

'Well that's the plan now according to Doyle,' Flann said. 'What's your plan, Scobie?'

Gerry thought. What was his plan? Did he back off as he had been instructed to do and leave it to Maguire and co? To hell with that for a game of snooker! This was his turf and this was where the kidnapping had occurred and no pumped up peacock from outside was going to keep him in a box. Others had tried before. 'I know it'll be a complete waste of time but I'm going to tell Doyle he should instigate an immediate search of the area, put out a bulletin on the limo and have every station on the alert for it. I don't think they've taken her to Dublin. Remember, they've two people to cope with and logic dictates that you don't try and move them around too much and risk getting spotted. For my money, they're holed up somewhere within a twenty or thirty-mile radius and after the ransom's paid, they'll ditch them and then they're free to travel without having to worry about hiding bodies in their car or truck or whatever.'

'You could be right. Sorry, can you hold a minute, sir.'

Gerry listened as Flann had an off phone conversation with someone and then he was back. 'That was Doyle. Asking me if that was you I was talking to.'

'So that was what the hold on sir bit was for.'

Flann snickered. 'Yeah. I told him it was a local shopkeeper reporting a bit of shop lifting. Bollocks had no interest in that. He told me if you rang in, you're to get your arse back here asap.'

'Feck him and the high hobby horse he rode in on. I'll be back when I'm good and ready and not before.'

'So – what are you going to do?'

'Think I'll do a bit of driving around. We know they wouldn't have headed back to town and we know they didn't go on towards the woods so chances are, they're holed up somewhere not too far away. I know there's a lot of old abandoned sheds and outhouses around. I'll start with them.'

Flann's voice reflected his doubt. 'Bloody hell, Scobie. With just you on your own, that's like looking for the proverbial needle in the haystack. Would you not come back and try and convince Doyle to organise a proper search? Get everybody out looking.'

'I would if I thought the bollocks would listen to me, and I will suggest it later just to get it on record that I did request a full search but for now, I'll do a quick recce myself. You never know what I might spot.'

'Right,' Flann said. 'If anything happens here, I'll give you a shout.'

Gerry ended the call and got back into his car. He drove back a few hundred metres and then took the old spur road to the left. It was just wide enough for his car and was deeply rutted in spots. He cursed as he hit a particularly deep pothole and his head bounced off the roof. He slowed down a bit as the road worsened even further. It wasn't a road now. It was more a series of potholes held together by small strips of stones and tightly packed earth. A few miles further on, he pulled up outside an old hayshed. Some of the corrugated sheets which made up the back and sides were hanging loose and more from the roof were missing altogether. He got out and walked in through the open front. It was empty except for a few rotting bales of hay stacked in one corner. He walked over and idly kicked at one of them and then jumped back as a large rat scurried out from underneath and ran across the floor. It was nearly big enough to put a saddle on. Satisfied that the place was deserted, he got back into the car and drove on. About a mile further on, the road veered at right angles to the left and after he had negotiated the tight turn, he saw the farm buildings ahead. Jamesie McCracken's place. He drove into the yard and stopped in front of a small thatched house. He had seen bigger sheds in the back gardens of terraced houses in town. There was no sign of life, either human or animal, around the place. He got out and went up to the front door and gave it a few thumps with his fist. 'Hello. Anybody home?'

The only response was a bird flying out from under the eave of the thatch. He peered through the grimy window to the left of the door. It was an old kitchen cum living room with a big high open fireplace which housed a pile of old ashes. Beside it was a blue plastic bin which was almost full to the top with black turf. There was a small rough wooden table in the centre with two timber chairs, a side cabinet with cups hanging from hooks along the front, a sideboard with a small television set with a rabbit ears aerial on top and a battered leather armchair to the left of the fireplace with some of the stuffing visible through worn patches on the arms. Over the fire was a large picture … he had to peer hard to recognise the figure … of Patrick Pearce in military uniform and draped over that was a small tricolour. He walked over to the other window on the right and peered in. There were lace curtains on the window but it was a long time ago since they could claim to have been what he presumed had been an original white colour. A single bed stood against the opposite wall with a heaped bundle of blankets on top. There was a large wooden cupboard which was closed with a blue striped shirt hanging on one of the door knobs and a black tie on the other. And that was it. Just the two rooms. He looked around the yard. Slightly to the left of the house was a small concrete building, not much bigger than a phone box and a quick examination of this showed it to be an outside toilet. He wrinkled his nose as he took in the deeply stained toilet bowl which stood alone in the centre. It had no seat and the cistern at the back was missing its top as well. A few rolls of damp stained toilet paper were on the ground beside it as well as an old folded yellowing newspaper. He quickly closed the door.

Across the yard was a large mound of silage which was a few feet high and swarming with flies and close to it was a large shed. He walked over and in through the open doorway. It was a cowshed with stalls down one side. Each of the stalls had a slatted pallet and he could see the watery cowshite underneath. The stink was quite horrific. He quickly went back outside. He was just getting back into his car when his phone rang again. It was Faye Knight. 'Scobie. Have you heard anything?'

'Nothing, Faye. They're working on the assumption that she's been taken to Dublin and they're now talking about tracking the money when the ransom is paid. Have you heard anything on that?'

'Nothing yet,' Faye said. 'Harold and Sam have both been talking to Mr. di Angelo. He's working on it but the story is he won't have it by Sunday. The studio are a bit cash poor at this precise time.'

'Any word from her husband?' Gerry asked.

'He's over in England. His father has just died and the studio are trying to get word to him.'

'Any money there?'

'Not from what I know,' Faye answered. 'According to Sabrina herself, the old man frittered most of it away. Where are you now, Scobie?'

'Out in the country. Just checking around. See if I can spot anything.'

'But I thought you said they had taken her to Dublin?'

'That's what Maguire and Doyle think but I still think she's still around here somewhere.'

She was silent for a minute and then, 'God, it's a mess, isn't it, Scobie? Poor Sabrina. I can't imagine how she must be feeling.'

Gerry tried to sound more positive than he felt. 'We'll find her, Faye. And in the worst case scenario, she'll probably be released anyways after the ransom has been paid.'

'They won't ... you know ... hurt her or anything like that?'

'No,' he said. 'She's their cash cow. And after they get the money, well, they'll just release her somewhere isolated or else ring a newspaper and tell them where she is.'

'Will I see you soon?'

'Yeah. I should be back in about twenty minutes. I'll see you then.'

'Bye, Scobie.'

He closed his phone. Feck it! Flann was right. He was wasting his time looking on his own. He would have to bite his lip and try and get Doyle to organise a proper search of the area.

He got into his car and drove out of the yard and back down the narrow laneway.

*****

CHAPTER 26

Spence angrily switched off the television in his office up over the Doonwell Arms pub which was one of the three he owned. The kidnapping had been the lead story. But it was the announcement at the end of the bulletin which was now both angering and worrying him at the same time. There had been an interview with the head of the studio in Hollywood, a guy called di Angelo, and he had as much as said that they were not going to be able to raise the money in time to meet the Sunday drop in the National Stadium. And that would rightly screw up his plans which were now all meticulously in place. He knew the cops would be thick on the ground in the stadium, the money under close surveillance. But he had that covered. He had paid a sizeable sum of money to a casual worker at the stadium to hit the main switch after the money drop. It would plunge the whole stadium into darkness allowing the ransom to be picked up unseen by one of his men who would be close to the drop zone and equipped with night vision goggles. By the time the stadium staff and the cops realised what had happened and got to get the lights back on, his lad and the money would be well gone. But now it looked like the guy in America was stalling for time. And that could screw up everything. Everything was geared to the Sunday night pick-up. The quicker this whole thing was over, the better. In his experience, the longer things dragged on, the greater the risk of something going amiss. He had masterminded four successful kidnappings of bank personnel and some of their families and in all four, everything was concluded in a three-day time frame. But now, here was this American guy pissing around and trying to drag things out. They were a Hollywood studio, for crying out loud! They had to have plenty of dosh. This was all just a delaying tactic, possibly at the behest of the police. He would have to talk to O'Driscoll. Maybe get him to do a recording of the distressed actress appealing for the ransom to be paid and shoot it off to the television people. He knew O'Driscoll had a few untraceable phones with him. He himself had suggested that. And it would be no problem for O'Driscoll and his lads to get her looking a tragic figure. A few slaps across the kisser would do just that. Once the public saw that, the pressure would be on the studio to pay. He took out his phone and dialled.

O'Driscoll answered almost immediately. 'I thought we weren't supposed to have any contact until all this is over?'

'We got a problem,' Spence said. 'Just watching the American studio boss on television. Looks like they're going to stall paying the ransom.'

'Fuck that,' O'Driscoll said as he walked out into the tunnel to avoid being overheard. 'We can't stay holed up in this shithole much longer.'

Spence snorted. 'I got everything set up for Sunday night. If it doesn't happen then, a lot of planning goes down the tube. We gotta convince them to stick with the schedule.'

O'Driscoll grimaced. He knew what was coming.

'You gotta take a video of Metcalfe for the television. She's got to be a sorry looking sight and pleading for the ransom to be paid. Get the public screaming for her release. They'll have to cough up then. And it might be no harm show the driver as well. Make it a double whammy.'

O'Driscoll said nothing for a minute. He knew he would have to tell Spence. He swallowed hard. 'We got a problem here too.'

'What?' The single word dripped with ice.

'The driver had a heart attack. He's dead.'

In his office, Spence closed his eyes. He didn't give a shit about the driver dying but it was another complication he could do without. His voice stayed cold. 'Anything else you need to tell me?'

O'Driscoll's voice dropped to a whisper. 'I think she might have heard your name. Fatty let it slip by accident.'

Spence felt the blood rush to his head in a red hot flush. But it wasn't fear. It was sheer anger. Christ! How had he let himself get involved with this shower of amateurs. One of the hostages already dead and now, his name bandied about in front of the other. The stakes had just dramatically increased. And because of that, there was only one course of action. He just hoped they had the balls to do it. 'Then she doesn't come out of this.'

O'Driscoll took a sharp intake of breath. The words had been said in a matter of fact voice but they had sent an avalanche of ice coursing through his body. It was all getting out of hand. Spence was talking about murder! He knew that was nothing new to Spence – he had been involved in many deaths when a member of the Provisional IRA and as O'Driscoll also knew, had taken out some competitors as well, since swopping his national aspirations for criminal ones – but he himself had never been involved in anyone's deliberate death. He was a thief and a thug but he wasn't a murderer. He was sorry now he had said anything. 'Jesus, Harry, she's a Hollywood star, a world-famous actress. We can't just snuff her out like that. There'd be hell to pay. She mightn't have heard anyways,' he said.

Spence's voice remained calm, as if he was discussing the swatting of a troublesome fly. 'She has to go. It's my name that's in the frame and if she gets to tell the cops, my life won't be worth living. The bastards will hound me morning, noon and night until they get me, one way or the other. I can't take that chance.'

O'Driscoll felt the beads of sweat break out on his forehead despite the chill in his body. He knew if Spence's name did get out, it wouldn't be just his life that wouldn't be worth living. They would all be finished. Spence would see to that. Silently, he cursed Fatty again for his big mouth. Well if the deed had to be done, Fatty could bloody well do it. This was all down to him. But he still had time. 'We need her for the moment, Harry. In case they look for proof of life.'

'I bloody well know that. I'm not fucking stupid. But you make sure that when you leave that rathole you're in after we get the money, you leave two bodies behind. Now get that video made and in to the television crowd. I want to see it on the news tonight.' He didn't wait for an answer, cutting off the call.

O'Driscoll slowly pocketed his phone and walked back into the cellar and sat down on one of the chairs next to their captive. He was actually feeling quite faint after that conversation with Spence. He looked over to where Ratser and Fatty were sitting on one of the bunks next to the wall, playing cards. He looked back at the actress. She was still tied to the chair, the sack still over her head and the top part of her face. Her chin was down on her chest. He thought she might be asleep but then she lifted her head and twisted her head around a few times, probably trying to ease the stiffness in her neck. He sat looking at her, a mixture of emotions running through his head. He had seen her in a few of her pictures and she was some woman all right. Even now, sitting hunched on the chair in her now dirty clothes, there was something about her. She still oozed a sexuality that refused to be neutered by the situation she was in. He could see that her lips were dry and the red lipstick was beginning to crack a bit but even that couldn't take from the fullness and sensuality of the perfectly shaped generous lips. And that figure. Smallish but perfectly shaped and firm breasts, a slim waist and strong rounded buttocks and long slender legs. Up close, he could still get the faint whiff of her scent despite the cloying smell from the scented candles lighting on the table and the strong stink of silage. But he could smell her too. Pheromones, isn't that what they called them? He looked as her head lifted again and turned to face directly at him. She had obviously sensed his proximity to her.

'Please,' the voice low and rasping, completely unlike the sultry voice which had oozed from the big screens and sent male hearts racing into overdrive all over the world. 'Please let me go. I'll do anything you want. I can get you money. Leave it anywhere you want. Nobody needs to know. I swear.'

He said nothing for a minute and then stood up and went over to one of the boxes and took out one of the new mobile phones. Ratser and Fatty gave him a quizzical look but he ignored them. He switched on the phone and then walked back over and stood in front of her. 'Right, lady. I want you to sit up straight and when I say go, you start begging that head guy in Hollywood to pay the ransom immediately so that you can be released. Make it good. Tell him that if it isn't paid on Sunday night, you are afraid of what is going to happen to you.'

He held the phone in front of him. Spence had told him to have her crying but to hell with that. He wasn't going to hit her. She looked tragic enough anyways.

'Right,' he said. 'Off you go.'

Sabrina looked in the direction of the voice. Her mouth and throat were bone dry and she tried licking her lips but her tongue was like a piece of sandpaper. 'Please,' she said. 'Could I have a drink of water.'

O'Driscoll reached for the bottle on the table but then stopped. A croaking voice would add to the pathos of the appeal. 'Afterwards,' he said. 'Now, get on with it. And make it good.' He gave a dry laugh. 'You're an actress after all, aren't you?'

Sabrina ran her tongue over her lips again and then started. 'Enrico, Sam, Harold. They have told me that if the ransom isn't paid on Sunday night as asked, they will hurt me. I'm begging you. Please do as you've been asked. I fear for my life. Please, Enrico. Do what they ask.'

O'Driscoll pressed the stop button. Short and sweet. He looked over at Fatty. 'Get on the laptop and get me a mobile number for anybody at the television station. I want this to go straight away.'

Fatty got up off the bunk and came over and opened up the laptop on the table. He punched a few keys and then looked up. 'There's a number here for a Hillary Devine. She's a researcher for some new cookery programme being planned. Looking for people to text in old menus handed down from parents or grandparents. Will she do?'

'Doesn't matter,' O'Driscoll said. 'Whoever gets it will go straight to the news editor.'

Fatty read out the number. A minute later, the short recording was sent.

Ratser came over. 'Why are we sending that? They dragging their heels on coughing up the dosh or what?'

O'Driscoll ignored the question. 'Give her a drink and then the two of you come over to the stairs. I want a quiet word with you.'

He walked over himself and waited. He didn't like what he was going to tell them but he had no choice now. Because of Fatty's slip up, Spence was calling the shots now.

*****

CHAPTER 27

Gerry walked up the stairs to Doyle's office. Flann had told him he was up there along with the three from Dublin. He gave one short rap on the door and then walked straight in, not waiting to be invited.

Doyle was behind his desk with Maguire and Casey sitting in front of the desk. There was no sign of Fogarty. The three heads looked at him. 'This is a private meeting, Tierney,' Doyle said.

Gerry ignored the comment and walked over to the side of the desk. 'Flann told you I found the spot where the abduction took place.'

It was Maguire who answered. 'Yes. Detective Inspector Fogarty is out there now assessing things. We should have his report shortly.'

'He'll have feck all to report,' Gerry said. 'As I'm sure Sergeant Flannery also told you, there's nothing to see out there. Not a clue as to where they went.'

Maguire's lip curled. 'Be that as it may, we still like to check things out for ourselves. We do have considerable experience in such matters, Sergeant Tierney, and it is quite possible, you may have overlooked something and if you did, the detective inspector will find it.'

Gerry refrained from correcting what he knew was the deliberate downgrading of his rank. He looked straight at Doyle. 'I think we should organise an immediate and thorough search of the area within a twenty-mile radius of the old railway crossing at Crotty's bridge. Get every available man on it first thing in the morning and maybe pull in a few more from some of the city stations. I still think...'

Doyle cut across him. 'What you think is of no relevance in this investigation, Tierney. I thought I had already made that clear to you. Superintendent Maguire and myself here are of the firm belief that Miss Metcalfe has been moved to Dublin. Obviously, it would be impossible to carry out a search of the whole of Dublin city so the best course of action now is for the ransom drop to proceed and for us to track it. We are both of the belief that with covert monitoring, it will lead us to the perpetrators of this abduction after the release of Miss Metcalfe. And of course, Mr. Donovan.'

Gerry tried to suppress his rising anger. He mentally counted to five before speaking again through virtually clenched teeth. 'I have to disagree. I don't believe whoever snatched her would have taken the chance on driving to Dublin with her and the driver. I think they're holed up somewhere in the vicinity. Somewhere previously identified by them when they were planning all this. There's a lot of old deserted buildings and outhouses all around here. With a proper search, we might just get lucky.'

Doyle looked at Maguire who in turn, looked at Casey. It was he who spoke, a condescending tone to his voice. 'I'm sure we all appreciate your fervour, Detective Sergeant Tierney, which I'm sure, is well intentioned, if a little misplaced. But let's face it. You don't really have much experience in these situations, do you? Whereas the superintendent, Inspector Fogarty and myself ... well this is what we do every day. We've dealt with literally hundreds of such cases and, if I'm not being too modest, with quite a lot of success as well. We understand the mindset of these people. And we believe that letting the ransom be paid is now the best way to effect Miss Metcalfe's release and tracking it afterwards is the best way to apprehend the culprits.'

Gerry gritted his teeth. They were treating him like a half-wit. He was about to argue but stopped as the door opened and Fogarty walked in. He strolled over and took the vacant chair beside Casey.

'Well, Larry,' Maguire said. ' See nything of interest out there?'

The detective inspector threw a glance at Gerry and then looked back to his superior. 'It's obvious the gate was pulled across the road to stop the car. The gate is fairly dilapidated and hanging off its hinges. It was obvious it hadn't been moved for a long time prior to that and the dirt was disturbed when someone dragged it from its position. Obviously, when the driver got out to pull it back, that's when they were grabbed.' He folded his arms and sat back.

When Maguire just nodded and said 'Thanks, Larry', Gerry couldn't hold back. 'And that's it? That's the extent of your investigation down here where the actual abduction took place? You send a man out and he comes back and tells you exactly the same thing I told you over an hour ago. And then it's just 'Thanks, Larry'. And now you're all going to hotfoot it back to Dublin to stake out the money? And that's assuming the studio come up with it for Sunday night.' He shook his head in exasperation. 'I don't feckin' believe it.'

Doyle quickly jumped to his feet and gave him a hostile look. 'Be careful, Tierney. In case you've forgotten, you are addressing senior officers. I won't stand for your smart mouthed subordination.'

'You just did stand for it,' Gerry muttered, as he thought, under his breath, but when Doyle's face started to turn a bright red, he knew it hadn't been low enough.

'Right,' Doyle said. 'That's it. I've had enough of your impertinence. Consider yourself on immediate suspension.'

Maguire held up a placating hand. 'Gentlemen, gentlemen. Can we all stand back and take a breath here.' He looked at Doyle. 'I'm sure, Freddie, the detective sergeant didn't mean to be offensive.' He looked at Gerry. 'Did you, Tierney?'

Gerry knew he was on wafer thin ice that was already melting. Getting suspended just couldn't be an option at this stage. Though it would stick in his craw, he knew he wold have to eat a large slice of humble pie. 'No, sir. No offence was intended to anybody. I'm sorry if offence was taken. I just got a bit carried away.'

Maguire looked again at the inspector. 'There you are, Freddie. The detective sergeant didn't really mean any offence. Let's all just put this behind us. We are after all, all on the same team. What do you say?'

Doyle glared at Gerry but he didn't want to go against Maguire. 'Perhaps you're right, Pat. This situation has left us all a bit wound up.'

Maguire looked from one to the other, a wide smile on his face. 'Good. That's the way.' He focussed his attention on Gerry. 'I know you think we're ignoring your suggestion but you have to trust that we know best. As you yourself have said, there are I'm sure, a lot of old sheds and the like around the place but can you really see them holing up in one of them? They wouldn't be too secure, would they? They would know that they could easily be found. No. The most likely thing is that they went straight to Dublin where they could have a million different hiding places. Our best bet now is to stake out the National Stadium where the drop is to take place and take it from there.'

'Well should we not rule these places out anyways?' Gerry said. 'And what about the limo? Has its description been circulated?'

Maguire looked at Casey. 'Noel?'

He nodded. 'The registration and description of the limo were put up on the system...' He looked at his watch... 'forty three minutes ago.'

Maguire looked at Gerry. 'There you are, detective sergeant. And...' He looked at Doyle … 'I'm sure the inspector here won't object to you and a few of your colleagues doing a local search. Just to rule out the slim possibility that they are still in the area. It shouldn't take too long, should it?'

Doyle coughed. 'I had intended to do that anyways. I just didn't get time to say it before certain conclusions were jumped to.' He looked at Gerry. 'I'll sanction a search for tomorrow. That should be long enough to rule out around here.'

Maguire beamed again. 'That's it so. We will let you organise a local search and we will head back to Dublin shortly and set things up for Sunday night. It's going to take a lot of careful planning. Of course, we will liaise the whole time with you, inspector. We will keep you informed and you can let us know how your search went.' He extended his hand to Gerry. 'Nice to have met you, Tierney.'

Gerry shook his hand. 'Superintendent.' He nodded to Fogarty and Casey, deliberately ignored Doyle and turned and walked out, closing the door quietly behind him.

Downstairs, Flann came up to him. 'Well? How did you get on?'

Gerry gave a derisive snort. 'Those gobshites up there couldn't be trusted to find an apple in a feckin' orchard.' Then he grinned. 'But at least we can do an official search around here now. At least I got that out of them. Can you tell the lads that are out on patrol that I want them here at the station first thing in the morning? And call in anybody who's off tomorrow. I want to get this under way before Dithery Doyle up there decides he's going to take over. Once his three new Dublin amigos leave, he'll be down here like feckin' General George S. Patton.'

He left Flann and walked over to where Elsie Masterson was sitting at her desk, her eyes focussed on the flickering computer screen in front of her. 'Hey, Elsie,' he said. 'Check and see if there's been any response to the posting of the limo details. Somebody has to have seen it. It couldn't just feckin' disappear.'

The policewoman grinned at him. 'Heard what you said to Flann. I take it you and Doyle aren't seeing eye to eye on things. Now why does that not surprise me?'

Gerry rolled his eyes. 'He's about as useful as a rubber fork in a steak house. Still, we forget about him and do our own thing.'

'Just like we always do, eh Scobie?'

He grinned at her. 'Exactly, Elsie my girl. And that's why things get done around here.'

She was peering at the screen. 'Look, Scobie. The limo was stopped just outside Dublin this morning at a traffic checkpoint. It was showing tax and insurance so they waved it on.'

'Who posted that?'

She scrolled down. 'The Naas station. Garda Anne Kelly.'

'Get her on the phone for me,' he said.

A few minutes later, he was talking to the young female officer on the mobile number the Naas station had given Elsie. 'Can you describe the driver?'

'Medium height I think, although it was a bit difficult to tell as he was sitting down. Didn't really see his face as he was wearing a chauffeur's hat and dark sunglasses. He had a beard though.'

'Anybody else in the car?' Gerry asked.

'No. Just the driver,' was the reply.

'You check the boot?'

Her voice took on a defensive tone. 'No I didn't. I had no cause to. We were just on a routine tax and insurance check.'

Gerry assured her he wasn't being critical, thanked her and hung up. Elsie Masterson looked at him. 'You going to tell Doyle and Maguire?'

He grinned. 'They have access to computers themselves. If they bother their arses looking, they'll see it.'

'So what do you think it means?' she asked. 'Do you think they're right when they say she's been moved to Dublin? Could she have been in the boot of the car?'

Gerry shook his head. 'No. That would have been too risky. And remember, they have two people to hide. Let's not forget about Donovan. I think it was just the car. Easier to lose that in Dublin than down around here. And as you've seen, even when it was stopped, they had nothing to hide.'

Flann came over. 'I've gotten six. Smithy, Hartigan, O'Dowd and Reilly will be here at eight in the morning and Flynn and Dowling are off but they'll come in as well.'

'Good,' Gerry said. 'Tell the lads in the squad cars that they needn't come in. Get them to organise themselves in pairs and start checking old houses and sheds in the Menlough and Kilglennon area and when Flynn and Dowling come in, have them search down in the Callows area and then work their way across to meet the others.'

'How about me?' Flann said.

'You better stay here with Elsie. If we strip the place completely, Doyle will be like a feckin' lunatic. And if he does start acting up, you can block for me.'

Flann snorted. 'So Batgirl and me, we're to take the shite for you.'

Gerry grinned at him. 'Sure, don't you always, Flann. That's why you're as brown as a berry and I'm still a milk bottle.'

'Fuck off,' Flann said, although it was said in a good-natured way.

'I'll keep in touch with the others and report back to you if we turn up anything. And if flutehooks upstairs gets up to anything, make sure you tell me.'

'Will do,' Flann said. 'Now go on, get your ass out of here. I don't want to have to referee another dogfight between you and the wanker upstairs.'

Gerry started towards the door and then stopped and turned. 'We've got to crack this one, lads. I know everyone expects Metcalfe and Donovan to be released unharmed as soon as the money is paid but we don't know who's involved or what has happened since they were snatched. It's usually scum who do these things and if they think either of them could finger them later on, well, it might not just work out the way Maguire and his boys seem to think.'

When he had gone out, Elsie Masterson looked up at Flann. 'God, do you think he's right? Would they... .do something to them?'

Flann rubbed a weary hand across his eyes. 'You've seen it yourself, Elsie. Ireland is fast breeding a new type of criminal without any scruples. Some of them would slice your throat for a fiver without giving it a second thought and then go home and play happy families with their kids. Scobie is right. If it's some of that breed that's involved, God knows what they'll do to protect themselves.'

Elsie Masterson gave a deep sigh. 'It's at times like this I wish I'd listened to my father and taken the job he had set up for me in the creamery.'

Flann laughed. 'Arra you'd have gone mad after a week. Talking shite about spuds and cows and pigs to all them farmers.'

She laughed herself. 'I still wouldn't have heard half the shite I hear from you and Scobie. Ye come out with more shite than a herd of elephants with chronic diarrhoea. Now feck off and let me get on with my work. Seeing as Scobie has commandeered everybody else for tomorrow and you do fuck all anyways, I've to keep this place going.'

Flann was about to continue the banter but when he heard the door of Doyle's office opening, he walked to his own desk and sat.

*****

163

CHAPTER 28

Fatty couldn't believe his ears. He looked at Ratser who didn't appear to be too upset by what O'Driscoll had just told them. But then, why would he? It wasn't him O'Driscoll had said had to ice the woman. Fuck! It had been just a temporary lapse in concentration. And that was because of Leery's selfie with the pint. But he had said Spence's name in front of the woman. He knew that. But why the hell had O'Driscoll to go and tell Spence? He should have known that that mad fucker would go ballistic. Everybody knew he was a dangerous nutcase. He looked at O'Driscoll. 'But she mightn't have heard. I only said it the once. And people in stressful situations don't really be concentrating, do they? Fuck it, Billy. I've never killed anybody. I don't think I can do it.' But he knew he was lying. He hadn't technically killed anybody but there was that day all those years ago when he had gone swimming with Laura Fletcher and Rocky Donovan. He had been twelve years of age. The other two were fourteen and something of an item together. They had let him tag along, probably for their own amusement at his expense. But he was infatuated with Laura who lived in a flat just three doors from his own. Rocky Donovan was the school and the flats bully and it was him who had first called him Fatty and the name had stuck. He hated him with a vengeance but despite his obesity, was in no condition to take on the stronger older lad. They had gone down to a stretch of the Liffey river which was popular for swimming. Shortly after getting there, it had started to rain. Laura and three other kids who were there had decided to go home but Rocky wanted another swim while in the water and had asked Fatty to hang on for him. He had been too afraid to say no. And then when Rocky had gotten the cramp and had called out to him to throw him the lifebuoy from the pole. He had taken it down and then stood with it in his hands, looking at the thrashing Rocky who was yelling at him to throw it. But he hadn't. He had held it to his chest and just watched as the bane of his life eventually went down for the third time and didn't surface any more. He had hung up the lifebuoy and gone home. When Rocky's body was recovered and the Guards questioned him, he had claimed that he had left shortly after the others and Rocky had told him he was just having one last swim and was then going home himself. He had never felt an ounce of guilt. So – technically, he had never committed murder but he had been very instrumental in someone's death.

O'Driscoll's eyes bored into him.

'Do you fucking think I'm happy about it? But you know Spence. If we don't do what he says, we'll all be wearing wide grins on our throats. He'll slice the lot of us from ear to ear.'

'You shouldn't have told him,' Fatty said.

'And then what?' O'Driscoll said. 'Let the cops go after him and tell him she heard his name from one of us. He would skin us alive and then cut our fucking heads off.'

Fatty shivered. He knew O'Driscoll was right. Even if Spence was locked up and the key thrown away, he would still get them. He had even madder fuckers working for him. 'When?' he asked.

'After the money is paid and Spence gives us the green light.'

'And after I.....I do it, what do we do with the bodies?'

'We leave them here,' O'Driscoll said. 'We go over this place with a fine-tooth comb to make sure we leave nothing behind only the two bodies. And who knows. With Lugser's step uncle the way he is, it could be months or even years before anybody finds this place.'

Ratser gave him a sly look. 'If we're going to get rid of her, maybe we can have a bit of fun first.' He licked his lips. 'Not too often you get a chance to screw a Hollywood sex bomb. Whad'ya think?'

Fatty looked hopefully at O'Driscoll. Just hearing Ratser mention the possibility had caused a slight stirring in his nether region. It had even put having to kill her out of his head.

O'Driscoll looked from one to the other. 'We don't touch her until we get the call. After that... He shrugged his shoulders. If they were going to kill her, what did it matter? 'After that, we'll see.'

He started back into the cellar and the two followed.

Sabrina had heard the muted voices coming from, it seemed, far away. But she knew they were back now. She could sense their presence. Her whole mouth and throat were parched dry and she couldn't even conjure up even the slightest bit of saliva. And she had a headache from the continued presence of the sack around the top part of her head and the sickening smell permeating all around her. And her head was roasting hot and itched like mad. She had lost all track of time, now completely disorientated. She lifted her head and ran her dry tongue over her even drier lips. 'Please.' Her voice was now a rasping croak and it hurt to speak but she continued. 'Please let me go. I'll give you anything you want. Pay it whatever way you say. And I won't go to the police. Please. I'm begging you.'

O'Driscoll took a bottle of water from the table, unscrewed the cap and put it to her lips. 'Here. Drink this.'

She parted her lips and as he tilted the bottle, she slurped greedily from it. Even the small amount that dribbled down her chin was an additional relief. When the bottle was empty, it was pulled away. She licked her lips, her tongue tracing over the cracked lines of her lipstick. She tried again. 'Please. I'm begging you. Please let me go. I haven't seen you and I don't know who you are. I swear I won't tell anybody anything. I don't know anything.'

Fatty stood looking down at her. Was there any way he could find out if she had heard him saying Spence's name? He leaned in closer until they were virtually head to head.

Ratser and O'Driscoll sat down at the table and watched but neither spoke.

Sabrina thought she would faint from the smell of stale body odour and rancid breath. She could feel the hot fetid breath on her cheeks. 'Please. Help me.'

Fatty gripped her under the chin and tilted back her head. 'How could we trust you? You'd no sooner be out of here than you'd have every copper in the country chasing us down.'

She stifled a sob of hope. 'I swear. I wouldn't say anything. I don't know anything. You have to believe me.'

Fatty took a deep breath. 'You did hear a name mentioned, didn't you?'

Sabrina gulped. She had heard some names mentioned. Lugser and Spence. Something about making a call. It was probably her acting training which had registered them with her once she heard them. Her memory and recall were two of the attributes which had helped her make it to the top of the Hollywood tree. But did she admit that? Wouldn't that only make things worse? 'No, I didn't hear any names.'

Fatty squeezed her chin with his stubby fingers. 'See! You're promising the sun, moon and stars and still you're lying. There's no way we could trust you. We know you heard. '

She tried again. 'I swear. I didn't hear any names. You have to believe me.' She gagged as the hot foul breath hit her again from even closer range. He had to be nearly nose to nose with her. She tried to twist her head away but it was roughly pulled back.

'You can swear all you like, lady but we don't believe you. We know you heard and nothing you say will convince us otherwise.'

She felt the tears sting her eyes. His pinching grip on her chin was actually hurting her. But that wasn't what was generating the tears. She was now fearful that she mightn't get out of this alive. Up until this, she fully believed that she would be released once the ransom was paid but now, if they believed she had heard names, they wouldn't be taking any chances on her getting to tell the police. Had Sean Donovan heard the names as well? There hadn't been a sound out of him since the whole thing had started and that was very strange. And then the thought hit her like a bolt of lightning. Was he dead? Had they killed him? The tears flowed quicker. If they had killed the driver, there was no way they were going to let her walk. Even after the ransom was paid. She lapsed into silence. There was no point begging any more.

Fatty gave her chin one final rough squeeze and then walked back to the table.

O'Driscoll and Ratser looked at him but didn't speak but he knew by the look on their faces that they didn't believe the woman either. He looked back over at her. She was hunched on the chair, her head bowed, her shoulders twitching as the occasional big sob came from her lips. He had seen the tightening of the mouth and the turning of the head when he had gone face to face with her. The same reaction he had gotten from Laura Fletcher over thirty years ago when he had tried to cop a kiss from her when he had walked her home from Rocky's funeral. She had been crying a lot during the funeral mass and at the graveside. He had worked his way up beside her when the grave was being filled in and her parents had been happy to let him. It was nice that Laura's friends be with her. They themselves had never liked the Donovan boy and it was obvious from Laura's demeanour that she resented their efforts to be sympathetic. Maybe this fat boy could settle her a bit. She had refused to go home with her parents and he had been over the moon when she had taken his hand and said that he would walk her home. He had stopped at the bike shed on the way into the flats complex and tried to give her a kiss. And she had reacted just like the big actress had a few moments ago. Pulled away from him in disgust. He felt his resentment rise. She wasn't so high and mighty now, was she? She was just a prick-teaser like Fletcher had been but while Fletcher's teasing had been confined to Rosamunde Flats, hers was on a worldwide scale. But unlike Fletcher, she couldn't slap his face and walk away. No siree! She was at his mercy. And that was something he had little of for her now. Sure it would only take a matter of minutes, maybe two or three, and hadn't he watched Donovan struggle for close on ten minutes without a trace of compunction. He felt the stirring in his loins again as he contemplated what he would do to her before it was time to put a final end to things. And how would he do it? He considered the options. The obvious one was to strangle her. It wouldn't take much effort to wring that scrawny little neck. Or he could stick her with the pitchfork. It was still in the cellar. Or maybe he would smother her. Pinch her nose and clamp a hand over her mouth and hold it for the few minutes it would take. Of course she would struggle but it would only be much the same as a chicken flapping its wings as the farmer wrung its neck. The thought of having that power now began to excite him almost as much as the sexual one. Yes, he could do this.

O'Driscoll could see that Fatty was drooling over something in his mind. And he could also see the lasciviousness on Ratser's face as he leered at the bound figure on the chair. They were obviously contemplating what they would do to her when the time came to leave. He himself had no interest in any sexual exploitation of the actress. He actually even felt a bit sorry for her. He couldn't imagine what must be going through her head. One day, you're the sexiest and most adored actress in the world and the next, you're a broken wreck shortly to be raped and abused by two lecherous morons before finally being killed. She mightn't know that last bit but he was sure the thought would have crossed her mind. Again he cursed Fatty for being so loose with his big mouth. And he cursed Spence as well. He should never have gotten him involved. But the die was cast now. Unless they saw it through to the end, they were all in jeopardy. And he would much prefer to have to deal with the police rather than have to deal with Spence. One only meant incarceration but the other meant obliteration. And it wouldn't be done in a painless way either. Spence would see to that. And even if he did opt for the police option, Spence would still find a way to make them pay. He just hoped the ransom drop went as planned on Sunday night and they could get to hell out of this shithole and back to civilisation.

*****

CHAPTER 29

Enrico di Angelo took a deep breath and picked up the phone and dialled. He glanced over at the large television screen on which he had paused the picture on the news report from Ireland after playing and rewinding it a few times. Sabrina Metcalfe's drawn face looked out at him – well the bottom half did but there was no mistaking it was her all right. Even if her face had been fully covered and despite the hoarseness, it was definitely her voice that was making the appeal. When the phone was answered, he said, 'You've seen the latest report from Ireland?'

In his office in the penthouse suite of the Golden Peacock Hotel and Casino in Las Vegas, Ernesto Gratelli took a deep pull on his $79 Arturo Fuente cigar before answering. He blew out a stream of blue grey smoke. 'I've seen it.'

Di Angelo took another deep breath. 'We gotta pay. If we don't, the whole damn world will be against us. It could ruin us.'

Gratelli twisted the fat cigar between two stubby fingers. He had to agree with di Angelo. That last piece of footage would have every male and quite a few females all over the world clamouring for the studio to quickly pay the ransom demand and get Sabrina Metcalfe free. He didn't give a damn about the woman. They could carve her up and feed her to the fish for all he cared. But if they didn't pay, di Angelo was probably right. The whole world would turn against the studio. Probably boycott all their productions. And they couldn't allow that. Global Pictures was too important. It was the main vehicle through which they washed a large proportion of their drug money. He put the cigar to his mouth and sucked in another mouthful of rich smoke and then exhaled it loudly. 'Okay, we pay. I'll arrange for the money. Should have it sometime early tomorrow. You arrange for the jet to be ready for take-off as soon as I let you know. And you better be ready yourself. You have to be seen to play a high profile in this. I'll be in touch.'

He terminated the call and then picked up the phone again and punched in an extension number. 'Lenny. We need two million by tomorrow. That broad Metcalfe has got herself kidnapped over in Ireland and we have to cough up to get her released'.

Deep down in the basement of the casino, Lenny Kassman, the casino's chief financial controller, didn't raise an eyebrow at the news or the request. 'We have about a mill and a half here. I'll have to get the rest from the bank.' He paused for a few seconds. 'We do have about three hundred thous'nd of that euro money. I could use that as the balance. I wouldn't mind getting rid of it.'

Fifteen floors above him, Gratelli blew out a stream of smoke.

'Do it.'

He hit the end call button and then dialled a mobile number. 'Frog? I need you and a few of your boys to be ready for a trip to Ireland. As you've heard, that actress broad Metcalfe has gone and gotten herself kidnapped and we now have to cough up two and a half million dollars, in euros. I want you and two of the boys and you know who, to be on the plane with the money. We ain't got time to look into this as we'd like to before the loot has to be handed over but I want you to stick close to di Angelo. If the cops keep him up to speed on their investigation as he'll ask them to, I want you to get to the fuckers who did this before they do. No fucking Irish micks are going to get two mill outta me and waltz off into leprechaun land without me getting a chance to track 'em down and get it back.'

Johnny 'Frog' Frogatti stuck the mobile phone back in his pocket. He had expected the call. He, like most people in the western world, had heard about the kidnapping of Sabrina Metcalfe while over in Ireland making a movie. It had been headline news on all the channels. He knew the studio would come to Gratelli for the ransom money and he knew that the mafia boss wouldn't part with that kind of loot without sending someone to lurk in the background and be ready to move when the time was right. And he knew it would be him. He finished off his drink and threw a ten dollar bill down on the counter. The barman looked at him. 'You want another?'

He shook his head. 'Naw. Gotta go.'

He made his way out of the bar and stood at the pedestrian crossing waiting for the light to turn green. He didn't draw even one glance from the throng of other people waiting to cross. He was of nondescript appearance, of average height and build and – dressed in a grey suit, white shirt and blue tie – could pass for your average white-collar worker. His face was clean shaven and without any outstanding feature. His black hair was short and neatly cut. He was just like one of the hundreds of thousands of faceless people who peopled the gambling capital behind the neon lights. To look at him, it would be hard to believe that he had killed over thirty people. Now forty six years of age, he had joined the Gratelli family thirty years earlier as a runner. He was taciturn by nature, even as a youngster, and went about his business quietly and efficiently. He was respectful to all, never complained and always showed up on time. This quiet reliability saw him move up through the ranks and just before his twenty first birthday, Gratelli made him his own personal aide. In this position, he was often in the company of Lucas 'The Bull' Paruzzi, the main enforcer for the Gratelli family. Paruzzi, as his nickname implied, was a bear of a man. He stood over six foot four inches in height, weighed in excess of 260 lbs and didn't have one shred of human decency in his entire body. He controlled a team of ten button men who were equally ruthless. Such was their fearsome reputation that other families always deferred to Gratelli and he was looked on and referred to as the don of dons. For some strange reason, Paruzzi took a liking to the new quiet member of Gratelli's inner sanctum and for his part, Frogatti cultivated this odd friendship. He wanted to learn everything. When Paruzzi had asked him one night if he wanted to come with him and three of his men to 'sort out' a black drug dealer who was encroaching on Gratelli territory, he hadn't hesitated. They had driven to an apartment building in a black Ford transit van and made their way to the tenth floor. Paruzzi had kicked in the door of one of the apartments and they had all stormed in. There were three men and a woman in the apartment, all young and black and all sitting around a low table on which there was a large bowl of white powder and a pile of small cellophane bags, some of which already contained about a spoonful of powder. One of the men had dived for a gun which was on the armchair behind him but Paruzzi had swung his leg and kicked him in the head before his hand had gotten anywhere near it. The four had their hands taped behind their backs and were then bundled into the elevator and down to the van where they were pushed into the back and followed in by Paruzzi's men. Paruzzzi himself had gotten in behind the wheel and told Frogatti to get into the passenger seat. They had then driven out to the desert where the four were pulled out of the van and thrown down on the sand. Paruzzi's three men had then taken shovels from the van and started to dig.

He had stood to one side, beside Paruzzi who was nonchalantly smoking a cigarette and occasionally picking at his large nose. When one of the men and the woman had started pleading, one of the diggers had lashed out with his shovel and hit the man across the face, nearly slicing off half his cheek. Both he and the woman had immediately gone silent, only their eyes now reflecting their absolute terror.

Paruzzi had turned to him and said, 'This is a lesson for you,

Frog. If you're dealing out retribution for the boss, you gotta make it hurt as much as possible. Now we could have just shot these bums at the very start but that would have been too easy for them. Seeing their own grave being dug, well that I'm sure just adds that extra little layer.'

Half an hour later, the three diggers had climbed out of the rectangular pit which was just over six-foot long, four-foot wide and two foot deep. When Paruzzi gave a nod of the head, they had pushed the four into the hole. Paruzzi had then walked over, pulled a gun from his underarm holster and shot the three men in the head. He had then turned to Frogatti and held out the gun, a crooked smile on his face. 'You up for it?' And he hadn't hesitated. He had walked over and taken it from him and calmly shot the woman through the left eye just as the second high pitched 'please' plea left her mouth. Paruzzi had laughed and said, 'I always knew it was ice that was behind that quiet demeanour of yours.'

When Paruzzi had died of a heart attack a year later, he had seamlessly moved into the position.

He crossed with the crowd and then turned left and made his way to Harty's Irish bar. He stood just inside the door and quickly scanned the room. As he suspected, Hegarty was there, sitting at a table on his own in a booth near the back, a mug of beer in front of him and a newspaper open on the table. He walked over.

Hegarty looked up. 'What gives, Johnny?'

He gave him a wry grin. 'This is your lucky day, Shaun. We got a job and it's over in your old homeland. The boss wants you in on it.'

Hegarty's eyes widened. 'Fuck sake! Back in Ireland? What's the gig?'

'You not been watchin' the news? Seems some of your crowd took a particular shine to the actress Sabrina Metcalfe. Snatched her and her driver and are lookin' for the equivalent of about two and a half million dollars to release her. It's got to be delivered Sunday night over in Dublin. The studio guy di Angelo, he'll be carrying and you, me, Montello and Schwartz are ridin' shotgun. And the boss wants us to find out who did it, get back the money and deal with them.'

'Won't be easy,' Hegarty said. 'Unless the cops over there identify who's behind it and we get to find out, we could be pissin' in the wind.'

Frogatti shrugged his shoulders. 'That's why you're along. It's time you stated earning some of that money the boss pays you.'

Hegarty stood up, a vexed look on his face. 'I pay my way and you know that.'

Frogatti's face remained impassive. 'Well now's your chance to impress the boss and maybe earn a pay rise. You help get that money back and the bastards responsible, I'm sure the boss will be only too happy to flesh out your envelope even more. I'll ring you later with the details.'

Hegarty stood watching as he walked out of the bar. He picked up his glass and drained the last of the beer and walked over and left the glass on the bar in front of the bartender. 'Give us a shot of Irish, Arty.'

'Sure thing, lieutenant.' He picked up the glass, left it aside and took up a small shot glass. He picked a bottle of Jameson whiskey from the shelf behind him and filled the glass and slid it in front of Hegarty.

Hegarty took it up and downed it in one mouthful. He put it back on the counter. 'Gotta go now and arrange for a few days leave. I'll be seeing you, Arty.'

'Yeah, see ya,' the barman replied and stood watching as Hegarty went back, picked up his paper and left.

'Fucking leech,' he said to himself. He didn't like any of the cops who frequented his bar and drank his booze without any attempt to pay but he particularly didn't like bent ones and Hegarty was as crooked as a corkscrew. But it was Gratelli's pocket he was in and that just about made him untouchable. He took the two empty glasses and rinsed them out in the sink.

*****

CHAPTER 30

Gerry pulled up outside the hotel at eight thirty the next morning. The other teams were already out on their searches. He wanted a quick word with Faye before joining them. He found her in the small dining room which was used for private dinners and small functions. She was sitting at a table which also had Harold Zwimmer, Jerome Scott, Syl Carpenter, Harvey Rockwell, Harriet Taylor and Ruby Lipman around it. A large urn of coffee sat in the middle of the table and each had cups in front of them and plates with varying remains of breakfast on them. He walked over. 'Any word on the money?' he asked.

It was Zwimmer who answered. 'Sam's up in the room now talking to the studio. He should be down shortly. You guys turn up anything?'

Gerry shook his head. 'Not yet. We've just started a search of the area. We're going to check old sheds, farmhouses, outhouses and anywhere else that's secluded.'

Carpenter gave him a surprised look. 'I thought you were working on the theory that she has been taken to Dublin? At least, that's what that guy Maguire told us. That you're going to let the ransom be dropped off where they said and follow it.'

'That's one course of action being followed,' Gerry said. 'Meanwhile, we're doing a search around here just in case.'

Zwimmer looked hard at him. 'You think she might still be held in this area?'

'No harm checking,' Gerry answered. 'We still have all day today and tomorrow. Until 9 o'clock anyways.'

Harriet Taylor gave him an anxious look. 'They won't hurt her, will they?'

Gerry tried to raise a reassuring smile. 'I wouldn't think so.'

He didn't expand any further and Ruby Lipman picked up on it. 'But you're not sure, are you?'

Gerry gave her a resigned look. 'There are so many variables, it's impossible to say. It depends on the individuals themselves, the pressure they feel under, whether or not she's seen a face or heard a name. There's really no way of telling. But our experience in most of these situations is that the person is released unharmed.'

Carpenter banged a large fist down on the table. 'I should have been with her. It was stupid us using two different cars. If I'd been there...' He didn't finish the sentence but the implication was that he would have stopped it.

Lipman reached over and patted his back. 'It's not your fault, Syl. And if you had been with her, you could have been snatched as well or worse still, hurt.'

He rolled his broad shoulders. 'Wouldn't have happened. I'm well able to take care of myself.'

Lipman patted his hand. 'Of course you are. I wasn't saying you couldn't.'

Gerry was about to remind the actor that this wasn't one of his films. The baddies in this situation weren't working to a script and he was damn lucky he wasn't in the car with Metcalfe. All his macho posturing wouldn't have counted a toss with the lowlife gangs now operating in Ireland, one of which had to be behind this.

The door opened and Sam Brookman came in. He strode over to the table, acknowledging Gerry's presence with a curt nod of the head. 'The money is on its way. Enrico himself is flying over with it in the company jet. They should get into Dublin early tomorrow morning.' He turned to Gerry. 'Enrico has a few colleagues with him including a lieutenant from the Las Vegas police department. He hopes you will include him in the loop of your operations.'

'That's for Maguire and Doyle to decide, 'Gerry said.

'Can you ask them?' Brookman asked.

Gerry curled his lip. 'I think it would be better coming from the studio.' He nodded to Faye to follow him over to the door.

'I'm going out to join the lads on the search. Will you keep me informed if anything happens here?'

She put a hand on his arm. 'Be careful, Scobie. I think you really believe they are still around here. I don't want you to get hurt.'

He grinned. 'There's many a scumbag tried to scupper the Scobie but I'm still here. Don't worry that pretty little head of yours on my account. I mightn't be built like a brick shithouse like Carpenter over there but I think I have a bit more...' He tapped the side of his head...'up there than machoman.'

She looked over at Carpenter and gave a little laugh. 'Well that wouldn't be too hard. Syl might have the body of an Adonis and heartthrob looks but when the Good Lord was handing out brains, I think he was in a different room.'

She stood on her toes and gave him a quick peck on the cheek. 'Stay safe, Scobie Tierney.' She walked back over and sat down.

Gerry left the room and crossing the hotel lobby, he met Jeremy Clarke, the manager of the hotel. He stopped in front of him. 'This is a terrible state of affairs, Scobie. Has there been any word?'

Gerry shook his head. 'Nowt as yet, Jeremy. The ransom money is on its way from the States and Maguire and his team are setting up a monitoring operation for the drop at the National Stadium tomorrow night. They won't make any move until Miss Metcalfe has been released and is back safe and sound.'

The hotel manager looked hard at him. 'God, I hope this all works out as your colleagues are hoping it will. I know it's an awful lot of money but the main thing is to get her back safe. Getting those responsible and the money back has to be the lower priority. If anything was to happen to her, God it's just unbearable to think what the consequences for Ireland would be. It would kill the American tourist industry straight away.' He gave Gerry an embarrassed look. 'God, that sounds awful, doesn't it? As if all I'm worried about is the tourist industry and not poor Miss Metcalfe.'

Gerry gave him a light punch on the arm. 'Arra will you whist. Sure we all know you treat all your guests like family. We'll leave no stone unturned, Jeremy. The lads are even out now, searching all the old farmhouses and outbuildings within a twenty-mile radius of where she was snatched. I still believe they're holed up somewhere in the area. And even if we don't find her before Sunday night, at least when the ransom is paid, she should be released. And that, as you say, is the main priority.'

He gave the manager one final pat on the arm and then went out and got into his car. He took out his phone and dialled. Smithy answered almost immediately. 'Yeah, Scobie?'

'How are ye getting on?' he asked.

'We're almost finished the Menlough area and we're going up soon to join the lads in Kilglennon. No sign of anything unusual though.'

'Right,' he said. 'Keep going. I'm heading down to the Callows to meet up with Dodo. I'll see you when we meet up.'

He terminated the call and threw the phone down onto the passenger seat.

As he drove out towards the low-lying land which formed the Callows, he went over the events of the past thirty hours or so. So much happening in such a short space of time. About thirty hours since Sabrina Metcalfe was kidnapped. Only about half that time since they had found out. Plenty of time for her to be moved to Dublin. Was he right in his belief that she was still in the area? It was his gut feel and his gut had always been relatively reliable in the past. He slowed down as he saw a car ahead pulled into the side of the road, a woman standing beside it, frantically waving her arms. He eased to a stop behind it and as he got out, he immediately saw that her front passenger side wheel was as flat as a pancake.

Terry Nolan breathed a heavy sigh of relief when she saw the car stop and pull in. Nothing had gone right for her since she arrived the previous evening. She had gotten directions to the location where the film was being shot from a man she had stopped and asked near the town but had been stopped herself about a half mile from the site by some security men. Her press pass hadn't cut any ice with them and they had refused to let her pass. She had then come back to Kilbracken and gone to the local police station where a female Garda officer had only offered the information that the investigation into the kidnapping of Sabrina Metcalfe was ongoing and she couldn't comment any further. When she had asked to see a senior officer, an Inspector Doyle had been even more abrupt. She had then gone to the Cloisters hotel where, after booking in for the night, she had chatted up the receptionist who had been a bit more forthcoming until the manager had come along and interrupted the conversation. However, she had learned that the producer and director were staying in the hotel along with some of the cast including Syl Carpenter. She had felt herself go a bit faint when she heard this. Syl Carpenter was one of the sexiest men in Hollywood in her opinion. What she wouldn't give for an interview with him. But the manager had told her that the film people had expressly said that there would be no interviews. The receptionist had also told her before the manager's arrival, that the local guards were doing a search of the area the next morning. She had sat in the bar for the next two hours hoping that some of the film crew would come in but they hadn't so she had gone to bed. She was getting desperate at this stage. She had hoped to have had something to file but so far, she had diddly squat and Rhino would be down later on so time was running out for her. And so she had come out early hoping to come across some of the search party and maybe get permission to tag along. And now she had gotten a bloody puncture.

Gerry got out of his car and walked up to the young woman who gave him a wide relieved smile. He looked down at the flat tyre which had a long, jagged scar around the rim. It was obvious she had driven on for some time after it had happened. 'You did a right job on that,' he said.

She made a face. 'I know. I was hoping to reach a house or somewhere.' She looked down at it. 'It's fairly flat, isn't it?'

'It's fecked,' Gerry said. 'Only good for a bonfire now. You got a spare?'

She shrugged her slim shoulders. 'Don't know. It's my mother's car. I don't drive it very often.'

Gerry walked over and popped the boot. He lifted out the set of golf clubs and pulled up the mat. The wheel well was empty. He took up the bag of clubs and put them back in and then closed the boot. 'You haven't got a spare. I'm going to have to get someone to come out and bring a new tyre.'

He got down on his haunches and checked the tyre size and then stood up and took out his phone and punched in a number.

She watched as he spoke into the phone. 'Yeah, Hank. I'm out here on the Slipwell road, about a mile past Haslam's old quarry. Got a young lady here needs a new tyre. It's a Toyota Corolla. Tyre is a 155/80 R13. Can you fix her up?'

When he closed the phone, she smiled at him. 'I'm really very grateful for your help. Will he be long?'

'Says it could be an hour and a half or so. He's already out on a call and has another one waiting. Guess the old roads around here aren't the best but he's not complaining. They're good for his business.'

She bit her lip with annoyance. What the hell was she going to do for an hour and a half? Maybe she could head back to the hotel and with a bit of luck – she was overdue some of the good type – she might just bump into one of the film people who might be willing to talk. God! She might even bump into Syl Carpenter. She looked at him. 'I don't suppose you could run me back to town, could you? Back to the Cloisters Hotel.'

It would set him back about half an hour but Gerry wasn't the type of man to leave someone stranded. Particularly a good looking young one, even if she was too young for him. He nodded to his car. 'Okay, come on.'

As he drove back down the road, she glanced over at him. He was quite good looking. There was something roguish about him that was quite attractive. She wondered if he knew anything about the kidnapping. He was a local after all. 'That's awful about that actress that's been kidnapped down here, isn't it?'

Gerry gave himself ten out of ten in his own mind. He had spotted the small recorder and the notepad on the passenger seat of her car beside her handbag. He had fully expected her to take the handbag and the small recorder – you wouldn't leave them visible in an empty car – but when she had taken the notepad as well, he just knew. He had bet himself that she was a reporter down in Kilbracken because of the kidnapping. He decided to play along with her. 'Bloody awful all right, God love her.'

'Do you know if the police have any idea who did it?'

'Don't think so,' he said.

'I heard the local police are doing a search around here.'

Gerry feigned surprise. 'Is that right? God, you seem to be more informed that I am.'

She allowed herself to feel a little bit of smug satisfaction at this comment. Maybe if she told him something that impressed him, he might tell her who she could talk to that might know something. 'I have a small confession to make. I'm actually attached to the American Embassy. I've been sent down to look into the kidnapping of Miss Metcalfe.'

Gerry managed to keep a straight face and looked at her with raised eyebrows. 'I'd never have guessed. An American investigator? Well fancy that! And you so young!'

She gave him her most winning smile. 'It's really my first case and I would be very grateful for any help I could get.' She looked at him coyly. 'You seem to know people around here. You wouldn't... you know.... know anybody who might know what's going on? Somebody who might have a bit of inside information. I would be ever so grateful.'

Gerry pretended to think for a minute. 'Have you been to the police station? There's an Inspector Doyle who's supposedly in charge of the case. He might give you the laydown of what's going on, seeing as you're both sort of on the same side.

She shook her head. 'Been there already. Got nothing from him only rudeness. But then I couldn't really tell him who I was. We don't want to upset the local police by having them thinking we are sticking our noses in. Politics and all that. '

Gerry shook his head. 'I can understand that. I'm sorry to hear he was rude to you though. But then, he's only a blow-in. Only here a wet week.'

'Anybody else?' she asked.

He pretended again to think for another minute. 'There's a retired postman in town. His name's Billy Hamilton. Knows everybody in Kilbracken and knows everything that's going on. If you get him talking, you'll be listening for a long time.'

'Really? You think he'll talk to me?'

'Yeah. I'm sure he will. And after that, you could talk to a guy called Dick Larkin. He's a retired police detective. Carries a lot of weight around Kilbracken.' He had to stop himself from sniggering at this last sentence.

She glowed at him. 'Oh God, that's great. Thanks a million.'

'No bother,' he said. 'If you ask around town, somebody will tell you where you can find them. They're always hanging about.'

'There is one other person I've heard about,' she said looking over at him. 'A Detective Sergeant Tierney. The hotel receptionist was telling me he's a man I should try and talk to.'

'Tierney! That gobshite!' He shook his head. 'Wouldn't be wasting my time there.'

She gave him a surprised look. 'You don't think much of him?'

'Listen,' he said. 'I see that ... if you'll excuse my French. I see that bollocks every morning. First person I see is him. And all he does is stare back at me and if I say anything, he just mimics exactly what I say.'

She gave him a puzzled look but said nothing. The guy sounded a bit cracked.

He pulled up in front of the hotel. 'Here you are.'

He waited as she got out of the car.

She stood with the door open. 'I don't know how to thank you Mister ... Sorry, I never even asked you your name.'

'Scobie,' he said. 'Everybody calls me Scobie.' He reached across to close the door. 'And don't forget to call down to Kilbracken Tyres. Hank won't be there but the girl on reception will tell you what you'll owe. And if you talk nice to her, she might just organise a lift back to your car for you.'

He pulled shut the door and drove off.

Terry Nolan watched the car drive away, a smile on her lips. God, country people could be so gullible. Still, she now had two names to talk to. With a bit of luck, one of them would have some information she could build an article around.

In his car about a few hundred yards down the road, Gerry was still chuckling to himself.

*****

CHAPER 31

They did every farmhouse, outhouse, hayshed and derelict building within a twenty-five-mile radius but turned up nothing. Gerry was feeling deflated. Maybe Maguire and Doyle were right and she was now in Dublin.

They were all parked in the rear car park of The Wayside Tavern, a halfway house about two miles from Kilbracken which had been closed for over a year. They had already searched it. Smithy looked at him. 'So what do we do now, Scobie?'

He shrugged his shoulders. 'We call it a day. Not much else we can do.' He looked from one to the other. 'Appreciate it, lads. Particularly those of you who were off today.'

'How about tomorrow?' Dodo Donoghue asked. 'We could widen the search.'

Gerry shook his head. 'I don't think there's much point. We would need a lot more manpower and Doyle certainly wouldn't sanction that.'

Hartigan voiced his own earlier thought. 'Maybe the Dublin crowd are right and she has been taken to Dublin. If she has, there's fuck all we can do now except leave it to them. It's out of our jurisdiction.'

Gerry could see that the rest of them were nodding their heads in agreement. But still something nagged at his gut. He turned to Smithy. 'Will you do me a favour, Smithy? You might drop in to the station and tell Doyle the search didn't turn up anything. I just couldn't face the smug bollocks now. '

'Course I will,' Smithy said. 'And you were right to check things out here, Scobie. I'm just sorry it didn't turn up anything. We all are.'

There was a general murmur of agreement.

'Right,' Gerry said. 'I don't know about you guys but I'm gagging' for a pint. Anybody interested?'

One by one they all declined, most saying they had to go home to their families.

Gerry looked at Smithy. 'How about you, Smithy? You've neither chick nor child to rush home to. Fancy meeting me in Macker's after you see Doyle?'

Smithy shook his head. 'I'd love to, Scobie but I promised Trish I'd take her out for a meal. It's sort of our anniversary. A year going out together.'

'No sweat,' Gerry said. 'I'll see ye, lads and thanks again.' He got into his car and drove away.

He pulled up outside the Cloisters Hotel and parked.

Jeremy Clarke was standing at the reception desk. When he spotted Gerry, he came over. 'Any luck on your search, Scobie?'

Gerry shook his head. 'Nothing I'm afraid.'

'Sorry to hear that,' the hotel manager said. 'I know you were sort of hanging your hat on the belief that she was being held around here.'

Gerry chewed on his lower lip. 'And despite the search throwing up nothing, my gut feel is that she is around here somewhere. I don't buy the Dublin theory. It would have been too risky to chance driving the two of them that distance after snatching them. These guys don't take chances like that.'

'But you've searched everywhere, haven't you?'

'I know,' Gerry said. 'I just can't figure it out.'

'Well please God, it will all be resolved tomorrow night when the money is paid and they'll both be released unharmed from wherever they're being held.'

'Aye, let's hope so.'

'Your American friends are in the bar,' Clarke said, a ghost of a smile on his lips.

Gerry grinned himself. 'Maybe I'll just pop in for the one. Even if your pint is shite.'

Clarke feigned an insulted look. 'There's nothing wrong with our pints I'll have you know. Our taps are serviced regularly and our lines are cleaned every four weeks by the brewery rep.'

'Yeah,' Gerry said. 'But where's your bar staff from? I don't think you've one Irish person working behind the bar, have you? And pulling a pint of Guinness is an art form in itself. It comes naturally to us Irish but I'm afraid foreigners don't have the same knack. They don't let it settle long enough and it never has the right sized head.'

Clarke gave a little laugh. 'Most of our clientele are not expert Guinness connoisseurs like you, Scobie. Few people are. Our staff serve a very acceptable pint but I will admit, it wouldn't be up to McCluskey's standard. That, I think, has spoilt you for everywhere else.'

'You're probably right,' Gerry said. He started off towards the bar and then turned. 'Sure there's nothing to stop me having a Jameson anyways. That's one thing they can't screw up.'

Clarke gave a resigned shake of his head. 'Go on with you.'

Gerry stopped at the bar door and scanned the room. They were all down the end, seated around a table next to the large window. A few other tables were occupied around the room, some by local people he recognised. At one in a corner, he saw the young woman from the tyre incident that morning. She was in deep conversation with two men, one of whom had his back to him. There was no not recognising Moby Dick Larkin though and when the other man turned slightly reaching for his drink, Gerry saw that it was the councillor, Handy Andy. But at least, both his hands were in view. For the moment anyways. He grinned, wondering how the young girl had gotten on with Billy Hamilton. At least, she still had hair on her head so she hadn't pulled it out in total frustration.

He walked over to the bar, got himself a Jameson whiskey and ice, added a small amount of water from the jug on the bar and then walked over to the American group.

All eyes turned on him. It was Faye who asked the question which was on all of their faces. 'Any luck with your search?'

He pulled out a chair and sat. 'Afraid not. Not a sign of anything.'

Harold Zwimmer left down his glass of beer. 'Guess we will just have to wait until tomorrow night when the ransom is paid. Hopefully, she will be released shortly after it's handed over.'

'I'd imagine the film will be put on hold then. She'll be in no fit state to continue. Not for a while anyways,' Sam Brookman said.

Ruby Lipman gave a little snort. 'Particularly after the studio has stumped up over two million buckaroos. Enrico will be looking to cut costs in a big way. We could all be out of a job in a few days.'

'Dammit,' Harvey Rockwell said. 'I turned down a part in a Paramount production to take this one. Just my damn luck.'

Harriet Taylor gave Gerry a hopeful look. 'But aren't your people going to track the money? There's a good chance they'll get it back, isn't there? After Sabrina is released.'

Gerry didn't get a chance to answer.

'I wouldn't be counting on that too much,' Syl Carpenter said, his voice slightly slurred. 'From the little I've seen of these guys, they're certainly not the LAPD.'

'That's not fair, Syl,' Faye said, casting Gerry an apologetic look. 'They're doing their best.'

'Well their best isn't damn well good enough,' he replied, his look at Gerry a challenging one.

Gerry took a drink of his whiskey. He could see that the big actor was a little the worse for wear from drink and was spoiling for an argument. Well he was just in the mood to oblige. 'I've seen how the LAPD work. Can't say I was over impressed generally, although one officer did impress me quite a lot.'

Carpenter glared at him. 'Whad'ya mean you've seen the LAPD work? I'm not talking about what you've seen on television or in films. I'm talking real policing here.'

Gerry took another slug of whiskey. 'I'm not talking about television or films either. I worked side by side with them for a few weeks in Hollywood. I even contemplated joining them at one time.'

'And why didn't you?' Carpenter asked. 'Decided it was too tough for you? You wouldn't be able to cut it with the big boys. Was that it?'

Gerry felt a pang of pain as Gloria Ballantyne's image floated into his mind. The Los Angeles policewoman with whom he had fallen head over heels in love with while over at a police convention. The one and only woman he had ever asked to marry him. And then, on the night he had bought her the ring, in the fancy restaurant celebrating their engagement and her stepping in to try and prevent a hit on a mobster and getting the bullet intended for him. He shook his head to try and clear the painful memory.

Carpenter continued to prod. 'If this was America, Sabrina would probably already have been rescued by now. But you guys … you're just a joke. And what kind of police go around without being armed anyways? This is the twenty first century for Christ sake.'

Gerry kept his voice calm. 'The kind who think with their brains and not their itchy gun fingers.' He tossed off the last of the whiskey and stood up. 'Now, if you'll all excuse me. I've better things to be doing than listening to a big gobshite talking through his fat arse.'

Carpenter jumped to his feet, his fists clenched 'You better take that back, buddy.'

'Or what?' Gerry said.

Harold Zwimmer stood up, his two hands raised in a placating manner. 'Please, Syl, Detective Sergeant Tierney. Let's all try and compose ourselves here. Sabrina's abduction has upset us all and we're all on edge.' He looked at Gerry. 'I'm sure Syl didn't mean any offence to the Irish police force,' He faced the other man. 'Did you, Syl?'

The scowl didn't leave the actor's face. He stayed standing, still glowering at Gerry but didn't say anything. Gerry stared right back at him.

Zwimmer gave a heavy sigh, shrugged his shoulders in resignation and sat down.

'Well?' Carpenter said belligerently. 'You gonna take that back?'

Gerry deliberately ignored him and turned to Faye. 'I'll talk to you tomorrow.'

Faye nodded. 'Okay.' She looked at Carpenter who still stood angry faced. 'Let it go, Syl. As Harold said, this thing has us all spooked. I know Scobie is doing his best to try and find Sabrina and we should support him and the other policemen as best we can.'

Gerry didn't wait for the actor to respond. He gave the others a brisk nod and then walked off.

He was half way across the lobby heading for the door when he heard his name being called. He turned to see who it was.

Terry Nolan came over. 'So Detective Sergeant Tierney, also called Scobie. You sent me on a right goose chase, didn't you?'

Gerry grinned at her. 'Did I? I better ring the American ambassador so and apologise for wasting one of his investigator's time.'

She gave a little chuckle. 'You knew, didn't you? I'm sorry about that. Just thought if said I was a reporter, people wouldn't talk to me.' She glanced back towards the bar door. 'Although that Mr. Larkin had plenty to say but it was all about himself. And then when he introduced the councillor to me . . .' She gave a little shudder. 'There's something creepy about that man.'

'And how did you get on with Billy Hamilton?' Gerry asked, the grin still on his face.

'Ah that poor man. God! He really has a very bad stammer, hasn't he? But he was still very interesting. It was hard at times to know what he was saying but I think you were right when you said he knew everybody's business.'

She gave him a questioning look. 'He mentioned something about three IRA men being hidden around here by a local farmer a good few years ago, right under the noses of the local police and nobody knowing a thing about it. You ever hear that story?'

But Gerry's attention was elsewhere. Syl Carpenter had just come out of the bar and was glaring over at him.

She followed his line of vision and gasped when she saw the actor. 'Oh my God! That's Syl Carpenter. What I wouldn't give for an interview with him.'

'Would it help?' Gerry asked. 'You know, with your career.'

'Are you serious?' she said, looking over at the actor again. 'It would only be mega. The paper's hot shot reporter is due to take over and that'll be me finished on the Sabrina Metcalfe story. But an interview with one of the hottest actors in Hollywood! God, the editor would take my arm off.'

'Slap my face and give out to me,' Gerry said.

She gave him a wide-eyed look. 'Slap you? What for?'

Gerry leaned in closer. 'Carpenter hates my guts and if he thinks you do as well, well, he'll be very kindly disposed to you. Just do it and then walk away but make sure you walk in his direction. And if you're snivelling a bit, all the better.'

She gave a quick glance over at the actor. He did have a sour look on his face and it was definitely focussed on Scobie.

'Thanks, Scobie. I owe you,' she whispered and then raised her hand and smacked him across the face. 'You're nothing but a chauvinistic pig,' she shouted and then turned on her heel and rushed over in Carpenter's direction, her hanky now out and up to her eyes.

Gerry made a face as his jaw stung from the slap. For such a slight young one, she certainly packed a wallop. She didn't have to have hit him that feckin' hard.

He looked after her and masked a grin when he saw her with Carpenter, his big arm around her shuddering shoulders. The actor gave him another baleful look and then the two of them walked back into the bar, the reporter still dabbing at her eyes with the hanky.

'The things I do for women!' Gerry said to himself as he went out through the main door. Feck it! He would hit McCluskey's for a few quiet pints before calling it a night and to hell with the world.

*****

CHAPTER 32

Sabrina woke, surprised to find that she had actually slept. And, judging by the way she was feeling, it looked like she had slept for a few consecutive hours at least. Up until this, she had only dozed for short periods. But now, her neck was as stiff as a board and as she slowly moved her head from side to side, the movement sent a bolt of pain shooting though her neck and down between her shoulder blades. Her hands and legs were virtually numb from being tied for so long and the sack on her head was making her scalp hot and uncomfortable and as itchy as hell. What she wouldn't give to be able to rip it off and give her head a good two-handed scratching. She sensed someone moving close by. 'Please. I need a drink.'

Ratser took a bottle of water from the table, screwed off the cap and then stuck it between her lips. He tilted it as she greedily swallowed big gulps, both ignoring the overflow running down her chin and onto her chest. To Sabrina, it was a small bit of cooling relief. To Ratser, it was a big enhancement of her breasts. He would have loved to have dowsed her completely, just like those women in wet t-shirt competitions whose outlined breasts through the wet material often had him drooling. He took away the now empty bottle and just stopped himself throwing it on the ground. Instead, he walked over and placed it in the bag which was already nearly full of rubbish.

O'Driscoll and Fatty were both still stretched on the bunk beds. They had moved the driver's body to the floor. Fatty was snoring loudly but he could see that O'Driscoll was awake. He walked over and gave Fatty's bed a kick. 'Wake up, ya noisy bastard. Do you want every cop within a few miles of here to hear ya snorin' like an elephant?'

'Fuck off,' Fatty said drowsily, sitting up and rubbing his eyes with two fat thumbs. 'Yer no fuckin' sleepin' beauty yerself when yer throwing up the z's.' He swung his feet on the floor. 'Thanks be to Christ, this is the last bloody day down in this shithole. I think I'll be smellin' cowshite for months after this.'

O'Driscoll got up off the bed. He nodded to Sabrina. 'Get her something to eat.'

Ratser went back over to one of the boxes against the wall and rooted around in it. He took out a tin of beans, pulled on the tab and peeled back the top. He then took a spoon from the table and went over to her. He tapped the spoon off her lips.

'Open up, darlin'. I've got a bit of grub for you.'

Sabrina opened her mouth a little and when he put in a spoonful, she chewed on them even though she was sick of the taste of cold beans. They seemed to have nothing else in the line of food. She took another three spoonfuls and when the next one was put to her mouth, she clamped her lips shut and shook her head.

Ratser stuck the spoon into the half empty can and left it down on the table. He didn't blame her. He was sick of beans himself. All the sandwiches they had brought were long gone and it had been beans for everyone for the last few meals. The first thing he was going to do when they got back to Dublin was to go to the Red Rooster restaurant up the road from his flat and order the biggest T-bone steak on the menu. Just the thought had his mouth salivating.

O'Driscoll finished off the last of his tin of beans and then took the half empty tin from the table and went over and put the two cans into the rubbish bag. Like everyone else, he was sick of the taste of beans and swore he would never ever look at a tin again. But at least they were down to the last day. All going well, they would get the phone call tonight that the ransom had been paid, safely collected and that they could leave. He glanced over at the woman. He didn't like the thought of her being killed but he knew they had no choice now. None of them believed her when she said she hadn't heard any names. And even if they did, Spence had decreed that she die and that was that. If she didn't, they would. It was as simple as that.

He stood up. 'Let's start going over this place again. I don't want anything left behind. Not a scrap.'

Fatty gave a loud belch, scooped the last spoonful of beans from the tin and shovelled them into his mouth. He took a swig of water, belched again and then twisted on the chair and loudly broke wind in one long protracted fart which nearly burned the hole off him. He shimmied on the seat and breathed a sigh of relief when he felt no wetness. At least he hadn't shit himself.

Ratser gave him a disgusted look. 'Ya poxy git ya, Fatty. As if the stink down here wasn't bad enough without you adding your shit to it.'

His comment only drew a smirk from Fatty. 'Well as me auld lad always said, better an empty flat than a noisy tenant.'

Ratser wrinkled his nose as the new smell hit him. 'Ah for fuck sake, Fatty, your hole must be diseased. You're fuckin' rotten.'

Sabrina heard this exchange and it sent a flash of terror coursing through her. This was the first time they had used names. And it hadn't drawn any reprimand or warning from the voice belonging to the man she knew was the boss. That could only mean one thing. They weren't afraid of her repeating the names to anybody. And she didn't believe it was because they were nondescript names which could be applied to anybody. No. There was only one conclusion.

She wasn't going to leave here alive. Her panic increased and tears of fear and self-pity rolled down her cheeks. She tried to speak but the words stuck in her throat. She swallowed a few times to clear the phantom lump. 'Please. Please let me go. I swear I won't say anything to anybody. Please.' Her body heaved as the tears increased and she started sobbing loudly.

The three men looked at the pitiful figure on the chair, her racking sobs echoing around the low-ceilinged cellar, the tears coursing trails of black mascara down her already dirty face. She was a sad and pathetic figure, now worlds removed from the sexy woman whose image adorned billboards and magazines across the world and whose smouldering presence on the big screen was the image a lot of men brought to their marital or bachelor beds.

Ratser looked at O'Driscoll and Fatty to see what their reaction was. All of a sudden, he himself had no interest in doing anything to the woman, sexual or physical.

Fatty stared at her. He just wished to fuck she would cut out the whining. It was beginning to really get on his nerves. And he could see it was affecting the other two as well. Maybe they should gag her until it was time.

O'Driscoll steeled himself against the pathetic sight in front of him. She seemed to have physically shrunk and now looked almost childlike on the chair. He glared at Fatty and mentally cursed him again for letting Spence's name slip. And why the hell had he himself told the psycho. He should have known how he would react. He gritted his teeth. The die was cast now. He got up and without a word, walked over to the stairs. He took out his phone and punched in the number.

Danny Corbett answered after a few rings. 'Yeah?'

'I want you to come out here. Drive around a bit to make sure the coast is clear and then come and open up. I just need to get out of here for a while.'

'Are you sure that's wise? We've only today to go.'

'At this stage, I don't give a fuck. Just get here. I need to tell you something anyways.'

He ended the call. The constant sobbing had audibly stopped and now there was only a periodic gulp followed by a shiver. But that made her even more pathetic looking. He tore his eyes away from her and looked at the other two. 'Start packing up everything into the boxes and bring them out into the tunnel.'

The two jumped up straight away, anxious to be doing something that heralded their impending release from the claustrophobic and perennially stinking confines of the cellar.

O'Driscoll sat down at the table and looked at his watch. Just approaching eleven o'clock. Only another ten hours until the money was to be dropped off at the National Stadium. He didn't waste time wondering how Spence planned to get away with the money. Nor had he any worries on that score. Spence had written the handbook on kidnapping and collecting ransoms. What did worry him was the fact that when there was no sign of the actress after the money being paid, the search would intensify dramatically. He estimated that by ten o'clock, or eleven at the latest, when there was no sign of the actress, there would be massive police activity all over the place with checkpoints everywhere. They had to be back home in their own places before that. He hadn't told the other three but he planned for them to leave early in the evening. They wouldn't take the direct route through Naas but would swing up through Athlone and Longford and across into Louth and come into Dublin from the north. But it would only be Corbett in the van after Athlone. Himself, Ratser and Fatty would get out there and get the train up. There was one at eight fifteen. He had already checked. One man in a van was a lot less suspicious than four if the van was stopped. They would travel separately. He watched as Fatty and Ratser moved around the cellar, gathering up everything and carrying the boxes over to the bottom of the stairs. No more than himself, they were still wearing their gloves so there was no need to wipe down the place. When they were finished and sat down, he stood up. 'I'm meeting Corby shortly. You keep an eye here.'

He walked over to the stairs and waited.

A few minutes later, he heard the movement up top and shortly afterwards, the hatch opened and Corbett's face appeared. He quickly hopped up the stairs and when he was out, he stopped Corbett from dropping back down the hatch cover. 'Leave it.'

He walked over to the doorway and Corbett followed.

'Any sign of any activity around?' he asked.

'Nothing,' Corbett said. 'I heard yesterday they did a search all around but there was no sign of anything today.' He gave O'Driscoll a questioning look. 'Why we meeting so early? I thought the plan was for me to come back after getting the call from Spence that the money was in hand and then we'd drop Metcalfe and the driver's body up to the old shed.'

'Plan's changed,' O'Driscoll said.

Corbett looked hard at him but said nothing.

'Fatty fucked up. Mentioned Spence's name in front of her.'

Corbett winced. 'Oh bollocks! Does Spence know?'

'Had to tell him,' O'Driscoll said. 'If we didn't and he found out later, he'd have all our guts for garters.'

'Wouldn't think that went down too well. What did he say?'

O'Driscoll's eyes closed to a slit. 'We get rid.'

Corbett winced again. 'Oh fuck! I was afraid you were going to say that.'

They both went quiet for a few minutes and then Corbett turned to him. 'You gonna do it?'

He shook his head. 'It's Fatty's fuck-up. He's doing it. But the reason I called you now is, we're leaving earlier than planned. I want you to fill the tank and be back here at five. We're going to swing north towards Athlone where you'll drop us at the train station and then you head up through Longford and Ardee and come into Dublin from the north.'

Corbett nodded. 'Yeah, that's good thinking. And I presume we leave the two bodies here? The longer it takes to discover them, the better chance we have.'

O'Driscoll looked back over at the open hatch. 'The stuff is all packed. I'm trying to decide what to do with it. Ideally, I'd like to burn it but we can't do that here.'

'How about I take it now and bring it up to the old shed we were going to leave Metcalfe and the driver's body in? It's well isolated and I can burn it in the shed. Nobody will see it and with a bit of petrol, it should burn out fairly quickly.'

'Good thinking,' O'Driscoll said. 'Let's do it now.'

They both walked back over to the hatch and O'Driscoll went back down. Corbett stooped down as the first box emerged and took it from O'Driscoll. He quickly walked out to the yard where the van was parked and opened the side door and pushed it in. O'Driscoll and Ratser appeared out with two more boxes with Fatty following with a full black refuse bag. When all were loaded into the van, O'Driscoll slid across the door. 'Right, you put the pallet back after we're in and then go to the shed and burn the stuff. We'll see you back...' He glanced at his watch...'in exactly four hours.'

'And don't be fuckin' late,' Ratser said.

'I won't,' Corbett said.

He reached back into the van and took out a white plastic rubbish bag, the size used in pedal bins. 'Here. That should do for any last few bits of rubbish. Bring it with you when you're leaving.'

Fatty took it from him and stuffed it into his back pocket.

Corbett followed the three back into the shed and when they were down, he closed the hatch and dropped the pallet back down.

He was up at the old derelict shed fifteen minutes later. The door was open. He looked nervously at it. When they had come across it on their recce a few days earlier, they had left it closed. And then he remembered yesterday's police search he had heard about. They had obviously checked it. He got out of the van and cautiously made his way to the door and peered in. It was empty. He quickly went back to the van, unloaded the boxes and the refuse bag and carried them in. He retrieved the can of petrol from the van and sprinkled the contents over the pile and then took out a box of matches, struck one and tossed it onto the heap. The petrol ignited in a sudden whoosh and soon the boxes and bag were burning too. He went out and closed the door.

Back in the van, he looked over at the shed. He could see the flickering light of the flames through the cracks in the door but there was no tell-tale smoke coming out. Satisfied, he started the van and drove off.

*****

CHAPTER 33

Gerry woke late on Sunday morning. Because he had been so down after the fruitless search and then the argument with Carpenter, he had stayed a lot longer than he had planned to in McCluskey's and he now had more than a bit of a head on him from a generous mixture of Guinness and Jameson. He quickly showered and dressed and then brushed his teeth. He didn't feel a whole lot better but at least he was beginning to feel a bit more human. He checked his watch. Eleven thirty. Did he have breakfast now or hold on an hour or so and have dinner? His stomach was still a bit queasy and in truth, he didn't think he could look a fry in the face. Deciding on the latter which he could have with Faye up at the hotel, he made a quick decision to walk down to the station and see if there had been any developments in the case. He knew in his heart and soul that there hadn't – somebody would have rung him – but sure he hadn't much else to do. Matters were all but out of his hands now. He sucked in great mouthfuls of fresh air as he walked the short distance. By the time he walked through the door, the headache was gone and he was feeling a lot better, if still a bit seedy.

Elsie Masterson and Smithy were on duty when he walked in.

Smithy grinned at him. 'Fuck sake, Scobie. I've seen eyes on corpses with more life in them. You hang one on last night?'

He grinned himself. 'Had a few all right.'

Elsie Masterson gave a snort. 'A few? By the look of you, I'd say the sales charts in Arthur G's and Johnny J's went up a fair bit last night. You're like an extra from that series, The Walking Dead. How the hell you manage to put so much away, I still can't understand. You must have hollow legs and a ten-gallon bladder.'

Smithy laughed. 'Did you not know, Elsie? Scobie here had a surrogate mother. His umbilical cord was attached to a Guinness tap. And then when he was being breast fed, it was off a Jameson optic.'

'Feck off the pair of ye,' Gerry said good naturedly. He nodded to the stairs to the office upstairs. 'Flutehooks in today?'

Smithy shook his head. 'No. He was in earlier but said he was going to Dublin to meet up with Maguire and his lot.'

'Feckin' wanker,' Gerry said. 'Thinks he's going to be involved in the action. Those boyos will feed him a load of shite just to keep him sweet and he'll go around so full of his own self-importance that if you pricked him with a pin, he'd blow up like a grenade. God preserve me from luders like him.'

Big Pat Hartigan walked in, a few copies of the Sunday papers under his arm. He picked one out and held it out to Gerry. 'See your name in the paper this morning, Scobie.'

Gerry grabbed it off him and sat down at his desk.

The big man winked at the others. 'Page 8, Scobie.'

Gerry quickly flipped to the page. It was an interview with Syl Carpenter under the heading

TINSELTOWN'S FAVOURITE MACHO MAN
WORRIED FOR HIS CO-STAR.

He grinned when he saw Terry Nolan's name under the heading. So she had got her scoop. He quickly scanned through the article. It detailed Carpenter's early life as a college basketball star, his move from Nacogdoches in Texas to Hollywood to work as an extra, primarily in Westerns, and culminating in his selection by a well-known director to play one of the lead roles in another Western film about Billy the Kid. That had led to further lead roles until now he was the main go to man for directors looking for an all action hero for their movies.

He had been delighted to be in Ireland to star with the beautiful and talented Miss Sabrina Metcalfe but now he was just totally distraught at the ordeal the poor woman must be going through now. If he had been with her that morning, he was damn sure it wouldn't have happened. And if he had been with her and they had still tried, they would have been damn sorry. You could bet your bottom dollar on that. And much and all as he hated to criticise the local Irish police, he felt they weren't doing all they could to track down her whereabouts and arrest the scum responsible. He knew that a local detective called Tierney had organised a bit of a search around the area where the abduction had occurred but he thought the whole thing had been done in a haphazard fashion and had been totally lacking in professionalism. He had sat in on cases with the LAPD himself back in Los Angeles when getting background for a few roles in which he played a police officer and one of these had been a kidnapping. The cops had solved that case within eight hours, successfully rescuing the girl involved and apprehending the perpetrator. He had taken great pleasure in playing some small part in that case. When Terry had asked him for details of the kidnapping, he had cited police confidentiality for not being able to give those details.

Gerry snorted. Probably a girlfriend dragged off by an ex-boyfriend who'd had too much to drink. A dog with a mallet up its hole could have solved that. Carpenter was asking all his many fans in Ireland, and those of Miss Metcalfe, to pray now for her safe release. The ransom was due to be paid that night and God willing, his much-loved co-star would soon be back safely with her colleagues and friends. When Terry had asked him if he had spoken to Sabrina Metcalfe's husband, he had said not yet. As far as he knew, Mr. Tremayne was in England following the death of his father but he believed he was in constant contact with the studio's people back in Hollywood and would travel over to Ireland as soon as his father was laid to rest. As far as he knew, that would be on Tuesday morning. He just hoped and prayed that Sabrina would be back safely by then.

In the last paragraph, he eulogised about how beautiful Ireland was and how friendly all the people were and how it was such a shame that this had happened. He sincerely hoped that it wouldn't have a negative effect on the Irish movie industry or on American visitors coming over to Ireland.

The article was accompanied by a colour picture of Carpenter standing outside the Cloisters hotel, one cowboy booted foot up on the fender of one of the limos, his thumbs hooked into his belt. Gerry noted that he had changed his clothes for the photograph. He was wearing a pale blue shirt with button down pockets which looked like it had been moulded to his muscular body, tight blue jeans and a wide belt which, when you examined it closely, featured a big buckle of a cowboy on a bucking bronco. He had a yellow neckerchief tied loosely around his neck and a large Stetson hat sat at a rakish angle on his head. He wasn't quite smiling but there was still enough to show off his gleaming white teeth. For all intents and purposes, the quintessential American cowboy. High, wide and handsome.

'And boy do you know it,' Gerry said to himself as he closed the paper.

Elsie Masterson held out her hand. 'Here, give us a look.'

Gerry handed her the paper and she quickly opened it up. She let out a low whistle. 'You have to admit, lads, Carpenter is quite a hunk. I wouldn't kick him out of my bed, that's for sure.'

Smithy leaned in and looked over her shoulder. 'Arra he looks like he's full of himself. Look at the way he's sticking out his chest.'

'Yeah, but look at the muscles,' Elsie said. 'Shoulders, chest, biceps. He's bulging everywhere.'

Smithy gave a snort. 'His jeans are as tight as his shirt but there's no bulge there, is there?' He laughed and looked over at Gerry and Hartigan. 'Looks like all the furniture was put upstairs and downstairs is empty.'

'Yeah,' Hartigan said. 'You get him in bed, Elsie girl, you might have a great selection of muscles but not the one you want.'

She closed the paper. 'You're all just jealous, that's what's wrong with ye.'

Gerry stood up. 'Well riveting and all as this conversation is, I've more to be doing with my time than discussing the physical attributes or lack of, of that gobshite. I'll talk to yis later.'

Smithy looked at him. 'You going to have another look around? Not that I think we missed anything yesterday but knowing you, I'd say you'll give it another go.'

He shrugged his shoulders. 'Haven't decided. Might take a spin around later.' He patted his stomach. 'Right now I think I need a bit of soakage. Ye hear anything here, give us a bell on the mobile.'

Outside, he decided to stay on foot. The Cloisters was about a fifteen-minute walk from the station and the fresher air he got, the better.

He stopped outside Supermacs and peered through the glass door to see if Tina Dolan was working. He was expecting the signed Papal bible any day now and wanted to tell her. When he saw her come out from the back, he opened the door and went in.

The place was fairly full of a lot of young teenagers sitting at tables in small groups, talking animatedly and laughing. Boss O'Connor was at another table with another man almost as big as himself, both bent over the table with big burgers up to their mouths. The plate on the table in front of each of them boasted another large burger and a pile of chips. Boss had a dribble of red ketchup from both sides of his mouth, which, with his long jet-black hair and the black leather jacket with the collar turned up, gave him something of a Dracula look. Even his incisor teeth were a little bit longer than the others. He paused in his mastication of a mouthful of burger and gave Gerry a big grin. 'How's it goin', boss?'

'All right, Boss,' Gerry said.

Some of the kids gave them a curious look and then whispered between themselves and started laughing. Probably thought it funny that the two were calling each other 'boss'.

'What's the story on this auld fillum me dogs are supposed to be in? Is it held up on account of yer wan that's missin'?'

'Afraid so,' Gerry said. 'Hopefully she will be released tonight and maybe then in a few days, they might start filming again. I'll let you know as soon as I hear anything.'

The other man wiped a smear of ketchup from his chin and looked at Boss. 'What's this about yer dogs being in a film? Ya never told me about that.'

'I don't have to tell you everything, do I, Jamesie Breen?' Boss replied. 'Yer not me fuckin' manager or anything like that, are ya?'

'I'm yer fuckin' cousin, ain't I?'

Boss finished off the remains of the first burger and picked up the second one. 'Arra I was goin' ta tell ya. The fillum crowd need a couple of auld dogs for a while. Boss here told them about Sampson and Hercules.'

Breen gave a laugh. 'Ye think them two are goin' ta be the new Lassies?'

'Lassie me fuckin' arse,' Boss said, a disgusted look on his face. 'Sure my lads would chew that poofter up and spit him out as cat food.'

Breen nodded knowingly. 'That they would all right.' He too started on his second burger.

'I'll see ye lads,' Gerry said.

The two just nodded, both now hand shovelling chips into their already bulging mouths.

He walked up to the counter.

Tina Donovan spotted him and came over. 'Bit late for the breakfast, Scobie but seeing as it's you, I'll get one done for you. The usual, is it?'

Gerry shook his head. 'Not this morning, Tina, thanks. Just popped in to tell you I should have that item we were talking about in a couple of days. How are things going on that front?'

She made a face. 'We were supposed to go to the funfair Friday night but Larry rang to say the old witch wasn't feeling well and he had to stay home and mind her. That's how it's going.'

Gerry gave her a grin. 'Well let's just hope your little present to her in a few days will see a complete transformation in the old witch, as you call her. She might even be going wedding dress shopping with you.'

'God, I hope not. I think I'd nearly prefer her the way she is than for her to become buddy with me. Anyways, thanks for all your doing, Scobie. I really appreciate it.'

'No bother,' he said. 'I'll be in touch.'

He left the fast food outlet and headed for the hotel. He was feeling much better now, head fully clear and the seedy feeling gone. He was looking forward to dinner with Faye. Hopefully, they could get away from the others.

He was whistling as he went in the door.

*****

CHAPTER 34

The film crew were gone, including Faye. Jeremy Clarke told Gerry this when he stuck his head into the dining room to see if any of them were there. They had left about twenty minutes before his arrival, leaving for Dublin where they believed Sabrina Metcalfe would be released and they wanted to be on hand to comfort and support her after her ordeal. It had been Syl Carpenter's idea. Not all of them had agreed at first but when Zwimmer and Brookman said that they should be there for Enrico di Angelo as well, nobody had wanted to disagree – Gerry's good humour dissipated. Feck it! He had been looking forward to a long leisurely lunch with Faye, albeit it, with the cloud of Sabrina Metcalfe's kidnapping hanging over it, but at least the company would have been a distraction for them both. But now it looked like he was eating on his own. And it looked like everyone now believed that Sabrina was in Dublin. Maguire and his crew, Doyle, the film crew now and he suspected, even some of the lads at the station. Was he the only one who thought she might still be held around Kilbracken? Could he be that off beam?

He went up to the carvery counter and ordered a plate of beef, mashed potatoes and mashed carrots with a liberal pouring of gravy and carried it over to a table in the corner of the dining room. When one of the waitresses passed by, he called her. 'Hey Sharon, would you get us a glass of milk.'

Sharon Gleeson grinned at him. 'Milk? For you, Scobie? Are you sick or what?'

When she didn't get one of his usual smart answers, she gave him a raised eyebrow look and then hurried away and came back a minute later with a pint glass of milk and left it down in front of him. He just nodded his thanks but did manage to accompany the nod with a smile. He ate quickly, eager now to be out of the hotel. He had decided now to do another sweep around the area. He hadn't much else to do.

After he had finished, he was just about to stand up when Dora Donovan, her daughter and the boyfriend came into the dining room and after a quick look around, came over to his table, the two obese women waddling like ducks, the stick thin man like a spacer between them. Dora was dressed in a floral patterned cavernous summer dress which was like a tent on her large frame. It stopped just above her ankles which, in Gerry's opinion, was a good thing as it probably concealed legs which were like tree stumps. But it had short sleeves which gave full view of her flabby arms on which the flesh wobbled like jelly. Her daughter hadn't been quite as considerate of other people who would see her as her short black skirt stopped a good six inches above her large knobbly knees and her bare legs were thicker than Gerry's thigh and looked like somebody had pumped them full of water the way the flesh wobbled on them. She wore a white blouse through which the shadow of a blue bra could be seen. The bra was failing miserably in its effort to support two bulbous drooping breasts which nearly reached her naval. A small red heart was tattooed on one. Her myopic eyes were further enhanced by a pair of thick framed black glasses. Her short hair was platinum-blonde, but the roots of her naturally black colour were very evident,

The boyfriend was smaller than Dympna and as thin as a whippet. He had a ferret face with long black hair tied back in a rat's tail. He had a thin moustache which was so uneven, it looked like it could have been drawn on by a four year old child. He was dressed in denim jeans, black shirt and a black leather jacket. Gerry spotted the end of a tattoo on his arm when he lifted it to pick at his nose. All this he quickly noted as the three formed a formidable wall in front of him.

'They told me at the station you were here,' Dora said. 'I want to know why you're all not out looking for Sean. Everybody is talking about that actress but nobody seems to be giving a shit about my poor husband. Even the papers didn't mention him. It's all about her.'

'It's Inspector Doyle you need to be talking to,' he said. 'He's in charge of things down here.'

'Yeah,' she said derisively. 'And where is he now? Up in bloody Dublin, that's where. How the hell are we supposed to ask him anything when he isn't even here!'

'We did a big search yesterday,' he said.

'I know that,' she said. 'So why aren't ye all out searching again today?'

Before Gerry could answer, Dympna Donovan started to blubber. 'Poor daddy. Where is he? We're so worried about him.' She stuck a pudgy knuckle up under her glasses and rubbed an eye.

The boyfriend put an arm around her shuddering shoulders. 'Hush, pet. He'll be home soon. I'm sure he will.'

She gave him a withering look. 'That's a stupid thing to say. You don't know that.' She started to cry again.

Gerry wanted to get away from them. People were looking over and he could see the whispered conversations and the heads nodding. 'I'm going to have another look around myself. I'll let you know if I find anything.'

'On your own?' Dora Donovan said, her incredulous voice ringing around the now silent dining room as everybody sat watching. It wasn't often there was lunchtime entertainment at the Cloisters. 'What bloody good is that? Why aren't the rest of your lot going out as well?'

'You'll have to ask Inspector Doyle that when you see him,' Gerry said, edging away. 'Now, if you'll excuse me.'

He left the three of them standing there and quickly left the dining room, all eyes following his departure. He could nearly physically feel them boring into his back. He went out and walked back to the station.

Elsie Masterson looked up from her desk when he walked in. 'The Donovan's get you?'

He made a face. 'Yeah. The Double D's got me all right. And I'm not just talking about their initials. I honestly don't know how they manage to walk straight with them big bazookas in front of them. They could breastfeed an orphanage between them.'

Masterson laughed. 'Sure ye men don't know how lucky ye are. The only dangly bit ye have is like a finger, and in a lot of cases, a little finger. Us poor women have a lot more to cope with than that.'

Gerry grinned at her. 'You speaking about them fingers from experience, Elsie?'

'Feck off, Scobie,' she said laughing. 'I'd say you've handled a lot more bazookas as you call them than I have little fingers.'

'What's this about fingers?' Smithy said, coming out of the Incident room, a marker pen in his hand.

The two looked at each other and laughed.

'What?' Smithy said.

Elsie chewed her bottom lip to keep a straight face. 'Ah we were just saying that you can tell a lot about men by the size of their little finger.'

Smithy held up his hand and studied it, his little finger extended. He looked at it and then over at her, a puzzled look on his face. He held up the finger. 'So? What does mine say about me?'

All she could do was burst out laughing.

Gerry gave him a thump on the back. 'It just says you're a big prick, Smithy. But take it from me, I mean that in a good way.'

Smithy stared at him. 'Were the two of ye smoking funny stuff or something? I don't know what the fuck you're talking about. And if it was anybody else called me a big prick, Scobie, they'd be chewing on more than my little finger.'

Elsie went into another fit of laughing and Gerry too couldn't stop himself.

'Arra fuck off the two of you,' Smithy said. He picked up a sheaf of papers from his desk and went back into the room.

Gerry looked over at Elsie. 'Give him a few minutes and then explain it to him, will you?'

She laughed. 'God, that's the best yet. It's not often you get to get one up on him.'

Gerry headed for the door. 'I'm on the mobile. If you hear anything, give us a bell.'

'You going looking again?' she asked, her face now serious.

He stopped at the door and turned. 'I know everybody thinks I'm wasting my time but my gut instinct is that they're still holed up somewhere around here. I just can't see them having risked taking them to Dublin. I could be wrong. Maybe I am. But I just have this feeling and it won't go away.'

'Well if there's one thing I've learned since coming here, Scobie, is that that gut of yours has led to more cases being solved than any amount of police think tanks. You go for it.'

He gave her a grateful look. 'Thanks, Elsie. That means a lot.'

She waved him away. 'Go on. I'm going in to Smithy now. He's probably in there giving out all kinds of shite to himself about us.'

Gerry left and walked back to his apartment where his car was parked. His thoughts turned to the article in the paper. He grinned. He had at least got one up on Carpenter. Macho man didn't know that he had orchestrated the whole thing. But he was glad that Terry Nolan had gotten her article. She seemed a nice young one. He thought back to their conversation in the hotel. When she had come out to him in the lobby after talking to Moby and Handy Andy. Something niggled in his mind. Something she had said. He rewound back to the hotel lobby. She had called after him as he was going out. And she had said that all Moby could talk about was himself. And Handy Andy had given her the creeps. But she had something just when Carpenter had come out of the dining room and distracted him. What the hell was it? And then it hit him. Billy Hamilton, the stuttering ex postman. Something about him knowing about some IRA men being hidden right under the noses of the police. He took out his mobile and rang the hotel. He recognised Jeremy Clarke's voice straight away.

'Jeremy. It's Scobie. You double jobbing now?'

The hotel manager laughed. 'Just giving the girls a break. What can I do for you?'

'You have a girl, Terry Nolan, staying there. Is she there now do you know?'

Clarke answered straight away. 'No. She checked out just after breakfast. Told Eileen that another reporter from the paper was taking over the Sabrina Metcalfe story. But she was happy she had gotten her interview with Syl Carpenter. And that was down to you, she told Eileen.'

Gerry silently cursed. He would have to talk to Billy himself. He thanked the manager and terminated the call.

Billy Hamilton lived only a short distance away, within easy walking distance. He was knocking on his door five minutes later. And a few minutes after that, he was still knocking. He cursed again and was just about to walk away when the next door opened and Mrs. Relihan stepped out. Her late husband had been a guard for over thirty five years. Her hands were white with flour and there were white handprints on the blue apron she wore and a smudge on her nose. 'He's away, Scobie' she said, rubbing her two hands together to remove the flour. Him and Geraldine have gone to Lourdes on the parish pilgrimage.'

'Any idea when they'll be back?' he asked.

'Seven days. I was hoping to go on it myself but...........' She gave a resigned shrug of her shoulders. 'I've the grandchild's birthday on Wednesday and I said I'd go up for it. You want me to give him a message when they're back? I presume it's Billy and not Geraldine you're looking for?'

'It was,' he said. 'Nothing important though. I'll get him again.'

She studied him. 'You're looking a bit peakey, Scobie, if you don't mind me saying. Why don't you come in for a cuppa. I've just made a few nice rhubarb tarts. The first one's fresh out of the oven.'

He gave her a regretful look. 'James Street, I'd love to, Nancy, but I'm a bit tied for time.'

'Always the same with you guards,' she said. 'Arthur was the same. Always rushing around.'

'Arthur was a great guard, Nancy. One of the best. And a good friend to me.'

She gave a wistful look into the distance and then re-focussed on him. 'He liked you too, Scobie. Always said you were one of the best detectives he ever worked with. Said you had a knack of figuring things out when nobody else could.'

She put a floury hand on his arm. 'Hold on a sec. I'll pop a tart into a bag for you. You can bring it home and eat it when you're not so busy.'

She was gone back in before he could answer but he hadn't been going to decline the offer. It would have been insulting to Nancy to do that. Her tarts were prize winners every year at the Kilbracken agricultural show and at the big show in Kilkenny city.

He waited at the door and a couple of minutes later she was back out, a puffed up white plastic bag held flat on her hand like a waiter's tray. She held it out. 'Here. And keep it like this. If you turn it sideways, the juice will only run out and spoil it.'

He balanced it on his hand. 'Thanks, Nancy. I'm looking forward to eating this tonight when I can sit down and enjoy it.'

Her face clouded over. 'You still working on that poor woman's kidnapping?'

He nodded. 'Yeah. Just going to do another sweep around. I still think they've all got it wrong by thinking she was taken to Dublin. It's just a gut feeling but . . .' He shrugged his shoulders.

'Well you stick with your gut, Scobie Tierney. My Arthur said you had the gut of a bloodhound and there weren't too many things he was wrong about.'

'Thanks, Nancy. The ransom is due to be paid tonight anyways so please God, she'll be released before the night is out.'

She crossed herself. 'And please God again.' She made a shooing sign. 'Now, off with you. And be careful with that tart.'

He quickly walked back to his apartment and went in and left the tart in the kitchen. He took out his phone and rang directory enquiries. When it was answered by what sounded like a bored female voice, he said, 'Can I have a number for the Sunday Chronicle.'

A few seconds later, the monotonous voice said, 'Would you like to be connected?'

'Please,' he said.

Another few seconds and he heard another female voice, much

younger and perkier than the previous. 'Sunday Chronicle. How may I help you?'

He took a deep breath. 'I'm looking to speak to one of your reporters, Terry Nolan. Would she be there?'

'Terry's not in today. Can I take a message?'

He took another deep breath. 'I wonder could you give me a number for her. It's extremely urgent that I talk to her.'

'I'm sorry. I can't give out her number.'

'I'm a Garda detective sergeant calling from Kilbracken station,' Gerry said, hoping the official title and address would change the girl's mind.

He was mistaken.

'I don't care if you're the Angel Gabrial calling from beside the throne of God. It's more than my job's worth to give out anybody's personal number. But if you give me your number, if I track her down, I'll tell her you called. She can ring you then if she wants.'

He had to grin at her response, despite his disappointment. He quickly gave her his number, thanked her and ended the call. There was nothing more he could do but wait and hope that she called him. He had to find out if Billy had told her the name of the farmer who had hidden the IRA guys. In the meantime, he would drive around and keep looking.

*****

CHAPTER 35

Enrico di Angelo and his three companions stepped off the plane at Dublin airport. It was just after four o'clock. Two Garda squad cars were waiting for them on the tarmac.

Maguire and Fogarty got out of the first one and walked over to where the four were standing, Di Angelo with the large suitcase standing beside him. The superintendent introduced himself and the inspector and then nodded over to the other car. 'Sergeant Noel Casey, one of my team and Inspector Doyle, the officer in charge down where the incident occurred, are in that car. Maybe you'd like to split up, two with us and three with them. We're going to go to Crumlin Garda station. We've set up an incident room there.'

Di Angelo introduced himself and then Frogatti, Montello and Schwartz as associates of his. He then nodded at Hegarty. 'This is Lieutenant Shaun Hegarty of the Las Vegas police department. Because of his experience of hostage situations and his Irish background, he's agreed to accompany us and act as our liaison with you guys, if that's okay.'

Maguire shook Hegarty's hand. 'Delighted to meet you, lieutenant. Glad to have you aboard.'

Hegarty made a self-deprecating gesture. 'It's your show, guys. All I'm asking is to be allowed ride along with you and if there's anything I can offer, I'll be glad to do so.'

'Good,' Maguire said. 'Now, how about we head back to the station and we'll bring you up to speed on things and what we plan for the handover.'

It was Hegarty who answered. 'As I've said, it's your show, superintendent. Whatever you say.'

Fogarty opened the back door of the car.

Hegarty stood to one side and nodded to di Angelo, 'After you, Enrico.'

When the studio boss had climbed in and settled himself; after stashing the suitcase in the trunk, he slid in after him. Maguire got into the front passenger seat.

Fogarty indicated for the other three men to follow him to the second car where, after brief introductions, the three got into the back. He returned to the first car and got in behind the wheel. He drove off and the other car quickly slipped in behind. As they travelled along the M50, Maguire turned back to Hegarty. 'So, lieutenant, what's the Irish connection?'

'Parents were from Ballina in Co. Mayo,' he replied. 'But they left for the States a month after my mother became pregnant with me so I'm not a hundred per cent Irish I suppose.' He gave a little laugh. 'Still, at least I was conceived here. That's a lot more authentic than a whole lot of other Americans who have to go back three and four generations to find their link.'

'And you're with the Las Vegas police department. How long have you been a cop?'

'Just shy of twenty-five years now but twenty-four of them were with the LAPD in Los Angeles. I only moved to Vegas a year ago.'

'Why the move?' Maguire asked.

Hegarty shrugged his shoulders. 'Just a bit of burnout I suppose. Los Angeles is a tough city. It can grind a man down, particularly one in law enforcement.' He wasn't going to tell him that his captain had strongly suggested he think about moving to somewhere else after his name was linked to a corruption probe by Internal Affairs. He wanted him out of the way to take the heat off as he himself also received a fat envelope from Gratelli. And it was Gratelli who had set up his job with the Vegas police department where his tentacles reached even further than in the LAPD.

'I can imagine,' Maguire said. 'Dublin is getting a bit like that. The criminals we're dealing with now are younger, more arrogant and better armed. The older guys were a lot easier to deal with. There was a certain - you know – code that existed between us and them. A certain level of mutual respect I suppose you could call it.' He shook his head. 'But the young scumbags that are out today – well they're just pure fucking evil, if you'll pardon my language. They respect nothing, least of all the law and the cops.'

Hegarty grunted sympathetically. He didn't give a fish's tit what went on in Dublin or anywhere else in Ireland but he had to lick up to make sure he got into the loop on this Sabrina Metcalfe case. That was what he was here for. 'I can imagine. And your regular guys don't carry guns. That must make things a whole lot tougher. I have to say, you guys over here have my complete respect.'

'Any idea yet who's behind the kidnapping?' di Angelo asked.

Fogarty threw a quick glance over at Maguire before focussing back in the road. 'We're working on a few theories,' he said. 'But our main focus now is the ransom drop tonight. Once that's done and we get word that Miss Metcalfe's been released, then we move.'

Hegarty sat forward a bit. 'So you have a plan to track down the perps?'

Maguire turned around to face him, a smug look on his face. 'Let's just say, where the money goes, we won't be far behind. And sooner or later, the cheese Mr. di Angelo brought with him, will lead us to the vermin.'

Hegarty sat back in the seat, a wry grin on his face. It was obvious that, as well as planning to have eyes on the money at all times, there was probably also going to be a tracking device planted somewhere in it or stitched into one of the bags. It was all basic police procedure in cases like this. The question was, how smart were the gang behind it all? If they had an ounce of cop on, they would be expecting both these things.

'This stadium where the drop is supposed to take place, is it big?'

Maguire turned around again. 'It's big all right. And it's going to be packed tonight. There's a big boxing competition on.'

Hegarty nodded. 'Right. That could be a doubled-edged sword. In one way, it provides plenty of cover for your men who no doubt, you'll have strategically placed near the drop off point but by the same token, it equally could provide cover for the pick-up man.'

'True,' Maguire said, a small smile on his lips as he and Fogarty shared another look.

Hegarty looked hard at him. 'So… A tracking device. Am I right?'

'Yes. One in with the money and another stitched into the bag.'

Hegarty nodded. 'Good thinking. They probably won't be expecting two devices.'

They all stopped talking as Fogarty pulled up in front of a big building which had the Garda symbol over the door and parked in one of the spots with the reserved sign stencilled on the road. The other car pulled into another reserved spot behind and all got out.

Maguire led them into the building and up the stairs, nodding and exchanging the odd greeting with uniformed men and women whom they passed. He opened a door and he and Fogarty stood aside as the others filed in.

It was a big room, about fifteen foot square, with a large table in the centre and a row of six chairs each side and two at each end.

There was a large whiteboard and a felt covered noticeboard

taking up a sizeable portion of one wall, a half dozen filing cabinets along another with the wall opposite the door having a big window which looked directly onto the street below. The noticeboard had a picture of Sabrina Metcalfe pinned to it along with a map of Ireland on which someone had drawn a big red circle around County Kilkenny.

To the left of the door, there was a smaller table with a coffee machine and a selection of cups and a tray on which there was a box of Barry's tea bags, a half full litre bottle of milk and a large jar of Nescafe coffee. There was also a stack of transparent plastic cups. Beside the table was a water dispenser.

Maguire indicated for everybody to sit down and when they had, he quickly introduced everybody again.

He took a chair at the head of the table. 'Right. The first thing we have to do is plant the tracking devices. The bag one is already stitched in so we just have to stick one into one of the bundles of money.' He gave the assembly an expansive smile. 'And if I say so myself, the one in the bag is somewhere it won't be found.'

Hegarty decided to give another few strokes to the Irish copper's ego. 'So one of them is a decoy tracker. I like it. Good thinking. When they find that and dispose of it, they'll think they're home and hosed.'

Maguire visibly preened in front of him. 'Exactly. And we will still have the other tracker telling us exactly where they are. As soon as Miss Metcalfe surfaces, we move in. Any questions?'

Hegarty glanced at Frogatti who gave him an almost imperceptible smile.

What they weren't telling the Irish cops – for now anyways – was that they had their own tracking device planted in the money. And it was a type they were very confident wouldn't be found. It was the latest invention from Silicon Valley and wasn't even in the public domain yet as it was still in prototype stage. Gratelli had gotten wind of the invention and a honey trap had been set for the chief executive officer of the company. Married with a wife and four kids, when they had shown him the video of his drug enhanced tryst with the two black hookers, it had been easy to get him to sit on the invention and Gratelli was currently buying up as many shares as he could in the company before the device was launched into the marketplace. When it was, the value would rocket, and he stood to make millions.

The tracker was about half the size of a sim card and half as thin but round in shape. It was more like a blister and it was virtually transparent. It was undetectable by all existing scanning equipment. It had a tracking range of fifty miles and could be tracked on a mobile phone using an app which the company had also developed. It had been inserted in the middle of one of the banded bundles of money and unless you peeled off each note individually, it was impossible to spot it, and even then, could quite easily be overlooked. It had cost over $180,000 to produce this final prototype. Hegarty, Montello and Schwartz had the app on their phone as had Frogetti himself. di Angelo didn't as he was only the cash carrier.

Frogatti had decided to play a waiting game. He suspected that if the people who had abducted Metcalfe had half a brain between them, they would scan the money for tracking bugs. Maguire's belief that they would stop checking after finding one was just plain stupid. He would bet a dime to a dollar that whoever they were, would find both of the bugs. But they wouldn't find his. When the cops lost the signal, he knew there would be panic and he planned to exploit that. Maguire was a smug ambitious cop whom he believed, would be desperate to avoid being seen as a loser which he would be, if they ended up losing the money. At the right time, a deal could be done with him. They still needed his knowledge of the city. He would be told of the other tracking device and allowed to join up with them. When their bug showed that the money had reached its final destination, he would then be allowed call in his team and make his arrests but only after Frogatti and his guys had the money back and had dished out a bit of retribution. How Maguire explained the state the men would be found in, well that was his problem. Frogatti didn't think the Irish cop would be too bothered anyways. He looked at his watch. Just under three hours to the drop. With a bit of luck, they could be on their way back to the States in the morning.

*****

CHAPTER 36

Gerry cruised around the area which Smithy and the other guards had checked before his arrival yesterday. He did a cursory check of some old outbuildings but he knew he was only killing time and that they would have been well checked out. He looked at his watch for about the fifth time. It was now just after five o'clock and Terry Nolan still hadn't rung. 'Where the hell are you?' he said to himself. He pulled into the car park at the back of The Wayward Tavern and parked and killed the engine. He had never felt at such as loose an end before. He got out of the car and lay back against the side. About forty thousand feet above his head, a jet was like a tiny silver speck, its long white trail petering out near the end and breaking into small rings which looked like smoke rings from a cigarette or cigar. He wondered where it was heading. Maybe it was time he took a holiday himself. Jet off to some exotic place and forget about the world and all its problems for a week or two. He sighed as the plane disappeared from view and took out his phone and dialled.

Flann answered almost immediately. 'Hey, Scobie. What gives? Where are you now?'

'Sitting behind The Wayward waiting for a young one to ring me. You at the station?'

'Just left,' Flann said. 'Nothing much new there apart from the news that the ransom money has arrived in Dublin. Doyle rang while I was there. He told me there's a Las Vegas cop with the four from the film studio who brought over the money, whatever the feck he's doing over here.'

'From Las Vegas? James Street! This is turning into a right feckin' carnival so it is.'

'Aye,' Flann said. 'It's beginning to look like a Hollywood production all right. Tell me, why are you waiting for a call from a young one? You up to something I don't know about?'

Gerry laughed. 'I am in me arse. No – this young one was down here yesterday and was talking to Billy Hamilton. Just something she said he told her I want to follow up on. Might throw a bit of light on this Sabrina Metcalfe case.'

'And can't you ask Billy himself,' Flann said and then laughed. 'Although I suppose by the time you get the answer, you could be ready to strangle him.'

Gerry grinned. 'Yeah, you would be tempted all right, wouldn't you? No – I found out himself and the queen are gone on that diocesan pilgrimage to Lourdes. Probably praying for reprobates like you and me. Won't be back for a week. Although if he decides to say a full rosary, he mightn't be back for a month.'

'Not much you can do so unless your girl rings you,' Flann said.

'I'll give it another while,' Gerry said. 'You interested in meeting up in Mackers for a few scoops later on?'

Flann gave a heavy sigh. 'Nothing I'd like better but tonight is out I'm afraid. Lucy is in this show they're putting on down at the school hall. And after it's over, there's a sort of reception. Could be late before it's all over.'

'Ah that's lovely,' Gerry said. 'What's the show?'

'As if you give a shite,' Flann said.

Gerry pretended to be vexed. 'I asked, didn't I? If I can't show an interest in my best friend's family, what the hell can I do!'

'Don't bullshit a bullshitter, Scobie,' Flann said laughing. 'You've as much interest in St. Fiachra's senior infants production of Sleeping Beauty as I have in the mating habits of pregnant snails. Now – you might have feck all else to do but I have to go soon and start pretending I'm looking forward to spending over an hour on a hard seat for probably less than five minutes of my own daughter's stage time. And I wouldn't mind but that's in the first fifteen minutes, so for the other hour or so, I'll have to sit and coo and smile with all the other parents. So good luck.'

Gerry grinned as the call was ended. Poor Flann. He would be like a hen on a hot griddle. And because he was the local sergeant, all the mothers would be clucking at him as much as to say, 'Isn't my little darling the best, sergeant?' And it would be worse for him at the reception afterwards. At least while the show was on, it could only be simpering looks and proud nods of the head over at him but without the restriction of having to remain seated, he would be the target for a lot of one on one conversations. God, he was glad he didn't have to put up with all that bullshit. Nobody expected it off a singleton considered by a lot of the locals to be as feckless as you could get. And that suited him just fine.

He gave a little start when his phone interrupted his thoughts. He looked at the screen. A number he didn't recognise. It had to be Terry Nolan. He quickly pressed the answer ikon. The first thing he heard was a babble of voices and loud banging music. She must be in a club somewhere. 'Terry? Is that you?'

'Detective Sergeant Tierney.' She had to shout to be heard over the background noise. 'I'm sorry. I should have rang you much earlier to thank you for setting that up with Syl Carpenter.' She gave a little laugh. 'Although I have to say, it was a rather unorthodox way of getting an interview. But it worked and I'm very grateful.'

'No problem,' Gerry said. 'But that's not why I'm calling. You told me Billy Hamilton ... ' He gave a little laugh himself. 'You know, the p-p-p-p post-m-m-m-man. He told you about some IRA guys being hidden down here years ago and nobody knowing a thing about it. Did he say where they were hidden?'

'No, he didn't say where.'

Gerry felt his heart sink. It looked like he would have to wait for Billy himself to come back from Knock and that would be a good while after the ransom drop in Dublin.

He heard the excitement in her voice. 'God, Scobie! Are you thinking what I think you're thinking? That Sabrina Metcalfe could be hidden in the same place?'

'Well if it worked years ago for the provos, what's to stop it working now if somehow, whoever grabbed her, had heard about Billy's hiding place? It could even be a gang of ex provos. But Billy didn't tell you where the hiding place was so that fecks that.'

'No,' she said, her voice even more excited over the pounding beat of the background music which was still rattling his eardrums. 'But he did let slip the farmer's nickname.'

Gerry felt his own excitement shoot up. 'And can you remember it?'

'I'm a newspaper reporter, Scobie – well I am now thanks to you. The name was Crackers. That ring a bell with you?'

The name reverberated in his brain. Jamesie 'Crackers' McCracken. The bachelor farmer who had the small farm about fifteen miles outside of Kilbracken that he himself had checked. He had to have missed something. 'Thanks, Terry. I'll let you know if it leads to anything.'

This time her voice was laced with disappointment. 'Shite on it anyways, Scobie. I'm over in Ibiza. Came over last night after leaving Kilbracken and sending in the piece on Syl Carpenter. And knowing 'm here drinking Tequila shots and fending off pimpled faced leaving cert students and dirty old men who....

He heard her gasp. 'Oh my God! Oh my God!'

'What?' he asked, pressing the phone as tight as he could to his ear.

'Oh my God, Scobie! You won't believethis. There's a naked woman on the stage and she has a mouse and she's putting it...Oh my God! I don't believe it!'

'Putting it where?' He was almost shouting into the phone.

'Putting it where the sun doesn't shine,' she said. 'You know, into her ...her privates.'

'Arra how can you see that if it's a mouse she has,' he said. 'Sure there's probably a few thousand people in that place. Aren't all them clubs the size of Croke Park? I'd say you can barely see the stage, never mind a feckin' mouse.'

'Yeah, I know,' she said. 'But I can see one of the twenty foot by ten foot screens they have all around the place and believe you me, it's a mouse and she's putting it in there.'

Gerry laughed. 'Must be a mickey mouse so.'

She didn't catch the pun. 'It's disgusting, that's what it is,' she said. 'All you can see now is the poor thing's tail. Oh God! Listen, I'm going, Scobie. I'm getting out of this bloody place. Let me know how you get on.'

He was still shaking his head and grinning when he put the phone back in his pocket. A feckin' mouse! He had read a lot in the papers about the bizarre carry on in these clubs but a woman and a feckin' mouse! The world wasn't half settled.

He got back into the car. He would be at McCracken's place in less than fifteen minutes.

*****

CHAPTER 37

Danny Corbett pulled into the yard and parked around the back of the shed. He was feeling a mixture of relief and trepidation. He was glad that the whole thing was coming to an end and that they would all soon be a great deal richer but he didn't like the fact that the woman had to be killed. That had never been part of the plan. But Fatty's loose mouth and Spence's callous nature had dictated otherwise. But he didn't want to be in the cellar when Fatty did it.

He took the surgical gloves from the dash and put them on and got out of the van. He walked around and into the shed and went to the last stall and stood the pallet up on its edge. He had to step aside quickly as the cover was immediately pushed up and O'Driscoll climbed out. Ratser followed him and when he was out, he let the cover back down. None of them spoke as they walked out of the shed.

'I parked around the back,' Corbett said. 'Just in case.'

They all walked around to the back of the shed and Ratser pulled back the side door of the van and sat down on the edge. Corbett followed O'Driscoll around to the front where they both leaned back against the bonnet.

'I told him ten minutes,' O'Driscoll said.

Corbett's lip curled. 'What the hell does he want to do that for anyways? We should be getting the hell out of here now and not sitting around twiddling our thumbs while that perv screws her. He should be just getting on with what he has to do.'

O'Driscoll shrugged his shoulders. 'It sticks in my craw as well but I couldn't really say no to him, could I? Seeing as he's the one that's topping her.' He nodded back to where Ratser sat. 'We're lucky Ratser changed his mind or we could be waiting even longer. Why did you change your mind anyways, Ratser?'

Ratser looked over. 'Didn't really think it was right doing that to her and then killing her. I just wouldn't have been able to...you know.' He gave a little snigger...rise to the occasion.' He sniggered again. 'And I'd say Fatty will have shot his bolt after a minute or two, that's if he can find it underneath that big slab of fat he has hangin' down.'

Down in the cellar, Fatty cut the restraining tape and hefted the actress out of the chair and dropped her down on one of the bunk beds. He pulled her arms up over her head and taped one each side to the tubular frame. He stood back and looked down at her. He was as nervous as a young lad entering a brothel for the first time but was equally as excited. The last time he had sex was over six months ago and it certainly wasn't with a woman as good looking and sexy as the one stretched out in front of him. It had been with a pock faced junkie with oozing needle sores on her arms and who had been as thin as a whippet and out of her mind on the coke he had given her earlier. He could still nearly feel her razor sharp bony body cutting into him. He reached down.

Sabrina winced and closed her eyes tight as the dirty sack was whipped off her head. She blinked a few times to acclimatise her eyes to the light, weak and all as that light was. When she could keep them open, she looked at the man standing over her. He was as obnoxious looking as he smelt. Small, obesely fat and dirty looking, his face had a good growth of stubble which made him look even dirtier. He was wearing baggy denim jeans and a dark t-shirt which bulged at his midriff. But it wasn't his appearance which frightened her most. It was the leering lascivious look on his face. She looked up at him, tears welling in her eyes. 'Please. Please don't hurt me.'

She let out a shriek when he suddenly reached down and tore her blouse open and then roughly grabbed her bra between the cups and pulled. The single hook at the back was no match for the brute force and it easily came away in his hand. When he pulled down her leggings and thong and threw them aside, she started to cry loudly and beg. 'Please. Please don't hurt me. I'm begging you. I'll give you anything you want.'

Fatty ignored her cries and feasted his eyes on the gorgeous body. He had never seen one as beautiful. The smallish but firm breasts with the prominent nipples, the hourglass waist, the shapely legs, the blemish free and deeply tanned skin without even a bikini line. Even her tear stained and dirt smudged face didn't detract from the overall perfection. He felt himself stirring and quickly unbuckled his belt and dropped his jeans and kicked them off. He stepped out of his boxer shorts and then lowered himself down.

Sabrina tried to fend him off with her legs but his weight quickly flattened her and knocked the air out of her lungs. She felt his hand groping between her legs. His breath was hot and foul smelling and she tried to turn her face away but it was roughly pushed back. She saw him brace himself for penetration and it was then that the serene actress Sabrina Metcalfe and recently elevated Lady of the realm disappeared and the tough hard bitten wildcat called Mary Harte returned. As his face hovered over hers, she snapped her head up and clamped her teeth over his nose. She held on grimly as he tried to pull away, his animal cry of pain reverberating around the confines of the cellar as blood poured from between her teeth and down her chin and onto her breasts. He grabbed a fistful of her hair and pulled but still she clung on, her sharp teeth biting through cartilage and into the septum and as she shook her head from side to side, he heard the sharp snap. It was only when his large fist smacked into the side of her face that she released her grip but as she did, a large strip of flesh peeled off in her teeth.

He jumped up off her and put a hand to his face which was now just a pulsing ball of intense pain. His nose felt like it was hanging off and was still pumping blood and staining his t-shirt and sprinkling her body and the floor around him. He gingerly probed it with the tips of his fingers and groaned as the slight touch increased the already intense pain. He felt a large deep gash up over the now broken bridge and as he probed lower, he groaned as he felt the wet ragged flesh just over his upper lip. It felt as if he just had one big nostril now with the lower part of the septum completely bitten through. He was glad he didn't have anything to look at himself in.

He pulled up his boxers and jeans and buckled the belt. His lust had fizzled out as quickly as its physical manifestation had shrivelled. Now all he felt was intense hate for the face looking up at him with blood stained lips and teeth. His blood. The side of her face where he had punched her was rapidly swelling. She shrunk back on the bed as he moved over her again. He gripped her around the throat and began to squeeze.

Sabrina said a silent prayer to a God she had abandoned many years earlier. She knew she was about to die. She closed her eyes as she struggled for breath as his fingernails bit into her flesh and the pressure from the two thumbs on her larynx increased. And then suddenly, the pressure and his hands were gone. She opened her eyes. He was standing looking down at her, a grin now on his mangled and still bleeding face. Like her own jaw, his nose was badly swollen which made the two bloodied wounds even uglier looking.

He saw her eyes open and the puzzled expression on her face and he gave a little sneering laugh. 'You think I've changed my mind, do you? Well I haven't, bitch. Strangling is too good for you after what you've done. That would be over too quick and I've got a better idea.'

She watched with fear filled eyes as he reached into his pocket and took out a white crumpled ball of something. When he shook it out, she saw it was a plastic bag. He saw in her eyes that she knew. He laughed, despite the fact that it hurt his face to do so. 'That's right, Miss famous American actress. With this little baby tied over your head, it will be slow and painful. They say your life flashes in front of your eyes before you die. Well this way, you'll be able to do a good few reruns of yours.'

He deftly slipped the bag over her head, smoothed it down to remove as much of the air as he could and then pulled the two handles together and quickly knotted them tight under her chin. He gave a harsh laugh as he saw the plastic being sucked in and blown out with each of her panicked breaths. As time went on, it would blow out less and less as the small amount of oxygen ran out and the way she was breathing now, that wouldn't take too long and then it would be like cling film over her mouth and nose. And when that happened, it was sayonara. He gingerly touched his throbbing nose. He would love to be able to sit down and watch but O'Driscoll had said ten minutes and it was nearly fifteen now. He cinched his belt tight and giving her one final look, he headed for the stairs.

Behind the shed, O'Driscoll looked at his watch. 'That's it. He's had his ten minutes and more.' He straightened up and then stopped and stood listening. Corbett had his ear cocked as well.

Ratser saw the two tense bodies. 'What?' he said.

'Quiet,' O'Driscoll hissed. 'There's a car coming.'

The three of them stood frozen like statues, listening as the sound of a car engine increased. They heard the tyres displace gravel as it swung into the yard and then the engine was switched off.

O'Driscoll nodded to Corbett as they heard the car door slam.

Corbett nodded back in tacit understanding and crept forward and peered around the building. The other two watched as he stooped down and picked up a rock and then disappeared around the corner.

*****

CHAPTER 38

Gerry slowed down as he turned off the road and onto the narrow laneway which led up to McCracken's farm. He cursed as he hit a big pothole which rattled his teeth and bounced his head off the roof. He drove into the empty yard and stopped. It all looked still and deserted, the very same as before.

He got out and stood beside the car examining the buildings. There was really only the three, the small house, the shed and the outdoor toilet which you really couldn't call a building. It didn't look like any of them could have a secret hiding place. And maybe they didn't. Perhaps old Jamesie had a secret hiding place in some of the fields. If that was the case, he would need the bloody army to search for it. He should have checked that with Terry Nolan. He decided to start with the shed, it being by far, the biggest building.

He stopped at the door and cast his eyes around. It all looked same as the last time. There was no loft, only the rectangular shed with the stalls on one side. The cart still sat with its shafts up on blocks opposite them. He walked in a bit and then stopped. There was something different. The timber pallet in the last stall was up on its edge. Somebody had moved it since he was here. He quickly went over and straight away, he saw the trapdoor. But he also saw the scuffed footprints in the slurry coating covering the concrete floor around the trapdoor. His heart started to race. He reached down and gripped the lip of the handle and hefted it up, ignoring the slime which immediately stained his fingers. He saw the stairs but what he also saw were the brownish partial footprints on the steps. He stepped down onto the top step and slowly and as silently as he could, began to make his way down. He winced as one of the treads creaked as he put his foot down on it. He held his breath as he paused listening but he heard nothing. Another four steps and he would be able to see around him. He realised he was still holding his breath so he exhaled as quietly as he could through his nose. He stepped down the last few steps and into the tunnel and then as he emerged into the room, stopped when he saw the man in front of him. They both looked at each other, one face more surprised than the other. He hadn't even time to take in the other man's full details or scan the rest of the cellar when the blow came crashing down on his head. The bolt of intense pain shot though his skull and he pitched forward, his brain and vision scrambled. He felt the warm wetness, which he knew was his blood, trickling down his neck. He wasn't fully unconscious but he lay still, his eyes closed. Whoever had hit him could do it again if they thought he was still conscious and he was now in no fit state to defend himself. And another similar blow could kill him. His only chance was to lie comatose which, the way he was feeling after the blow, wasn't a problem. When he got the violent kick in the stomach, he bit down on the cry of pain which would have betrayed him.

Danny Corbett stood over the prostrate body, the rock poised in his hand for another blow. When his kick didn't elicit any sound or movement from the man on the ground, he lowered it. He looked at Fatty. 'What the fuck happened to you?' He looked over to the bunk where Sabrina Metcalfe was squirming, mewling sounds coming from the plastic bag over her head. He looked back at Fatty. 'Jesus! What the hell went on here? Did she do that to you? And what the fuck are you doing to her?'

Fatty touched his face. 'Bitch nearly bit my nose off. So as payback, I decided to let her suffer a little herself. She should be dead in another few minutes.'

Corbett shook his head in a mixture of disbelief and anger. 'Fuck sake! Can you do anything straightforward? All your fucking around nearly got us all caught. Only we heard the car and I had parked around the back, we could all be in trouble now. I can tell you, the boss ain't very happy with you. Now come on. We're running behind time as it is.'

He stooped down and quickly went through the unconscious man's pockets and when he found the phone, he dropped it on the floor and then smashed his heel down on it. He ignored the man's wallet but took the car keys and stuck them into his pocket. He kicked the remnants of the phone away and then turned on his heel and went back up the stairs.

Fatty gave a last look around and followed.

O'Driscoll looked questioningly at Corbett when he came out of the shed. 'Well?'

'I got him. He's out cold.'

'Who...' He stopped when Fatty came out. 'What the fuck? What happened to your face?'

When Fatty just shrugged his shoulders, Corbett answered. 'Seems our American actress took exception to Fatty's amorous advances and had a bit of fight in her. She had a chew on his nose.'

Ratser cackled. 'Fuck sake! She did a right bloody job on it.' He laughed again. 'Bloody job all right. Looks like a raw burger. A burger bite. Bet ya that wasn't on your menu, Fatty.'

O'Driscoll glared at him. 'Shut the fuck up, Ratser. This isn't a joke.' He looked at Corbett. 'You think that fella's a cop?'

Corbett nodded. 'I'd say so. Nobody else would have a reason to be around here. I smashed his phone. What are we going to do?'

O'Driscoll threw Fatty another dirty look. 'Fuck you, Fatty. I should never have given in to you.' He rubbed a hand across his eyes. 'He can't be allowed leave here. He's seen Fatty and presumably the two bodies.' He looked at Corbett. 'There are two bodies down there now, isn't there?'

Corbett threw a quick glance at Fatty who stood with his head bowed, his hand still delicately nursing his nose. If she wasn't dead yet, it wouldn't be long before she was. No point going into the details of Fatty's little bit of inventiveness. O'Driscoll was pissed off enough. He nodded. 'Yeah, two bodies. Could even be three in a while. The copper's skull was bleeding quite heavily.'

O'Driscoll massaged his chin, thinking. He looked at his watch. They had already lost valuable time. If they didn't leave soon, they would miss the train in Athlone. He looked into the shed and then nodded as he made a decision. 'Right,' he said. 'The three of you put the pallet back and then push that cart on top. If the copper doesn't bleed out, at least he'll be stuck down there. With a bit of luck, they might never be found.'

The three went into the shed and Corbett got between the shafts. He nodded to Ratser. 'Drop the pallet and then the two of you grab a wheel each.'

When Ratser had the pallet back in place, he stooped down and lifted the shafts. The other two went each side and gripped a spoke of a wheel and braced themselves.

'Right, come on, push,' Corbett said, his voice strained from his own effort between the shafts.

Between them, they slowly pushed the cart over to the edge of the pallet.

'Right, one last effort.'

With a lot of grunting and panting, they worked the wheels up onto the pallet until they were fully on and centred. He let the shafts drop down and stepped out. All three were breathing heavily.

'It must have been some fuckin' horse to have pulled that bastard thing,' Ratser said, wiping sweat from his brow. 'Must weigh a fuckin' ton.'

O'Driscoll waved them all out. 'Come on. Let's get moving.'

'What about his car?' Corbett said. 'We can't leave that in the yard.'

O'Driscoll made a face. 'You're right. Did you think of getting the keys?'

Corbett took them from his pocket and held them up.

'Right,' O'Driscoll said taking them from him. He tossed them over to Ratser who wasn't expecting them and they fell at his feet. He stooped down and picket them up and then looked questioningly at O'Driscoll.

'You drive it up to that old shed where we burned the rubbish. We'll follow in the van,' O'Driscoll said, already opening the passenger door and getting in.

Corbett got in behind the wheel and Fatty crawled in through the open side door and slid it shut after him.

Ratser walked around to the front and got into Gerry's car. He cursed as he adjusted the seat nearer to the steering wheel. That copper had long fuckin' legs. He started the engine and drove out of the yard. The van came around from the back of the shed and followed him out.

Down in the cellar, Gerry shifted on the ground and groaned as the slight movement sent shards of piercing pain through his head. He sat up and gave himself a minute to clear the fog in his brain. His eyes were like lead and the urge to lie down again and just close them was overwhelming. But he knew if he did, he would quickly sink into unconsciousness. He put a hand up to the back of his head. His hair was matted with blood and the wound was still oozing. He blinked a few times to focus his blurred vision and looked around him. He gasped as he saw the two bodies, one on a bunk bed and the other on the floor across from where he sat. He recognised Sean Donovan straight away. He looked again at the body on the bunk bed.

Sabrina Metcalfe was naked but he didn't really notice that. His full attention was drawn to the white plastic bag tied over her head. He got onto his hands and knees and ignoring the increased pain, crawled over close to the bunk. Her body was unmoving, the plastic bag tight to her face, like shrink-wrap put on with a heat gun. Her mouth was open but full of sucked in plastic which wasn't moving. Was he too late? He pulled himself up onto his knees and quickly punched a hole where her mouth was. He saw the blood staining her mouth. Had she coughed it up in her struggle for air? But the plastic had been clear so there was some other reason for the blood. Maybe she had bitten her tongue or something. He untied the bag and pulled it off and then leaned over her and pinched her nostrils with his thumb and forefinger. He gulped in a large lungful of the stale air and then putting his mouth to hers, he exhaled it into her mouth. He repeated this a half dozen times. He was about to do it for a seventh time when she gave a little cough and then gasped a huge chesty sounding wheeze. He sat back on his haunches, watching closely as she coughed a few more times and her gasping gave way to short laboured breaths and her eyes opened. He saw the brief look of surprise in them and then sheer relief take over as they welled up with glistening tears which were soon trickling down her face. With his mind now freed from the intense concentration on his resuscitation efforts, it once again gave its full attention to the throbbing pain in his head and all of a sudden, he felt weak and dizzy, the lead weights now back on his eyelids and even heavier than before. He didn't hear her speak his name. The blackness was descending like a dark veil and he could fight it no longer. He sank sideways to the ground.

Sabrina called his name but he didn't move. She craned her neck to look down on him and a wave of relief washed over her as she saw that he was still breathing. Her relief turned to anxiety when she saw the bloodied head with the hair now stiff with dried in blood. She pulled against the restraints binding her hands to the frame of the bunk but she knew it was a useless exercise. All she could do now was wait and pray that the Irish detective would come to again. But at least they were both breathing and the men had gone. She lay back and closed her eyes.

*****

CHAPTER 39

The drive to Athlone went without incident. They had put the cop's car in the shed and Fatty's face was now cleaned up as best they could get it, with ointment on the deep gashes which were concealed under plasters they had bought in a chemist's shop in Mountmellick. He still looked a sight but as they waited for the train, he sat on one of the benches with his head bowed, his chin down on his chest. Ratser stood outside on the platform while O'Driscoll stood at the small shop counter, sipping a cup of coffee. They had bought their tickets at separate times and didn't acknowledge each other. When the train pulled into the station ten minutes later, they got into different carriages. They were now on the home run.

Seventy odd miles away, Spence was going through things with Jordie Tumulty, Nippy Cleary and Mark Breen, the three men who would pick up the ransom money. The drop was less than an hour away.

Tumulty was one of his most trusted lieutenants and had been with him from day one. A wiry man of short stature, his heavily lined face and sparse grey hair belied his forty nine years of age and most people thought he was well over sixty. His weathered appearance was accompanied by a rather high pitched voice which added to people's perception of him as a harmless little old man. But nothing could be further from the truth and some young Turks in the gangland world had found this out the hard way. Jordie Tumulty was as vicious as a snake but his fang was a six inch long switchblade knife which had left many a scar on many a smart mouthed lout who had thought they could ridicule him.

Nippy Cleary was twenty nine years of age and was the complete opposite to Tumulty. He stood just a fraction of an inch under the six foot mark and had a round baby face under a head of thick curly black hair and myopic eyes behind Buddy Holly glasses. He looked like your typical gangly twenty first century nerd. And he was a nerd, or to be more precise, a technical wizard. Computers and gadgetry of all types were his forte and there were few things in the world of modern technology that he couldn't master. His value to Spence was immeasurable.

Mark Breen was muscle, pure and simple. He had started pumping iron in the gym at fifteen and had never missed one of his thrice weekly sessions in the following twenty years. He was only five-foot seven-inches tall but he was like a lump of granite with bulging biceps on deeply veined muscular arms, shoulders that looked broad enough to carry a large bull and a rippling torso which he unashamedly displayed in tight white t-shirts. He finished off his 'Mr. T' look with three strands of gold chain around his neck, a small one of fine filigree, a thicker one of connecting links and a large ostentatious one of thick gold with a large cross pendant which dangled down and was housed between his pronounced pecs.

Spence opened a drawer in his desk and took out a box and slid it across in front of Tumelty. He took it up and opened it and pulled out the contents. Spence nodded to Breen who stood up and went over to the window and pulled the curtains closed and on his way back to his chair, he diverted over to the door and turned off the light.

Tumulty slid the goggles over his head and adjusted them over his eyes. The room immediately appeared in front of him, everything and the other three men highlighted in a bright green light. The night vision goggles were working quite satisfactorily. He gave a thumbs up sign.

'Take them off,' Spence said, walking over to the door.

He checked that Tumulty had them off and then turned on the light and walked back to his desk and sat down. 'Right,' he said. 'Jordy has a ticket for a front seat in the block adjacent to the one at the back of which the money will be dropped. The power will be cut at exactly 9.15 which is the time the third fight is scheduled to start so the boxers should be in the ring. That should have most people's attention focussed on the ring.'

'Apart from the cops,' Tumelty said. 'I'm sure they'll have their eyes on the bag of loot.'

'Apart from the cops, Spence agreed. 'I estimate you have a five minute window, maybe ten, but you shouldn't need ten, or even five for that matter. The corridor is right behind you and it's a straight forty feet to the fire exit door. It will probably take fifteen or twenty minutes for them to restore the power but it is very likely, the cops will be scrambling for torches before that. All you have to do when the power goes is to stick on them goggles, run around the back, grab the bag, hit the corridor and out through the fire exit. You should do it in two.'

He switched his attention to the other two. 'You will have the van at the door at the exact same time as the power goes, with the back door open. When Jordie comes out, you take off and head for Swords.' He looked at Cleary. 'You will check each bundle of money for a bug.

With your equipment, you should find it fairly quick. I know they will probably have one in the actual bag itself but you toss that as soon as you've emptied it. They'll probably have another somewhere in the money. When you find it, don't bother ripping it out of the bundle. You toss the complete bundle but you wait until you're passing the derelict Megastore complex in Santry. There's always a clatter of scumbags and junkies hanging around there. Look for one hanging on his own and toss it in front of him.'

'How soon do you think they'll come looking?' Cleary asked. 'Assuming O'Driscoll releases the woman soon after he knows we got the money.'

Spence looked him straight in the face and then looked deliberately at his watch. 'I'd imagine an hour or so after your pick up. O'Driscoll will release her as soon as you confirm to me that you have the money, have found any bugs in it and have ditched them as we've discussed. That should be well within the hour.'

Cleary nodded. 'Shouldn't be a problem so. I'll ditch the bag fairly early and if there's a bug in the money, I'll have it located within a couple of minutes. I should be tossing it out at the Megastore complex within twenty minutes of leaving the Stadium.'

Spence gave a derisive laugh. 'Imagine the look on their faces when they come charging into some grotty squat or kip of a flat and find some toerag with just one bundle of notes and their magic bug! Wouldn't you just love to be a fly on the wall to see that.'

'So, where to after we do that?' Cleary asked.

'The lock up in Balbriggan. The plates will be changed on the van there just in case. Towser will have a car waiting for yourself and Mark. You two head home or to a pub or wherever you want to go. Jordie and Towser will stay with the money. So? We all good to go?'

The three heads nodded and Tumulty stood up and the other two followed. When they reached the door, Spence called after them. 'Jordy, will you hang on a minute. He'll follow you down, lads.'

Tumulty waited as the other two left.

'Close the door,' Spence said.

When Tumulty was back in front of his desk, he slid the goggles over to him. 'You were going without these.'

'Oh fuck! Sorry, boss.'

Spence gave him a grim look. 'Get your mind on the game, Jordy. There's two million big ones at stake and a lot of them are mine. We can't afford any cock-ups.'

Tumulty made an apologetic face. 'Just a temporary lapse, boss. Won't happen again.'

Spence smiled, although it never reached his eyes. 'There's one other thing. The American woman – there's been a bit of a problem there.'

'What kind of problem?' Tumulty asked.

'A serious one,' Spence said. 'Seems one of O'Driscoll's morons let my name slip in front of her. That sort of changed matters.'

Tumulty's face remained impassive, registering neither shock or surprise at this piece of news. 'I take it she's been dealt with so?' he said in a matter-of-fact voice, as if he was talking about a stray dog or cat who had become a nuisance.

Spence nodded. 'As of a few hours ago. I didn't tell the lads. There's no reason for them to know yet. They'll find out soon enough.'

He got up from behind his desk and walked over to the window and pulled back the curtains. The street below was busy, a lot of the Sunday night crowd out and about. He could see a small group of elderly men just below him, outside the door of his pub, the smoke from their cigarettes wisping up into the air. The pub had a smoking area around the back but most of the male customers preferred to stand on the street where they could ogle the young ones heading to the trendier pub straight across the road and make lewd comments to them. His was a working mans' pub, frequented in equal numbers by tough men who worked the docks and building sites and a cross section from the criminal world. The pub also boasted some female customers, most of whom were girls and older women who worked the streets, in for a few gin and tonics before heading for the park area at the end of the road. He stood watching as a group of five young ones staggered up the road, their micro miniskirts leaving little to the imagination. And the cluster of men underneath his window didn't need much to stimulate their imaginations.

'Where'd ye buy them, girls?'

He recognised Rasher Deegan's voice and then saw him as the big man moved out on the footpath. Deegan worked sporadically, only taking casual work on the docks when he ran out of drinking money. Married with seven children, his wife supported herself and the children from her work as a seamstress. All Rasher's money went on drink. But Spence wasn't complaining. His pub got most of it. He stood watching as the young ones stopped in front of Rasher.

'Buy what?' one of them asked. No more than sixteen or seventeen, her skirt was the size of a postage stamp and her blouse had a plunging neckline almost down to her naval. But she had little in the boob department. More buds than boobs.

'The greyhound skirts,' Rasher said.

'Whad'ya mean greyhound skirts?' another of the girls asked.

'Arra ye know,' Rasher said. 'Wans that give ye a glimpse of the hair.'

'Fuck off,' the girl said. 'Yer nothin' but a dirty auld perv.'

There was a general guffaw from the men.

Spence grinned himself.

One of the other girls raised her hand with the middle finger up and gave the leering group the bird, then all five linked arms and crossed over the road to the other pub.

He turned away from the window.

Tumulty still sat at the desk. 'You better go,' he said. 'The lads will be waiting for you. Ring me as soon as it's all done.'

Tumulty stood up and took the goggles from the desk. 'Don't worry, boss. It'll go just as you've planned.'

He opened the door and went out.

Spence went back to his desk, opened a drawer and took out a bottle of whiskey and a glass. All he could do now was wait.

*****

CHAPTER 40

Sabrina's arms were beginning to ache unbearably. She shifted on the bunk to try and get some relief but the movement only served to intensify the pain. She groaned loudly as one of her legs cramped to add to her distress. She lifted the leg into the air and flexed it a few times and sighed with relief when she felt it unlock and the pain ease almost immediately. Gingerly lowering the leg, she craned her head again to look at the prostrate body on the floor. How long had he been out now? She had virtually lost all concept of time. It could have been a half hour or two and a half hours. She just didn't know. She called his name again, probably for the ninth or tenth time and when yet again, there was no response, she flopped back on the bunk. She didn't know how much longer she could stick the pain in her arms. She heard a low groan. Had she reached the stage where she was now groaning unbeknown to herself? It wouldn't surprise her. She was so disorientated now after the last few days, she could be doing anything without conscious thought. Then she heard the groan again and she knew it wasn't from her mouth. It could only be the detective.

'Detective Tierney, can you hear me?'

Gerry heard the voice as if it was coming from a long distance and being filtered through a series of sound buffers. The pain in his head was so severe, it felt as if all his past hangovers had come together to make one concentrated assault on his sensory system. He blinked a few times to get his blurred vision into a clearer focus. He heard his name being called again. It all slowly began to come back to him. The phone call from Ibiza, the trip to the farm, the hidden cellar, the brief glimpse of the man and then the crashing blow and after that, the kick in the gut, the woman on the bed with the plastic bag over her head and Sean Donovan. He struggled to sit up and groaned louder as ragged shards of pain lanced through his head. He held himself propped up on an elbow, allowing the pain to level out to a bearable level. When he felt he could cope with it without adding sound effects, he slowly sat up.

'Oh thank God,' Sabrina said as she saw him sit up. 'Please, my arms, they're killing me. Do you think you could untie me?'

Gerry thought about nodding that he could, but caught himself in time. He just knew a nod would push the pain altimeter even higher up the red zone. He kept his head straight as he slid over. It took him a few minutes to untie the hand tied to the side of the bunk beside him and he felt the heavy dizziness return along with increased pain in his head. His stomach and shoulder were now also beginning to pain him. He didn't think he would be able to reach the other hand as it would mean either crawling around the bunk or over her body and he didn't have the strength for either.

Sabrina saw that the effort of movement had drained the policeman and she could see the pain in his face. He had flopped back down on the ground and was now lying with his eyes closed. She rubbed her free hand against her naked leg to get some circulation back into it. It was only then the fact that she was completely naked entered her mind. She turned on her side and began untying her other hand. When she had successfully done this, she gave the freed wrist a few rubs and then swung her legs off the bunk and stood up. She saw her clothes in a heap on the floor and quickly grabbed them and pulled on her thong and leggings. She ignored the broken bra and slipped on the blouse. Most of the buttons had popped when it had been pulled off her so she grabbed the two ends and tied them in a knot at her midriff. She then walked around to where the detective was lying on the floor. She could see that the wound on the back of his head had started to bleed again. She looked around her for something to use to cover the wound but the only thing visible was her bra which was too lacey and flimsy. A search of the policeman's pockets located a hanky and she folded it into a small square and then gently pressed it over the wound.

Gerry felt the slight pressure on his head and opened his eyes. He saw the face just above his own, the eyes filled with concern. He made to move but she pressed a hand onto his chest. 'Stay still. You've lost a lot of blood and we need to stop any further bleeding.'

Gerry relaxed his body. He wasn't going to argue. He felt as weak as a mouse. He grinned a little as he thought of Terry Nolan's phone call from the club in Ibiza. He wouldn't mind being in that mouse's position now.

Sabrina saw the smile on his lips. 'What's the joke?'

He grinned again. The pain in his head had now settled to a dull but bearable ache and once he didn't move his body too much, the pain in his gut and shoulder was more a burning sensation now than actual pain. He looked up at her. 'Just thinking about something someone said to me a while ago. How are you feeling?'

She allowed herself a smile. 'Tired, stressed, dirty, traumatised, thirsty as hell, but I'm alive and that's down to you, detective sergeant.'

She glanced over at the body on the floor. 'And that's a lot better than poor Mr. Donovan over there.'

Gerry gingerly turned his head to look. 'Did they do that?'

She shrugged her shoulders. 'I don't think so. There wasn't a word or a sound from him since they stopped the car. I think he might have had a heart attack.'

She removed the now red stained hanky and looked at it. 'I need something else to keep it in place. Something to make a bandage from.'

Gerry eased himself up onto his elbow. He looked over at Sean Donovan. 'I don't think poor old Sean will object if you take his shirt. And he should have a hanky too. You can use them.'

She went over and quickly located the hanky in his pocket. She grimaced as she worked to get the jacket off the stiff body, deliberately averting her gaze from the ghostlike frozen face. It took her another few minutes to get the shirt off his back. She made a face as she pulled it off him. His chest, back and shoulders were covered with a heavy coating of thick black hair. She had never seen anybody so hairy. He was like a gorilla. She walked back over.

Gerry pushed himself up into a sitting position and shuffled over until his back was to the bunk. He watched as she made a square of Sean Donovan's hanky just as she had his own. She folded the shirt into a rectangular shape and then put the hanky over the wound on his head, put his own blood stained hanky over that and then draped the shirt over both. She pulled the two sleeves taut and then tied them under his chin. She sat back on her haunches, a little grin on her face. 'There, you look a bit funny but that should stop the bleeding in a while.'

'Thanks,' Gerry said.

They both went silent for a while, each wrapped up in their own thoughts.

Sabrina's were on her husband. Was he in Ireland now, chasing the authorities to find her? Or was he still in England? If the old man was still alive, she just knew Richard would stay over there. She would come a poor second, even despite Richard obviously knowing by now, her situation. She knew he only stayed with her because of her standing in Hollywood and the money she made. And she knew that she had only hung with him because of the titles he would inherit by birth and her by marriage, when the old man died. But maybe the old man had now died. She allowed herself a wry grin. Maybe Mary Harte, aka Sabrina Metcalfe, was now also Lady Tremayne. Her grin widened.

Wouldn't the other Lords and Ladies of the realm choke on their gin and tonics now if they could see the possible latest addition to their ranks with her dirty face and clothes and the ripped blouse with boobs nearly hanging out. But maybe she was still a commoner which, at the moment, would be a lot more in keeping with her appearance. She was surprised to find that she really didn't care anymore. Lady or not, she would file for divorce from Richard as soon as she got out. The hitherto highly coveted title of Lady Tremayne seemed to have lost all its allure in the last couple of days.

Gerry wondered what time it was. His watch showed 5.46 but the glass was cracked and the second hand wasn't moving so he knew it had stopped. He must have hit it off the floor when he fell. Multiple hours could have passed or maybe just a single one. He had no way of telling. And Sabrina Metcalfe wasn't wearing a watch so she couldn't shed any light on it either. His head was settling down a bit and he found he could move a bit without the pain getting too intense. He slowly pulled himself up onto the bunk bed and sat down.

Sabrina walked over to the stairs and went up. She knew the detective was in no shape to check out the exit so it was up to her. She reached up and pushed as hard as she could on the cover but it didn't move. It was like pushing against a concrete wall. Disappointed, she went back down. She sat down on the bunk beside him. 'I can't shift it. They must have blocked it on top.'

Gerry nodded. 'Course they did. They wouldn't want us hopping out a few minutes after they've just left.'

'Did you tell any of your colleagues where you were going?'

'Afraid not,' he said. 'I told Flann that I was waiting for a phone call but I didn't give him any details and in hindsight, that was stupid of me. I should have filled him in.'

She patted his arm. 'You weren't to know what was going to happen. Don't start blaming yourself.' She ran her tongue over her dried and cracked lips. 'God, what I wouldn't give for a glass of nice cold water now.'

He gave her a lopsided grin. 'Yeah. Never thought I'd say this but a glass of water would probably be more welcome now than a pint of Macker's finest or a Jemmy.'

She gave him a quizzical look. 'And what pray is a pint of – what did you call it? – Macker's finest or a Jemmy?'

It was his turn to run his tongue over his lips. 'A pint of creamy Guinness and a Jameson Irish whiskey. Two of the greatest inventions in the world.'

She smiled. 'Well it will be my pleasure, Detective Sergeant Tierney, to buy you some of each when we get out of here. I certainly owe you that and an awful lot more besides. If you hadn't arrived when you did, I would be dead now.'

He waved a dismissive hand. 'All part of the job.' He looked closely at her. 'Tell me, I noticed there was blood around your mouth. Did he hit you or what?' He then shook his head, remonstrating with himself. 'Arra that's a stupid question. Sure I can see the bruising on your cheek.'

She gave a little laugh. 'He hit me all right but not in the mouth. The blood was his. I sort of clamped my teeth over his nose when he started to try and rape me and he hit me to get me to let go.'

'James Street! Now I remember. I only got a quick glimpse of him before the other bugger crowned me but I did notice his snotser was a bit mangled looking all right.'

She laughed again. 'Well it did cool his ardour. And that was why he decided to use the plastic bag. He wanted me to suffer before dying.'

Gerry shook his head. 'Feckin' bastard! I hope you got a right chaw on his nose.'

'Well let's just say, he won't be smelling any roses for a while.'

Gerry looked at her again and she could see a dawning respect in his eyes. It made her feel good. Most men – no, all men – who looked at her, normally did so with only lust or desire in their eyes. Only ever saw her as a desirable sex goddess. And that had been okay. But the last few days had changed that, had changed her. All of a sudden, the reality of how close she had come to death hit her like a sledgehammer. She had been only minutes away from it, maybe even seconds. Only for the man beside her coming when he did, she would be another corpse on a bunk bed in a hidden cellar. The shock raced through her like an electric current and she started to shake. The tears welled up in her eyes and within seconds, she was crying uncontrollably.

Gerry knew it was delayed shock. He had expected it and was a bit surprised it had taken so long to come. He put an arm around her quivering shoulders and pulled her into to his chest, ignoring the dizziness this movement brought with it. He felt her tears dampen his shirt as she sobbed into it. He stroked her hair but said nothing.

They sat there for the next few minutes, she pressed into his chest, he holding her and gently stroking her hair until her body stopped shaking and her sobs gradually faded.

She pulled back a little from him and wiped her eyes with the back of her hand. 'I'm sorry. I didn't mean to break down like that.'

He smiled at her. 'I don't know what you're apologising for. If anybody was ever entitled to a little breakdown, it's you, after all you've been through. I might even have one myself when I get the chance.'

Her smile reflected her gratitude. 'Thank you, detective sergeant. If I was rude to you before – and I know I was – I apologise. I'm only here now because of you. I'll never forget that.' She scrunched her face. 'Oh God! That didn't come out right. I don't mean I'm in this place because of you. I mean I'm alive because of you.'

Gerry laughed. ''Arra will you stop. You're here because you had the savvy and the balls to fight and take a chunk out of that bugger's nose. As you said, that was why he used the plastic bag. If he hadn't, he'd have probably strangled you before I got here. And it would have taken more than the kiss of life to bring you back if he'd done that.' He grinned at her. 'And just so you know, there was no tongue.'

She laughed. 'You could have sucked my tonsils out and I would still be grateful. So thank you again, detective sergeant.'

Gerry smiled. 'My pleasure. And my friends call me Scobie.'

She leaned in and kissed him on the cheek. 'Thank you... Scobie.' She reached for the tied shirt sleeves under his chin. 'Now, let's have a look at that head of yours. See if the bleeding has stopped.'

He made a face. 'Yeah. And see if the few brains I have, haven't oozed out. And if it has stopped bleeding, don't put that feckin thing back on me. I must look like one of them old fashioned nuns that used to wear the wimple.'

She laughed and it surprised her how genuine her laugh was and how good it made her feel. Despite all that had happened and the fact that they were still trapped in the cellar, she was now feeling more relaxed than she had ever felt before. She looked over at Gerry. 'You're some man, Scobie Tierney.'

He grinned back at her. 'And you're not half bad yourself either, Miss Sabrina Metcalfe of Hollywood.'

She gently began removing the makeshift dressing from his head.

*****

CHAPTER 41

Superintendent Maguire sat in the end seat in the back row of Tier 11 in the National Stadium. He was dressed casually in denim jeans, open necked shirt, sports jacket and Nike runners. Beside him, Inspector Doyle sat, he too eschewing his normal civilian uniform of suit, white starched shirt with sombre tie and heavy black brogues for slacks, sports shirt, V-neck jumper and slip-on shoes. But he looked more like a golfer than a boxing fan. Shaun Hegarty sat beside Doyle. It had been no trouble getting the invitation to join Maguire's team. The Irish superintendent was only too happy to, as he had put it himself, 'welcome the experience and input of a fellow officer from the States.' All three could see the two large holdall bags with the studio's money that di Angelo had just left down at the back of Tier 12. The studio head was now heading back to the hotel where the film crew from Kilbracken had assembled. Maguire checked his watch. It was just a minute after 9 o'clock.

Other plain clothes officers sat in various seats close by and Fogarty and Casey were outside in two unmarked cars, the scanner on the each of the dashboards showing static dots for the two bugs planted in the bag. What they didn't notice was the car parked close behind them in which Frogatti, Montello and Schultz sat, Frogatti's phone in his hand and their own secret bug in the money also showing as a static dot on the small screen.

'Shouldn't be long now,' Maguire said to Doyle and Hegarty. He looked at Doyle. 'And remember, we don't move a muscle until whoever picks it up has gone outside. The boys will have it on monitors, so we don't need to be on their heels, okay? We just follow in the cars and don't make a move until we get word that Sabrina Metcalfe has been released and the bugs show us they've stopped somewhere. We don't just want the carrier. We want the whole bloody lot of them. You understand?'

Doyle felt more than a little resentment that Maguire had addressed his comments to him and not to the American. As if he was a raw recruit just out of the training college who needed to have things spelled out for him. But then, Maguire had been fawning over the Yank and licking his arse since his arrival. He seemed totally overawed by the hot shot lieutenant from Las Vegas. And he could see that Hegarty was playing the game as well, massaging Maguire's ego at every turn. They were both so far up each other's arses, it was just plain sickening. He was forgetting he had been just as sycophantic to Maguire before Hegarty had come on the scene.

He bit down on this resentment. 'Of course. I'm fully aware of the plan. You needn't worry about me.'

Maguire smiled over at Hegarty. 'You'll travel with me and Larry, Shaun. Doyle here can go with Noel.'

Hegarty returned the smile. 'Appreciate that, Pat.'

Neither of them noticed the thunderous look which clouded Doyle's face. Everybody else was Shaun and Pat and Larry and Noel, but he was Doyle. He didn't merit a first name reference. He ground his teeth behind clamped lips and then winced as a loose one sent a shot of pain up into his jaw. Fuck it! He had been threatening to get that seen to for weeks. He should have stayed in Kilbracken. At least he was the top dog there, even if he did have to put up with Tierney. He allowed himself a grin despite his tooth still aching. When Sabrina Metcalfe turned up in Dublin, hopefully in the next half hour or so, and they apprehended the gang and retrieved the ransom money after that, he could return to Kilbracken a hero. He didn't have to tell anybody he was only a ride along passenger. And he would take great pleasure in putting that smart mouthed upstart firmly in his place then. He should make superintendent soon after that and hopefully, get a station in one of the bigger cities. He still had the smug smile on his face when the whole place suddenly went black.

'What the hell?' Maguire said.

'Looks like a power cut,' Hegarty said.

About ten feet below them to their left, Jordie Tumulty grinned as he slipped the goggles out from inside his jacket and put them on. The glowing green vista immediately opened up in front of him like an old 3D film and straight away, he saw the two bags sitting on the floor behind the tiered seating. He went over and grabbed it and quickly dragged then through the door and into the corridor. Lucky for him, the bags had small castors on one end. He was at the exit door less than a minute later and when he pushed through it, he whipped off the goggles. The van was straight in front of him with Nippy Cleary in the back holdings the door open. He hefted the bag in and quickly followed himself. Cleary pulled the door shut just as Breen put the van in gear and drove off. The whole thing had taken less than two minutes.

Back in the stadium, now with flickering cigarette lighters like fireflies in the night, Maguire heard the call on the walkie talkie in his pocket. He quickly pulled it out. 'Talk to me'

'It's Fogarty, guv. They're on the move.'

'Right,' Maguire said. 'We thought there was a power cut in here but it was obviously them cutting the power. It's pitch black in here. Grab the torches from the boot and come in here. You'll have to guide us out.' He was just about to disconnect when the lights came back on. 'Forget that,' he said. 'The back-up generator has just kicked in. We'll be out shortly.'

Doyle and Hegarty were looking at him.

He stood up and glanced down where the bag had been left. 'They're moving,' he said. 'The blackout was obviously their cover for the grab.'

The three quickly made their way through the crowd and out to the front where Fogarty and Casey were waiting in the cars.

'You see what they were driving?' Maguire asked.

Fogarty shook his head. 'No. Just know from the monitor.'

'Doesn't matter,' Maguire said, opening the passenger door. He went to climb in but then stood back and nodded to Hegarty 'You ride shotgun, Shaun. Give you a chance to have a look at Dublin while we're tracking.'

'You sure, Pat?' the American said, but he already had one leg in the door.

Maguire hopped into the back. He let down the window and beckoned Doyle over. 'Tell Noel to follow us.' He didn't wait for an acknowledgement, closing the window again.

Doyle quickly went over and hopped into the passenger seat of the second car, again silently fuming inside at the haughty attitude of Maguire to him. He was a bloody inspector, for crying out loud! Only one rank behind Maguire. He deserved to be treated with respect and not ordered about like a red arse recruit just out of training college. He looked straight at the dashboard as Casey eased the car into line behind the one in front, his eyes fixed on the small sat navy type screen on which the red dot was flashing. He knew it was actually two red dots but they were one on top of the other because of the close proximity of the bugs to each other in the van.

He listened as Maguire's voice came over the walkie talkie which sat on the dash in front of Casey, to the left of the sat-nav screen. 'Mobile 1 to base. Do you copy?'

A static accompanied but still clear voice answered. 'Roger that, Mobile 1. Reading you loud and clear.'

'As soon as you get word of Metcalfe being released and seen, advise us immediately. Acknowledge please.' Maguire's tinny voice again.

'Roger that, Mobile 1. Will do.'

'Mobile 1, over and out.'

Doyle allowed himself a sneering smile. Who the bloody hell did they think they were? The fucking A team?

He looked out the window as Casey drove across O'Connell bridge and into the heart of the city. All of the shop windows and fast food outlets were brightly lit with the only dark building, the towering GPO which, despite its lack of light, was heavily thronged with people milling around its imposing pillars. It was still a popular meeting and gathering place for the night revellers as well as being a base for the beggars, do-gooders and religious crackpots.

They continued on to the end of the main thoroughfare and swung around into Parnell Square. He glanced over at Casey whose eyes were fixed on the road ahead. The man hadn't said a word to him since he got into the car. But that suited him too.

They swung into Dorset street and it was then Casey interacted with him for the first time. He gave him a nudge with an elbow and nodded to the small screen just as Maguire's voice crackled over the walkie talkie beside it. 'They found one.'

He could see that the two dots had separated with one now static while the other continued to move.

'Yeah. They've found one all right.' Casey said. 'Looks like they've ditched it.'

Maguire's voice was back. 'Mobile 1 to base.'

'Go ahead, mobile 1.'

'Looks like they've found one of the bugs. Location is Upper Drumcondra road. I suspect they've hefted it over the wall into the training college. Have that checked out immediately and advise.'

'Roger that, Mobile 1.'

Doyle looked at the small screen again. The single red dot was continuing to head north. He wondered was it a gang of ex provos from the north. If they crossed into the six counties, Maguire would have to contact the Northern Ireland police to take over. He wouldn't like that. And neither would he himself. The only reason he was putting up with Maguire's bullshit was because a positive result would reflect well on him as well. He slumped a bit in his seat. But he jolted up when Maguire's strident voice came bursting through the walkie talkie. 'Signal's stopped. Mobile 2, pull over while we assess.'

Casey put on his indicator and eased the car over to the side and stopped.

He followed Doyle's eyes to the screen. The red dot was pulsing on the one spot. They sat with their eyes glued to it, Doyle mentally begging it not to move. He hoped and prayed this was the final destination. The dot continued to remain static for about five minutes and then it began to move but it's movement was almost imperceptible.

'They're on foot,' Casey said.

Maguire's voice came over the walkie talkie like an echo. 'They're on foot, Mobile 2. We're pulled in at the Comet pub. Meet us there.'

Doyle felt his heart rate increase as Casey pulled out into the traffic and within a couple of minutes, he was pulling back in behind the other car which sat in front of the pub, two wheels up on the footpath, the other two straddling the yellow lines on the road. The three men were standing to the front of the car.

As soon as Casey killed the engine, they both hopped out and joined the other three. Maguire had the small sat nav in one hand, the walkie talkie in the other. He lifted the latter to his mouth. 'Mobile 1 to base.'

'This is base. Go ahead, Mobile 1.'

'Any word on Miss Metcalfe?'

'Negative on that, Mobile 1. There's been no word and no sighting.'

Maguire didn't acknowledge this transmission. He shook his head in frustration. 'Fuck it! I thought they'd have released her by now.'

'Maybe they're waiting until the money arrives wherever it's going,' Fogarty said. 'We should keep on it.'

Maguire nodded. 'Yeah. That's probably it. But we can't.........'

He stopped as a mobile phone rang. Hegarty made an apologetic face and took his phone from his pocket and answered it. The other four waited.

They watched as the American policeman listened for a few moments and then just said 'okay' and put the phone back in his pocket. 'Sorry about that,' he said. He didn't say anything about the call which had been from Frogatti telling him that their own tracking device was showing the money still moving north. They were going to keep on it until it stopped and when it did, they would ring him again if he hadn't already rang them.

Maguire looked again at the small screen in his hand. 'Yeah, they're definitely on foot. And not that far away either. Come on. Follow me but keep close.'

They moved off in double file, Hegarty sticking beside Maguire. He wanted to be near him when they found out that they had followed a bum steer.

They moved off, away from the main thoroughfare and as the houses thinned out and the streets darkened, they found themselves facing an old shopping centre which was dark and abandoned looking with the main store having shutters down in front of all its large windows and in front of its entrance. The graffiti artists had been to work on the shutters and all were covered in a variety of roughly sprayed drawings and disjointed words in foot high lettering. Both the drawings and the text were primarily lewd in content with random dates testifying to the times that someone had shagged someone else and underneath these momentous dates were short critiques. The name Sharon was predominant among these testimonies and at least four of them classed her as a 'great ride'. They could see small groups of people in the shadows of the buildings and as they moved closer, it was obvious that this was a hangout for winos and druggies. Some lay on the ground in moth eaten sleeping bags, their hands clutching the wine bottle close to their chests as if afraid that it was going to be snatched from them. They watched with hostile eyes as the five men passed by. Most of these were middle aged and older, their dirty and unshaven faces showing the wasted look of rough living and the mosaic of broken blood vessels from the rot gut wine. There were younger people further back in the shadows and as the more curious of these moved forward, Hegarty immediately recognised the zombie look of people lost to the ravages of either cocaine or heroin. He came across it quite often in the States. He ignored this sorry gathering of the detritus of humanity as the other four did and soon they were facing onto a large flats complex which, judging by its very run down appearance, certainly wasn't a private one. There were four large towers of flats in a rectangle with a concrete square in front of them. They rose about thirty stories high and each flat had a very small balcony, some of which sported assorted clothes and sheets draped over the railings. The square had some benches set around it but most were broken. Each tower had an arched entrance with weak yellow lighting and even from a distance, they could see that the walls were covered in graffiti.

Maguire stopped and held the small screen up so that they all could see it. The pulsing red dot was unmoving. He looked from one to the other. 'It's stopped.'

'So what now?' Casey asked. 'We've still no word on Metcalfe being sighted anywhere. We don't know if she's been released or not.'

Fogarty looked at his watch. 'It's been over an hour now. If they were going to release her, she would have been spotted by now. I say we move now. At least if we get hands on the perps, we can find out where she is.'

Maguire scratched his chin. 'Fuck it! Why hasn't someone seen her.' He looked at Hegarty. 'What do you think, Shaun? What would you do?'

Hegarty pretended to think for a minute. He wanted them to discover that they had been duped. Watch them all deflate like burst balloons. At least then he could have a private word with Maguire and get him on board for their own operation. 'It's your call, Pat. It would worry me that Miss Metcalfe hasn't been spotted by now. Begs the question, were they ever going to release her.'

Maguire nodded. 'I was thinking the same thing myself.' He rubbed his chin. 'Fuck it. We can't afford to lose track of the money. We lose that and we've nothing. No Metcalfe and no money. We move now.'

He started off and they all followed.

*****

CHAPTER 42

Harry 'Snotser' Dooley sat in the living room of his council flat
on the fifth floor of Block Two in the pretentiously named
Bougainvilla Towers, named by one of its designers after attending a
conference on urban designs in the luxury Barbadian resort. The name
was the only fancy thing about the flats complex. He sat back in the
grotty armchair which boasted a mixture of stains on its faded floral
patterned covering as well as numerous cigarette burns and worn
patches where the padding protruded in wiry tufts. For about the fifth
time, he stroked the bundle of notes in his trembling hands. For the
very first time in all of his thirty eight years, lady luck had at last
nodded in his direction. He reached down and took the wine bottle
from the floor where it sat beside the chair and took another deep pull.
He wiped his sleeve across his mouth and nose, adding another silvery
green trail to the already hardened section of coarse material and put
the bottle back down. He stroked the bundle again. All of them were
hundred euro notes and quite a thick bundle. He didn't have to count
them to know how much was in the bundle. It was written on the
paper band which held them together. Ten thousand euro. He had
never seen the colour of that amount of money in one go before. And
the way it had come to him. Being thrown out of a van as it drove past
the doorway in which he had been huddled, sucking the last dregs of
nicotine from the cigarette he had bummed from Megaphone Mag
who had nicked nearly a full packet earlier that day from an untended
table outside one of the bars in the city centre. Like manna from
heaven. Had it accidently been thrown out or was it one of these
anonymous do-gooders whom you read about travelling around
looking for worthy causes to give some of their money to? Either way,
he didn't give a shite. It meant a good supply of drink and fags. And it
wouldn't be the normal bargain basement wine either. With this
windfall he could treat himself to some decent rum. He grinned to
himself. Only for a stuck zipper, he might have missed out on this
windfall. The money had landed nearer to where Noddy Dobson was
huddled down in his old sleeping bag in the same doorway as himself.
But Noddy's zipper had stuck and he couldn't get himself out of the
bag before he had grabbed the money and taken off. He took another
deep pull from the wine bottle which finished it off. He slid a single
note out of the bundle and stuck the rest into a tear in the arm of the
chair and pulled some of the stuffing out to fill the hole. Satisfied that

his cache was out of view, he pulled himself out of the chair with a grunt and stuck the notes into his pants pocket. The all -ight filling station on Whitehall road had an off licence.

It was then he heard the movement outside his door. He cursed to himself. It had to be Dobson. Coming up to see what he had gotten. What he himself had missed because of his stuck zipper. He felt a shiver of apprehension. Noddy was as rough as a bear's arse but had the bulk, the temper and the fists to back it up, while he himself would struggle to make nine stone even when wet. If things got physical, he knew he would cave in like a burst balloon. Had he time to grab the bundle and split it? Hide it in two places? At least that way, he would still have a couple of hundred. He jumped when a fist hammered on his door.

Maguire banged on the door again. 'Police. Open up.'

The others stood behind him, all eyes focussed on the closed door with the peeling paint. They weren't worried about whoever was in the flat dodging them. They were on the fifth floor. Unless the occupant or occupants could sprout wings and fly, the door they were looking at was the only way in or out of the flat.

Doyle stood with the other three behind Maguire. He felt his excitement rise. If they found Metcalfe in the room as well, well that would be just the icing on the cake. It would be kudos all round from the brass and he would get his fair share. He watched as Maguire stepped back a pace when the door cracked open.

The superintendent flashed his police id card in front of the puzzled face which appeared in the gap. 'Police.'

He didn't wait for a response, putting a hand out and pushing the door open and as the man inside stumbled back, he followed him into the flat. The others piled in after him.

Snotser stood looking at the five unexpected visitors. The police! What the hell was that about? He sneaked a look at the armchair. It had to be about the money. What else would bring five of them to his flat! His dreams of good rum and cigarettes began to fade. But he could see that the other men seemed to be as confused as he was. They were looking at each other with puzzled expressions on their faces. He looked at the first man who had come in. He was looking at something in his hand.

Maguire had a terrible sinking feeling in his gut. The monitor was showing that the bug was right in front of him but he knew in his heart and soul that they weren't going to find two million in this grotty fleapit. The man in front of him was a down and out for fuck sake! A fucking wino! Somehow, they had been conned. He nodded to Casey. 'Check that chair.'

His colleague went over and after giving the chair a brief once over, stuck a hand into the ripped arm and pulled out a heap of the stuffing. A few seconds later, he had the bundle of notes in his hand. He snapped off the band and fanned through the notes and then extracted the small tracking device and held it up. He didn't say a word. There was nothing to say. They all knew they had been fooled.

Maguire glared at the dishevelled man who stood in front of him, a frightened look on his face. 'Where did you get that?'

Snotser struggled to keep his heart from racing. The coppers were his least favourite people. Always hassling him on the streets. Always telling him to move on. Move on to fucking where? And here they were now, even in his own pit, hassling him again. He glared sullenly at the man who had asked the question. 'Found it on the road.'

What happened next took him completely by surprise.

The five men shared another series of quick looks between them and then walked straight out of his flat without another word. He flopped down into the chair, his heart still racing, his legs suddenly becoming like jelly. He hadn't expected that. He had fully expected to be subjected to a battery of questions and then possibly taken down to the station. But they had left. He fingered the note in his pocket and grinned. At least he still had them. The cops weren't so fucking smart after all.

Outside in the hall, Maguire took the bundle of notes from Casey. He did a quick count, more to hide his acute embarrassment than anything else. This was his case and now all he had were these few poxy notes in his hand. No Metcalfe and no two million. He was rightly fucked. He finished the count. Nine thousand nine hundred euro. Based on the amount written on the band, there was a hundred missing. And he had a fair idea where it was. He turned to the others. Casey and Fogarty stood beside each other, their eyes down, shuffling their feet. They knew the whole thing was a screw up. His screw up. And that meant he would be like a bear with a burr up his arse. Ready to snap the head off anybody who even looked sideways at him.

Maguire glared over at Doyle who stood beside Hegarty. This whole thing was his fuck up. It had all happened on his patch down in the sticks. If he had been more proactive a lot earlier, there might not have been any need for him and his team to go down from Dublin. But now he was going to be seen as the failure. He continued to stare belligerently at the other man until he broke eye contact. He turned back to Casey and Fogarty. 'Let's head back to the station. There's not much point hanging around here. Maybe Metcalfe has turned up by now. You three go ahead. Shaun and myself will follow.' He sincerely hoped the actress had turned up. If she hadn't, it would be a right royal fuck up. No actress and now no ransom money. It could finish his career. He looked at Casey and held out a hand. 'Give us your keys.'

Casey handed over the keys and himself and Fogarty started down the steps. Doyle paused for a minute. He didn't want to be as sheepish as the other two. They reported to Maguire but he didn't. Technically, he was an acting superintendent. Maguire should be treating him as an equal. But then again, it was Maguire who was now leading the investigation. This fuck up was now all his. Best leave it at that. He could say that he would have handled things differently but the matter was taken out of his hands. That way, he could avoid the shit that would undoubtedly be flying in great big bucketfuls. Somewhat buoyed by this thought, he followed the other two down the steps.

Snotser stood inside his door listening. He grinned when he heard the decision being made to leave. Sure, the bastards had taken the wad of notes, but he was still a hundred euro richer than he had been an hour ago. He took the note from his pocket and kissed it. He would give the cops another ten minutes to clear the flats and then he would head down to the off licence. He actually felt the drool build up in his mouth at the prospect of sitting back with a full packet of fags and a bottle of Bacardi rum. He couldn't remember ever having such a luxurious prospect in front of him before. He was still holding the note in his hand when there was another fist pound off the door which startled him. He cracked open the door and then stumbled back as it was pushed open.

Maguire saw the note in the other man's hand. He gave a satisfied snort and then reached out, grabbing the hand holding it.

'What the fuck are you doing?' Snotser said, trying to keep a hold of the note which was, even as he spoke, being prised from his fingers.

Hegarty stood at the door watching, a smile on his lips. He knew Maguire was in a foul mood. This petty act of coming back in and taking the hundred euros off the bum just proved that. It was just pure vindictiveness. Maguire needed a kicking target and this poor bum just happened to be the ideal candidate. It would be easy to get him on side for their own little operation.

Snotser felt the tears sting his eyes and then trickle down his stubbled cheeks. Life was a bitch and this cop was one fucking miserable bastard. Coming back in for the hundred euros. Probably meant fuck all to the cop but to him it was a fortune. A fortune which was now in the cop's pocket. He massaged his fingers which were still sore from being forcibly forced open to release the notes. He felt his nose start to run, as if it was now acting in sympathy with his eyes which were still streaming. He sniffled loudly and then rubbed his sleeve across his face. 'That's my money.'

Maguire sneered. 'Don't push your luck, buster. Just be thankful I'm not taking you in and charging you.'

He turned to Hegarty. 'Come on, Shaun, let's go. If we stay any longer in this flea pit, we'll be scratching all night.'

They both walked out, Maguire slamming the door closed behind him. They made their way silently down the five flights of stairs and only when they had gotten into the car did Hegarty speak. 'There's something I have to tell you.'

Maguire sat and listened, his eyes widening. But when Hegarty had finished, he was smiling broadly. He knew he should be pissed at the Americans subterfuge but that wasn't important now. They were giving him a lifeline. He could still come out of this smelling of roses.

*****

CHAPTER 43

Frogatti took his phone out when he heard it ring. 'Yeah?'

He listened for a minute and then spoke again. 'We're parked behind a bar.' He looked out the window, over to the brightly lit building over which a flickering neon sign showed the name. 'It's called The North County Inn. He know where that is?'

About five miles away, Hegarty repeated the name to Maguire who nodded. 'It's just this side of the airport. Have they still got the signal?'

Hegarty repeated the question into his phone and then nodded. He listened for another minute or so and then said 'right' and ended the call. 'They still have a signal. It's still moving but they'll wait for us at that bar.'

Maguire started the engine and drove out of the complex.

As they made their way along the road, Hegarty turned to him. 'It will have to play out just as I've said. You okay with that?'

Maguire's lip curled. 'I don't give a rat's arse what happens to them. I'll just say I got a tip-off and that's how I found them. Once I get the money back and the perps, that's all that matters.' He looked sideways at the American. 'Maybe your guys … you know… could find out where Metcalfe is being held as well, assuming she still hasn't shown up anywhere. I'm sure their methods would be – how should I put it – a lot more productive than us sweating them back at the station. We'd all be winners then.'

Hegarty smiled. 'I'm sure that can be arranged.'

Ten minutes later, they pulled into the car park of The North County Inn. Hegarty pointed to a car parked to the rear, three men visible inside. 'That's them.'

Frogatti, Montello and Schwartz watched as the other car pulled up beside theirs. They waited as Hegarty said something to the driver and then got out and came over. Frogatti pressed the button to wind down the window.

Hegarty leaned down so he was face to face with Frogatti. 'He's on board. Wants you to find out where Metcalfe is being kept as well. Seems she hasn't been released.' He gave a smirk. 'And he doesn't care what persuasion you have to use.'

Frogatti nodded and then took his mobile phone from where it sat on the dash and handed it to Hegarty. 'You guys follow the signal and we'll follow you. Your Irish friend over there should be a lot more familiar with the area than we are. We're lucky we even got to follow them this far. Fucking roads over here are crap. We nearly lost the signal a few times because we had to make diversions because of road works. There's more craters in this bloody city than there was in Baghdad after Desert Storm. Digging up the roads must be a national pastime over here. It'll be easier all round if we follow him.'

Hegarty took the phone. 'Right. We'll lead so.'

He went back and got in beside Maguire and put Frogatti's phone up on the dash. 'We're taking the lead. The boys will follow us.'

Maguire nodded as he put the car in gear and drove slowly out of the car park. 'Fine by me.' He looked at the small screen. 'Looks like they're just passing the airport, heading along the old Swords road.'

They drove in silence; the other car close behind.

Some twenty miles ahead of them, Mark Breen pulled the van up in front of the closed gate into the large industrial estate on the far side of Balbriggan. Tumulty took a small piece of paper out of his pocket and handed it to him. 'That's the code.' Breen hopped out and keyed the code into the digital panel on the pillar which operated the electronic sliding gate. As it slowly rolled back, he got back into the van and drove just inside. He got back out and keyed in the code again into the panel on the inside and watched as the gate slid closed. A few minutes later, he pulled the van up in front of a small unit near the back, the name COMET COURIERS up over the door. This was one of Spence's other legitimate businesses which he used to move his stuff around the city. He hooted the horn twice and a minute later, the roller shutter door started to slowly roll up, the light from inside the unit gradually illuminating the area in front of the rising door. When the door was fully open, he drove quickly in and parked beside a small Renault Clio and a Toyota Corolla. There were rows of steel shelving down one side of the unit, all laden with different sized packages and cartons.

Towser Finnegan pressed the door close button, then walked over to the van. He stood waiting as the others got out. 'Any problems?'

Tumulty shook his head. 'Naw. Everything went like clockwork.'

'Any bugs in the money?'

Tumulty shared a grin with Cleary and Breen. 'Just as the boss predicted. One in the bags and one in the money. Some poor bum in

Santry is probably still getting the third degree from the cops.'

Finnegan laughed. 'I'd have loved to have seen their faces when they found out they'd been conned. I'd say they were mad as hell.'

Tumulty reached into the van and took out the plastic bag into which they had transferred the bundles of money from the dumped bags. 'You got those two counting machines set up?'

Finnegan nodded. 'In the office. You still think they're needed?'

'Spence does,' Tumulty said, heading for the small office. 'And as we've often found out before, he's never too far wrong.'

Breen called after him. 'What's this? Whad'ya want counting machines for?'

Tumulty stopped. 'You know the boss. He's a belt and braces man. Never leaves anything to chance. I know we found two bugs on the money but he still wants every single note checked and the quickest way to do that is to run it all through a counting machine. With two of them, we should get through it quick enough.'

Cleary nodded his head. 'Have to hand it to Spence. He's certainly leaving nothing to chance.'

'That's why he's still livin' life in his luxury apartment in Ranelagh and not sloppin' out with all the other so called smart arses who found out they weren't that smart after all. Spence thinks in the box, outside the box and all around the box. That's what keeps him one step ahead of all the cops who have tried to nail him down through the years. And that's why you and me and the other lads aren't shittin' in a bucket up in Mountjoy either.'

Inside the office, he upended the bundles of money out onto a large table on which two counting machines stood, already plugged into a double socket on the wall. 'Right,' he said looking at Cleary. 'You and Towser work one machine and we'll do the other.'

Finnegan picked up a bundle. 'Jasus, lads. These are hundred dollars.' He rifled through the large heap of bundles. 'There's a lot more dollars than euros here.'

Tumelty nodded. 'We saw that. Yanks probably couldn't come up with the two mill in euros in the short time they had. Doesn't really matter. Spence will be able to handle it. He laughed. 'And I'm sure he'll charge O'Driscoll a hefty exchange rate.'

They quickly set about taking the bands off the bundles and slotting them onto the back trays of the counting machines. The notes quickly flew through the two machines and all four had to work fast to keep them fed at the back.

'What the hell?' Towser said as his machine stopped spitting out the notes and began emitting a whining sound.

Tumulty quickly reached over and turned it off and then carefully extracted the note jammed in the mechanism. He held it up and examined it. 'Fuck sake! The crafty bastards.'

The other three peered closely at the note in his hand. He pointed to the raised blister on the note which was now split and showing barely visible broken thread- thin wires. 'I've never seen a bug like this before. You would probably never detect this in a manual check. Jammy buggers are gone all high tech by the look of it.' He carefully put the note down on the floor and then stamped his heel down on it a few times. He looked at the other three. 'Let's finish the rest quick to make sure there isn't any more and then let's get the hell out of here. You go back outside, Towser and have a look. If there's any traffic outside, it has to be the cops. Nobody else would be around here at this time. Hopefully, we found it in time.'

Finnegan quickly went out of the small office and over to the small side door, which he unlocked and cracked open a few inches. He peered outside and satisfied that it was safe to do so, fully opened the door and stepped out. He quickly scanned all around him. There was no sign of anything so he edged his way out towards the main entrance, making sure to keep close to the walls of the buildings. He exhaled a sigh of relief when he saw that the gate was still closed and the road outside was empty of any traffic. He slowly walked towards the gate.

Back in the shadows of the large supermarket car park across the road from the entrance to the industrial estate, Frogatti stood at Hegarty's open window. 'It just disappeared?'

Hegarty glanced at Maguire and then looked up. 'Yeah. It was flashing good and strong and then just disappeared.'

'And it was showing in that estate across the road?'

'Yes,' Maguire said. 'Definitely in there when it vanished. And that was only a few minutes ago.'

'Looks like they found it,' Hegarty said. 'They're a lot smarter than we thought. There must be over a hundred units in there.'

Frogatti glanced over at the dark estate. 'Don't matter. It did its job. All we have to do is wait. They're not going to stay in there all night. We just have to sit back and watch. Sooner or later, they'll come out.' He hunkered down until he was face to face with Hegarty.

'We'll do the grabbing. Be ready to provide back-up if needed.'

'Do you think Metcalfe is in there?' Hegarty asked.

Frogatti shrugged. 'Maybe. Maybe not. We'll find out one way or the other. Just you be ready to follow our lead.' He stood up, not waiting for a response.

Hegarty watched as he walked over and got into the other car which was parked just a few feet away from his.

Beside him, Maguire sat behind the wheel, his eyes glued on the estate across the road. His heart was racing with nervous excitement. Maybe Metcalfe was in there. Wouldn't that just be the icing on the cake. He would have all three. The actress, the kidnappers and the ransom. He felt almost dizzy with anticipation. He'd be fucking famous! The man who cracked the biggest kidnapping case in Ireland. It would be world news because of who Metcalfe was. And after this, he would nearly be as famous as the actress. He would be a celebrity himself. The media people would be going mad to get his story.

Hegarty glanced over and grinned to himself. He could almost see what was going through the Irish copper's mind. The nervous excitement was coming off him in great waves. You could almost smell it. He glanced back over at the gate into the estate. There was someone moving just inside it. He glanced over to the other car and he could see that they too had their eyes on the gate and the moving figure inside. He watched as the dark figure looked up and down the road and then looked over to where they were parked but he knew they were too far back in the shadows to be visible to him. He felt his own excitement mount. It had to be one of the kidnappers checking the lay of the land after finding the bugging device. They were obviously still inside. What they did next was up to Frogatti.

The three looked up as Finnegan came back in.

'Well?' Tumulty asked.

Finnegan shook his head. 'Not a sign of anyone. Quiet as a graveyard outside.'

'Right,' Tumulty said. He nodded to Breen. 'You and Nippy take the Toyota and head home. Towser and myself will wrap up things here. Give him the keys of the van. He'll change back the original number plates and leave it here.'

Finnegan was already peeling off the white adhesive sheets of paper which covered the Comet Couriers name, the logo image of a shooting comet, the address at the industrial estate, phone numbers and e-mail details on both sides of the van. He balled up the paper and walked over and tossed it into a small skip to the left of the entrance door. Breen took the van keys from his pocket and tossed them the ten or so metres over to Finnegan who deftly caught them in a snatch grab. He walked over to the corolla at which Cleary was already standing.

'Keys are in it,' Finnegan said, already down on one knee unscrewing the front number plate of the van.

Tumulty went over and pressed the button to raise the main door and waited as Breen fired up the engine and reversed out. When the car was outside, he pressed the close button.

'I'll be glad to get home after all this,' Breen said as he drove through the estate, heading for the main entrance gate. Beside him, Cleary nodded. 'Yeah. Who would have thought they'd have three bloody bugs in the money and that last one such a high tech piece. We were damn lucky Spence is such a nit picker. If he hadn't thought of running all the notes through the counting machines, we'd never have found it and would be well and truly screwed now'.

'He's obsessive all right,' Breen said as he moved down a gear approaching the gate. 'And thanks be the fuck for that. As you say, we would probably be up to our arses in cops by now if he wasn't.' He pulled up at the gate and quickly hopped out and went over to the control panel and punched in the code. As the gate slowly started to slide back, he turned and got back into the car. He drove through and then stopped outside. 'Won't be a tic,' he said to Cleary as he hopped out again. He walked over to the other control panel located on the road side of the entrance and entered the code again. As the gate started to close, he started back to the car and then stopped when he heard the high-pitched rev of a car engine and his eyes widened in shock when a large car lurched from out of the dark across the road and headed straight for the corolla. He jumped through the still open driver's door but the other car had crossed the short distance and was now nose to nose with his own. With the gate almost fully across, his car was now effectively sandwiched between it and the other car leaving no room to manoeuvre. His fear grew when three men hopped out of the other car. Beside him, Cleary sat in his seat watching the three men outside the car, his shoulders slumped in accepted defeat. He fully expected to now hear the wail of sirens and to see a couple of marked squad cars race up the road and totally surround them. He threw a quick questioning glance at Breen when this didn't happen and then looked back at the three who were now standing at the doors of their car, two on Breen's side, one on his, their hands down by their sides and not visible to him or Cleary.

'They're not cops,' Breen said out of the corner of his mouth as he reached inside his coat pocket.

'Aw fuck no,' Cleary said as he saw the gun emerging from the pocket.

'Aw fuck yes,' Breen said but those were to be his last words as one of the men on his side whipped open the door and pointed his own gun straight at Breen's head and fired.

Cleary recoiled in horror as Breen's head exploded in a mass of pulped flesh, bone, brain matter and blood, a big chunk flying right by his face and slapping into his side window where it momentarily clung for a few seconds and then slowly slid down leaving a red viscous trail on the glass.

He stayed frozen as his own door was yanked open and he was roughly pulled from the car by one of the men.

Schultz looked up from the open trunk of the corolla. 'No money here,' he said.

Frogatti stuck his face in front of Cleary's. 'Where's the ransom money?'

Cleary swallowed hard to dislodge the phantom lump threatening to cut off his airway. His mind was racing. Who the hell were these guys? They sounded American. And this guy had just shot Breen without blinking an eye. He would do the same to him unless he gave him a reason not to. But if he told them, Spence would kill him just as quick. He had to stall for time. 'It's gone. But they're going to ring me later on to tell me where we're to meet for the divvy up.'

He held his breath as the man in front of him digested this information. It had been the best he could come up with on the spot.

'How did it leave? Nothings passed us.'

Cleary swallowed again. 'By motor bike. He used a back pedestrian entrance.'

'Where's the broad?' The switch in question eased his fear a touch.

'We don't know,' he said. He quickly continued when he saw the other man's face cloud over. 'She was snatched by another crew. We were only brought in afterwards to handle the ransom pick-up. That's the truth. I swear. She's probably been released by now anyways.'

Frogatti tossed this information in his head. Realistically, he didn't give a rat's ass about the actress. Recovery of the money was his main concern. But if they were able to get her as well, that would be all the better. It looked like they would just have to wait another while until this guy got the phone call about the meet. He looked over at Schultz and indicated Cleary with a flick of his eyes. Schultz sidled up to Cleary and before the man knew what was happening, Schultz's gun butt whacked down on his head. Montello grabbed him as he fell and bundled him onto the back seat of the car. Frogatti indicated Breen's body slumped over the wheel of the other car. 'Stick that in the trunk. I'll be back in a minute.'

Breen's body was unceremoniously crammed into the trunk.

Hegarty and Maguire watched as Frogatti came walking across the road, their facial expressions in complete contrast to each other. Hegarty's was benign, the killing of one of the guys not fazing him one iota. This was Frogatti and where Frogatti went, violence was never too far behind. He had seen it many times before. In contrast, Maguire's face still registered the total shock and disbelief the sound and flash of the gunshot had engendered. His heart was still racing and he was still hyperventillating. He hadn't even been able to speak.

Frogatti hunkered down as Hegarty let his window down. 'Money's gone. We need somewhere to get rid of the body and then we hold the other guy until he gets a phone call.' He looked directly across at Maguire. 'This is your turf. You gotta know somewhere.'

Maguire threw a horrified look at Hegarty and then at Frogatti. He gulped a few times to clear the knot in his throat. 'Jesus! You shot one of them! I can't be involved in this.'

'Bum pulled a gun on me,' Frogatti said.

Hegarty looked hard at the Irish officer. 'You are involved. You wanted in on this.' He gave a mirthless laugh. 'These situations are like wedding vows. For better or for worse. Now snap the fuck out of it and tell us where we can go.'

Maguire felt the sweat run down his face. He knew now that Frogatti and his two henchmen had to be mafia types and Hegarty was obviously in cahoots with them. If he didn't play ball, they were just as likely to shoot him as well. He ran his tongue over his dry lips. 'Up the mountains. There's places up there.'

His voice was barely little more than a rasping whisper.

Frogatti stood up. 'Right. You lead, we'll follow.'

He turned on his heel without another word and crossed over the road where Schwartz and Montello were slouched against their own car. 'I'll take the Corolla,' he said.

Across the road, Hegarty just sat back in his seat. 'Right. Let's go.'

Maguire gave him another incredulous look, shook his head and exhaled deeply and then turned on the ignition and eased the car onto the road. The other two cars got in behind him and the three of them drove off down the road in procession.

Tumulty and Finnegan emerged from the shadows of the nearest building to the entrance and walked over to the gate as the tail lights of the third car disappeared in the distance.

'What do we do now? Are you going to ring Spence?' Finnegan asked, his attention still focussed on the now empty road.

Tumulty shook his head as he too looked down the empty road. 'No. Not by phone. This is one story that needs to be told face to face. Come on. Let's get the car and go.'

*****

CHAPTER 44

Gerry opened his eyes and blinked a few times to clear his focus. Sabrina Metcalfe sat cross legged on the bed looking down at him. She gave him a small smile when she saw him look at her. 'You passed out again for a while.'

He carefully pulled himself into a sitting position and put a hand to his head and gingerly felt around the blood matted hair. He was able to trace the deep jagged gash with his fingers through the raised roughness of the clotted blood. The pain was still there but it was now a dull constant throbbing. He allowed himself a wry grin. He'd had hangovers nearly as bad. He still had the soreness where he had gotten the kick in the stomach but it was very tolerable. Lucky the man had missed his ribs or that would be a different kettle of fish. He smiled over at her. 'Sorry about that. Was I out for long?'

She shook her head. 'No. Fifteen, maybe twenty minutes. That's all.'

He wrinkled his nose. 'God, it stinks in here, doesn't it? As if a herd of cows had an attack of diarrhoea all at the same time.'

She surprised herself by laughing, despite the seriousness of their predicament. 'It's pretty bad all right. But you get used to it after a few days. I did.'

'Feck that for a game of snooker,' Gerry said, carefully getting to his feet, a hand pressed to his stomach. 'I don't plan on spending a few days here.'

'There's no way out, Scobie,' she said. 'And we don't have any way of getting a message out unless....' Her voice took on a hopeful note...'unless you have a mobile phone. Have you?'

He pointed over to the scattered pieces on the ground at the bottom of the stairs. 'That's mine. And as you can see, even Alexander Graham Bell and all the techies at Apple and Samsung wouldn't be able to get a peep out of it.'

'They took mine from my bag,' she said, the disappointment evident in her voice. Gerry looked over to where the leather bag was thrown on the floor. He slowly walked over and picked it up and then looked over at her. 'I know it's not gentlemanly to go through a lady's handbag but I hope you don't mind me having a look.'

0 She shrugged her shoulders. 'Go right ahead. Nothing in there

except a bit of make-up, a hanky and a mouth spray.'

Gerry upended the bag onto the bunk beside where she sat and then gingerly sat down at the other end, the contents of the bag in a little heap between them. He poked a finger through it. There was a flimsy lace handkerchief with the initials S M embroidered on it, a lipstick tube with a bright red cap, a compact, a small bottle of nail polish in a similar red colour to the lipstick, a similar size bottle of clear nail varnish, an eyebrow pencil, a few loose cotton swab tips, two foils of condoms and a mouth spray.'

He held up one of the condoms and grinned. 'You don't trust your menfolk, do you?'

She gave a little snort. 'I've found out that you just can't rely on men to be responsible when their dicks are ruling their heads.'

He grinned again. 'Can't argue that one with you. I've been guilty myself of forgetting the little safety net once or twice.'

She saw him look around again and when he got up and walked over and lifted his hand and held it in the aperture at the top of the wall, she gave him a puzzled look. He answered the unasked question. 'There's a good flow of air in the wall. Has to be a sizeable gap to the outside somewhere near the top.'

'So?' she said. 'Unless we can shrink down to bird size, it's not of much use to us, is it?'

He didn't answer but did another quick glance around the floor. He walked over to where she sat on the bunk and stooped down and picked up the white plastic bag he had removed from her face. He left it down on the bunk, carefully got down on his knees and then flattened it out with the palm of his hand, paying particular attention to the ragged hole where he had pushed his fingers through. He pulled the jagged edges together as best he could. She watched in silence as he took up the small bottle of nail varnish, removed the cap and then liberally brushed the torn edges with the clear varnish. He blew on it a few times and then leaned back on his haunches. 'We'll give it a few minutes to dry completely.'

She looked at him, her face reflecting her total puzzlement at his actions. 'What are you doing, Scobie? Has that bang to your head made you a bit crazy?'

He grinned and tapped the side of his nose in a conspiratorial manner. 'The shell might be cracked a bit but the yoke inside is still working okay. Trust me, okay?'

She watched as he took up the tube of red lipstick, took off the

258

cap and then leaned over the plastic bag and began to write slowly. When he was finished, he picked it up, blew on it a few times and then wafted it in the air another few times. He laid it down flat on the bunk so she could read what he had written. She leaned over and read the vibrant red, hand-printed message on the white background.

HELP
RING SGT. FLANNERY
087198428
Mc CRACKENS
SCOBIE

A look of hope spread across her face. She sat watching as he took up the bag and shook it so that it opened out as it took in the air. Her eyes stayed glued to him as he walked over to the wall and took up the fork and carefully draped the bag over the prongs. She held her breath as he pushed the fork into the opening and slowly pushed upwards. He stood for a few minutes with his arm extended, the fork raised to the highest he could get it and then quickly jerked it down. She was still holding her breath as he gently eased it out of the aperture. The prongs were empty.

She exhaled a relieving sigh which came out like a gush of air and looked at him. 'Do you think it's gone out?'

'Can't be sure but I think so,' he said, leaving the fork down on the ground. 'If it has, let's just hope the wind takes it somewhere somebody might come across it. It's a long shot but I've backed longer odds horses.'

'And did they win?' she asked.

He laughed. 'Naw. Feckin' donkeys are all still running. But who knows! Today might be the day Lady Luck decides to give us both a break.'

He shucked off his jacket and standing over her, he draped it over her shoulders. 'Here., You must be bloody freezing with only that flimsy yoke tied around your belly.'

She pulled it tight around her. 'God, yes I am, now that you mention it.' She gave a little laugh. 'I didn't really dress for this unplanned few days stay in such salubrious surroundings.'

He walked over to the other bunk where Sean Donovan's stiff body lay like a male mannequin. He unhooked the little clasp on his trousers and pulled down the zipper and quickly pulled them off. He carried them over and held them out. 'Put these on. They mightn't be the fashion you're use to but at least they'll keep your legs warm.'

She didn't argue. Her body was losing the insulation brought on by the shock of her ordeal over the past few days and she was now feeling all the physical discomforts. Apart from the cold, she was hungry, thirsty and aching all over. But mentally, she was now in a much better place. And that was down to Scobie Tierney's presence with her. He generated confidence without probably being aware of it himself. There was just something about him. She bit her lip when she again thought of how rude she had been to him before. How high and mighty she had behaved. But she was a much different person now. She had had her road to Damascus experience. She pulled up the trousers and then grinned over at him when she held the top out, displaying that it was probably a good six inches too wide around her thin waist.

He laughed. 'Guess poor old Sean over there was a bit fonder of the doughnuts than you are. That's why he didn't need a belt to keep them up.' He unbuckled the belt from around is own trousers and sleeved it out of the loops and held it out to her. 'Here, use this.'

She took it hesitatingly. 'Don't you need it?'

He laughed again. 'I haven't needed a belt to hold up my pants for a hell of a long time now either. I only put one on for appearances. I hate to see trouser loops without a belt through them. It looks so... don't know... incomplete I suppose. Just another of my many idiosynchrasies. She cinched the belt around her waist. 'Thanks, Scobie.'

He sat down on the bunk beside her. 'So tell me. How did you get into movies? Did someone discover you or what?'

She knew he was just trying to get her to relax, to concentrate her mind on something other than the situation they were in. And she was very grateful for that. His demeanour was that of a man with no apparent worries. His head and stomach had to be hurting like hell and he had to have his own doubts about getting out of the cellar but none of it showed. She soaked in his positivity.

'It's a long story,' she said.

He grinned at her. 'And sure haven't we plenty of time. It could be a little while before the cavalry come.'

And so she told him all about her early days in Bixby, Oklahoma, her shoplifting, getting caught by the store, the modelling deal she agreed to, to keep the cops from being called, her pictures being seen by Imogen Meyers and her subsequent affair with the woman to get her start in the movie business.

Gerry listened without interrupting and when she had finished, he gave her a wide smile. 'Well that's some story all right. A real Hollywood fairy tale. But fair play to you. You got to the top of the tree, and that's for sure.'

She gave him a coy look. 'You don't seem shocked about my using the Meyers woman to get into movies.'

He shrugged his shoulders. 'You do what you have to do and no matter what I or anybody else thinks, it's your business and nobody else's.'

'Would you… you know… have an affair with another man further your career?'

'I would in me arse,' he said and then stopped abruptly and burst out laughing. 'I think I should re-phrase that, shouldn't I?'

She laughed herself and God, it felt so good. There was just something so therapeutic about this man.

Gerry could see that the actress was in a far better place now. The anxious look in her eyes was gone and her whole body language was a lot more relaxed. Talking was having the effect on her that he had hoped it would. He had to keep it going. 'I was in Hollywood once,' he said.

She looked at him with surprise. 'You were? When? And what were you there for? Did you like it?'

He held up a hand. 'James Street! Take your time.'

He gathered his thoughts for a minute and then began to tell her. But he didn't mention Gloria Ballantyne.

*****

CHAPTER 45

Flann parked in his customary spot at the rear of the station and went in. He nodded to Guard Donoghue at the public counter who was helping an elderly lady fill out a passport application form. Elsie Masterson was in the main office along with three other guards when he went in.

She sat at her desk, a polystyrene cup in one hand and a half eaten croissant in the other. The front of her blue tunic had a light covering of pastry flakes. 'Didn't have time for breakfast,' she said.

Flann rubbed his stomach. 'Had a Scobie breakfast meself. The works. Eggs, sausages, black pudding, tomato, hash browns and toast.'

Masterson made a face. 'Bloody hell, Flann. Just listening to that lot has my arteries already hardening. I take it your good lady's away?'

Her colleague grinned. 'Herself and the kids have gone down home to see her folks. Dropped them to the train station for the eight o'clock. Thought I might see Scobie in the diner. He in yet?'

Masterson shook her head. 'Haven't seen sight nor sound of him since yesterday morning.'

Flann's forehead furrowed in puzzlement. 'I spoke to him on the phone yesterday. He was waiting for a phone call from some young one. Something about Billy Hamilton and the Sabrina Metcalfe case. And he hasn't rung in or anything?'

Masterson raised her voice. 'Any of you guys seen or heard from Scobie lately?'

Two of the other men shook their heads.

'Maybe he's eloped with that film one he's been sparkin' lately,' Smithy said, walking over. 'You know Scobie. When he falls for a bit of fluff, everything else takes a back seat.'

'He hasn't fallen for anyone,' Flann said. 'And Scobie, as well you know, is always on the case.'

'Arra I'm only joking,' Smithy said. 'Sure I know that. And speaking of film ones, any word on the Metcalfe one. Wasn't the ransom being paid last night? '

'It was,' Masterson said, popping the last piece of croissant into her mouth and licking her fingers. She stood up and swiped a hand down her front to brush off the pastry flakes.

'Doyle was up there but hasn't appeared back yet.'

'Strange there was nothing on the news about Metcalfe being released,' Flann said taking out his mobile phone. 'I'm going to try Scobie. Maybe he went on a bender last night and he's still in the scratcher nursing one of his customary hangovers.'

He scrolled though his contact list and pressed the call button.

'That's strange,' he said after a few seconds. 'Not a peep.'

'Maybe he didn't pay his bill,' Smithy said with a laugh.

'Or maybe he just has it turned off,' Elsie Masterson said. 'If he does have one of his hangovers, the last thing he'll want is people ringing him. Not until he morphs back into a human being again anyways. And as we all know, if he's been mixing pints and whiskeys the way he can, that can take the guts of a day sometimes. And with Doyle in Dublin, he won't be too bothered about appearing.'

Flann laughed. 'You could be right. Maybe I'll call around to his pad later. Roust him out of the scratcher in time for dinner. He'd normally eat a farmer's arse through a ditch after one of his on the piss nights.'

Masterson was about to make another comment when her phone rang. She picked it up. 'Manor Street Garda station, Guard Masterson speaking.'

She threw a quick glance at Flann, rolling her eyes. 'No, sir. He's just not here at the moment. Can I give him a message?'

Flann watched as she listened and when she said 'Right, sir' and hung up, he grinned at her. 'Doyle checking up on Scobie, was he?'

She gave a derisory snort. 'Not even a hello or good morning, Guard Masterson. Just 'Put Tierney on'. Fecking ignorant git.'

'What does he want Scobie for?'

'Didn't say. Just said to find him and get him to call him.'

'I better call around now so,' Flann said.

Smithy took his tunic jacket off the back of his chair. 'I'll walk around with you. Have to do me ramble around the town anyways. Let the good people of Kilbracken see that the men in blue are on the job.'

Flann stood waiting as Smithy shucked on his jacket and buttoned it up and then took his hat from the desk and put it on. He grabbed his own hat off the top of one of the filing cabinets. 'Right. Let's go.'

The two walked out of the station and headed up the street.

Flann groaned when he saw Councillor Andy Hogan step out of

Comer's newsagents' shop up the street in front of them, a folded newspaper in one hand, the other thrust deep in his trousers' pocket. 'Here's fecking Handy Andy. Probably after giving himself a good jerking inside.'

Smithy laughed. 'Well you have to admit; Geraldine Comer is a fine looking young one. There's more than Handy Andy who lust after her.'

'Yeah,' Flann said. 'But they don't go around with their hand through a big hole in their pocket fiddling with themselves like that fucking perv.'

The councillor planted himself in front of them, a smirk on his face. 'Well now. Isn't it great to see our Garda out patrolling our streets in such force. Gives one a warm feeling of security. I will have to commend our new inspector.'

Flann ignored the comment but Smithy responded. 'Aye, he has us out all right. Seems there's a right wanker going around making the town's womenfolk – and even some of the young men – very uneasy. You haven't seen anything in your travels, have you, councillor? We would be delighted to get a hand from a responsible person such as yourself.'

Hogan gave a spluttering cough, a deep red colour suffusing his face. He quickly pulled his hand out of his pocket. 'I haven't seen anything. Now...' He cleared his throat again...' Must run. Things to do, you know.'

They both stood watching as he quickly walked away.

Flann grinned at Smithy. 'I thought I'd wet meself when you said that about getting a hand from him. I think he knew you were hinting at him.'

'Fuck him,' Smithy said. 'It's time someone put it up to the weirdo.'

Flann laughed again. 'I don't think anybody's going to be putting it up to Handy Andy. I think that's his problem. He's just a frustrated auld git who's never been with a woman and so he relies on the five fingered widow.'

They separated when they reached the main junction, Smithy heading right towards the town square, Flann going left to the little cluster of shops, one of which was Miss Timoney's travel agency. He stopped at the door to the left of the shop entrance and rang the doorbell. He gave it a minute or two and then pressed it again, this time keeping his finger on it for over a minute. When there was no reply, he opened the door into the shop and stepped in, the bell overhead tinkling his arrival.

Lucy Browne looked up from behind her computer screen, a wide smile breaking across her round cherubic face 'Hiya, sergeant. To what do we owe the pleasure of this visit?'

Flann grinned at her. Lucy was one of Kilbracken's bubbliest young ones, always in an infectious good humour. Eighteen years of age, just an inch over five feet tall, she was at least four stone overweight but she didn't let her obesity define her. She oozed self-confidence and Flann knew that many a young smart mouthed lad had come off second best when making disparaging remarks to her about her weight. And when words weren't enough to put someone in their place, a pudgy fist was sometimes employed.

'Just wondering if you've seen Scobie this morning, Lucy. There's no reply from the flat.'

She shook her head. 'No. Not since I came in anyways. Hold on and I'll ask Miss Timoney. in the back office. She was in before me.'

Flann watched as she extricated herself from her chair and went over to a closed door and opened it without knocking. He could see Miss Timoney's grey head look up from some papers on her desk.

Lucy held the door open so he could hear the conversation. 'Sergeant Flannery's wondering if you've seen Detective Sergeant Tierney this morning?'

The elderly woman got up from her chair, came out of the office and over to the counter. 'No I haven't, sergeant. I've been here since shortly after eight and I haven't seen him. I take it you've rang his bell?'

Flann nodded. 'Long enough to wake the dead so doesn't look like he's up there.'

'And no doubt you've tried his phone?'

Flann nodded again. 'Yeah. Not a meg out of it.'

Miss Timoney's mouth quirked into a small smile. 'Have you tried Supermacs? You know how much the detective sergeant loves his fry in the mornings.'

Flann laughed. 'That was the first place I tried but they hadn't seen him.'

'I will tell him you are looking for him if I see him,' Miss Timoney said. She gave a little sniff, wrinkling her nose. 'You do know he has been seeing one of that film crowd. Maybe she is making breakfast for him,' the disapproving expression on her face confirming the implication of impropriety by the two. She gave another little sniff of disapproval and walked back into her office and closed the door.

Lucy grinned at Flann. 'Her ladyship doesn't think much of Scobie's philandering ways, does she? But she could be right you know. He could be shacked up with that film one. You know Scobie. He'd get up on the crack of dawn given half a chance. And I've seen that one. She's quite the looker.'

Flann laughed again but then shook his head. 'All the film crowd went to Dublin. They went up to be there when Sabrina Metcalfe was released.'

'Oh God, yeah. And has she? I didn't hear anything on the news this morning.'

'Don't know,' Flann said. 'I haven't heard anything either.'

Lucy raised two thinly pencilled eyebrows in disbelief. 'Arra you must have heard something, sergeant. Ye lot have to be in the know. Come on – spill the beans. Where did they find her and why is it being kept quiet?'

'I swear to you, Lucy. We don't know anything. Maybe when the inspector comes back from Dublin, we'll know a bit more.'

The young girl was about to say something else but stopped when Miss Timoney's door opened again. The elderly lady gave Flann a deliberate look. 'You're still here, sergeant?'

Flann took the hint. 'I was just leaving, Miss Timoney. Thanks for your time. And if you do see Scobie, please ask him to give me a call.' He nodded to the young girl. 'I'll see you, Lucy.'

He quickly went out and closed the door behind him.

l He strolled back towards the centre of town and stopped at McCluskey's pub across the road. He hadn't thought of Mackers. It wouldn't be the first time Scobie had gone in the side door for an early morning cure. How the hell had he not thought of that sooner!

He walked across and went around to the side door which was also the entrance to the living quarters upstairs and gave it a few hefty bangs with his fist. He waited a few minutes and then banged again and was just about to lift his fist for a third barrage when the door opened and Macker's annoyed and unshaven face appeared. 'What the hell, Flann! What are you bangin' on me door for at this unearthly hour?'

What d'ya mean, unearthly hour?' Flann said. 'Sure it's nearly ten?'

'Yeah,' the publican said. 'And it was nearly four when I got to bed. Had a Dublin stag party here last night and apart from not getting rid of them until nearly two, it took me another two hours to clean up after them. One little bastard got sick all over one of the seats. Took me nearly an hour to clean it up and get rid of the smell. Had to use a full bottle of vinegar. And someone broke the handle of the jacks and some other dirty little fucker obviously burst at the seams and got shite everywhere. I nearly got sick meself cleaning up that mess.'

'Ah me heart is breaking for you, Macker, you poor auld devil. And on top of all that, you probably had trouble closing the till as well after jacking up your prices.'

'What d'ya mean?' Macker said. 'I'm an honest publican.'

Flann grinned. 'It's me you're talkin' to, Macker. I know you jack up your prices when you get a stag or hen from the city. I'm not criticising. But you know I know so don't try and bullshit me.'

McCluskey gave a shrug of the shoulders. 'Well we have to allow for breakages and things. And for some of them puking over the seats and shitin' all over the jacks. They're extra overheads we haven't allowed for. All of the pubs do it. And it's only for the out of towners. You locals still get excursion rates. Anyways, what do you want me for?'

'I'm lookin' for Scobie. He's not proppin' up your bar in there, is he? In for the cure.'

'No he's feckin' not,' Macker said. 'Haven't seen him since Saturday. You try ringing his mobile?'

Flann slapped the side of his head with his open palm. 'Oh my God! Now why didn't I think of that! Silly me.' He gave an exasperated shake of the head. 'Of course I tried ringin' him, ya gobshite. Do you think I'm feckin' stupid?'

Macker grinned. 'I refuse to answer that on the grounds that it might get me in trouble.'

Flann snorted. 'Arra feck off, ya big northern prick ya. If you had a single brain cell in that big head of yours, it would die of loneliness.'

They both laughed. 'If I see or hear from him, I'll tell him you're looking for him,' McCluskey said.

'Thanks, Macker.

*****

CHAPTER 46

Spence stood at the window and watched the last of the stragglers leaving the disco attached to the bar across the road. He allowed himself a wry grin when three young ones staggered out holding on to each other, one drunker than the other. Not for the first time, he considered whether he should add a disco to his bar. He had the space. There was no doubt they were a big money spinner with the youth of today seemingly unable to get enough of exorbitantly priced cocktails and shots to pour down their scrawny necks. But discos meant security, age checks, police monitoring and parents. No. It wasn't worth the hassle and a lot of his existing clientele wouldn't take too kindly to any of that. His lip curled in disgust as one of the three young ones squatted down on the footpath and relieved herself while her two mates stood looking at her and laughing. No. He definitely wasn't going to get into that.

He turned back from the window. 'And you have no idea who these guys were?'

Jordie Tumulty shook his head. 'All I know is they weren't cops anyways. Not the way that guy took Breen out. Spoke with American accents. What the fuck are Yanks doing over here?'

Spence sat down in front of him. He idly fiddled with one of the bundles of money which had slipped out of the plastic bag when Tumulty had lobbed it onto the desk. The other bag sat on the floor. 'Have to be guys who came over with the ransom. Probably hired by the studio.'

'So what do we do now?' Tumulty asked. 'They still have Cleary. That's if they haven't shot him as well.'

Spence continued to fiddle with the bundle, flipping it over and back like a card dealer. He gave it one final flip and then reached down and opened a drawer and took out a mobile phone. He slid it across to Tumulty. 'Ring him.'

Tumulty took the phone and keyed in the numbers. He pressed the speaker button and then put the phone back down on the desk between the two of them. They both listened as it rang.

'Yeah.' Hoarse and hesitant but they both recognised Cleary's voice.

Spence nodded to Tumulty.

'You okay?' Tumulty said.

There was no reply for a few seconds and then another voice came on the phone. There was no mistaking the American accent. 'We want our money back.'

Tumulty looked at Spence. It was he who spoke. 'And if you don't get it?'

The laugh was short and brittle. 'Then your friend here bites a bullet. But not before he's told us who you are and where we can get you.'

It was Spence who laughed this time. 'Then you'll find out that I'm not a man to mess with. Cleary will tell you that. You guys might be big shots in America but you're on my turf now and believe you me, my resources are widespread and if I say so myself, quite effective in resolving issues.' He allowed a few seconds of silence and then spoke again. 'But I'm a business man, as I'm sure you are. We go head to head and we both lose. Where's the purchase in that?'

A slight pause and then 'I'm listening.'

Spence winked at Tumulty. 'I was only contracted to do the ransom pick-up. I had nothing to do with the abduction of the Metcalfe woman. As I've said, I'm a business man and business is business so if I was to get a better offer now, well, isn't that how business is done?'

'Go on.'

Spence leaned in closer to the phone. 'My collection fee was twelve and a half per cent. If someone was to better that offer, well as I've said, I'm a business man. '

'You have the money?'

'Sitting right here in front of me,' Spence said.

'Ring back in ten minutes.'

The phone on the desk went dead.

Spence sat back, a wide smile on his face. He rubbed his two hands together. 'What do you think, Jordy? We got them thinking, I'd say.'

Tumulty grinned. 'Sounded like it to me. If they do bite, what about O'Driscoll and his lot?'

'I'll clear his debt. Fuck him after that.'

'He won't be happy.'

Spence sneered. 'O'Driscoll is a small time punk and the crew he has are a shower of wasters. He'll take the debt relief and be damn glad to get it.'

'What if this crowd ask for their names and ask about Metcalfe?'

Spence shrugged his shoulders. 'I'll tell them she's dead and I'll make an agreement to give them one name.'

'McGivney?'

'McGivney. The fat fuck that killed her. And all because he couldn't keep his big stupid mouth shut. He'll get what he deserves and it'll save me having to do it. If they wheedle the other names out of him – well, it wasn't me who squealed on them.' He looked at his watch, leaned down and opened the large bottom drawer and took out a bottle of Powers whiskey and two glasses. He uncapped the bottle and poured out two large glasses and pushed one across to Tumulty. He lifted the other in a toast. 'To the next few minutes when hopefully a quarter mill will increase another twenty per cent or so.'

Tumulty raised his glass and took a slug. 'Pity about Breen.'

Spence shrugged his shoulders again. 'Stupid bollocks shouldn't have gone for his gun when it was two to one. That was always his trouble. Body of a bull, brain of a flea.'

Tumulty looked at his own watch. 'Ten minutes. Will I ring?'

Spence nodded. 'That's what the man said.'

Tumulty picked up the phone and hit the redial last number button. It was answered almost immediately. 'You keep three hundred thou. You hand back the rest.'

Spence smiled over at Tumulty and gave him a thumbs up. 'Deal. You come to my place. Cleary will show you the way. And remember guys, my guys are all hardened ex provos so don't plan any little surprises. And if you don't know what a provo is, ask Cleary.'

'We know what a provo is. We'll be there in an hour.'

'See you then.'

'Wait. Where is Metcalfe? We need to know that.'

Tumulty gave Spence a quick worried look but Spence only smiled. 'Miss Metcalfe unfortunately had a fatal accident. You'll have to take my word for that.'

'And the body?'

'Let's just say, somewhere where it won't be found for quite a long time, if ever.'

There was a slight pause and they both could hear a muffled off phone conversation and then the voice was back. 'Someone has to pay.'

'Indeed,' Spence said. 'And when we conclude our deal, I will give you the name and address of the person responsible. You can deal with him as you see fit. And my name never gets mentioned. Do we have a deal?'

'Yes. We do. We will see you in the hour.'

Again the phone went dead.

Spence picked up the bottle and topped up both glasses. He looked over at Tumulty. 'Ring Quirke. I want him and his lads over here in the next fifteen minutes. And tell him I want them all tooled up. I want this place tighter than Fort Knox.'

Tumulty took out his own mobile and scrolled down through the long list of names. When he got to Quirke's, he hit the name.

Spence took another pull of whiskey as Tumulty spoke to the former provisional IRA commander. He sat back, a grin on his face. Three hundred thousand. Not a bad evening's work. Fifty more than he would have gotten from O'Driscoll. As he sipped his whiskey, little did he know that his betrayal of O'Driscoll had cost him another two hundred thousand.

Tumulty put away his phone. 'They'll be here in ten.'

Spence nodded. 'Good. Now give Bowen a ring in The Fenian. He'll know Fatty's address.'

'Will he be there now? It's nearly three o'clock.'

'He'll be there. He and his buddies always play cards after hours.'

Tumulty took out his phone again.

*****

271

CHAPTER 47

Gerry could see that Sabrina was beginning to lose hope. Her demeanour had changed again and she was now very quiet in herself. He didn't feel all that good himself. His head had started to pound again and he wasn't bubbling with confidence himself. But he knew despondency was the biggest threat to their survival. If hope left, then the will to live went hand in hand with it. He had to keep positive himself and instil it into Sabrina. He pulled himself up a bit and looked at her. 'So, when we get out of here, what's the first thing you're going to do?'

She gave him a sad look without even the ghost of a smile. 'We're not going to get out of here, are we? I don't believe that now and I don't think you do either.'

He forced an incredulous look on his face. 'What are you talking about? Of course we're going to get out of here. I haven't a shadow of doubt about that. Now come on. What will you do first?'

It was so fleeting that he almost missed it but it was a smile. 'A bath. A long, long soak in a bath full of bubbles with a bottle of champagne at the side.'

'And after that?'

'A full makeover. Make-up, hair, manicure and my sexiest outfit and then a meal of beluga caviar on crisp bread, roast duck in a wine sauce, baby potatoes, roasted vegetables and finished off with a delicate chocolate mousse.' She sat up a bit straighter on the bunk and pulled Donovan's coat tighter around her. And you, Scobie? What would you do?'

He noted her saying would instead of will. He gave her a wide dimpled grin and then lifted an arm and sniffed underneath. 'Well I suppose a shower will have to be the first thing. But after that …' He gave a little laugh. 'After that, I'll go straight to Macker's and sit at the counter and watch while he fills a big creamy pint. And after he puts it in front of me, I won't touch it for a minute or two. I'll just sit there and stare at it. And then I'll pick it up and neck it in one. And then I'll have a few more while Macker goes down to Luigi's and brings me back a cod and chips with mushy peas and I'll eat them sitting at the counter while drinking my pints. I'll finish off then with a couple of Jameson whiskeys.'

She laughed and it was the like a ray of bright sunshine breaking through a black cloud. 'God but you are a man of simple tastes, aren't you, Scobie Tierney?'

He laughed himself. 'I suppose I am. But sure that's the way God made me.'

'Do you believe in God?'

The question surprised him but he didn't let it show. He chewed on his lip as he thought about it. 'Well I suppose I do in a way. Not the big man with the flowing hair and beard but I do believe there's something or someone who dictates our lives to some extent.'

'So you and I ending up here was predetermined by some mystical entity?'

He laughed. 'Naw. That was down to a couple of low-lifes.' Everyone has the ability to make choices. Those scumbags choose to snatch you to make money and one of them choose to acquaint my head with a rock. And when we get out of here, I'll choose to find the bastards and see that they're locked up for a very long time. We all have free choice. Some choose to abuse that gift. That's human nature.'

She laughed again. 'My God, Scobie! You're a philosopher as well as a super-duper policeman?'

He gave her a little bow although the movement made him a bit lightheaded. He camouflaged the grimace. 'I have my moments.'

Her voice went serious again. 'Do you really believe we will get out of here?'

He nodded, this time sending pain coursing through his head. 'I do. Even if my plastic bag message isn't found, Flann will be leaving no stone unturned in finding me. He's as relentless as a bulldog. You would swear I was one of his children the way he's always checking up on me.'

'He's a good friend so?'

'The best. He and I go back a long way. I'd do anything for him and he for me.'

She gave a little sigh. 'That must be nice.'

He caught the pathos in the voice. 'I take it you don't have too many real friends in your life?'

She shook her head. 'Certainly none like that. Hollywood is a very fickle place with very fickle people. But you have to live there to know that.'

'I've been there as I've told you,' he said.

She gave him a quick look. 'Yes you have. I'd forgotten. When was that again?'

'A little over a year ago. Went over to that police convention.'

'And would you agree that the people you met there were fickle?'

He made a face. 'Some. But no more than anywhere else in the world. Sure, Hollywood is built on make believe and a lot of people are as shallow as a saucer but there are good people as well.' He didn't make her aware of his first impression of her.

'And you met some good people while you were there?'

His look became wistful. 'I did. I made some very good friends and one in particular.'

It was her turn to notice the change in his voice. 'Someone special?'

'Very special. A lady whom I instantly fell in love with. And strange as it may seem, she fell in love with me too.'

She sensed there was not a happy outcome to this story. It was written all over his face. 'I'm sorry, Scobie. I'm not trying to pry. You needn't tell me if you don't want to.'

'Her name was Gloria. Gloria Ballantyne. She was an officer with the LAPD, Hollywood division. I met her at the convention the first day and I was instantly smitten. We were inseparable after that. Got engaged within the week.'

He looked her straight in the face. 'Did you ever know when something was just so right. That this person was the one you had been waiting for all your life. Well that was how it was with me and Gloria. It was as if we had known each other all our lives. We were the perfect fit.'

She remained silent, giving him time to tell her at his own pace.

'It was the night we got engaged. We went to a fancy restaurant to celebrate. She pointed out some mafia people to me but we didn't pay them any attention. Though the restaurant was packed, as far as we were concerned, we were the only two in it.'

Again she didn't prompt him, giving him time to come to terms with it in his own mind before telling her.

'There was an attempted hit on the main mafia guy. Some Chinese hit man. Gloria got in the way and the bullet meant for the mafia guy ended up in her head. She died later that night.'

She felt the tears trickle down her cheeks as she saw the slump of his body, as if his retelling the story had hollowed out all his insides. She wanted to move next to him and embrace him but she held back. She sensed it would not be the appropriate thing to do. But she had never felt such feeling for another human being as she did now for Scobie. It was obvious the man had loved this woman with all his heart and her loss was still a source of deep upset to him, even after this length of time. Her thoughts drifted to Richard. But not because Scobie's total love for this woman had rekindled any of her own feelings for Richard. It was for the complete opposite. She knew she didn't love him. Never had. And she also knew that he didn't love her and never had. Theirs had always been a cosmetic marriage. Like a lot of things in Hollywood, all front and no substance. Unlike Scobie and this woman Gloria. It was obvious that this had been a total mingling of body and soul. A meshing of two hearts into one. Her tears fell quicker. God, what she wouldn't give to experience a love like that. She would give it all up. All the fame. All the glory. Just to have someone speak about her as Scobie just had about Gloria Ballantyne. That was true stardom.

Gerry blinked hard a few times to stop his own eyes from betraying the pain his recollection had engendered. He had thought he had come to terms with it but obviously he hadn't. Maybe it was just because of the circumstances they were now in. He looked at Sabrina and saw the tears. Feck it! He was supposed to be trying to keep her spirits up. 'God, what am I like,' he said. 'That's enough of that stuff. So – you looking forward to being a lady of the realm?'

Her voice was low. 'Thank you, Scobie.'

He gave a little laugh. 'For what?'

'For sharing that with me. I know it wasn't easy. But she had you for that week or whatever it was. She knew how much you loved her. You have to take comfort from that. You are a very good man and I know I have been so rude to you. I suppose I am one of those shallow people as well. Please forgive me.'

He didn't answer but eased himself over beside her. He looked her straight in the face. 'Let me tell you something, Miss Sabrina Metcalfe. Yes, I did think you were a pain in the arse when we met the first few times. And I did think you were shallow and full of your own importance. But now I have seen the real Sabrina Metcalfe and believe you me, the real woman is a very nice lady indeed. You've allowed me to see beneath the Hollywood veneer and what I see now is not only a physically beautiful woman, but a woman of great inner beauty and depth as well. So when we do get out of here, embrace that other woman and keep her to the fore. I know the film industry is a dog eat dog world but you have the ability and the humanity to rise above that and be the beautiful person you are.' He gave a little laugh. 'And there ended the first sermon of Saint Scobie to the Hollywoodites.'

She leaned over and kissed him very briefly on the lips and then pulled back. 'Thank you, Scobie Tierney.'

He laughed. 'Did I ever tell you I can do Joe Dolan impressions?' He laughed again when he saw her puzzled look.

*****

CHAPTER 48

Billy Melinn and Geraldine Phelan both jumped off their bikes at the same time and left them lying in the ditch. Billy took the plastic bucket off his handlebars and together they carefully stepped through the nettles up to the bramble bushes.

'Aw Shite!' Geraldine shouted leaning down and slapping her bare leg on the calf. 'I've just got a bloody sting.'

Billy laughed. 'I told you to wear long pants and not that skirt. It's your own fault.'

She rubbed the reddening spot on her leg vigorously. 'Pants are for boys and in case you hadn't noticed, I'm not a boy.' Giving the stinging spot one last rub, she gingerly stepped up to the bramble bushes where Billy was picking blackberries, popping every second one into his mouth which now already boasted red stains at the corners.

'If you keep eating them like that, we'll never fill the bucket,' she said.

He picked another big fat berry and stuck it in his mouth. 'Well it's your mother wants them for her tarts and she gives me feck all although I pick most of them.'

'You do not,' Geraldine said. 'Last time I picked twice as much as you did.'

Billy gave her a scornful look. 'No you didn't. You had that stupid skirt on again and it was me who went into the big clump of nettles to get them big juicy ones that almost filled the bucket. Even your mother said they were the biggest she'd ever seen.'

Geraldine carefully picked a berry and dropped it into the bucket and then stretched in to get another. She let out a yelp as the stretch brought her leg again into contact with a nettle. She pulled her arm back and then carefully stepped back out onto the road. 'I'm not picking any more. There's too many nettles around.'

Billy laughed scornfully. 'And still you'll tell your mother that you picked most of them when we get back. You're an awful liar at times, Geraldine Phelan.'

She didn't look up at him and stayed bent over, concentrating on rubbing her leg. Eventually she straightened up. 'Mammy always gives your mother a tart so you can't complain.'

'Yeah,' he said. 'But I never get a bit of it. Father Meehan always seems to come around just when it's out of the oven and he bloody eats the lot.'

She giggled. 'Yeah. He's a devil all right. Comes to our house too and eats all around him. Daddy says he's like a human dustbin with a white collar.'

'It's no wonder he's as fat as he is,' Billy said, adding a handful of berries to the bucket. He stretched out again and pulled the white plastic bag which was stuck in the hedge. He scrunched it into a ball and threw it on the ground.

'That's litter,' Geraldine said. 'You're littering the place. Miss Healy said we should always take litter to the nearest bin.'

He snorted. 'And do you see a bin anywhere? We're in the country for crying out loud. And it wasn't me who left it here anyways.'

She stooped down and picked it up. 'I'll bring it home and bin it.'

'Suit yourself, Miss Envriment,' he said and went back to picking berries.

'It's environment, stupid,' she said testily. 'I'm going to sit down for a while.' She walked over to the grass verge on the other side of the road. She uncrumpled the plastic bag and put it on the grass and ironed it out with her hand so that she would have something to protect her dress from grass stains. She stopped as she saw the red writing. 'Billy,' she called. 'Come and have a look at this.'

He turned back to her. 'What?'

'There's something written on the plastic bag.'

'So?' he said, the disinterest evident in his voice. 'Probably someone's shopping list or something.'

'No,' she said. 'It's a message from someone called Scobie and it mentions McCracken's shed.'

Billy carefully pulled his jumper free of the thorny bush it had caught on and came over. 'Here, give us a look.'

She held out the bag and he took it from her. 'Jesus! It's asking for somebody to ring Sergeant Flannery.'

'Who?' she said.

'Garda sergeant. You know yer man. He came to the school once talking about what to do if strangers approached us and that. And I think there's a detective called Scobie. I've heard dad mention his name a few times. 'He grinned. 'Likes his drink apparently. Never takes any names when he raids a pub after hours. Dad got away a few times.'

'What'll we do?'

'You got a mobile?'

'No. I'm not allowed get one until I'm twelve.'

'I haven't one either. We'll have to go home and get someone to ring from there.'

He stuck the bag into his pocket and went over and grabbed his bike and hopped onto the saddle. 'Come on,' he said, already starting to pedal.'

She got her own bike and pedalled hard until she had caught up with him.

'Aw damn!' she said.

'What?'

'We forget the blackberries.'

He glanced back over his shoulder. 'Feck 'em. Father Meehan can just settle for Kimberly biscuits.'

'Whoa,' Tommy Melinn said as the two came hurtling into the yard and nearly knocked him over where he was hunched at the rear of the tractor fixing the coupling which had gotten a bit bent. He straightened up. 'Is Mahon's bull after ye or what?'

Billy hopped off his bike and let it fall with a clatter. He pulled the plastic bag from his pocket and thrust it at his father, his face flushed with excitement. 'Here, Dad. We found this in the bushes. It's a message from Scobie. You know. The policeman you're always talking about.'

Tommy took the bag from the excited boy. 'A message from Scobie Tierney you say?' He straightened out the bag and quickly read the red print. 'Bloody Hell! Where did ye find this?'

'Up at Donegan's field. It was stuck in the bushes.'

'That's not too far from McCracken's place,' he said, already taking the mobile phone from his pocket. He looked at the bag again and punched in the numbers.

The two children watched expectantly as he spoke. 'Sergeant Flannery. It's Tommy Melinn. Yeah, I'm fine. Listen – the kids were out picking blackberries and they found this plastic bag stuck in the bushes with a message on it. It says to contact you and just says under the shed, McCrackens, Scobie. That mean anything to you?'

The two youngsters watched as his eyebrows rose and when he

ended the call, they looked questioningly at him. 'Well?' Billy asked excitedly. 'What did he say.'

'He said thanks and just hung up.'

Billy looked at Geraldine. 'Will we go back and get the blackberries?'

She picked up her bike. 'Might as well. I don't think mammy has any Kimberly biscuits anyways.'

Tommy Melinn watched the two of them mount their bikes and cycle away. He stood watching them as they cycled out of the yard but his mind was elsewhere. Sergeant Flannery had just indeed said thanks but the intensity and emotion with which it was said conveyed a lot more than a simple word of gratitude. There definitely was something going on. He wondered if it had anything to do with the recent kidnapping of the Hollywood actress. Well he had done his bit anyways. He hunkered down again, picked up the wrench and gripped the coupling. If somehow he had helped Scobie Tierney with something, then he was glad about that. The detective sergeant had helped him out many a time.

*****

CHAPTER 49

Flann raced into the station. He did a quick look around. 'Smithy. You and Hartigan come with me right now. I'll explain on the way.'

Elsie Masterson looked up from her computer. 'What gives, Flann? What's the big panic?'

He stopped at her desk. 'Tommy Melinn's kid found a plastic bag with a message from Scobie. It said to ring me and then had something about McCracken's shed.' He didn't wait for her to comment, grabbing the keys for one of the squad cars off the board and heading out the door with Smithy and Hartigan hot on his heels.

Masterson shook her head. 'Is there ever anything straightforward with you, Scobie?' she said to herself.

Flann revved the engine as Hartigan squeezed his big body into the passenger seat and Smithy got in the back. He drove out of the yard and headed down the road.

'So tell us, Flann? What the hell is up?' Smithy asked leaning forward.

'Yeah,' Hartigan said. 'What's with this *Starsky and Hutch* routine?'

Flann negotiated the tight corner and headed out of town, the speedometer quickly rising to over a hundred kilometres an hour. 'It's Scobie. I think he's up at McCracken's farm and is in trouble.' He quickly explained about the phone call from Tommy Melinn.

'Jesus!' Hartigan said. 'That's why we haven't seen him around for the past while. You think he's hurt or what?'

'We'll find out soon,' Flann said as he screeched around another tight bend. He jammed a foot on the brake when the tractor and trailer loomed up in front of him. He switched on the siren and pressed the horn. He kept the horn pressed until the tractor and trailer edged over to the side, it's big wheel scraping against the stone built wall and dislodging some of the big stones. He flew through the narrow gap, the other big wheel of the tractor almost scraping paint off the side of the car and accelerated again as the road stretched clear in front of him.

Smithy looked back through the rear mirror. 'I'd say auld Christy Doonan will need to change his pants when he gets home. He's still sitting there in shock.'

Hartigan sniggered. 'Well if he does, it'll be the first time in yonks. He's a scuttery auld bastard who thinks water is only for putting in whiskey.'

Flann didn't comment, his eyes firmly fixed on the road in front. The other two went quiet as they sped along the road.

'Down to the right,' Hartigan said as they came to a junction. 'It's not much of a road so for fuck sake, take it easy.'

Flann turned onto the grass covered lane and slowed down as the car bounced over the rough surface. He swung it into the yard at the end and cut the engine.

All three quickly got out of the car and went straight into the shed.

'Scobie. You here?' Flann shouted, his eyes doing a quick scan around.

Hartigan studied the ground. 'Looks like that cart has been moved recently. Look here. See where the imprint of the wheels is in the ground. It's been sitting in this spot for a long time. But now it's over there in one of the stalls.'

All three walked over. Hartigan got between the shafts and clamped a big hand under each and then hefted them up. 'Get each side of a wheel and shove. Let's shift this baby and see what's underneath.'

They had it moved in a few minutes.

Flann lifted the slatted pallet and then gave the other two a look when all three saw the cover. 'Fuck sake!' Smithy said. 'Who'd have ever thought.'

Flann was already lifting the cover. 'Scobie. You down there?'

A big grin split his face when he heard Scobie's voice. 'What the feck kept ye?'

Flann stepped down with Smithy and Hartigan right on his heels.

'Sweet Mother of Divine!' he said as he saw the three bodies in the cellar. He rushed over to Gerry. 'Jesus, Scobie. You alright?'

Gerry gave him a grin. 'No, ya big gobshite. Half of me is left. Now why don't you ring in for an ambulance. Miss Metcalfe here is in need of medical attention and I might need an aspirin or two myself.'

Flann quickly turned to the other two who were looking at Sean Donovan's body. 'Smithy. Get up top and call in. I want an ambulance here as of ten minutes ago. Ring Elsie. I don't want any of this getting out. Tell her to tell them no siren or anything like that. I want this done quietly. Pat, you carry Miss Metcalfe outside.' He smiled at the actress. 'I'm sure a breath of fresh air would be very welcome.'

Sabrina returned the smile and then smiled over at Gerry. 'This is Flann I presume.'

'Flann the man,' Gerry said. 'I told you he'd find us.'

Flann grinned at him. 'An SOS on a feckin' plastic bag! They'll be telling this one for years to come.'

Smithy raced back into the short tunnel and up the steps as Hartigan went over and in a sweeping movement, gently picked up the actress as if she was a doll. He nestled her in his big arms and carefully made his way to the stairs and up. He carried her out of the shed and over to the open back door of the squad car and eased her down on the back seat. Smithy turned around from where he sat in the driver's seat and smiled at her. 'Won't be long now, Miss Metcalfe. Ambulance is on its way. We'll have you safe and sound in the hospital before you know it.'

Sabrina gave him a weary smile and then lay back against the seat and closed her eyes for a brief moment. She luxuriated in the fresh air blowing in through the door. It had never smelled as good or so refreshing before. She opened her eyes and looked to the shed door as the sergeant came out with Scobie held around the waist. Scobie had one arm draped around the other man's neck, his other hand pressed into his stomach. She could see the pain etched on his ashen face.

Flann eased Scobie down on the ground, his back against the front wall of the shed.

'Hang in there, mate. The ambulance should be here shortly.' He nodded at the other two guards. 'The two of you go back down and bring up Donovan's body.'

Gerry's head lolled forward, his chin on his chest. His head was splitting and his stomach hurt and his eyes felt heavy and leaden. He vaguely heard Flann call his name. His voice seemed to be coming from a million miles away.

He tried to open his eyes and focus but the effort was beyond him. The dark cloud rolled in and he let it envelop him.

Smithy and Hartigan emerged from the shed and eased the driver's body down on the ground close to where Scobie was slumped against the wall. Smithy threw a worried look at Scobie and then looked at Flann. 'He's all right?'

'He's passed out,' Flann said. 'Poor bugger has one hell of a gash on his head and he could have internal damage as well.'

Hartigan glanced over to the open door of the squad car.

Sabrina's body was slumped down on the seat. 'I think Miss Metcalfe has passed out as well.'

Flann nodded. 'Just as well. God only knows what the two of them have been through.' He looked down at Sean Donovan's body, the mouth locked open. 'Heart attack I'd say. Looks like he's been dead for a while.' He rubbed a weary hand across his face. 'Jesus, this is some mess.'

'But at least we found Scobie and Miss Metcalfe and they're both alive,' Smithy said.

Flann looked down at his friend and colleague. 'Aye, we did. And thank God for that. Now where the feck is that ambulance?'

As if on cue, the ambulance came through the gate and pulled up in front of them. Two men in white and green paramedic uniforms hopped out. Flann recognised both. 'Eddie, Harry. Donovan is dead – heart attack I'd say – and both Scobie and Miss Metcalfe have passed out but I think they're okay. I want them taken to the hospital very quietly without word getting out. We don't want to turn this into a circus. You tell them at the hospital that if any of them breathes a word about Miss Metcalfe, I'll personally have their guts for garters.'

Eddie Slevin and Harry Crenshaw both nodded. 'We'll make sure it's done discreetly, Flann,' Slevin said. 'We'll take them in through the back door straight into two private rooms.'

'Right,' Flann said. 'They're all yours.'

*****

CHAPTER 50

Superintendent Maguire sat at his kitchen table, his head in turmoil. He grabbed the bottle of vodka and tilted another big splash into his glass and gulped half of it down in a single mouthful. The fiery liquid burned its way down his throat but it did little to ease the tension in his body. What had started out as a straightforward surveillance operation the previous evening with him in charge, had spiralled into a nightmare where a dodgy cop from Los Angeles and some mafia types were now controlling everything and telling him what to do. And he had witnessed a cold blooded killing. He wiped a hand across his clammy brow. After they had left the industrial estate out past Balbriggan, he had led them up the Dublin mountains where Hegarty had left him sitting in the car while he conversed with the other men. When Hegarty had come back, he had told him to give him his mobile number and to go home and wait for further instructions. When he had asked the American cop about the second man they had brought with them, he had been told that no harm was going to come to him. That they were going to use him to get to the ransom money. And so he had driven home. He had a series of missed calls from his colleagues back at the station but he had satisfied these with a simple text saying he was checking out a few things himself and would report in the morning. But what the hell was he going to say? No ransom money. No Sabrina Metcalfe – he would have heard if she had turned up – and no kidnappers except for one guy now buried up in the mountains and another in the hands of Hegarty and his cronies. And it seems these guys were only involved in the ransom collection. He was definitely hanging with his arse out the window. The commissioner would be looking for an update in the morning. What the fuck was he going to tell him!

He jerked as the kitchen door opened, startling him.

His wife stood at the door in her dressing gown, a worried look on her face. 'Pat? Are you all right? It's nearly four o'clock in the morning. Are you coming to bed?'

He forced a smile to his lips. 'Just unwinding, Claire. It's been a hell of a long night. I'll be up soon.'

'You'll find her, Pat. I know you will. I'll see you in a little while.'

He watched her turn and close the door. He finished off the last of the vodka and reached for the bottle. It was then his mobile rang. It was Hegarty. 'We've recovered most of the ransom but as far as the public are concerned, we've recovered it all. You won't like to hear this next bit but it seems Miss Metcalfe met with an accident while being held and unfortunately didn't survive.'

Maguire felt a rush of ice down his spine despite the sudden outbreak of beads of sweat on his brow. 'Sweet Jesus! You can't be serious!'

Hegarty's voice was calm and controlled. 'Afraid so. The beautiful Miss Metcalfe has made her last picture. What's this they say in the theatre – she's exited stage left.'

Maguire struggled to control his breathing. 'What happened and where is she now?'

'I don't know the details and her whereabouts are still unknown but we do have a name and address for the man that killed her. We are just about to visit him. Here's how you're going to tell it in the morning. You received a tip from one of your snitches that he had overhead two men arguing in a pub. Both were very drunk and Sabrina Metcalfe's name was mentioned. He noticed one of the men pay for drinks from a thick wad of notes. He thinks it was this that started the argument. They both left shortly afterwards and they were still arguing but he knew the flat where one of them lived and gave you the address.

You were on your way home so you decided to check things out. When you got to the flat, you were just about to knock when the door was flung open and a man rushed past you with a black plastic bag in his hand. You gave chase and caught up with him but he got away after a brief struggle but you had pulled the bag from his hand. You instantly recognised the bundles of money from the ransom. You went back to the flat and found the rest of the ransom money and known criminal Fatty McGivney dying from a stab wound to the chest. Before he died, he confessed that he had killed Miss Metcalfe but passed away before he could tell you where the body was or who else was involved. You rang it in straight away and then rang me as the official security representative of the studio to take charge of the ransom money. So, superintendent, you better get your arse straight over to 29 Cheadle Road in Rialto, the downstairs flat and do just that. And it might be no harm if you banged your face off something. An injury from the struggle is always a good prop and generates sympathy for the brave cop. Believe me, I know. And if you haven't the guts to do that, I'll be only too happy to oblige. See you shortly.'

Maguire sat with his phone still to his ear though Hegarty had ended the call. His mind was racing. The whole bloody thing was one big shambles. He was getting in deeper and deeper. But what choice had he? He really didn't have any. He had to run with the ball the way it had been passed to him. He got up from the chair. Rialto was only ten minutes away.

Frogatti inserted the pick into the lock and with a few deft twists, eased the door open after he heard the click. He stepped in quickly followed by Hegarty, Montello and Schwartz. The room was about fifteen feet by ten with a sink, stained cooker, short worktop with two single drawers and a cupboard and two high stools behind a kitchen counter on which the remnants of a fast food pizza meal was scattered along with over half a dozen crumpled empty beer cans. There was a small coffee table with a newspaper on it, a two seater couch and one armchair, all badly worn and filthy dirty. Against one wall, there was a narrow bed and the fat figure sprawled on it was snoring loudly with his mouth open. His nose was badly gashed and discoloured and still slightly swollen. It looked like teeth marks across the bridge. There was a small cubicle with a curtain on a rail and this was partially open revealing a toilet and a small wash hand basin. The four men gathered in front of the bed. Frogatti tiptoed back to worktop and opened one of the drawers. He reached in and took out the long bladed kitchen knife and then walked back over to the bed. Hegarty took the paper from the coffee table and draped it over one arm of the chair and sat on it. He watched as Frogatti nodded to Montello and Schwartz who nodded to each other and then reached down and each grabbed an arm of the sleeping man.

Fatty woke with a start and tried to lift an arm but found he couldn't. He blinked a few times to focus his eyes which widened further when he saw the men around him. 'What the fuc …' The fist to the jaw cut off the end of the expletive.

Frogatti leaned in until they were almost nose to nose. He ignored the strong stench from the man's body and stale beer from his breath. 'This question gets asked once. I don't get an answer …' He moved the tip of the blade to within an inch of Fatty's left eye. 'You lose an eye. If I have to ask a second time, you lose the other eye.' He grinned as he saw the two eyes bulge. They might even pop out themselves. He scraped the tip off the sagging bag under the left eye. 'Names. I want the names of your accomplices.'

Fatty knew straight away he was going to tell them. He couldn't even bear to get a piece of grit in his eye. 'Billy O'Driscoll, Ratser

Whelan, Leery O'Leery and Danny Corbett.'

Frogatti grinned again. He knew he was going to get all his answers. The smell of fear from the fat body was almost as powerful as the stench of sweat and rancid body odour. 'I presume you have a meeting place. Where's that?'

'O'Driscoll's place. Flat over The Chinese Lantern restaurant on Pritchard Row. Down the road from here.'

'And where is Miss Metcalfe? Or to be more precise, Miss Metcalfe's body.'

Fatty's eyes bulged even further. How the fuck did they know? Someone had snitched. If this guy was looking for the other names, it had to be Spence then. Bastard was selling them all out. 'In a hidden cellar down the country. In a deserted farm shed outside of a place called Kilbracken. Corbett knows exactly. He drove us there. That's all I know about it. I swear.'

'I believe you,' Frogatti said and then in one swift motion, plunged the knife deep into the fat chest.

Fatty's breath caught in his throat as the pain sliced through his body like a red hot skewer. He tried to lift his arms to clamp his hands over the source of the fire but they were held fast by the other two men. He watched through fading sight as the three men leaning over him watched him die, their faces expressionless. He felt his sphincter relax and he knew he was going to shit himself. But for the first time in his soon to end life, he didn't give a shit. He smiled to himself at this ironic contradiction. Then he died, the smile still on his face.

Hegarty stood up. 'Leave the knife in him and throw him on the floor and then you three disappear. But wipe that fucking smile off his face. Maguire should be here soon. I'll catch up with you back at the hotel.'

Montello and Schwartz hefted the dead body up off the bed, dragged it a few feet and then let it fall to the floor. Schwartz leaned down and clamped a hand over the lower part of the face and pulled the mouth into a straight line.

Without another word, the three of them walked out the door.

Hegarty sat back down on the arm of the chair. He was still sitting there when Maguire came in a few minutes later. He stood up.

'Make your call to the station now.'

Maguire briefly closed his eyes after seeing the body on the floor and exhaled a deep breath. He was up to his elbows in it now. He took out his phone and brought up the station number and pressed on it. 'This is Superintendent Maguire. I want a response team over here to 29, Cheadle Road, Rialto. And have an undertaker put on notice. I'll give the team a full briefing when they get here.' He ended the call and looked at Hegarty and nodded down at the body. 'He tell you anything?'

Hegarty briefly looked down as well. 'Nothing that you need to be aware of just yet. When the time is right, I'll let you know.'

Maguire felt his anger rise. He was getting sick and tired of this blow-in bent cop pulling his strings. 'I'm getting a bit pissed off with all this cloak and dagger stuff. Either I'm in the loop fully or ye can all just fuck off. I've had a bellyful.'

Hegarty said nothing for a few moments and then came to a decision. 'We have the names of the other kidnappers and the whereabouts of Metcalfe's body. We want to get this first episode over with before we go down the next road. You sort this out and when the ransom money is officially returned to us and we can leave, we will give you all the details. The rest of it is your baby. How you tie them to the kidnapping is up to you. I'm sure you'll say fatboy's flat turned up some information that led you to the rest of the crew. Whether that'll be enough over here to convict or not, you know better than me.'

'And when do I release the whereabouts of Miss Metcalfe's body?'

Hegarty grinned. 'You can say a clue to that also turned up in your search of this place. I'll give you the details later on today but first, I want you to get the release of the money cleared and then me, Frogatti and the boys can get the fuck out of here and back to the States. After that, you can lead the posse to glory.'

Maguire knew he wasn't going to get any more. 'Fine. We'll play it that way so.' He glanced around the room and then staggered back as the blow caught him square on the jaw. He glared at Hegarty who merely gave him a disdainful look. 'I told you I would do it if you couldn't do it yourself.'

Maguire rubbed the now swelling jaw. He had forgotten about it.

*****

CHAPTER 51

Scobie woke up and the first thing to hit him was the complete contrast in smell. Instead of the overpowering stench of cow dung and silage, it was the crisp antiseptic hospital smell which filled his nostrils. He was in a gleaming white room, tucked into a bed with an array of equipment on a board over the bed. A clock on the wall opposite showed that it was a quarter to three. A plastic bottle hung on a drip stand beside the bed with the plastic tube hanging down and snaking into a needle inserted in one of the veins on the back of his hand and held there by a criss-cross of medical tape. His stomach was heavily bandaged and he also had a bandage turban on his head. His head and stomach still ached but the pain was very bearable. He looked over as the door opened and Mr. Pyne, the resident surgeon came in. 'Well, well, Scobie. You're welcome back. Had a good snooze, did we?'

Gerry grinned. 'Sure you know I always love a good kip in this place, Mr. Pyne. Better than a five star hotel.'

Pyne allowed his lips to crease slightly. 'Quite, detective sergeant. You're becoming quite the regular visitor here, aren't you? I do believe we've patched you up more times than Mr. Hamilton did his old post bike, and that's saying something. I think he spent half his working life feeding a tube through a basin of water down at Nolan's bicycle shop. At least, that's how it looked to me.'

'He was a bugger for getting punctures all right,' Gerry said.

'And you seem to be following his example. This isn't the first or second time we've had to fix you up. This time, a ruptured spleen and a quite severe head injury. Thankfully, the rupture to the spleen was of a minor nature so you'll be glad to know you still have it. I do wish you would be more careful when going about your upholding of the law. All of your colleagues seem to manage it without damage. Why can't you?'

Gerry grinned again. 'Guess I must just be a clumsy sod or something. How is Miss Metcalfe doing?'

'Ah yes, the beautiful Miss Metcalfe. Slightly traumatised and badly dehydrated but apart from that, considerably better than one would have thought, considering her ordeal.'

'And Sean Donovan? How did he die?'

'Heart attack. Under circumstances which we can only guess at.

According to Miss Metcalfe, she told your colleague Sergeant Flannery that she hadn't heard a word from him since the time they were kidnapped. It would appear to have happened then, poor man.'

Pyne walked over and flicked a finger a few times at the tube coming out of the drip bottle. Satisfied that the flow was as it should be, he took the chart from the end of the bed and jotted down something and then hung it back. 'You missed the news this morning. This Superintendent Maguire who was in charge of Miss Metcalfe's case was on it. Seems they recovered the ransom money and one of the abductors early this morning, although the man was dead. Apparently stabbed in an altercation with one of his co-abductors whom the superintendent chased and fought with but was unable to apprehend. He did get the money from him though. He is coming out as quite the hero.' He gave Gerry a raised eyebrow smile. 'And his only injury is a slightly bruised jaw.'

Gerry's brow creased in a frown. 'What time did all this happen?'

Pyne stopped at the door. 'Twelve o'clock news. About an hour after you were brought in. I am sure your inspector will fill you in. He was sitting beside the superintendent at the news conference. He seemed quite chuffed with himself. It was he who announced that his officers had located Miss Metcalfe and rescued her following his instructions that a thorough search of the local area be made. Afraid he didn't mention your name though for some strange reason. Nor indeed that of Sergeant Flannery or any of his colleagues.' He gave Gerry a smile. 'I wonder why that was?'

'Because the man is a pillock,' Gerry said.

The surgeon smiled again. 'Quite.' He opened the door and went out.

Gerry lay back against the pillow. His head was beginning to hurt a bit more. He closed his eyes and tried to clear his mind. It was in too much of a fugue to think clearly. He allowed himself drift off.

'Scobie! Scobie! You awake?'

He opened his eyes. Flann and Elsie Masterson were standing beside the bed.

He threw a quick glance at the clock. It was showing half past five. He had slept nearly two and a half hours. But at least his head wasn't as bad. He eased himself up into a sitting position. 'Flann. Elsie. Good to see ye again.'

Elsie Masterson gave him. 'Good to see us? God, you don't know how bloody good it is to see you, Scobie. We were all worried sick about you. You just seem to have vanished through a hole in the ground.'

He grinned at her. 'Well isn't that what I did? Down a shithole at McCracken's place.'

Flann pushed the easy chair over to his female colleague and he grabbed the straight backed chair and sat down. 'You missed the news.'

Gerry snorted. 'Pyne gave me a synopsis. Pair of feckin' pricks! How did they get the money back and find your man?'

It was Elsie Masterson who answered. 'Seems Maguire got a call from one of his snitches. A guy called Fatty McGivney was arguing in a pub with another guy and the snitch heard Miss Metcalfe's name being mentioned. The fat guy had a big wad of fifties and they seemed to be arguing about that too. Maguire went to the fat guy's flat to check things out and was almost knocked over by a guy running out the door with a big black plastic bag in his hand. Maguire chased him but he got away although Maguire got the bag. When he got back to the flat, he found the fat guy dead with a knife sticking out of his gut. And the plastic bag had the ransom money. That's the story apparently.' She stood up. 'Now if you two gents will excuse me for a minute, I have to strain the spuds as Pat Shortt says.' She went into the small bathroom and closed the door.

Flann gave Gerry an apologetic look. 'I had to tell Doyle that we found Miss Metcalfe and you. Apparently, it was just in time for the press conference. I'm sorry, Scobie. I know those pricks stole your thunder.'

Gerry shook his head slightly, still aware of its fragility. 'You had to tell him, Flann. You had to follow procedure. But Maguire's story! That's awful neat isn't it?'

Flann nodded. 'Yeah. I thought so too. And there's something else we schmucks down here didn't know. Apparently, Maguire's sidekick during all of this is that detective from the Las Vegas police department. In on the action from the very start. He and the other four he came over with are taking the ransom money back to the film studio in the states. And wouldn't you just wonder who the others are and why they had to come over? I'm sure they weren't sitting on their thumbs while all this was going on.'

Gerry looked at him. 'You were talking to Miss Metcalfe. Pyne told me. Was she able to tell you anything?'

Flann snorted. 'Talking to her me arse. All she got to tell me was about not hearing a peep from Sean Donovan from the time they were grabbed. Pyne stepped in and told me she was in no fit state to answer any questions and I had to leave. I haven't had a chance to go back yet. The film crowd are in and out of her room like feckin' flies around a cowshite. And Doyle the bollocks rang from Dublin and told me he wanted to be present for her interview and I or nobody else is to go near her until he gets here. He's supposed to be down later.' He gave Gerry a steady look. 'But surely you were talking to her while ye were both down in that cellar. She must have told you all she knew.'

'I didn't ask her and she didn't volunteer any info. We kept it light and sometimes personal. It wasn't the time or place to be quizzing her about her kidnapping. There wasn't much point anyways. Not until we got out.'

Flann nodded. 'I suppose. Are you going to wait for Doyle?'

Gerry rolled his eyes. 'I am in me arse! Ever since Clancy retired, we've had nothing but a procession of brainless peacocks pumped full of their own importance. Well he can go and piss into a force ten hurricane. I'm going to have a word with her now before he gets here.'

'Feck sake! What are you doing?' Elsie Masterson shouted as she came out of the bathroom door and saw him pulling the drip needle out of the back of his hand. He rolled back the blankets and swung his legs out of the bed. 'I'm going down to have a word with Miss Metcalfe before that bollocks Doyle comes back.' He looked at Flann. 'What room's she in, Flann?'

The other man grinned. 'Ah Jaysus, Scobie, you'll never make it. She's away down in the room right next door.'

Gerry nodded to the back of the door on which there was a dressing gown although he knew it wasn't his. 'Get me that yoke 'til I put it on. You know how windy these hospital gowns are at the back. Wouldn't like poor Elsie there to see what a bum I am.'

She gave a little laugh. 'I've seen an awful lot worse than your fat arse, Scobie.'

He grinned at her. 'And as the nurse with the enema in her hand said to the patient as she pulled up his gown, I'm only here for the crack!'

Flann brought over the dressing gown and he slipped it on. The sleeves were a bit short but it covered his decency. They both held out an arm for him to steady himself on as he stood up. He stood for a minute until he felt stable enough to move and then he shuffled towards the door. 'You two head off. Call back later and I'll tell ye what she had to say.'

Outside the door, they both said goodbye and strode off down the corridor towards the main exit. He stopped and looked at the closed doors each side of him. Feck it! He hadn't asked Flann whether it was the room right or left of his. He shuffled the few feet to the door on his left and opened it but when he saw the two heavily bandaged legs hanging from a traction device, he quickly closed it again. He shuffled past his own door to the door the other side and pushed it open. Sam Brookman, Faye Knight, Syl Carpenter and another man he hadn't seen before were all seated around the bed in which Sabrina sat propped up against a phalanx of white pillows. All eyes turned to him and Faye Knight gave a little cry and jumped up and came over to him, her face clouded with concern. 'Oh my God, Scobie. How are you? Sabrina was just telling us all that happened.'

He allowed her escort him over to the chair she had just vacated and ease him down onto it. She grabbed a stool and sat down beside him. 'Arra I'm fine,' he said. 'Nothing a few pints and a few whiskeys won't sort out. I've always found them to be the best medicine for everything.'

Brookman extended his hand. 'Sabrina told us what you did for her. We're very grateful.'

Gerry shook the extended hand. 'No bother.'

Carpenter shuffled his big feet and gave a little embarrassed cough. 'Yeah, Tierney. I guess I had you all wrong. No hard feelings I hope?'

Gerry didn't get a chance to reply as the man he hadn't seen before stood up and stood in front of him, his hand extended. 'Mr. Tierney. I'm Richard Tremayne, Sabrina's husband. I can't tell you how grateful I am to you for saving her.'

Gerry took his hand and shook it briefly. It felt soft and clammy. 'I did no more than anyone else would have done in my position, Mr. Tremayne. And if Sabrina herself hadn't been … if you'll all excuse my French … so ballsy, well, neither of us might be sitting here now.'

He looked at the actress who hadn't spoken. 'Do you think you and I could have a serious conversation now? You might try and remember all you can of all that happened before I arrived.' He looked at the others. 'Would you all mind if we had a quiet word?'

Faye Knight, Sam Brookman and Syl Carpenter immediately jumped to their feet, gave Sabrina a kiss in quick succession, said their goodbyes and then left the room. Richard Tremayne stood up as well but made no move. 'I think I should stay with my wife, detective.'

Sabrina looked at him, her face solemn. 'There's no need, Richard. You head back to the hotel. I'll talk to you later.'

The man hesitated. 'Are you sure, darling. You've been through an awful lot.'

She gave him a ghost of a smile. 'No more than you, Richard. You have just buried your father. No, I'll be fine.'

Scobie thought she stiffened a bit as her husband bent down and kissed her on the lips. He acknowledged the man's goodbye with a brief nod of his head and watched as he went out the door, gently pulling it closed behind him. When it had clicked, he turned back to Sabrina. She gave him a big smile. 'Thanks for that, Scobie. I was beginning to feel suffocated by all their attention.'

Gerry half stood up and gave her a little bow. 'But of course, Lady Tremayne. Will there be anything else?'

She playfully swiped his arm. 'I hadn't even thought of that you know. Doesn't seem important now somehow.' And then she went very quiet. She looked him straight in the eyes. 'I'm going to ask him for a divorce. I've only stayed with him for the title and after all that's happened, well it's just not important any more. And I know he doesn't love me either. I think I've changed, Scobie. For the better I hope. And a good part of that is down to you.'

Gerry felt a bit embarrassed. This was all getting too confessional for him. He looked back at her. 'You do what you feel is right, Sabrina. But wait a little while. Until you've put all this trauma behind you. Then make your decisions.'

Her smile was instant. 'As always, Scobie, pure common sense and I'll take your advice'

He grinned at her. 'Good. Now I'm going to switch into this more comfortable chair and you tell me all you can remember since the minute you were snatched. Try to remember anything you might have overheard. Any names, places, anything like that.' He eased himself into the soft chair, sat back and listened closely as she began.

*****

CHAPTER 52

'Thank you, sir,' Maguire said and shook the assistant commissioner's hand and waited as he left his office. He closed the door behind him and then went back and flopped down into his chair. What had looked like being a total and career threatening disaster had suddenly turned around and now he was the golden boy of the Garda Siochana. He thanked his lucky stars that Doyle had told him about the actress being found down the country before he had gone on national television and told the world she was dead. That would have been a right fuck-up. That was why he had allowed Doyle take some of the glory by saying he had initiated the search. Of course it was the mouthy detective sergeant but if Doyle wanted to screw one of his own, let him off. It was no skin off his nose. And now he had the names of the other three kidnappers and the address for the leader. Hegarty had given them to him as soon as he had cleared the official return of the money to him. They were now on their way to Dublin Airport and good riddance. He looked up when there was a knock on his door. It opened and Doyle came in. 'I'm heading back down the country now,' he said. 'I'm going to interview Miss Metcalfe. I'll fill you in on anything I learn.'

Maguire stood up and came around from behind the desk. 'Good. Keep me informed. I'll be heading back to McGivney's place to do a complete search soon. You never know what it might throw up.' 'If I don't throw up first,' he thought remembering the state of the place.

Doyle held out his hand. 'I appreciate you letting me ride shotgun on this one, superintendent.'

Maguire shook his hand. 'We made a good team, Freddie. And the name is Pat.'

Doyle visibly preened. 'Thanks, Pat. I'll be in touch after I've interviewed Miss Metcalfe.'

When he had gone out and closed the door, Maguire pressed the intercom on his desk. His secretary answered immediately. 'Yes superintendent?'

'Get me Detective Inspector Fogarty and Detective Sergeant Casey. Tell them to be ready to move in a few minutes. We're going to do a complete search of McGivney's place. And don't let anyone disturb me for the next few minutes.' He released the button and then opened the drawer of his desk and took out a Paddy Power diary he had found in McGivney's. In it, McGivney had listed some reminders for himself in a handwriting which was more print than script and very easy to copy. There were entries about meeting up with Leery for a few pints scattered throughout the pages, days to collect the dole, some names which looked like horses' names, the name and phone number of a Doctor Khan and some pages just had some idle childish looking doodling. All the entries were in blue biro. He took out his own and went to a clear page. Copying the handwriting as best he could, he wrote in Sabrina Metcalfe's name on a blank page and heavily underlined it. He thought for a minute and then flicked through to the page with the date a few weeks before the actual abduction and wrote

MEETING IN O'DRISCOLL'S PLACE
WITH LEERY RATSER & CORBY
ME TO BRING THE BEER

He moved on another few pages to the date two days before the abduction and wrote

DON'T FORGET BALAKLAVAS

Then, on the page with the date the day Metcalfe was kidnapped, he wrote

GRAB THE BITCH DAY
KILBRACKEN

He sat back satisfied with his handiwork. He knew it would never stand up in court and he had no intention of ever using it for that purpose but he could use it to sweat a confession out of one of them. Some of them had to be as thick as McGivney obviously had been. Everything he had seen in the grotty flat had pointed to a loser. He got up and stuck the diary into his pocket and went down into the main office. Fogarty and Casey were sitting waiting. 'Right,' he said. 'Let's get out to McGivney's hovel and see what we can find.'

The three walked out to the car parked at the rear of the building and Maguire got into the front passenger seat while Fogarty got behind the wheel and Casey into the back. They drove in silence, the quietness in the car only occasionally broken by static accompanied messages over the radio. There was a call for back-up to a row outside a pub in Ringsend and a call to an RTA on the M50 at Lucan.

Fogarty pulled up in front of the house outside which a very boyish looking uniformed Garda stood, his hands thrust deep into his pockets. He immediately straightened up and snapped to attention when Maguire got out of the car.

'All okay, guard?' Maguire said as he headed for the door which the young officer immediately pushed open for him. 'Yes, sir.'

'Nobody been here since we left this morning?'

'No, sir.'

'Good,' Maguire said. 'Why don't you get yourself a cup of tea or something. We'll be here for a half hour or so.'

'Thank you, sir.'

Maguire went in followed by Fogarty and Casey, all three of them pulling on disposable gloves as they went in.

'Jesus! Stinks in here, doesn't it?' Casey said, wrinkling his nose and throwing a disgusted look around the room. 'Even Dermot Bannon and an army of other architects would have their work cut out changing this place from the kip it is.'

'Pretty bad all right,' Maguire said. 'The late Mr. McGivney wasn't one to waste his elbow grease, that's for sure.'

Fogarty was over at the sink. 'Jaysus! There's fucking green mould in the sink. Not to mention a pile of dirty plates.'

Casey looked over from where he was standing at the cubicle, the curtain pulled fully back. 'You should see in here. Toilet looks like it's been spray painted brown and the dirty bollocks even left a few turds floating.' He pulled the flush chain but only a trickle of water flowed down the sides.

Maguire sneaked the diary out of his pocket. Casey was in the small cubicle, gingerly lifting the top off the cistern. Fogarty was down on his knees, rooting around in the cupboard under the sink. After another quick glance to see that the two's attention was focussed elsewhere, he deftly slid the diary under the mattress and then walked over to the cubicle. 'Come out of there, Noel, before you catch something.' Casey was quick to oblige.

'Then people wonder how things like the plague started,' he said.

Fogarty came over from the kitchen area. 'Nothing there but a heap of mouse droppings and the risk of cholera.'

Maguire poked a gloved finger through the detritus on the counter. 'Beer and pizza. No wonder he had the gut he had.' He looked over to where Fogarty was pulling the dirty blankets off the bed.

'Ah for fuck sake!' the inspector said. He nodded to the sheet on which long brown skid marks were clearly visible. 'The dirty fucker.' He gingerly inserted a finger under one of the corners and whished it off in one sweeping tug. There were damp stains on the mattress. Casey came over and grabbing one side, tilted it over onto the floor. They all saw the collection of adult magazines, all of which were well worn with the edges curling. They all saw the diary as well. Casey picked it up and flicked through the pages. He then flicked over a page at a time, a smile forming on his lips.

'What?' Fogarty said leaving down the Readers Wives magazine he had been flicking through himself. 'You find something?'

Casey held the diary out to Maguire. 'You'll like this, guv.'

Maguire took the diary and slowly went through the pages. He looked at Casey and then handed the diary over to Fogarty. 'Looks like we've struck lucky. It should be easy enough work out these names.'

Fogarty was grinning as he flicked through the pages. 'Lucky for us McGivney obviously didn't trust his memory.' He handed the diary back to Maguire. 'I checked McGivney on the computer back at the station. He's been in and out of the Joy a few times. Shouldn't be too hard to find out who his acquaintances were. Especially now that we have one name, O'Driscoll.'

'Right,' Maguire said. 'Let's get back to the station and get working on this. I want full names and addresses on these before the night is out.'

The young guard was back on duty outside. Maguire looked at him. 'When are you due relief, son?'

'Off at eight, sir.'

'Right. Carry on.'

All three got into the car and drove away. Guard Leslie Tuohy looked after the departing car. It must be great to be a superintendent. He was going to study hard for the sergeants' exam. Theresa could just accept that he couldn't be gallivanting every weekend.

*****

CHAPTER 53

Gerry lay on his bed and thought about all Sabrina had told him. She had heard two names mentioned, Lugser and Spence. A reference to Lugser ringing the paper and giving them Spence's instructions for the ransom. And she had seen the man who had tried to kill her. He had seen him himself but it had only been a fleeting glimpse before somebody else had crowned him with the rock. Lugser was probably a nickname but Spence wasn't. He would get Elsie to check the name out on the Garda computer. But something else she had told him was also weighing on his mind. The film was being cancelled. That meant that Faye and the rest of the cast and crew would be returning to the States within a couple of days.

The nurse came in and walked over to his bed. 'I hear you've been a naughty boy, Scobie. Interfering with medical equipment and going walkabouts.'

He grinned at her. 'Arra sure that auld bag was nearly empty, Emma. And I needed to have a word with Miss Metcalfe before a certain luder arrives back from Dublin.'

The nurse checked the bag on the drip stand and took it down. 'I'd say if we had some of McCluskey's Guinness in this, you would be looking for a refill instead of pulling it off.'

Gerry laughed. 'Can't argue with you there, Emma. I'd kill for a few pints now.'

She feigned a stern face. 'You men! You're all the bloody same. We're here doing our best to get ye back on your feet and all ye can think of are ways to get footless.' She smoothed out the blankets on his bed with her hand and tucked them in at the sides. 'Mr. Pyne says you'll be going home in a day or two. That's if you agree to take it easy.'

He was about to make another smart remark when the door opened and Flann and Elsie Masterson came in. Both were out of uniform.

The nurse gave a dismissive snort. 'I see we're going to have a police convention. I'll leave ye to it.'

When she had gone out, the other two came over and sat down.

Flann nodded to the door. 'Doyle will be in in a minute. Sabrina Metcalfe said she wasn't well enough to be interviewed by him yet. I'd say that wasn't her idea, was it, Scobie?

Gerry grinned. 'I just advised her that speaking to Doyle could be extremely tiring and could lead a body to mental debilitation.'

'Well he's just outside talking to her husband and told us to tell you he'd be popping in to see you in a minute.'

Gerry made a face. 'Do you think he'd believe I've had a relapse. I could pretend...' He stopped as the door opened and the inspector came in and walked over. He stood at the end of the bed. 'Well you're looking fine, Tierney. Not too much the worse for your experience.' He gave a little cough. 'On that, em, that was good work. Thinking of the plastic bag and all that. Tell me, how did you come to think of looking for the cellar out at that place – what's it called? Bracken's?'

McCracken's,' Flann said.

'Right. McCracken's.'

Gerry flashed a quick look at Flann. 'Just some local information I picked up on the way. More luck than anything I suppose.'

'Well it worked out fine, thank God,' Doyle said. 'Lucky we decided to do that search of the area.'

'Wasn't it just,' Flann said.

Doyle gave him a dirty look and then looked back at Gerry. 'Mr. Tremayne – or should I now call him by his title, Lord Tremayne – he was telling me you carried out an interview with his wife.' He gave Flann another dirty look. 'Did she have much to say?'

Gerry shook his head. 'It wasn't really an interview. We were just chatting in general.'

Doyle perched himself on the end of the bed. 'Well it doesn't really matter now. We won't need to interview her anymore. I have some good news that isn't common knowledge yet. Pat – Superintendent Maguire – as you've probably heard recovered the ransom money and found one of the kidnappers, albeit murdered by one of his colleagues. He has now identified the other four members of the gang and they are being picked up as we speak. I can honestly say that this unfortunate incident has now reached a very satisfactory conclusion with all the perpetrators accounted for.' He stood up. 'Well I won't bother you any longer, Tierney. Just wanted to see how you are and fill you in. I'll be back up in Dublin for a few days – have to help Pat nail down all the final details. Flannery here will be in charge in both our absence.'

Gerry couldn't resist bursting the man's bubble. 'That's good to hear. But what about the people who collected the ransom? And the one who made the phone call? Have you and Pat' – he put a little emphasis on the name – 'tracked them down yet?'

Doyle stopped on his way to the door and turned around. The other three could see that he was flustered. 'What do you mean? We've got the gang who did it.'

'I know that,' Gerry said. 'But three of the gang were down in the cellar when the phone call to the paper was made and when the ransom money was picked up. Miss Metcalfe told me that. So unless they were capable of bi-location, one guy could hardly have done all that by himself. And they had to have one guy on the outside locally to open up the cellar for them. So there had to be others who looked after those two things.'

He could see that he had stumped the other man. 'Oh! Miss Metcalfe told you that? Well maybe I should just have a quick word with her so when she's feeling a little better. Thank you, Tierney.' He quickly left the room.

'What a thundering bollocks!' Flann said. 'I'd say he's already on the phone to Pat.' – the name spat out like a bad taste.

'Forget him,' Gerry said. 'Listen. I want the two of you to check Mountjoy for an inmate with the nickname Lugser and if you find one, check if there was any way he could have had access to a mobile phone on the day the call was made to the paper. Then I want you to check the Pulse computer for a guy called Spence. Probably based in Dublin.'

'You got these names from Miss Metcalfe?' Flann asked.

Gerry nodded. 'Yeah. She heard both names mentioned. Lugser in connection to the phone call and Spence in connection to the ransom collection. And as you know, they traced the call to the newspaper to a mast at Mountjoy.'

Flann grinned. 'What do you think, Elsie? He's lying here with a ruptured spleen and a big feckin' hole in his conk and he can still think out things better than most of us.'

Masterson laughed. 'That's our Scobie for you. Always gathering like a squirrel.'

Gerry had to laugh himself. 'Feck off the two of you. Let me know how ye get on. I'm going to have a well-earned sleep now.'

The two stood up. 'See you tomorrow, Scobie,' Flann said. He nodded to Masterson. 'Don't forget to give it to him.'

She made a face. 'Jeez, I almost did forget.' She opened her handbag and took out the naggin bottle of Jameson and left it down on the bed. 'Here you are, Scobie. Put that into your drip.'

Gerry gave them both a wide smile. 'Arra the blessings of God on ye. Now before you go, Elsie, will you get me a glass from the bathroom and a small drop of water. Somehow I don't feel quite so sleepy now.'

While she went into the bathroom, he looked at Flann. 'I've an awful sneaking feeling I've heard the name Spence before. I think there was a provo guy with that name back at the time of the troubles that the special branch were keeping an eye on. If it's the same guy, we want to be very careful. From what I heard about him from some of the old guys, he was some feckin' animal.'

Masterson came out of the bathroom, two small glasses in her hand, one of them full of water. 'Here you go, Scobie.' She left them down on the locker beside him. 'Sorry about the size of the glasses but that's all that was in there.'

He was already twisting the cap of the small bottle of whiskey. 'That's the great thing about Jameson whiskey, Elsie. It doesn't give a shite what size glass it's poured into.'

He was tilting it into the empty glass when they left.

*****

CHAPTER 54

Maguire and Fogarty were in the small interrogation room with Leery O'Leary sitting at the table in front of them. Casey and Doyle were in the adjoining room, looking through the one way window. Leery's eyes were darting all over the place giving him the appearance of a trapped ferret. He jumped as Fogarty thumped a fist down on the table which made the Paddy Power diary and the small whirring tape recorder jump as well. 'We have it here in Fatty's own handwriting, Leery. All of your names and all the arrangements. Was it you that killed him? Saw him as the weak link?'

Maguire's voice was a lot more conciliatory. 'You're going down for this one, Leery. All of you are. And it's not just for kidnapping. There's the poor driver's death as well. But the one who tells us who killed the driver and Fatty – well, things will go a lot easier for him.'

Leery tried to look at Maguire but one eye was looking to his left. 'I swear Mr. Maguire. I didn't kill either of them. I don't know who did.'

Fogarty stood up and loomed over him. 'But you were there when Donovan was killed, weren't you? We have you as an accessory to murder. Unless you tell us otherwise.'

Maguire took out his phone when it rang. He listened for a minute or so and then said 'Right. Thanks.' He put a hand on Leery's shoulder. 'Come on, Leery. Do yourself a big favour here. We have Whelan in another room and from what I've just heard, he's asking what would be his deal for telling. If he tells us first, then the deal for you is off the table. The same offer is also being made to O'Driscoll and Corbett so it's a bit of a race between the four of you.'

Leery squinted to try and focus on the superintendent. 'What is the deal?'

'Tell him, Larry.'

Fogarty sat down again in front of O'Leary. 'Just the kidnapping charge with a request to the judge for a reduced sentence for co-operation. With a bit of luck, you could be out in three years. Otherwise, it's kidnapping and conspiring in at least one murder. That would carry twenty years minimum. Your decision, Leery. You either walk out of the Joy a relatively young man still or you crawl out a wizened old lag. But you better make your mind up pretty damn quick.

From what I know of your friend Whelan, he's not adverse to saving his own skin by fingering somebody else. And that somebody could be you and if it is, well – the only way you'll be coming out of the Joy then is in a wooden box.'

Leery felt the sweat roll down his back and drop down from his armpits. They had been at him for over an hour now. Again he mentally cursed Fatty for keeping a diary. He knew he was a forgetful bollocks but to have to write down things! And the things he had written down! Even after dying, he was still fucking things up for them. And he'd made a balls of killing the woman as well and it was probably her who had fingered Fatty himself. If he'd even managed to do that properly, none of them might be sitting where they were now. But he hadn't and here they were now all sitting on hard chairs being pressured to make a statement and take a deal. He didn't think O'Driscoll or Corbett would do a deal but Ratser was a different kettle of fish. He would sell his own mother to save his skin. And he knew that if he was going to finger anybody, it would be him. He'd be afraid of the other two. He made a snap decision. 'Yeah. We all did the kidnapping. It was Corby's idea. O'Driscoll owed some money and we thought this was a good way to get it and some more besides. It was Fatty and Ratser who did it for the driver. He had a heart attack while they were sitting on him. I don't know who killed Fatty himself. All I did in the whole thing was drive the limousine up to Lucan and leave it in a car park with the keys in the glove compartment. What happened to it after that...' He shrugged his shoulders ... 'I don't know.' He was damned if he was going to let Spence's name slip. That would be signing his own death warrant.

'You just left it in a car park in Lucan?' Fogarty said.

'Yeah, The one at the back of the big shopping centre. Left it there and got the bus home.'

'So who made the phone call to the paper and picked up the ransom?'

He shrugged his shoulders again. 'Don't know. As I've said, all I had to do was drive the limo up to Lucan. I wasn't in the loop on anything else.'

'It wasn't discussed at any of your meetings in O'Driscoll's place?' Maguire asked.

'Not while I was there anyways,' O'Leary lied.

Maguire stood up and picked up the tape recorder and the diary. He stuck the diary into his pocket and pressed the stop button on the recorder. 'Okay, Leery. I'll have your statement typed up and we'll get you to sign it in a few minutes. Sit tight and we'll be back.' He nodded to Fogarty and the two of them left the room, a uniformed officer coming in and standing at the door.

In the hallway, Fogarty punched the air. ;Yes! Didn't think we'd get him to break that quick. Nice touch with the bit about Whelan asking about the deal, guv. I think that's what put him thinking.'

Maguire allowed himself a smile. 'Well we can see what we get from him when we sit him down. He might be prepared to give us a bit more than O'Leary.'

'So Whelan next?'

'Yeah. But not for a while. I'm going to grab a cup of tea and a sandwich or something first. It'll be no harm to let him stew for a bit more anyways.'

Casey and Doyle came out of the observation room. 'Well done, guv,' Casey said.

'Yes, Pat,' Doyle said quickly. 'A lovely bit of interrogation with an excellent result.'

Maguire looked at him. 'You like to sit in on the next one, Freddie? Ratser Whelan.'

'If you don't mind, Pat, yes. I would like.'

Maguire turned to the other two. 'Freddie and myself will take Whelan. You two have a go at O'Driscoll and Corbett. We'll compare notes in...' He looked at his watch. 'In say an hour's time. That should give us time for a quick break before we begin. What say we meet in my office then?'

'Fine by me,' Fogarty said.

Casey nodded. 'Sounds good to me.'

'Right, Freddie. Let's you and I grab a quick cup of tea and a snack before we tackle the rat.'

Doyle followed him out of the station and around the corner to a coffee shop. 'You grab a table, Freddie. Tea or coffee?'

'A coffee please, Pat. White, no sugar.'

'You want a pastry or something with it?'

Doyle shook his head. 'No. Just the coffee is fine, Pat.'

Maguire was down to him a few minutes later with the coffee and a mug of tea and two long cream filled buns for himself.

He took one of them up and took a big bite, leaving a moustache of cream across his top lip. He took a swig of tea and then looked over at Doyle. 'I don't think we're going to get anything from any of them on the phone or ransom guys. In my opinion, O'Leary is the weakest of them and if we can't get the info from him, I don't think we'll get it from any of the others.'

Doyle took a sip of his coffee. 'Do you think he knows?'

'Of course he knows. It had to be discussed at their meetings. They weren't going to kidnap your woman without having the ransom arrangements in place. No – whoever they got to do it, they're not going to give them up for some reason.' He took another bite from the bun and licked the cream off his lip. 'Pity your guy had to open his mouth about it. As far as the press and public and the brass upstairs are concerned, we've successfully wrapped up this case. Everybody's feeling good about it. Why should we now fuck that up by looking for guys who were only bit players in the whole bloody thing. Even if we got them, they'd only get a slap on the wrist.' He looked at Doyle. 'Is there any way you think this guy might … you know… row in with us and not push this? After all, we got the kidnappers, got back the ransom money and got back the victim safe and sound. That's one hell of a result in any man's language. So what, if the guy who made the call and whoever picked up the ransom get away from us. What have they out of it? Zilch. Nada. As far as I'm concerned, they're not worth the effort now.'

Doyle nodded. 'I can only agree with you, Pat. The public are satisfied with the outcome as it stands. All we're doing by going after these others is taking the gloss off what we have achieved and leaving ourselves open to the perception that we didn't quite solve the whole case.'

'Exactly, Freddie. Couldn't put it better myself. The public hear about this postscript, then we'll have the press hacks looking for updates. And we don't catch these guys – and I'm of the opinion that we won't – then they'll only be too happy to turn our success into a failure. That won't do any of our careers any good.' He started on the second bun. 'Maybe it might be an idea if you went back down and had a quiet word with your people and particularly this guy Tierney. Show them that whoever made the call and collected the ransom have nothing out of it and it would be a waste of valuable police resources to spend time trying to find out who they are. What do you think?'

Doyle made a face. 'There 'd be no problem with most of them but Tierney? He's just a loose cannon. A fucking self-styled Don Quixote. He'd keep tilting at windmills until the cows come home. He'd keep after it just to spite us.'

Maguire finished off the second bun, using a finger to clear the cream from his mouth and then licking it clean. He took another slug of coffee. 'Yeah. My impression of that guy was that he was a smart mouth. Not a team player.' He leaned in a bit closer to Doyle. 'You got anything we could use? You know, anything that might make him reconsider his position?'

Doyle shook his head. 'Nothing of any significance. I know he turns a blind eye to afterhours drinking – he's the biggest culprit himself – and he's not adverse to cutting corners and skipping proper procedures but that's all mickey mouse stuff, isn't it? He'd only laugh at me if I started down that road.'

'And if we offered a carrot of some type?'

'He'd tell me to stick it up my arse.'

Maguire sat back. 'Then there's only one thing we can do.'

'And what's that?'

Maguire sniggered. 'I'll arrange to have him appointed as the officer in charge of the search for the phone caller and ransom guys. Let him bust his ass chasing a dead end and when the press guys start baying for blood, it will be his head above the parapet and not ours.'

'You can do that?'

'Listen, Freddie. After cracking one of the highest profile kidnapping cases in the bloody world, I can walk on water at the moment, as far as the brass are concerned. I'll tell them there are a few minor players outside the net but that they're not worth the time or effort of senior officers who are better deployed on more important cases.' He pushed his chair back and stood up. 'Come on. Let's have a crack at this Ratser Whelan. Maybe we might hit lucky and he might just tell us who these guys are. Then Tierney can go and kiss my ass.'

'He'll be on sick leave for a few weeks,' Doyle said.

'All the better. Maybe during that time, he'll forget about it.'

'I wouldn't be holding my breath,' Doyle said.

Maguire snorted. 'Fuck him. If he still persists, it'll be his ass on the line and not ours.' They walked out of the coffee shop.

*****

CHAPTER 55

Gerry was sitting in the chair beside his bed fully dressed. His bandaged gut was hidden beneath a crisp blue shirt and the bandage turban on his head had now been reduced to the size of a Jewish kippah, the skull cap worn by men. He was being discharged that afternoon. He looked to the door as it opened. It was Faye Knight. He gave her a wide grin. 'Hello, Faye. It's good to see you.'

He stood up as she came over. She sat down on the bed and patted the spot beside her. 'Sit down, Scobie.'

He eased himself down beside her and she quickly turned her head and gave him a kiss on the cheek. 'We're all going home today, Scobie,' she said, the disappointment evident in her voice.

Gerry nodded. 'Yeah. I heard. I'll be sorry to see you go, Faye.'

She gave him a smile. 'I'm sorry too, Scobie. We never did get to go to the funfair, did we?'

He grinned himself. 'No. We didn't.'

She took his hand in hers and stroked it. 'You're a good man, Scobie Tierney. It would have been nice to have enjoyed your company a bit longer but ...' She shrugged her slim shoulders ... 'The best laid plans and all that.'

He held her hand. 'Maybe you could stay on for a while. You know, go back later.'

She rubbed a hand across his cheek. 'I could, Scobie. But you know, and I know that there really would be no purpose in that. Sure, we would probably have a good time and enjoy ourselves but we both know nothing would ever come of it.' She put a finger to his lips as he started to speak. 'Shush. Let me finish. I had a long chat with Sabrina.' She grinned at him. 'I don't know what you did to her down there in that cellar, Scobie but she's one very changed woman. Anyways, she told me you told her about Gloria.'

Gerry went to interrupt again but she pressed her finger back over his lips. 'Please, Scobie.'

He went silent.

'You still love her, don't you? Even after all this time. You have to do yourself a favour, Scobie. Gloria is gone. It's good that you will always remember her but I think – and Sabrina does as well – we both think you're using her memory to keep yourself from allowing anybody else into your heart. You have to open yourself to other possibilities, Scobie. To other opportunities for a new relationship to develop. I'm sure Gloria would want that for you. You have to let go of her and embrace somebody new when that person presents herself. And someday she will.'

'It's not easy, Faye' he said, his voice little above a whisper. 'I think about her nearly every single day. And sometimes, the pain is as raw as the night she died.'

Faye put an arm around his shoulder. 'I know, Scobie. I know. But be honest. You do allow yourself to embrace the pain, don't you? You feel because she's gone, you have to suffer too. That's not the way she wants you to remember her, Scobie. She would want your memories of her to be happy ones. Not ones that cause you pain and keep you from opening up to other relationships. We both know life can be hard and cruel sometimes but we must put the pain behind us and move forward. Be kind to yourself, Scobie. Move forward.'

Gerry scrunched his eyes tight to hold back the tears. He knew everything she was saying was right. Others had said the very same many times before. And yes, he did know he sometimes used the memories as some form of self-flagellation for not saving Gloria on that fatal night. And he knew it was all holding him back from anything other than superficial relationships. Maybe now was the time to try and make the break.

Faye saw the tears glistening in his eyes and it broke her heart. It wasn't right that such a good man was shackled to a past love, the memory of which put a barrier between him and the possibility of finding a new love. She knew from all she had heard that Gloria had been a lovely person – she had to have been to have won Scobie's heart the way she did – but she was now a past love and that's where it should be left now, in the past. Life was too fleeting for the past to control the present and the future.

Gerry swallowed hard a few times to compose himself. He felt her embrace around his shoulders briefly tighten and then her arm slipped away. He took his hanky from his pocket and gave his nose a good hard blow. He shifted on the bed so that he was looking her straight in the face. 'I know you're right, Faye. And I promise I will do everything I can to get everything into perspective. But I want you to do something for me too.'

'And what is that, Scobie?'

'Go back to your man. Don't let him push you away again. He

needs you but like all of us men, he's too stubborn to admit it. He thinks he's doing the noble thing by pushing you away. Just like I'm doing with Gloria's memory. But we can't let the arrows of life pin us to the ground. That's what I've been doing and that's what your man back home is doing. Go back to him, Faye. And you tell him that you love him and that whatever the outcome, you are going to stay with him because that is the only thing that makes you happy.'

She wiped the tears from her own eyes. 'God, what are we like, Scobie?'

He put an arm around her and pulled her in tight and kissed her cheek. 'We're just two people, Faye, whose partners drew a bad card but you still have the chance to add your ace to his. And as we all know; an ace strengthens any hand. You just have to convince him of that.'

Her mouth tightened with resolve. 'You're right, Scobie. He needs me and I need him. And I will convince him of that.' She kissed his cheek. 'Thanks, Scobie. I'll never forget you.'

'And thank you, Faye. I do promise I'll put things in proper perspective.' He gave her a mischievous grin. 'You're sure you're going back? The funfair is still in town you know.'

She gave his arm a playful swipe. 'You're just incorrigible, Detective Sergeant Scobie Tierney. But I guess, that's what makes you what you are.' She stood up and hugged him tightly and then jumped back as he emitted a small groan. 'Oh my God! Your poor stomach! I forgot all about it. I'm so sorry.'

He pulled her back into the embrace. 'Sure it's only a feckin' spleen and half the jockeys riding today don't have theirs anymore.' He gently released her and stood back. 'Goodbye, Faye. I hope everything works out for you.'

'Goodbye, Scobie.' She patted his cheek with her hand and then turned and left the room.

He had only sat back down when there was a knock on the door and it opened again.

'Hello, Scobie,' Sabrina Metcalfe said.

He stood up and let out a long low whistle. 'God, Sabrina, you look a million dollars.'

And she did. Her face was perfectly made up with a light blue eye shadow and finely pencilled eyebrows giving her eyes an extra sparkle. Her lips were painted a deep red which with her naturally tanned skin, enhanced the whiteness of her even teeth and the wide smile on her face. Her hair shone with a healthy lustre and she was wearing a bright yellow coloured blouse, short bolero type blue suede jacket, tight blue jeans stuck into short cowboy style boots and a pair of hooped gypsy style earrings. Far removed from the dirty faced, stressed and tired woman in the pants and jacket of a man twice her size.

She walked over and kissed him on the lips. 'They tell me you're going home today,' she said.

'Yeah. Same as yourself, I believe. Although, I'll be home in ten minutes.'

She made a face. 'God, I wish I could say that.' She sat down on the bed and patted the spot beside her. 'Sit here beside me.'

He grinned. That was the second offer to get on a bed with a good looking woman in a matter of minutes. He sat down. 'I'm sure you're looking forward to getting back to Tinseltown and away from us country yokels. Not to mention a certain stinky hole of a cellar.'

She didn't laugh as he expected. 'Yes and no, Scobie. I'm certainly glad to be out of that awful cellar but I have to say, I've found this trip to be very cathartic in certain ways. I think I'm going back a nicer person than when I came.'

He smiled at her. 'I've told you, Sabrina. That woman was always there. It just took an emotional experience to burn away the outer Hollywood veneer to get down to the real Sabrina Metcalfe.'

She rewarded him with a glowing smile. 'Where did we get you, Scobie Tierney. How did you get to be so …so philosophical and yet, so down to earth?'

He grinned at her. 'You learn an awful lot looking into one of Macker's pints.'

She laughed. 'Ah yes. The famous McCluskey Guinness and whiskey. Part of your stable diet, I'm told.'

'Now who would tell you a thing like that?'

'Mr. Pyne. All the nurses. Your colleague Sergeant Flannery. Need I go on?'

It was his turn to laugh. 'Okay, okay. Point taken.'

She put a hand on his. He was getting quite used to this. 'I just want to thank you again for saving my life. Words seem so inadequate but I know if I was to offer you anything else, I would probably be offending you.'

He squeezed her hand. 'A thank you is more than sufficient, Sabrina. Now the less we dwell on that experience, the better for both of us. Is Richard going back with you?'

She shook her head. 'No. Richard is going over to England for a few months. He has a lot of family stuff to sort out.'

'And the divorce? You still going ahead with that?'

'Yes. And it will be by mutual agreement. Richard is happy to put it all behind us as well.'

Gerry nodded. 'That's good. It wouldn't have been very nice for two such high profile people if it got messy. The press would have feasted on it for weeks.'

'Yes,' she said. 'We both knew that. And with Richard now a Lord of the realm, well that was the last thing he wanted.'

'And are you Lady Tremayne still?'

She smiled. 'Until we divorce. Then his next wife can have it.'

'So? Back to the states and what then?'

She shrugged her shoulders. 'I don't really know yet. I'll check in with Marty and see if he has anything for me to look at. There's always a script, Scobie.'

'I know something you could do before looking at any more scripts.'

She raised a pencilled eyebrow. 'And what would that be?'

'You could always go down to Bixby. Maybe try and patch things up with your mother. Wouldn't that be a nice thing for the new Sabrina Metcalfe to do? Family is family after all.'

She closed her eyes for a few moments and when she opened them again, he could see the tears. He put an arm around her shoulder. 'She's your mother, Sabrina. And I'm sure she had never stopped loving you. Give her a chance. Give the two of you a chance. You've had a traumatic experience. And you're about to lose a husband. We all need somebody, Sabrina. And there's still nobody better than a mother. No matter how long or wide the rift has been.'

She gave a little cry. 'I will, Scobie. I will.'

He moved to lighten the moment. 'Well then. I'm glad that's all sorted.'

'And you, Scobie? Who's going to be there for you?'

He laughed. 'Sure I'm the Lone Ranger. Always have been. And I have my Tonto in Flann. There's not a loss on me.'

'I met Faye outside in the car park. She told me you and she had a good chat.'

'No more than you had with her earlier I believe. Telling her all my secrets.'

Her smile was almost shy. 'We both care a good deal for you, Scobie. We want you to be happy. And as Faye told you, Gloria would want that for you too.'

'It's all right, Sabrina. Faye got your message through.'

She stood up. 'I'm glad. And now I really have to go. Our flight leaves in less than three hours.' She kissed him again. 'Thank you again, Scobie, for everything you have done for me. No matter what happens in the future, I'll always know I have a leading man back in Ireland.'

'Good luck, Sabrina. I'm not one for reading movie mags but I'll keep an eye on your career. Have a good life. And give your mother a big kiss from me.'

The door opened and Sam Brookman's bald head appeared around it. 'Hello, Scobie. We really have to go now, Sabrina. The others are all gone.'

She walked over to the door and then turned. 'Goodbye again, Scobie. You'll always have a special place in my heart.'

Sam Brookman let her pass out by him, waved to Gerry and then pulled the door shut.

Gerry lay back on the bed. He wished Pyne would come and release him. He was gasping for a pint.

*****

CHAPTER 56

'Now, Scobie. Get your chops around that,' Macker said as he left the settled pint down on the table in front of Gerry. Gerry licked his lips, reached out, picked up the pint and took a deep pull which lowered it a good quarter way down the glass. He licked away the frothy moustache. 'Aaah! Mother's milk. Ye can't whack it.'

McCluskey grinned at him. 'Yerra it's a long time since you had mother's milk. Good to see you up and about though. You're a bit prone to getting the shite kicked out of yourself, aren't you?'

Gerry took another slug and left the glass back down. 'You and Pyne should form a feckin' duet.' He ignored the publican's puzzled look. 'Start fillin' another one, Macker. This one is nearly fecked.'

McCluskey went back behind the bar and picked up a fresh glass and held it under the tap and pulled the pump. He filled it up to just above three quarters way and left it down on the drip tray while the swirling Guinness settled. 'The film crowd are gone.'

'I know, 'Gerry said.

'Big loss to the town.'

'I'm sure.'

'Boss is a bit pissed off. Thought he had the two new Lassies on his hands.'

'He'll get over it, 'Gerry said finishing the last of the pint.

McCluskey topped off the fresh pint and brought it over. He left it down in front of Gerry and picked up the empty glass, the creamy white circles still lining its inside like a creamy spiral.'

McCluskey held it up and studied it. 'Ye won't see a better sign of a good pint that that.'

Gerry held out a tenner. 'Here. Take for the two.'

McCluskey waved away the money. 'You won't be payin' for porter in here for a long time. Or whiskey for that matter.'

'What the hell are you talking about?' Gerry said. He waved the note. 'Here, take it.'

The publican grinned at him and shook his head. 'No can do. It's already been paid for. As well as enough porter and whiskey to keep you comatose for the next twelve months.'

'What the feck are you talkin' about?'

McCluskey grinned again. 'I had that cowboy fella in this morning. You know, the big fella who was starrin' in the picture with Miss Metcalfe. Or was supposed to star in it anyways. He left a wad of notes with me. Said Miss Metcalfe asked him to do it for her. Something about making you a promise to buy you a drink.' He gave a laugh. 'So, Scobie. For the next twelve months or so, all your drinks are on Miss Metcalfe.'

Gerry shook his head in disbelief. 'Arra what the feck did she want to do that for? I can't accept that. How much did she leave?'

'Five thousand euros. All of them brand new from the bank.'

'Put them in a plain envelope and next time Dora Donovan comes in, slip it to her. Tell her Sabrina Metcalfe left it here for her.'

'You sure you want to do that, Scobie? It's a lot of money, you know.'

'Yeah. And if I drink it all, I'll be askin' Pyne to put me on the liver transplant list. No, give it to Mrs. Donovan. She has Sean's funeral to pay for.'

'Whatever you say.' He held out his hand.

'What?' Gerry asked.

'Eight euros for the two pints.'

Gerry had to laugh. He picked up the tenner and gave it to him. 'I'll never lose the run of meself with you around, Macker. That's for sure.'

McCluskey went back behind the bar to the cash register and was back a minute later. He left five two euro coins down on the table. 'Ye hardly think I'm that big a skinflint, Scobie? Fuck sake! I was only messin' with you. Those two pints are on me.'

'Ah thanks, Macker. Beneath that gruff exterior lies a heart of pure copper.'

The door opened and Elsie Masterson came in. She was in uniform.

McCluskey looked at her. 'Bit early for a raid, don't you think, guard? It's not even six o'clock yet.'

Elsie ignored him and sat down at Gerry's table. Macker went back behind the bar. 'Thought I'd find you here all right,' she said. 'Flann will be along in a few minutes. Doyle rang from Dublin just as we were leaving. How are you feeling?'

Gerry lifted the pint. 'How do you think I'm feelin'? Happy as bull in a field of randy cows.' He took a drink and smacked his lips. 'Need this to wash all that shite from McCrackens out of me lungs. You want a mineral or anything? Seeing as you can't have a proper drink while you're in uniform. Although, I could get Macker to put a gin and tonic in a tall glass. How about that?'

'You're all right. I don't want anything. We're just here to fill you in on what we've found out but I'll wait for Flann to come.'

Gerry took another pull from his pint. 'And have ye found out something?'

She gave him an excited look. 'We bloody well have. But Flann told me to wait for him.'

They sat in silence for the next couple of minutes during which Gerry finished off his pint and got another from McCluskey for which again, he wouldn't take any money. He was taking his second mouthful when Flann came through the door. He sat down beside Elsie Masterson. 'Have you told him anything?'

She shook her head. 'No. You told me to wait for you.'

'Right.' He looked at Gerry. 'We checked out the nickname Lugser with Mountjoy. They have a young buck called Harry Brennan, aka Lugser. He's awaiting trial for possession of drugs. Quite a considerable amount of drugs for a young fella of eighteen so he was probably just a courier. He wouldn't give up who he was delivering for though. Sad case really. I spoke to the arresting officer. The result of rape, his mother was only sixteen when it happened. She was a junkie and never took to the kid. None of her family would take responsibility for him so he spent most of his life in and out of foster homes. Supposed to be a cocky little bastard.' He edged forward on his seat. 'And this is where it gets interesting. A week or so before Miss Metcalfe's abduction, Lugser had a visit from a Danny Corbett.' He nodded when he caught Gerry's quick look. 'Yeah. The same Danny Corbett who is one of the four Maguire has nicked for the kidnapping. And ...' He paused for effect. '... and the day the call was made to the paper, there just happened to be a routine check for mobile phones and quite a few were found, most of them fecked out onto the landings. I got them to check all the phones against Lugser's prints and what do you think they found? You're right. One of them had his dabs.' He sat back, a very satisfied look on his face.'

'I don't suppose the sim card was in it?' Gerry said.

Flann snorted. 'Fuck sake, Scobie. You're not looking for much, are you? Brennan wasn't that stupid.'

'Pity,' Gerry said. 'If we had that, we'd know who rang him or who he rang to get the details for the ransom drop.'

Flann was grinning like a Cheshire cat.

'What?' Gerry said.

'Guess who's Brennan's step uncle and lives down the country?'

Gerry's eyes widened and a broad smile cracked his face. 'McCracken. It's McCracken, isn't it?'

The smug look on Flann's face answered him. 'Great work, Flann. Now, what about Spence?'

Flann nodded to Elsie Masterson. 'Elsie was on that.'

'Arthur Spence,' she said. 'Seventy three years of age. Former member of the provisional IRA. Served time in the Maze for murder. Freed under the Good Friday agreement. Has built up a major criminal organisation in Dublin and is suspected of being one of the main drug suppliers in the city. Was definitely involved in quite a few tiger kidnappings but they were never able to get any evidence against him. None of his people ever testify against him. He's supposed to be ruthless. Owns three pubs and a courier business. The serious crimes squad have been trying to nail him for years now.'

Gerry took a thoughtful pull from his pint. 'Brennan's the key. In my experience, cocky little bastards are so full of themselves, they think they're untouchable.'

'He wasn't that untouchable. He got nailed, didn't he?' Flann said. 'In the Joy awaiting trial.'

'In his eyes, that wouldn't be a negative. These guys think jail time makes them bigger men. Massages their macho image.'

'Well in his case, his image will get plenty of massaging so. He's probably facing five to ten years,' Flann said.

'And that might be just the bargaining tool we need. He won't like that. Flann – will you arrange a visit for me to see Mr. Brennan. Elsie – I need the name and a phone number of the main guy in the Serious Crimes Unit who's working on Spence.'

Masterson gave him a disbelieving look. 'You're on sick leave for a few weeks, Scobie. Doyle won't be happy if you poke into things while you're out. Nor will Maguire in Dublin. After all, it's his case.'

They both looked at Flann when he laughed.

'What's so funny?' Elsie asked him.

'That phone call from Doyle. He told me Maguire decided that since Scobie here brought up about these minor players, as he calls them – and whom in his opinion aren't worth police time – it should be him who takes charge of trying to find out who they are.'

Masterson snorted. 'They think they've it all wrapped up with the kidnapping gang in custody and if the phone caller and the ransom collector aren't found, it won't reflect on them now. That'll be your failure, Scobie.'

Gerry finished his pint and waved the empty glass at McCluskey who immediately started to pull a fresh one. 'Of course, Elsie. But what they don't know is what we do know. We have Brennan and Spence and I'll bet a penny to a pound, they're the ones we want. We just have to get Brennan to give us Spence. Now, why don't the two of you go off home and change and then come back and have a few scoops.'

Flann stood up. 'No can do I'm afraid. We've the in-laws coming this evening. It's their anniversary and we're having a meal for them at ours. In fact, I should have been home an hour ago. I'll catch ye tomorrow.'

Gerry looked at Elsie as Flann left. 'How about it, Elsie? You game for a few?'

She grinned at him and stood. 'And what do you think my Phelim would say? Me drinking alone with Kilbracken's own Gunga Din.'

McCluskey came over and left the pint down on the table. 'Gunga Din me arse. Sure all he ever did was give people water. Scobie here is more your W.C. Fields.'

Masterson stood up. 'Thanks but no thanks, Scobie. I'm going to head. Phelim's on his own with dad.'

'Ah fair enough, 'Gerry said. He turned to the publican. 'Turn on the old telly there, Macker. There's racing from Tramore this evening. Think I'll have a few punts.'

Elsie Masterson stopped at the door. 'You know what W.C. Fields said about horse sense, Scobie?'

'Go on. Tell me.'

She grinned at him. 'Horse sense is what keeps horses from betting on people.' She turned and left.

*****

CHAPTER 57

Two days later, Gerry was sitting behind the single table in an interview room in Mountjoy jail. He was feeling fresh as a daisy having had no drink the previous day. He had spent a couple of hours visiting his old superintendent, Clancy, and they had discussed the Sabrina Metcalfe kidnapping and Arthur Spence whom his old boss had known quite a bit about. It was Clancy who had rang Trevor Costigan, the head of the Serious Crimes squad who just happened to be an old friend and Gerry had asked him if he could make Lugser Brennan an offer of no charges if he had something they could use against Spence. The senior officer had gotten quite excited at the possibility of getting Spence but Brennan had been carrying just too many drugs, for him to be able to get the charge pushed aside. The best he could possibly swing was a reduced sentence, to be served outside of Dublin.

He looked up as the door opened and a young man was escorted in by a warder and pushed into the chair the other side of the table. 'You want me to wait?'

Gerry shook his head. 'No. I'll be fine.'

The warder went out and closed the door behind him.

Gerry looked at the young man sitting in front of him. Still more a boy than a man. He was of average height with a not unhandsome face despite still having some acne which he was obviously trying to hide behind a couple of days stubble and the sullen look. His hair was cut to the butt and as he slouched nonchalantly in the chair, his eyes roved around the room. His whole demeanour screamed 'I'm here but I don't give a shit.' Gerry took an instant dislike to him but smiled. 'How are you doing, Mr. Brennan?'

The young lad gave him a brazen look. 'As if you care. Now, it's chow time soon so let's not waste each other's time.'

Gerry grinned. 'Your time is that precious? You must have a full schedule here so. Your friends waiting for you? I would imagine a good looking fella like you would find quite a few of the older lags wanting to be – you know – sort of special friends with you.'

His comment only got a scowl.

'Okay,' Gerry said. 'Let me tell you what I know and why I'm here. You rang the Chronicle paper and told them that the actress Sabrina Metcalfe had been kidnapped and told them how much the ransom was and how it was to be delivered.'

Brennan just curled his lip in a sneer and folded his arms but made no comment.

'As I'm sure you've seen on television, your associates – if I can call them that – have all been apprehended and as you probably already know as well, Mr. McGivney is unfortunately dead. Murdered by person or persons unknown.'

A snigger. 'No loss, the fat fuck.' Obviously not a fan of Fatty's.

Gerry continued. 'Now we know you made the call and when you're up for the drug charge, a kidnapping charge will also be brought against you. I would safely say you're already facing five to ten years for the drugs. This additional charge should add maybe another five or so to it. That's a good slice out of your life, Mr. Brennan.'

For the first time, he saw the macho veneer crack a bit. Brennan unfolded his arms and sat up a bit straighter. 'So? I'll probably only serve half that, if that. I can do that standing on my head. Now, are we done here?'

'Have you heard of Deirdre Twomey, Mr. Brennan?' Gerry asked.

Brennan shrugged his shoulders.

'Well, Mr. Brennan, Deirdre Twomey is the new minister for justice. She's a bit of a Mrs. Thatcher. Ah wait. Sure you wouldn't know who Mrs. Thatcher was. Sure you're miles too young. Mrs. Thatcher was a British prime minister. Tough as nails she was. They called her the iron lady. Well Deirdre Twomey is our iron lady and three days ago in Dail Eireann she tabled a motion proposing that anyone convicted of drug related charges – carrying, supplying or just plain minding – will be sentenced according to the severity of their crime but – and this is the important bit – their sentence will not be subject to any reduction for good behaviour or any other reason. It passed through the Senate this morning and will be signed into law within the next two weeks. You're not due before the court for another three weeks I'm told so you'll be one of its first beneficiaries.'

The macho veneer cracked a good bit more. 'I didn't hear anything about that.'

'Oh! Was Mrs. Twomey supposed to clear it with you first? Guess she must have forgotten. How remiss of her. I'll tell her you're very annoyed with her when I see her.'

He got a sullen look but a lot of the initial bravado had gone. The starch was gone out of him.

'Of course,' Gerry continued. 'We Guards still have a bit of wriggle room when it comes to cases we bring before the courts. And I'm here, Mr. Brennan, to offer you some of the wriggle I've negotiated for you if you help me out?' He paused. He wanted Brennan to ask. A minute passed and then a second. He was getting a bit worried when a third minute passed but then he heard the magic words. 'I'm listening.'

Gerry leaned forward, his arms on the table. 'We have you for the phone call. I can guarantee you that. And you were caught with a shit load of drugs. What if I was to tell you that I could have things diluted in your favour. The DPP's office wouldn't oppose a recommendation to the judge that you serve only a short sentence, maybe in the midlands or Cork. Somewhere away from here.' He had his full attention now.

'Sure what can I do? You have O'Driscoll and the other lads. You want me to confirm they did it? I'll do that.'

Gerry shook his head. 'No. We don't need you for that.'

'For what then?'

Gerry gave him a small smile. 'Arthur Spence. The man who gave you the instructions for the ransom pick-up. We want him.'

Brennan laughed but there was no mirth in it. 'Spence! You want me to finger Spence? That bandage must be covering a hole in your head if you think I'm fingering that mad bastard.'

Gerry gave him a surprised look. 'I thought you young Turks weren't afraid of old men like Spence?'

The chest was pumped a bit. 'I didn't say I was. But why should I get the old bollocks' goat up just to help you lot out?'

Gerry looked him in the eye. 'Not just to help us, Mr. Brennan. You help yourself as well. Think about it. Ten to fifteen years in here, probably for the first few fighting off the randy lags who like to make special friends out of the young good looking new blood. You haven't been put into the main system yet, have you? But you will after your conviction. And that's where... well, I don't have to spell it out for a smart cookie like you, do I? Or ...?' He paused for effect. 'Or assuming that what you give us help us to nail the old bollocks as you call him – a few comfortable years in your own cell in Castlerea or Cork. You're a bright lad. You should be well able to carve out a new life for yourself somewhere else after getting out. You'd still be a young man.'

He could see he had him thinking so he stopped talking.

A few minutes elapsed. Gerry stayed quiet.

Brennan slowly shook his head. 'No. I don't think I'll take your offer. You'll have to sweeten it a good bit. No jail time and a payment of some kind but it would have to be a big one.'

Gerry stood up. 'Thank you for your time, Mr. Brennan.' He walked towards the door.

'Where are you going?' Brennan asked, his face reflecting a mixture of surprise and shock.

'I'm going home, Mr. Brennan.'

'But... but what about what I said?'

'You said you weren't accepting my offer. That's fine, Mr. Brennan. Enjoy your stay here.'

He knocked on the door which was opened by the same warder.

'Wait!' There was panic in the single word.

Gerry nodded to the warder who closed the door again. He walked slowly back and sat down. 'Well?'

Brennan licked his lips. 'No Money. Just no jail time.'

Gerry stood straight up again and made for the door.

'Ah Jeez! Wait!'

Gerry turned to face him. 'I think we've done enough dancing around here. You've heard my offer. You say either yes or no. If it's yes, I'll listen to what you have to offer and then it will be up to me to say yes or no.' He knew he had won when he saw the shoulders slouch.'

'I have the sim card from the phone. It has a recording of my conversation with Spence.'

Gerry shook his head. 'Not enough, Mr. Brennan.'

Brennan's eyes darted to the door as if he suspected someone was listening. 'But it'd be enough along with a tape recording. One that has Spence's name, his voice discussing the ransom pick-up and saying that the whole thing is his operation.' He gave a brittle laugh. 'And that's a good one because it wasn't his operation. He only arranged collection of the money. But you get that recording, you can pin the whole thing on him. And your lot wouldn't hesitate for a second to do that, would ye?'

'And where is this recording?'

Brennan gave him a sly look. 'I will get a reduced sentence, won't I? And I won't have to serve it here?'

Gerry nodded. 'Yes. You have my word.'

'Corbett has it. Himself and O'Driscoll made it in case Spence tried to keep all the money.'

Gerry stood up. 'Right. I'll pass on the info.' He walked over and knocked on the door which was again quickly opened by the same warder who stood to one side to let him out.

'Don't forget,' Brennan shouted after him as he walked down the corridor.

Gerry ignored the shout. He was already ringing Trevor Costigan.

*****

CHAPTER 58

Arthur Spence slugged down the whiskey his barman had poured for him and grimaced as another wave of acid reflux burned his gullet. Fuck it! He knew he was only making it worse by drinking whiskey but he was damned if he was going to drink milk. He took another couple of antacid tablets and popped them into his mouth and chewed on them and then took another slug of whiskey to wash them down and clear the chalky taste from his mouth. He looked over to the table where Jordie Tumulty and Nippy Cleary were playing pool. Apart from himself and the barman, they were the only other people in the bar which wasn't surprising as it was not yet twelve o'clock on a working day. It was normally after one before the regulars started to come in. He studied Cleary as he stretched low over the table lining up a shot. He thought about what Cleary had told him and smiled. He knew the three guys who had shot Breen and taken Cleary hostage were Americans. He had met them and a fourth guy himself when handing over the money. More than likely mafia. Particularly the guy who had done all the talking. He was straight out of Goodfellas. Connected in some way to the film studio. The film studio was probably like his pubs and courier business. A vehicle for rinsing drug money through. He had the whole conversation on tape. And now something that had been puzzling him from that conversation with the Yanks was solved.

It had taken Cleary a while to recover from his ordeal. He had been convinced that he would be shot like Breen. He had even been made help carry Breen's body and dump it in a ditch and then gather up rocks and branches and throw them on top of it. He had been so fucked up by the whole experience that this was the first day he had ventured out of his apartment and come to the pub. Spence smiled. But he had had some interesting things to tell him. The blow he had gotten hadn't knocked him out but he had feigned unconsciousness as he knew he would get another crack if they thought he was still conscious. The two guys were in the front and he was lying across the back seat. The driver had laughed and made a comment about Hegarty telling him that when Frog had shot the guy, the Irish cop Maguire had nearly shit himself. Spence had heard the name Hegarty before. It had been the fourth guy who had come for the money. He had introduced himself as a cop from Las Vegas. Obviously a bent one. But he had no problem with bent cops. He had a few on his own payroll.

But he had definitely heard Maguire's name before as well. It had been in the papers and on the tv. Superintendent Pat Maguire, the man in charge of the investigation into the Sabrina Metcalfe abduction. And the Yank had mentioned an Irish cop showing them where to hide Breen's body when he had asked him how they had thought of going up the Dublin mountains. Now he had the name. He smiled again. That was a tasty morsel of information. And something he could exploit some time. He had it all on the cctv camera that had been activated as soon as the Yanks had come into the room.

He made a face as another clot of burning acidic bile regurgitated up his gullet and he swallowed hard to force it back down. Fuck it. Maybe he would get a glass of milk or maybe get Jordie to run to the chemist shop for a bottle of Gaviscon. He casually looked over as the door of the bar opened and a group of men came in. His lip curled in annoyance when he recognised the man in front.

Gerry followed Trevor Costigan and his five plain clothes colleagues into the bar. He had planned to go back to Kilbracken after his visit to Lugser Brennan but after speaking to Costigan, he had agreed to stay over and had kipped down in Garda headquarters in the Phoenix Park. Things had moved very quickly after he had rung Costigan and told him about the existence of the set-up tape implicating Spence in the kidnapping. Costigan himself had gone straight out and interviewed Corbett who had been only too happy to cop a deal for himself when he found out that Lugser had told them about the tape recording. It was now every man for himself. And that was confirmed a while later when O'Driscoll eventually agreed to co-operate as well on the promise of not being charged as the ringleader and the assurance from Costigan that Spence would serve his sentence in a different prison to him. Spence had made a lot of enemies over his lifetime and a lot of them were already in Mountjoy. They would be very happy to see Spence arrive and his immediate future as an inmate might just come to an abrupt end. He certainly hoped it would. After these interviews, Costigan had sat down with Gerry and asked him if he had a problem with going after Spence as the main man behind the kidnapping although they both knew he wasn't. Gerry had listened as the senior man had recited a litany of offences they were convinced Spence had committed but they had never been able to prove any of them. It would be just poetic justice to eventually get him for something he hadn't done. Gerry hadn't had a problem with that. He wasn't shy about bending the rules himself when the occasion merited it. Any way you could take a low life scumbag out of circulation well –

in his eyes – the end always justified the means. Costigan had gone to a judge he knew and gotten the warrants. Judge Anthony Clohessy had lost a son to drugs and like Costigan, he too lived for the day they could put Spence away. It was his signature which were on all the previous warrants which had never gotten Spence in front of him or one of his colleagues. But the tape recording he had heard – well that was a different kettle of fish. Spence and his high priced mouthpiece might not be able to wriggle him out of this one the way they had all the others.

The small recorder now nestled in Costigan's pocket along with the arrest warrant and a search warrant for the pub and the office upstairs. Other crews were already on their way to the other pubs and the courier premises with other warrants.

'What the fuck do you lot want?' Spence said, a sneering expression on his face, although he had been expecting them. He was used to the cops hassling him and he knew Costigan in particular, was hell bent on catching him for something. But they never had anything. Okay, he knew Metcalfe had been found alive – Fatty couldn't even do that right – and would have told them she had heard his name being mentioned. That was obviously the reason they were here now. It was just going to be the start of a lot more hassle he could do without. But what they had was just hearsay and that and three euros, would get them a cup of coffee. It was actually all getting a bit monotonous now.

Tumulty and Cleary stood with the cues in their hands, looking from Spence to the group of new arrivals. The barman busied himself polishing glasses. They too had seen it all before.

Gerry lagged a little behind the other six men as they walked over to where Spence sat. He was really only a guest at this stage but that suited him fine. It was more than Maguire and Doyle were. They hadn't been contacted at all.

Costigan didn't stand on ceremony. 'Arthur Spence – I am arresting you for the kidnapping of Sabrina Metcalfe and as an accessory to the unlawful killing of Sean Donovan.' He nodded to one of the other men who took out a pair of handcuffs and started towards Spence.

Spence couldn't believe his ears. What was this crock of shit they were peddling? Trying to nail him for the kidnapping! There wasn't a shred of evidence to link him to the kidnapping. How could there be? He hadn't been involved except in arranging the ransom pick-up and they would have a damn hard job proving that unless they got their hands on the cctv tape and that wasn't going to happen. His heart rate settled a bit and he looked at Costigan. 'You're way off beam on this one, Costigan. I had nothing to do with the snatching of that broad. That's the truth.' He gave a little snigger. 'And for the first time in my life, I can put my hand on my heart and say that.'

The senior policeman sneered at him. 'You could put your hand all over your miserable body, Spence, but you wouldn't find a heart. You don't have one. There's nothing in that chest of yours only a lump of granite.'

Spence scowled at him. 'I'm not saying another word until my solicitor is present.' He shouted over to Tumulty. 'Ring Hardiman.'

Costigan raised his eyebrows in feigned surprise. 'Did I ask you to say anything?' He turned to the others. 'Did I ask Spence here to say anything?'

Gerry joined the others in a shake of the head. He was enjoying himself. He stood watching as the policeman with the handcuffs reached out towards Spence who instantly backed away. 'You can fuck off with those things.' He looked at Costigan. 'Unless you have a warrant, I'm not going anywhere with you.'

Costigan gave a protracted weary sigh and then reached into his pocket and produced the two pieces of paper and held them out. 'A warrant for your arrest and a warrant to search this place.'

Spence snatched them from his hand and quickly scanned each of them. 'Just as I thought. That high and mighty prick, Clohessy. You two should be rechristened Dumb and Dumber. You're fucking unbelievable. This is all just another of your big wind-ups, isn't it? Just out to cause me more of your fucking hassle.' He thrust them back at Costigan. 'You've never had anything on me, you've nothing now and you never will have.' He pushed out his two wrists. 'So go ahead. Let's play out this little charade of yours. I'll be back here drinking another whiskey before your frump of a wife puts the shitty kippers down in front of you for your tea.'

Tumulty came over as Spence was being handcuffed. 'Hardiman will meet you down at the station.' He gave Costigan a sneering look. 'It will be the same station as always, chief superintendent, won't it?' He looked at Spence then. 'Give me a ring when you're ready to come home, boss. I'll pick you up.'

Spence's nodded. 'Yeah. You do that, Jordie. I know I can always rely on you to know what to do.'

Costigan looked at Tumulty. 'You and your pool buddy can leave.

If we need to talk to you later, we'll know where to find you.' He turned to the man who had handcuffed Spence. 'Pete – you and Eddie take this can of piss down to the station and book him. If his brief turns up, let him see him but no matter what his brief says, he stays put until I get back.'

They all watched as the three men left followed out by Spence's two associates and then Costigan rubbed his hands together. 'Right, lads. Let's toss this place good and proper.' He looked over at the barman who was still standing behind the bar. 'You can go too. As of now, this place is closed for the next few hours. You can stand outside and tell that to your colourful customers when they start arriving. We'll let you back in when we're finished.'

Gerry stood thinking. He had seen the quick look which had flashed between Spence and Tumulty during their last exchange. There had been some hidden message in Spence's look to Tumulty. And the way he had said 'I know I can always rely on you to know what to do'. The words had been said in a very deliberate way. There had been a subliminal message there too. Nobody else had spotted it. But he had. He went over to Costigan. 'If it's all right with you, I'll grab a bit of air.' The chief superintendent, who was busy directing his other men, nodded. 'No problem, Scobie. We've it covered here. And thanks again for all your help.'

Gerry quickly went outside.

The barman was slouched against the litter bin in front of the pub, a cigarette in his hand. He glanced disinterestedly at Gerry when he came out and then looked away, his attention drawn to the much more interesting sight of two young girls in miniskirts who had just turned onto the street and were heading in his direction. Tumulty and Cleary stood at the corner talking to each other. Gerry was tempted himself to have a good look at the two young ones but kept his eyes on the two men. When Cleary walked off across the road and Tumulty went around the corner, Gerry went up to the corner and peered around. He was just in time to see Tumulty go into a Chinese acupuncture and herbal remedy shop next door to the window of the pub. He quickly followed and after a quick glance through the open door which confirmed that Tumulty wasn't in the main shop, he went in. The shop was only about ten foot square with a small glass counter and display case in which various boxes of potions and powders with such names as Ginseng, Ginkgo seeds, Goji berries and a lot more he couldn't even pronounce were on display. There was a large colourful poster almost six-foot high on one wall showing all the acupuncture points on a naked male body. A long thin table took up the other wall on which more remedies, potions, incense sticks, herbal teas and small books on the treatment of different ailments were displayed. There was a floor to ceiling beaded curtain which obviously gave entrance to a back area. Sitting on a small wooden chair beside the display counter was a small wizened Chinese man who had to be at least eighty years old. He had a flowing mane of snow white hair, a moustache which was long and silken and came down past his chin and a small goatee style beard. He was dressed in a gold and red traditional Chinese robe with white socks and gold coloured slippers on his small feet. He gave Gerry a yellow toothed grin and a slight bow of the head as he came in. 'You need medicine or acupuncture? You stressed? Sore body? Want give up smoking?' A little cackle. 'You need help get Johnny up? Make love with wife or girlfriend?'

Gerry laughed. 'No, I don't need anything. Just looking for the man who came in here a few minutes ago.'

The grin disappeared, and the eyes narrowed to thin pencil lines. 'No man here. Only me. Now – you not want anything, you leave.'

'I think it's your eyes might need some acupuncture,' Gerry said. 'I saw him come in and he hasn't come out. Let's have a look in the back, shall we?'

The small man stood up and planted his body in front of the beaded curtain. He was so small and thin, he was like a pipe cleaner. 'Private back here. You no come in.' He put his two hands up in front of him in a Kung Fu pose. 'You leave now.'

Gerry stopped himself from bursting out laughing at the comical figure hunched in front of him. He could drown him with a spit and still have saliva left. He reached into his pocket and produced his Garda identity card and held it in front of the old man's face. 'Listen Charlie Chan or whatever your name is, this is official police business. Now, please step aside and let me pass.' He fully expected the old man to stand aside and this time he did laugh when the only reaction he got was a series of slow deliberate hand movements accompanied by some kind of Chinese chant which were straight out of a bad Hong Kong martial arts film. He stepped in to brush past the little man. The kick caught him square on the thigh and this was quickly followed by a small fist to his chest which nearly cracked his sternum. If it had been a little bit left, it would have burst his spleen – again! He staggered back in shock, his leg numb, the card falling from his hand.

'You leave now,' the man shouted, his two balled fists held out in front of him.

Gerry raised a hand in apparent submission. 'Okay, okay, I'll leave. Just let me get my identity card.' He reached down to where the card was at the man's feet and picked it up and closed his fist around it. Then in a move – the speed of which even surprised himself – as he straightened up, he whipped his fist under the man's chin. The crack was like a rifle shot and the little man actually lifted off his feet before falling back through the beaded curtain. Gerry hobbled in after him dragging his still numb leg behind him but the man was out cold. He had never hit an old man before but his leg and chest still hurt and he had no doubt that if he hadn't taken the sly crack, the oldster would have wiped the floor with him. And he would have needed a lot more than acupuncture after that. He rubbed his knuckles which were now sore as well.

The back room was a little smaller than the front with just a treatment table with a small table beside it on which there was an array of long thin needles with little ball heads of assorted colours. There was another small table at one wall with a small tray of sand with a couple of what looked like joss sticks sticking out of it. There was a strong smell of incense in the room. But it was the door in the other wall that took Gerry's attention. He limped over and opened it as quietly as he could. It opened into a very short corridor with stairs in front. He held his breath as he clumsily made his way up the stairs and stopped as another small room came into view. Tumulty was bent over some type of recording equipment, a cassette tape in his hand. Gerry took another deep breath and then went up the remaining few steps and into the room.

Tumulty sensed the other presence while his back was still to the stairs. 'You should be down …' He stopped mid-sentence. It wasn't old man Chang. It was one of the guys who had come into the pub with Costigan. He had to be a copper. And if the cops got the tape in his hand, Spence was fucked and he might be as well. He began to edge his way along the side wall. At least there was only one of them. But where the hell was Chang? He kept his eyes on the other man as he called out. 'Chang! Chang!'

Gerry gave a little laugh to himself. Chang – not Chan. He had only been one letter out. He watched as Tumulty began to move slowly along the wall. He knew by the look in his eyes that he was calculating just when he would make a rush at him. He stayed blocking the stairs, balancing himself on the one leg which still had feeling in it, in expectation of a sudden rush.

Tumulty stuck the tape inside his jacket and as he did so, he felt for the knife in his pocket. He might have to use it on the cop. And if he had to, he wouldn't hesitate. As Spence always said, a dead cop was just another annoying splinter removed from their backsides. And dead cops couldn't tell who killed them. But with a bit of luck, he would get past this one and get away. He inched forward.

Gerry watched and waited. He turned his head slightly when he heard a sound coming from downstairs.

Tumulty saw the brief distraction and lunged.

Gerry felt the man's body crash into him knocking the breath from his own and he knew if he didn't move quickly, he would end up at the bottom of the stairs in God knows what condition. He swivelled using his good leg as a fulcrum and this shift saw him crash back against the wall instead of tumbling down the stairs. He got a hand up to the other man's face, got a finger up one nostril and pushed as hard as he could.

Tumulty roared with pain as he felt the man's finger push deep up into his nostril. He had never thought a nose could generate so much pain. He felt the nail on the finger cut through the lining and then the warm flow of blood. He threw himself backwards to free himself of the invading digit.

Gerry bent over gasping for breath. He lifted his head to see where his antagonist was and allowed himself a small smile when he saw the other man a few feet away holding a hand to his bloodied nose. But the smile quickly disappeared when he saw the hand go into the pocket and produce the knife and flick out a very ugly looking blade. He had feck all to defend himself with.

Tumulty saw the change of expression on the other man's face and it was his turn to smile. He swiped the air a few times with the blade for added effect. He knew that if the man had any back-up, it would have been here by now. And if he was armed, he would have produced it before now. Obviously just an ordinary plod. When he saw Chang's head start to appear up the stairs behind the cop, his smile widened.

*****

CHAPTER 59

Gerry heard the soft footsteps behind him but didn't take is eyes off the man in front. He knew it had to be the Chinese man. If it was Cormican or any of his men, they wouldn't be creeping up the stairs. It would be a full scale heavy footed stampede. His mind was racing. Would they just leave with the tape or would they feel they had to deal with him first? And was he going to just watch them leave with what he guessed was a crucial piece of evidence? But they held all the aces. He was alone and unarmed. Tumulty had a knife and Chang had a lethal pair of hands and feet, even if they were attached to a rag doll of a body.

'How'd he get by you?' Tumulty asked as Chang stepped into the room and stood a few feet away from him.

Chang shot Gerry a hostile look. 'Trick me.' He rubbed his chin which was now sporting a large bruise. 'Hit me when I not looking.'

Tumulty laughed. 'You're losing it, Chang. Letting the likes of him get the better of you. Guess you're getting a bit too old now for all that Kung Fu shit.' He looked at Gerry. 'Question now is, what do we do with him?'

Chang stroked his wispy moustache. 'He know too much now. We kill him.'

Tumulty looked at Gerry, a sneering smile on his face. 'Guess you really have upset Chang. You must be the first person to get past him. And he obviously doesn't like that.'

Gerry decided he needed to play for time. Give himself time to think. 'I'm a police officer and I'm arresting you both for conspiracy to conceal evidence and assaulting an officer in the course of performing his duty.'

The other two men laughed, Tumulty's a shrill cackle, Chang's a low titter. 'You hear that, Chang?' Tumulty said. 'We're being arrested. I suppose we better go quietly.'

Gerry watched from under hooded eyes. He knew that very soon they would get fed up with continuing this little scenario and when they did, he was going to be in serious trouble. If he was to get out alive, he had to take the initiative. Use the element of surprise. That was all he had. He knew with his dead leg, he couldn't outrun them. He winced and put a hand to his thigh and staggered a few steps which brought him close to Chang. 'My leg is killing me. Feels like I was hit with a sledgehammer. I think you might have burst something.' He watched as Chang preened a bit and glanced over at Tumulty, a smug look on his face. He didn't hesitate another second. He snapped out his arms and grabbed the small Chinaman and lifted him off the ground and threw him with as much force as he could muster into Tumulty. The two went clattering to the floor in a tangle of arms and legs. As they scrambled to get back onto their feet, he quickly shuffled in and delivered a sharp rabbit punch to Chang's neck which stretched him out on the floor again. He then quickly turned to Tumulty who was half way to his feet and without a moment's hesitation, he swung his dead leg and planted as hard a kick as he could right between the other man's legs. The almost animal howl which filled the room was music to his ears and he had to grin as Tumulty dropped the knife and grabbed at his crotch with both hands, his face contorted in pain. He grabbed the handcuffs he always carried from his pocket and quickly snapped one over one of Tumulty's wrists and then grabbed one of Chang's legs and snapped the other over the thin ankle. He picked up the knife and frisked Tumulty for the tape and then staggered back and sat down on the floor, his breath coming in ragged gasps from his exertions. The numb feeling in his leg was beginning to wear off and was being replaced by an ache which was nearly more acceptable than the dead feeling. His chest too still ached from the punch. He looked at the two who were on the floor a few feet away. Chang was still unconscious and Tumulty was still massaging his crotch with his free hand but his hate filled eyes were glaring over at Gerry. He saw the sudden switch in the eyes when their eyes met. A calculating look. 'What would it be worth to you to walk away?' Tumulty asked. He nodded to the tape now on the floor beside Gerry. 'To give that back and just pretend none of this happened. We could make it well worth your while. Spence would be very grateful.'

Gerry said nothing which prompted Tumulty to continue. 'What do you make a year? Forty, fifty thou? Wouldn't it be nice to get a few years wages all in one lump without any deductions? Your colleagues don't know you're here. If they did, they would have been here by now. You could just forget you were up here. I'd see to it that you're looked after. Think about it. Just imagine all you could do with that kind of money.'

Gerry rubbed his thigh which was now throbbing a bit more. He looked over to the table. Part of the equipment on it was a small television with a built in video player. He picked up the tape and lumbered to his feet. 'Let's see what we're bargaining for, shall we?' He hobbled over and turned on the small set and then inserted the tape into the opening under the screen. He sunk down into the chair and hit the play button.

The screen lit up and for a minute or so, was just snowy with the only sound an intermittent static. Then it crystallised into a wide angled scene of a room with Tumulty visible sitting in a chair directly facing the camera in front of a desk on which there were stacks of money. The back of a man's head was also visible and it didn't take a genius to know that this was Spence. The hidden camera was obviously positioned somewhere behind him so that it took in the whole room in front. He watched as the door opened and another man stuck his head in and said, 'They're here,' and then stood aside as five other men walked in. Four of them were well dressed and walked confidently into the room while the fifth was very dishevelled looking and looked somewhat cowered. He recognised him as the other man who had left the bar with Tumulty. He watched and listened.

'You okay, Cleary?' The question from Spence.

The dishevelled man nodded. 'Yeah. I'm okay.'

One of the other four spoke. 'I see you have our money.' A very strong American accent.

Spence waved a hand at the money piles. 'As agreed. I've taken my cut.'

'You got a bag?' The same American.

It was Tumulty who got up, picked up a bag from the floor beside his chair, walked over to the desk and scooped the money in. He then left it down in front of the American and went back and sat down.

One of the American's colleagues picked up the bag.

'I'm curious,' It was Spence again. 'You got rid of Breen's body up in the mountains. You're Yanks. Just arrived. How did you figure out going up there? You tell them, Cleary?'

This was answered by a quick shake of the head.

One of the four who hadn't spoken gave a little laugh. 'We had the services of a man who would know all about such places.' The other three with him laughed as well.

"Care to share the joke?' Spence asked.

'My name is Detective Hegarty. I'm a cop with the Las Vegas police department. I was sort of riding shot gun with the Irish cops on this one. It was one of them helped us out.'

'You got a name? Could be useful to me.'

It was the first man who spoke. 'You got your man back and your cut. We got our money. And you said you would give us the name of the man who killed Metcalfe. That was our deal. Nothing else.'

'I did, didn't I,' Spence said. 'It's McGivney. Fatty McGivney. Lives on Cheadle road in Rialto. Number 29.'

The American didn't acknowledge the information. He nodded to the other three and they all walked out without another word.

Gerry half nodded to himself. McGivney had probably told the others that Sabrina was dead. He continued to watch as the film rolled on.

'Thanks, boss. I was fully convinced they would top me too like they did Breen.' The man he now knew was Cleary.

'Breen was a stupid prick. He got what he deserved. You able to tell me anything?'

A sly smile. 'The Irish cop they said helped them. I know who he is.'

Gerry saw Spence sit up in his seat and he leaned forward closer to the screen himself.

'When we were driving up the mountains. Two of them were in the front and I was in the back. They'd coshed me but I wasn't out although I pretended I was.' Gerry saw him lick his lips. 'They were laughing and said Hegarty – the Yank cop – said Maguire nearly shit himself when Breen was shot.'

Spence's voice went up a couple of notches. 'Maguire? The superintendent in charge of the case? It was him? He was there when Breen got shot?'

Cleary nodded. 'Apparently himself and Hegarty were in another car across from the estate. I don't know how Maguire was tied in with them but he was.'

Spence started laughing. 'Superintendent Pat Maguire. Well, well, well.' The snowy screen returned and then went blank.

Gerry swung around in the chair and looked at Tumulty who was sitting up on the floor watching him. He gave him a sneering look. 'So you see, whatever your name is, even the high and mighty Superintendent Maguire has his secrets. There he is on national television, telling everybody what a great cop he is, but we know different, don't we? No reason why you can't have your secrets as well, and have a shitful of money with them.'

When Gerry didn't answer, he kept on. 'Come on, man. What do you say? It's the way of the world, isn't it? Look at that American cop, Hegarty. He's as crooked as a corkscrew. I'm not asking you to hide a murder like Maguire did.' His lip curled into a wider sneer. 'Or maybe two murders. He could have been involved with the Yanks in Fatty's death for all we know. Just give me the tape and walk away. Walk away a much richer man. And who's to know? We're certainly not going to say anything. Come on, man. Do yourself a big favour here.'

Gerry popped the tape from the television. He slowly stood up. His leg was a lot more painful now and he could see by the tightness of his trouser leg that it was swelling up. He limped over and looked at Tumulty. 'You're saying it was the Yanks killed McGivney?'

Tumulty made a face. 'They wanted a name. We gave them his. He winds up dead. You're the fucking policeman. You figure it out.'

Gerry wiped a hand across his face. He had thought the tape would just further implicate Spence and his lot, but Maguire! That was certainly a curve ball nobody had seen coming.

'Well? We got a deal?' Tumulty asked.

Gerry looked at him. Chang was beginning to stir and Tumulty shook him with his free hand. The Chinese man sat up and shook his head to shake off the stupor. He slowly rotated his neck a few times and then glared at Gerry with venomous eyes. Tumulty rattled the handcuff which tethered his wrist to Chang's ankle. 'Forget about it. Unless I carry you like a baby, you're not going to be able to move, never mind take him on.' He focussed on Gerry again. 'Come on, man. Take off the bracelets and let us walk with the tape. This is your big opportunity to get some serious money.'

'Do you think I came down in the last shower?' Gerry said. 'I let you walk with the tape and when I go looking for the money, you tell me to feck off. I'm not buying that can of smoke.'

Tumulty grinned. 'I can give it to you now. It's here. What about a hundred big ones with three zeros after them?'

Gerry felt his heart race. 'I prefer odd numbers. Make it a hundred and fifty.'

'All ye cops are grasping bastards, aren't ye?' Tumulty said in a sneering voice. 'Okay. A hundred and fifty thousand.' He rattled the handcuffs. 'Take this off and I'll get it for you.'

Gerry shook his head. 'You tell me where it is and I'll get it. Then you get to leave.'

Tumulty laughed. 'And you expect me to trust you?'

Gerry's leg was beginning to give him serious bother. His pants' leg was now like an elastic bandage around the thigh. All of a sudden, he was just so tired. He wanted to be back in Kilbracken. Sitting in Macker's having a pint and watching racing on the telly. He had done his bit and more. Let Costigan deal with all the rest. He looked at Tumulty. 'Your friend there has given me a serious pain in my leg and another one in my chest but you're giving me a king size pain in my arse as well as a headache. Now you either tell me where the money is or we just forget about the deal. Your call.'

Tumulty could see that the conversation had reached its end. He didn't really have any choice. He nodded over to a wall cabinet on one side of the room. 'Safe's behind that. It just swings out from the wall. Code is 6754. Each bundle has ten-thousand, so you take fifteen and no fucking more.'

Gerry didn't move but took his phone from his pocket. As he scrolled through the contacts list for Costigan's number, he glanced at Tumulty who was now looking at him with a wary look. 'Where I come from, we don't do deals with scumbags. I wouldn't touch your money with a barge pole.' He pressed the dial ikon. Costigan answered almost immediately.

'You find anything?' Gerry asked.

The disappointment was very evident in the other man's voice. 'No. Not a scrap of anything. And I don't think the audio tape on its own will be enough to nail the bugger.'

'You better comer here so,' Gerry said. 'Around the corner. Chinese medicine shop. Up the stairs.'

Costigan was there in a couple of minutes with two of the others and Gerry had the tape in the television and ready to play.

'Well? What have you got, Scobie? Please tell me you have something.'

Gerry just hit the play button and nodded to the screen. Nobody spoke as the tape played out and when it was finished, Gerry ejected it and handed it to Costigan who was grinning like a cat who had fallen into a vat full of cream. 'And there's a safe behind that wall cabinet. You might find some of the ransom money there.'

'Jesus, Scobie! We've got the bastard. Fair play to you, boyo.'

He looked again at Gerry, a concerned look replacing the wide grin. 'You all right?'

Gerry's leg was now pushing the pain barometer up into the red zone. He was hot and sweaty and if he didn't get some pain relief shortly, he knew he would start roaring. 'I need to get to a hospital.' He indicated his now massively swollen leg. 'Got Kung-Fu'ed on the leg by Bruce Lee's grandfather over there. Think he might have done some serious damage.'

Costigan whistled. 'Jesus! That leg's as fat as the mother-in-law's.' He gave an apologetic grin. 'Sorry, Scobie. Bad joke.' He turned to the other man. 'Eddie. You take Scobie to the Mater Hospital.'

Gerry allowed the other man to grip him around the shoulder and help him start down the stairs.

'And use the damn siren,' Costigan shouted after them.

Gerry gave a little snort. If his leg got any worse, he'd be making a lot more noise than any siren.'

*****

CHAPTER 60

Dooley – that was the name of the other cop helping him – linked him in through the doors of the emergency department and over to the reception counter. 'Got a man here needs immediate attention.'

The nurse looked up. 'He'll have to wait.' She waved a hand at the full room. 'As you can see, we're under a bit of pressure here.'

Gerry winced. His leg was just one big ball of intense pain which he thought might have plateaued at this stage but was continuing to find higher levels every few minutes. If someone offered to cut it off now, he would have gladly handed them Tumulty's flick knife which was still in his pocket. He was about to make his own plea but Dooley got in ahead of him. 'I can see you're busy, nurse. And I know it's the same every day for ye. But my colleague here is Detective Sergeant Scobie Tierney and he's been badly injured in a police operation in which he played...' He grinned at Gerry. '... a starring role. He's in an awful lot of pain so as a fellow public servant, I would be very grateful if you could have someone look at his injury straight away.'

The nurse came around from behind the counter and gave Gerry a quick once over. When she saw his leg, the trousers of which now looked so tight it could have been painted on, she clucked sympathetically. 'God yes. I can see he's in trouble.' She hailed a passing orderly who was walking by pushing an empty wheelchair. 'Tommy, where are you heading?'

'Up to St. Rita's ward. Bringing ...' He consulted the clipboard in his hand. '... bringing Mrs. Reilly down to Theatre 3 for a hip replacement op.' The nurse indicated Gerry. 'Take him down to 3. I'll ring ahead. This man needs immediate attention.'

Fifteen minutes later, Gerry was on the operating table, the warm glow from the anaesthetic spreading all over his body and bringing peaceful oblivion. He went with the darkness.

He opened his eyes and propped himself up on one elbow and looked around him. He was in one of the two corner beds next to the window in a room of six. There was a dull ache in his leg which – when he felt beneath the sheet and under the hospital gown – he discovered was heavily bandaged. He knew by the feel of it that the swelling was greatly reduced. He looked around the room. Lying on the bed directly opposite him was an old man who was pulling at his pyjama top while a young man in the green uniform of an orderly was restraining him as gently as he could. Gerry could hear the frustration in his voice. 'Now, Pat, I've told you. You can't be taking off your clothes.' He glanced over and caught Gerry's look and gave him a resigned smile and then turned back to the old man who now had a leg in the air and was pulling off his bottoms revealing a stick thin leg sticking out of an adult nappy. The orderly worked it back on and then quickly smoothed down the blanket and tucked it tightly in on one side and then walked quickly around and tucked in the other side, basically straitjacketing the man into the bed. He took up a small plastic dish and spoon from the tray to the side of the bed. 'Let's try another little bit of jelly, will we, Pat?'

Beside them, another old man lay asleep in his bed, the sheet tucked tightly up to his chin with only his head visible. His mouth was wide open and he was snoring, occasionally interrupting the sonorous sound with a high pitched snort.

Next to him, an overweight middle aged man in a very old fashioned wool dressing gown sat on the side of his bed, his feet in old slippers which matched the rusty brown colour of the dressing gown. He had a head of thick jet black hair which sat on his head like a tea cosy, indicating to Gerry that it had to be a wig, and a bad one at that. He had a paper open on the bed in front of him and all his concentration was focussed on it through heavy black rimmed glasses which rested on the tip of his nose. When he looked up and their eyes met, Gerry smiled over and said hello but the other man ignored the greeting and went back to his paper. 'Feck you, scrawhead' Gerry said to himself.

He turned to his own side of the room. The screen was around the bed beside him and this blocked off his line of vision to the third bed. He lay back and closed his eyes. With a bit of luck he would be able to get out later.

He opened his eyes when he heard his name being called and was surprised to find that he had dozed off. The screen around the bed beside him was pulled back and a young lad of about eighteen or nineteen was sitting up in the bed, his eyes on the television up over the door, earphones over his head. A quick glance at the screen showed he was watching a soccer match. The bed next to him was empty but the blanket was pulled back and the sheet was crumpled so it had obviously been recently vacated.

A nurse and a tall black doctor stood at the end of his bed.

'How are you feeling, Mr. Tierney?' the doctor asked in very refined, almost gentrified tone.

'Never better,' Gerry said with a grin. 'Feel as if I could give your man Bolt a run for his money over the hundred metres.'

The doctor laughed. 'Well I think you would need a ninety nine metre head start.' His face became more serious. 'You've had a serious injury to your leg. A ruptured muscle which was bleeding. And because it was an internal injury, the blood had nowhere to go, hence the massive swelling. I had to aspirate your thigh to release the blood. You had a considerable amount of pain, I would imagine.'

'You can sing it,' Gerry said. 'Felt as if it was about to explode any minute.'

'You sustained it in the course of your work, I believe? And I noticed a lot of other old and not so old injuries. Your work must be extremely dangerous or else you are very prone to misfortune, Mr. Tierney.'

Gerry grinned. This doctor must have the same hymn sheet as Pyne. 'I suppose the answer is sometimes and yes, doc.'

'Well it took a serious weapon to inflict that injury. What was it, an iron bar or something like that?'

'It was a thing called a Chinese cos,' Gerry said, remembering the Irish word for leg from his schooldays. He kept a straight face as the doctor's registered puzzlement. 'A Chinese cos!' He pronounced it cuss. 'Can't say I've ever heard of that. What is it like?'

How did he answer that one and still keep a straight face? 'It's about two feet long with a swivel type head which has five little stubs at the end with nails stuck to them.'

The doctor's eyes widened. 'My God! That sounds like a vicious weapon. You are lucky the nails obviously missed you as the skin wasn't broken. That would have been a lot more serious. Yes, a lot more serious. Very lucky indeed. And it is called a Chinese cos? I will have to google that.'

Gerry was beginning to feel guilty. And he could see by the look on the nurse's face that she knew he was taking the piss. It was she who spoke. 'When do you think we can let the brave detective sergeant go home, doctor?'

'I see no reason why he cannot go home tomorrow. He will be on crutches for a couple of weeks but other than that, there is no real need to keep him in.' He nodded to Gerry. 'We will organise the crutches for you but if you want to make arrangements for someone to collect you, tell them you will be free around twelve o'clock. I probably will not see you in the morning, Mr. Tierney, so I will say goodbye now. Nurse Dillon here will organise some pain killers for you in case you need them and maybe, will get the crutches for you now. You might need a few training runs before leaving.'

'Thanks, doc,' Gerry said.

'Goodbye, Mr. Tierney.' He strode out of the ward.

The nurse looked at Gerry, a smile on her face. 'I'll go and get you the crutches. I'm sure you would like to be using your own two Irish coses as soon as possible.' She giggled. 'For walking, that is.'

Gerry gave her a sheepish look. 'Ah God, I was only having a bit of a laugh. I didn't intend any offence to the good doctor. And it wasn't really a lie anyways. It was a Chinese foot that fecked up me leg.'

'He will google it, you know.'

'Ah feck! Let's just hope I'm gone home before he does.'

She laughed again. 'I better get you those crutches so. Let you have a few practice runs up and down the corridor before we cut you loose. How are you for pain relief? Do you need any?'

He looked at her name badge and then shook his head. 'No, Nurse Laura Dillon, I'm fine. It's not really pain as such. More just a dull throb, but it's nothing really.'

'Okay. I'll be back shortly.'

When she had left, the young lad next to him took off his earphones. Gerry could hear the muted match commentary coming from them. 'Hello. My name is Stevie.' He extended his hand. Gerry shook it. 'How are you, Stevie. My name is Gerry but most people call me Scobie.'

The young lad gave him a shy smile. 'You're a policeman.'

'So they tell me,' Gerry said. 'Now what's a fine young lad like yourself doing in here?'

'Burst appendix. But I'm fine now. Going home tomorrow.'

'That's good,' Gerry said.

They both looked as a man came in and climbed into the empty bed. He was probably in his mid-twenties but was emaciated looking, his face almost skeletal. He didn't say a word or even look in their direction, just climbed into the bed and pulled the blanket up over him and turned his back to them.

'Anorexic,' the young lad whispered.

Gerry shook his head. 'That's a bummer. Just can't understand how people don't want to eat.'

The nurse walked in carrying a pair of crutches and rested them at the head of Gerry's bed. 'There you go, detective sergeant. Take your time on these but be sure you don't put weight on that leg of yours.'

Gerry grinned at her. 'Thanks, Nurse Dillon. I'll try not to get a speeding ticket.'

She laughed and then looked around the room. 'Anything I can do for anybody else before I go?' The only response she got was from the young lad who smiled at her and said he was fine. 'I'll say goodnight so,' she said and left.

Gerry swung his legs out of the bed and grabbed the crutches. 'Time to give these yokes a test drive,' he said to his young neighbour who grinned at him before putting the headphones back on and returning to the television.

Gerry got his balance and with his injured leg bent slightly, made his way out of the ward. He navigated the long corridor down to the reception area and was just easing himself into one of the easy chairs when he saw Costigan coming through the main door. The chief superintendent spotted him immediately and came over and sat down next to him. 'Good to see you up and about, Scobie. How's the leg?'

'Arra it's grand,' Gerry said. 'Getting out in the morning. How did you get on?'

The smile was almost beatific. 'Couldn't have gone better and that's thanks to you. We have the bastard good and tight this time. Apart from the large amount of money and details of various bank accounts we found in the safe, there was a ledger listing a whole heap of drug transactions. We have the names of over half the drug pushers in Dublin now. The only way he's coming out of Mountjoy now is in a box. Apart from the recording and the cctv tape, the others are all now tripping over themselves to blame the whole thing on Spence. We owe you big time on this, Scobie. Only for you we would never have come across that Chinese shop.'

'What about Maguire?'

Costigan shifted in his seat. 'Can't help feeling sorry for him. Okay, I know he fucked up by going on a solo run with the Yanks – he should have called it in – but I think he just got caught up in a series of events over which he had no control. I spoke to the commissioner. Maguire's going to retire immediately. We think that's enough.'

'And the American cop and his buddies?'

Costigan made a face. 'All we can do there is tell the authorities over there. And I honestly don't think they'll be able to do anything.' He stood up. 'Anyways – we've had our own result and...' He stood up and stuck out his hand. '...I've said, we couldn't have done it without you so thanks again.'

Gerry shook the hand. 'Glad to have been of help.' He took up the crutches and eased himself up. 'Better get back. They're letting me out at twelve tomorrow. Do you think one of your lads could drive me down to Kilbracken?'

'No problem. Eddie will be here at twelve. He'll drive you down in your car and get the train back. Right. Best go. Thanks again, Scobie.'

Gerry watched him stride off and then slowly made his way back to the ward. The room was quiet with the television turned off. Stevie sat up in his bed fiddling with the earphones.

'Your match over?' Gerry asked as he got into his own bed.

The young lad shook his head. 'No. Still ten minutes left but ... ' He nodded to the bed in the opposite corner. '...he told me to turn it off. Said the glare was annoying him.'

Gerry looked over. 'Scrawhead' was lying back in his bed, his hands behind his head, his eyes open, a sour look on his face.

Gerry turned to the young lad. 'Put it back on if you want. Don't mind him.'

The young lad threw a nervous look over at the man across the room and then looked at Gerry. 'Ah no. It's okay. Sure it was nearly over anyways. I think I might get some sleep. Goodnight.'

'Goodnight, Stevie,' Gerry said. He lay back himself and began to go back through all of the events since word of Sabrina's kidnapping had filtered through. It had certainly been some roller coaster of a ride. He was unaware of the time passing as he relived his time with Faye, his time in the cellar with Sabrina and then the events of the last few days and when he looked at his watch, he was surprised to see that it was well after midnight. He glanced around the quiet room. All other five were sleeping. He looked over to Scrawhead's bed and smiled when he saw the hairpiece resting on the bedside locker along with the heavy glasses. He quietly got out of bed and grabbed the crutches.

*****

CHAPTER 61

He woke at seven when a new nurse came into the room. He watched as she quickly checked the young anorexic and the old man, both of whom were still sleeping. She then went down to Pat the stripper who was just waking up and already starting to try and get his pyjama top off. She pressed the call button beside his bed and then put a restraining hand on his arm. 'Now, Pat, you can't be taking off your clothes. We've told you that.' A man in the green uniform of an orderly came in and went over to help her and between them, they got the old man settled in the bed. The orderly sat in the chair beside him.

The nurse came over to Gerry. 'You're leaving us today I believe, Mr. Tierney.' She looked at the young lad in the bed beside him who was also awake. 'And you too, Stevie. You're going home today as well, aren't you?'

Stevie gave her a big smile. 'Yes, nurse.'

She fluffed up Gerry's pillow behind him and then went over and did the same to Stevie's. 'And where is home?'

'Lucan,' Stevie said.

'Ah that's grand. You haven't far to go so. How about you, Mr. Tierney? Where's home for you?'

Kilbracken. It's in Kilkenny,' Gerry answered.

'Nurse! Nurse!' The call came from Scrawhead's bed.

She went over. 'Yes, Mr. Guthrie? What is it?'

Gerry and Stevie watched as the big man whispered something they couldn't hear to the nurse.

'Are you sure?' the nurse said. 'You didn't put it in your locker or maybe leave it in the bathroom?'

There was a rigorous shake of the bald head. 'No. I left it on the locker here beside me. I do that every night. Someone has taken it.'

The nurse looked over at Gerry and Stevie who, apart from Pat the stripper, were the only patients awake. 'Mr. Guthrie is missing a personal item. You didn't see anybody come in here during the night?'

They both shook their heads. 'What's he missing?' Gerry asked.

The nurse pursed her lips to stop herself from smiling. She cleared her throat. 'His.... emm ...hairpiece.'

Gerry tried to keep the deadpan look on his face. 'Somebody

lifted his hairpiece?' He shook his head in disbelief. 'God, that's terrible. What's the world coming to when they'll even take the hair off your head!' He gave the nurse a small smile. 'Metaphorically speaking of course. I don't think someone is doing a Geronimo and going around the wards scalping people.'

Beside him, Stevie sniggered which earned him a thunderous look from Guthrie. 'It's all a big joke to you two, isn't it? Wouldn't surprise me if it was one of you took it.' He looked at the nurse. 'I think we should check their lockers.'

The nurse gave him a stern look. 'No, Mr. Guthrie. We cannot go searching other people's lockers.'

Gerry looked at Stevie. 'I've no problem having my locker searched, have you?'

The young lad shook his head. 'Wouldn't bother me. I know I didn't take it. Why would I do that?'

'There'll be no searching of lockers,' the nurse said. 'I'll check with the reception desk. See if anything was handed in there.' She looked to the door as a woman came in wheeling a breakfast trolley. She reached down and shook the man in the middle bed. 'Mr. Cummins. Breakfast is here.' When the man had opened his eyes and began to pull himself up into a sitting position, she crossed over to the opposite side where the anorexic was sleeping. 'Mr. Reilly. Mr. Reilly. Time for breakfast.' The only response she got was a dismissive wave of a hand attached to a skeletal arm. Gerry had seen more flesh on a chicken wing. The nurse persisted. 'Come on now, Mr. Reilly. You know what the doctor said. You have to try and eat.'

'Don't want anything,' the voice low and sullen.

Gerry got his crutches and made his way over. 'Hi, Mr. Reilly. My name is Gerry Tierney. I'm your neighbour from one bed up. The nurse here probably isn't allowed tell you this and maybe she doesn't know but I think you should know. I heard your doctor discussing you with one of his colleagues while you were asleep, and they were making arrangements for you to be fitted with a nasal feeding tube. Now I don't know about you, but I had one of them once and I wouldn't wish the experience on my worst enemy. They're a bitch to get in and are as uncomfortable as hell. All you want to do the whole time is pull it out and that hurts like hell as well but when you do – and I guarantee you will – they stick it straight back in. And that's even worse than the first time because your nose is a lot more sensitive. And you never get used to it. It's just sheer discomfort and soreness the whole time. If you want my advice, I'd settle for a few spoonfuls of porridge and a bit of toast a hell of a lot quicker than a big lump of plastic up my snout and down into my stomach. But it's entirely up to you. Just thought you should know.' He walked back and sat down on his bed and pulled in the trolley on which his own breakfast tray now sat. He lifted the cover off the plate and grinned when he saw the three rashers, two sausages, two eggs, two pieces of tomato and the white and black pudding discs. His flattering of the young girl who had taken the orders last night had certainly worked. He was hungry enough to eat a farmer's arse through a ditch. He quickly buttered one of the slices of toast, poured out a cup of tea and began eating. As he chewed on a melange of toast, egg, sausage and pudding, he covertly looked over at Reilly and allowed himself a small grin when he saw the nurse spooning some porridge into his mouth and he swallowing it. Beside him, Stevie stopped midway through his scrambled egg and toast and grinned over at him. 'You should take up motivational speaking, Scobie.'

Gerry grinned himself. 'I don't think it was motivation. More like frightening the shite out of him.'

They finished their breakfasts without any further conversation and as he pushed the trolley away from him, the nurse came over. 'Thank you, Mr. Tierney. That's the first bit of food we have managed to get him to eat in two days.' She gave a little laugh. 'Unorthodox but highly effective. What were the circumstances behind your own nasal tube experience? Did you have stomach problems or what?'

He gave her a mischievous smile. 'Never had anything up me nose except me finger. Except for the time when I was a nipper and pushed a pea up it. The mother had to use a tweezers to get it out. But other than that – no – never.'

'So, what you told Mr. Reilly was a pack of lies?'

'Guilty as charged,' he said.

She gave him a little laugh. 'Well in this instance, we forgive you your porkies. Now I better go, see if I can find Mr. Guthrie's crowning glory. But where to start looking, I haven't a clue. Who the hell want a hairpiece of all things? You're a policeman. What do you think?'

Gerry looked at her name badge. 'Well. Nurse White, in my humble opinion, I would say that someone took it as a joke or just to get back at Mr. Guthrie.' He glanced over to where the other man was lying on his bed. 'He is a bit of an obnoxious prick, if you'll pardon my choice of words. How long has he been in here?'

The nurse glanced over at the subject of their low conversation.

'Must be going on two weeks now. Came in complaining of pains in his chest and stomach. He's had all sorts of tests but so far, we haven't found anything wrong with him'.

'I'd say there's a lot of people whose noses he's gotten up in those two weeks.' He laughed. 'Feckin' up noses again! Although I'd say if it was a choice between him getting up your nose or having a nasal tube, most people would opt for the tube.'

She smiled. 'Well I better go and try and track down his missing wig or he'll be threatening all sorts of things on us. Thanks again for your help with Mr. Reilly.'

She turned to leave but Gerry stopped her. 'Might I make a suggestion, Nurse White?' He didn't wait for her to answer. 'If I were looking for a missing hairpiece, I'd be inclined to have a look in the children's play room down at the end of the corridor.'

She gave him a long look, a half smile twitching her lips. 'Is that right, Mr. Tierney? This would be your suggestion based on your long experience as a police officer and not on anything else? Is that right?'

Gerry grinned. 'Well let's just say, I have a gut feeling about things.'

She did smile fully this time. 'Thank you again, Mr. Tierney. I will certainly follow your gut feeling.'

She turned and left. Stevie looked over at Gerry. 'You took it, didn't you? You as much as admitted it to her.'

Gerry shrugged his shoulders. 'Maybe I did, maybe I didn't. The miserable bugger should have let you watch the end of the match. He's just a cantankerous auld shite.' He waved over to the man who had just come in, a bundle of newspapers under his arm. 'Over here. I'll take the Indo.'

The man came over and extracted a copy of the Irish Independent from the bundle and handed it to him. Gerry took a five euro note and handed it to him. 'Give Stevie here a Daily Mirror. I know he'll only want the soccer pages and won't even bother his arse looking at page three. Isn't that right, Stevie?'

The young lad grinned. 'Well sure if you're buying me the paper, Scobie, sure it would be bad manners not to look at it all the pages, wouldn't it?'

Gerry waved a dismissive hand when the man went to give him change. 'You're all right.'

'Thanks, mate,' the man said and then, after looking around to see if anybody else was looking for a paper, hefted the bundle under his arm and left.

Nurse White came in a few minutes later, the hairpiece in her hand. She walked over and put it down on Guthrie's locker. He grabbed it immediately. 'Where did you find it?' he asked as he settled it on his head.

She shook her head in puzzlement. 'It was down in the children's playroom. On top of a balloon on which somebody had drawn a funny face.'

Guthrie stared at her. 'And how the hell did it get down there? Who took it? I want to know.'

'I don't know, Mr. Guthrie,' she said. 'But you have it back now so that's the important thing. Now if you will excuse me, I have things to do.' She turned away before he could speak and came over to Gerry. 'You've everything you need now for leaving, Mr. Tierney? Enough painkillers and your crutches.' Her voice dropped to a whisper. 'The kids in the playroom really enjoyed their hairy headed visitor.'

Gerry grinned. 'Well sure wasn't it the same thing for the hairpiece there as here. It was still sitting on top of a windbag. No difference there.'

She laughed. 'Go on. I'll leave you to get dressed. It's been a pleasure, detective sergeant. Mind yourself and mind that leg of yours.'

He shook her hand. 'Thanks, Nurse White. And say thanks to the doc and Nurse Dillon for me.'

'I will.' She turned to Stevie. 'You're not leaving until this evening, I believe, Stevie. Doc wants to give you the once over before you go. I'll see you later on.'

She looked over at the orderly who was still sitting beside the old man's bed. 'I'll get someone to relieve you shortly.'

She got a very grateful look in reply. With a final look around the room, she left.

Gerry got up and pulled the curtains around his bed. He dressed as quickly as he could and then pulled them back again. He didn't have anything to pack as he had come in with only the clothes he was wearing. Everything else he had gotten from the hospital including a packet of disposable razors, shaving cream, toothbrush and toothpaste. These he left on the locker. He planned to wait for Eddie Dooley down in the main reception area. He had enough of Guthrie glaring over at him which he had been doing since the nurse left. He grabbed the crutches. 'Well, Stevie boy, time to rock and roll.' He extended his hand. 'It was nice to meet you. If you're ever down Kilkenny way, pop into Kilbracken and say hello.'

The young lad warmly shook his hand. 'Pleasure was all mine, Scobie.'

Gerry started for the door but stopped when Guthrie stepped out in front of him, blocking his way. He stuck out his chest in a belligerent manner. 'It was you, wasn't it? You took my hairpiece. Having a sick joke at my expense.'

'You're in my way, Guthrie,' Gerry said.

The big man sneered. 'So? I'll move when I get an apology.'

Gerry let out a long heavy sigh. He lowered his voice so that only the man in front could hear him. 'You're just a big bullyboy, Guthrie. Eighteen stone of pure sour bile. I've met a lot of your type before.' He inched forward until their noses were almost touching. 'Now I'm going to count to three and if you don't shift your fat arse out of my way, I'm going to take one of these crutches and ram it so far up your arse, you'll be able to take off the rubber tip with your teeth.'

Guthrie glared at him but his demeanour was totally different now. He stood his ground for a few seconds but when Gerry started to count, he stepped aside. 'Fuck you.' He turned around and flung himself into the easy chair beside his bed.

Gerry turned and waved to Stevie. 'See you, Stevie.'

'See you, Scobie.'

*****

CHAPTER 62

'Thanks for driving me down, Eddie,' Gerry said. 'The train should be along shortly.'

'No problem,' Eddie Dooley replied. 'Hope the old leg gets better soon. And thanks for all your help in nailing Spence. I've never seen the guvnor as happy.'

He grinned. 'You do know he'll probably take all the credit. You might get a passing mention if you're lucky.'

'Doesn't bother me,' Gerry said. 'I'm well used to that. Just glad everything worked out the way it did.'

'Right. I better get a ticket. I'm looking forward to this train ride. I haven't been on a train since I was a nipper in short pants.'

They shook hands and Eddie stood propped on his crutches as the other man went through the sliding door and into the station. When the door had slid shut, he started back up the street. Dooley had parked his car at the flat and they had walked the two hundred metres to the station. He was just approaching his door when Mr. Pyne came out of Miss Timoney's shop. He looked deliberately at the crutches. 'I see you've been in the wars again, detective sergeant. What is it this time?'

'Ruptured muscle,' Gerry answered, hoping the short answer would satisfy the surgeon. He was mistaken.

'And how did that happen?'

'Got a kick from a Kung Fu fighter.' He wasn't going to tell him it was an eighty year old man.

'And pray what were you doing fighting …what did you call him … a Kung Fu fighter?'

'It was all in the line of duty,' Gerry said. 'I was assisting some Dublin colleagues in apprehending a few nasty types.'

'I see. And where did you get your leg looked after?'

'The Mater hospital.'

The surgeon sniffed. 'Not too bad I suppose. Who did it?'

Gerry tried to hide his exasperation. He hadn't expected a long question and answer session. 'It was a Doctor Mabuto. Something like that anyways.'

Pyne sniffed again. 'Never heard of him. Still – sure all they had to do was aspirate it. Not what you would call major surgery, was it?'

'No,' Gerry said. 'Just stick a needle in it a few times to let the blood out.'

'Quite. Well I won't detain you any longer, detective sergeant. You should put that leg up and rest it. Good evening.'

'See you, doc.'

He rooted in his pocket for his keys and then groaned as Miss Timoney came out of the shop. He was gasping for a pint but he wanted a shower and a change of clothes first. Like Pyne, she too focussed first on the crutches. 'And what have you done to yourself this time, detective sergeant?'

Gerry was fecked if he was going to stand around for another twenty questions. He stuck the key in the door. 'Just a sprain. Right as rain in a day or two.'

'Oh. I see.' She sounded somewhat disappointed. 'A package arrived for you. I have it in the shop.'

Gerry stood waiting as she went back in and emerged a minute later with a small brown parcel. She made a show of studying it. 'From Vatican City, I see.'

She held it out, her eyes looking for more information.

His leg was beginning to throb a bit and his hands were sore from the crutches. He took the parcel from her. 'Thanks. Now I better get in. The old ankle is beginning to give me a bit of gyp.' He didn't give her a chance to say anything else, turning the key and pushing open the door. He could see by the look on her face that she was annoyed. And if he left her annoyed, she would be like a wasp for a good while. 'It's just a book from Monsignor Cunningham. A friend asked me to get it.'

The answer seemed to satisfy her. 'You better rest that ankle, detective sergeant.' She walked back into the shop.

Gerry picked up the small bit of mail from the floor and made his way upstairs to the flat. He flicked through the envelopes. Apart from an electricity bill and a circular from his union, the rest was all junk. He went into the bedroom and stripped and then went out to the kitchen and got the roll of cling film from the drawer and wrapped a few strands around the dressing on his thigh. Just as they had told him to do in the Mater. He grinned. The makers hadn't envisaged this use when they invented it.

Half an hour later, he was showered, freshly shaven and kitted out in a clean pair of jeans, t-shirt and casual jacket. He stuck his wallet into his jean's pocket and then grabbed the crutches and headed down the stairs. The shower had freshened him up no end and he was feeling pretty damn good in himself. He deserved a few pints. No – he deserved a good few pints. But first he had to call into the station and fill in Flann and the rest. He hadn't spoken to any of them since going up to Dublin. He didn't know if Doyle would be there and he didn't care. He had a cert from the hospital covering him for two weeks so he didn't have to stay put and listen to any of his crap. If he started mouthing off, he'd just plonk the cert down in front of him and walk out.

Elsie Masterson, Flann, Smithy and big Pat Hartigan were in the main office when he walked in.

'Well Holy God! If it isn't Long John Silver himself,' Hartigan said. 'Where's your parrot?'

'Feck off, ya big bollocks ya,' Gerry said good naturedly. 'Or I'll give you a crutch in the crotch.'

They all gathered around him. 'What the hell happened in Dublin?' Flann asked.

He sat down on a chair and rested the crutches between his legs. They listened without interruption as he filled them in on all that had happened, the interview with Brennan in Mountjoy, the raid on Spence's pub by Costigan and the serious crime team, his discovery of the Chinese shop, the discovery of the tape, the money and the ledgers.

Smithy whistled. 'Spence! I know that animal. They were even trying to nail him when I was stationed in Dublin and that wasn't today or yesterday.'

'Was Maguire's team and Doyle with ye on the raid?' Elsie Masterson asked.

Gerry shook his head. 'No. And Maguire's not in the force any longer either.'

Flann's eyes widened. 'What the hell do you mean, Scobie? What happened?'

Gerry quickly told them about how the superintendent got caught up with the suspected mafia guys and the crooked cop from the States and the killing of Breen and McGivney. 'He was just a stupid bollocks who let his quest for glory put him in a very compromised position. The poor schmuck didn't know his Yankee friends were as crooked as a horseshoe and when he did find out when they killed Breen, he was rightly caught. The heads up in the park accepted his explanation that he hadn't known they were crooked and that when he did find out, he was powerless to do anything. But it was only on the basis that he retired immediately. I don't know about Doyle. Didn't see him at all. Is he back?'

'No, thank God,' Flann said. 'We haven't seen him since he appeared on the telly at the press conference. He rang down two days ago and said he wouldn't be back for a few days. I'd say after hearing all that, he's probably afraid to show his face back here.' He nodded to Gerry's legs. 'So? What gives with the crutches? You fall off a high stool up there or what?'

Gerry grinned. 'Arra that's a long story, Flann. And one for over a few pints. And that's just what I'm heading for now. Anybody interested?'

Flann looked at his watch. 'Just about quitting time for me. I'll just give the queen bee a ring and tell her.' He walked over to his desk.

Gerry looked at the other three. 'Any of you interested?'

'I'm on until eight,' Smithy said. 'Might stick my head in then if you're still there.'

Masterson shook her head. 'No can do this evening, Scobie. Mrs. Dempsey can't sit with dad tonight so that's me tied up.'

'How's he doing?' Gerry asked.

'He's happy, Scobie. Happy in his own little world.' Her eyes glistened a bit. 'The Alzheimer's is progressing fairly quickly though. He doesn't even know who I am most of the time now.'

'I'm sorry to hear that, Elsie. Must be tough.'

She shrugged a shoulder. 'It is what it is, Scobie. And once he's not suffering – well that means a lot.' She looked to change the subject. 'How about you, Pat? You going with them?'

The big man made a face and shook his head. 'I am in me arse. Last time I went drinking with them two, I fell over the wall when I got home. And of course. it just had to be where all the wife's prize fucking tulips were growing. I made shite of the lot of them. She didn't talk to me for a week and for a week after that, she just kept going on and on about it like a broken record. She was like a bad case of tinnitus. I'm not risking that again.'

Flann came back shucking on his coat. 'Right. Mackers it is. Who've we got?'

'Just you and me, amigo,' Gerry said getting to his feet. 'Smithy might join us when he's finished.'

Flann gave him a disbelieving look. 'You can feck off if you think

I'm staying drinking until after eight.'

Pat Hartigan snorted. 'The little missus put you on the clock, Flann?'

Flann grinned. 'Just as well too. If I stayed drinking for that length with hollow legs here, I'd need his fecking crutches to get home.'

Ten minutes later, they walked through the door of McCluskey's.

The bar was fairly busy with a group of about twenty people of varying ages down the far end, clustered around a few of the tables which had been pushed together. A few balloons with 'Happy Retirement' across them floated above their heads and the tables were covered with glasses and bottles. Nearer to the door, Councillor Andy Horan sat with three other men, their heads close together in muted conversation. Old Charlie Mulqueen was in his usual place, the small table under the window which was recognised by all the locals as his sole preserve. It was he who spoke when they came in. 'Well if it isn't me two favourite peelers. Why don't you join me, lads?'

Flann looked at Gerry. 'What do you think, Scobie? Should we lower our standards and join this old reprobate?'

Gerry grinned as he left the crutches against the wall and swung over an easy chair to the table and eased himself into it. 'Might as well. At least this way we can strangle the little bollocks when he starts his usual singing.'

Flann pulled in another chair. 'I'll get the drinks.' He looked at the old man's near empty glass. 'And I suppose you wouldn't say no to another little Jemmy, would you, Charlie?'

The old man's face creased into a wide smile. 'You're right there, Flann. And I wouldn't say no to a large one either.'

Flann laughed and then walked over to the bar.

'So, Scobie?' Mulqueen said. 'What gives with the two sticks?'

'That's what I want to know too,' Flann said as he came back and sat down. 'Macker will drop over the drinks.'

Gerry was just about to answer when Horan and his three companions approached their table heading for the door. The councillor stopped. 'How are we today, gentlemen?' The other three waited at the door.

Charlie Mulqueen lifted his glass and finished off the small drop of whiskey. 'Well I can't speak for Scobie or Flann here but I'm the same today as I was yesterday and I was the same yesterday as I was the day before that. How about yourself, councillor? Anything new?'

The councillor gave him an expansive smile. 'Well now that you ask, Mr. Mulqueen, there is. I'm here with these three gentlemen who are from Finland. They are hoping to open up a new factory here to make men's clothing.'

'Hoping or going to?' the old man asked.

Horan's smile faded a bit. 'Well there's still a lot of negotiation to be done but I'm hopeful. Wouldn't it be grand if we could all walk down the street in new suits with the label 'Made in Kilbracken' on them? Well – mustn't keep my guests waiting. We're heading over to the Cloisters to meet up with the council chairman and some men from the IDA. I'll see you, gentlemen.'

McCluskey came over with the drinks as they went out the door. He left them down in front of them. 'Here ye go, lads. I'm afraid I can't tell ye that Councillor Horan paid for them.'

Mulqueen cackled. 'Sure he only puts his hand in his pocket for one thing and it isn't to get money out. I wonder if them fellas do start makin' suits and things here, will all the trousers have a big hole in one pocket?'

Gerry laughed. 'Only if they hire Handy Andy as their designer.'

McCluskey nodded to the crutches against the wall. 'What happened you, Scobie?'

'We're all waiting to hear that,' Flann said.

Gerry took a deep pull from his pint and licked the cream from his lips. 'Aaagh. I needed that.' He took another deep slug and then sat back. 'Well it was like this, lads. Ye've heard of Bruce Lee, haven't ye?'

'Yeah,' Flann said. 'The martial arts fella. Enter the Dragon. Died young.'

Gerry took another pull from his pint. 'Well, lads. I met his grandfather.'

*****

CHAPTER 63

Gerry blearily opened his eyes as his mobile rang and vibrated on the locker beside him. He groaned as a bolt of pain shot though his head. He groped for the phone and looked at the screen. Flann calling. He swiped his finger across. 'Feck sake, Flann! What the hell are you calling me for at this hour?'

'What d'ya mean at this hour? It's after one o'clock in the day. What the hell time did you leave Mackers at? Smithy told me he left at half ten and you were still knocking back the Jemmies.'

Gerry pulled himself up and lay back against the headboard. He hadn't a clue what time he had left or how he had gotten home. 'I left soon after Smithy,' he lied. 'Now – what's so urgent that you have to ring a man out on sick leave?'

Flann sniggered. 'I'd say you're sick all right but it's not from the kick you got from the old Chinaman. You had six pints while I was there and Smithy said you had another three with him before switching to Jemmies. I'd say you're as sick as a small hospital.' He laughed again. 'And I still can't believe a little oriental octogenarian put you on crutches.'

Gerry dragged his tongue across his teeth to try and clear the dry scum. His mouth felt like a bricklayer's armpit after a day hefting blocks up and down a ladder. 'Well are you going to tell me why you rang or am I supposed to guess?'

'Doyle arrived back this morning. Asked if you were in. I told him you were on sick leave.'

Gerry sat up a bit straighter. 'Did he ask what was wrong with me?'

'No. He knew. Apparently, your friend Costigan filled him in as a matter of courtesy seeing as he's acting superintendent here. He nearly choked on it but he said you had been a big help to the Dublin crowd.'

Gerry had to grin. 'I'd say that nearly killed him all right. Did he mention his buddy Maguire?'

'Yeah. Said he had to retire for health reasons. But that's not why I'm ringing. He's gone again. Cleared out his desk and told me he was being re-assigned and that I was in charge until further notice. Now what do you make of that?'

'Probably because he hitched his wagon to Maguire's train and now he's paying the price for that association.' He laughed despite his throbbing head. 'Still, as they say, behind every cloud etcetera. He was a right arse licker. I'm not crying after him, are you?'

'Course I am. Tears are runnin' down me legs. Anyways – thought I'd let you know.'

'Thanks, Flann. I might as well get up now seeing as you've woken me from my beauty sleep. Fancy meeting up later? Baptise your temporary elevation until they find another gobshite to foist on us.'

'No can do I'm afraid. The wife's night for her drama group so I'm babysitting.'

'Fair enough,' Gerry said. 'I'll catch you later.'

He swung his legs out of the bed and then closed his eyes and sat for a minute when a sudden dizziness hit him. It passed nearly as quickly as it had come. He gingerly got to his feet and then stood swaying as another wave hit him but it too passed quickly. He glanced around the bedroom. His shirt was in a ball on the floor but there was no sign of his jeans anywhere in the room. He opened the door into the living room. His jacket was thrown across the small glass topped table and he could see one shoe up against one wall and the other under a chair along with his balled up socks but there was still no sign of his jeans. What the hell had he done with them? And his wallet was in one of the pockets! He always carried it in his trousers pocket. He grabbed the jacket and quickly went through the pockets. His search yielded his keys, some loose change and a badly crumpled fiver. But no wallet. He limped over to the couch and pulled off the cushions but the only thing under them was a half-eaten ham sandwich which was flecked with mould and as hard as cardboard. He picked it up and walked over to the small kitchen area and binned it. And then something else struck him. There was no sign of his crutches. He hobbled back to the couch and sat down. He tried to piece together the previous night. He remembered drinking with Flann and then with Smithy after Flann had left. He remembered Smithy leaving and he vaguely remembered singing something. Singing with old Charlie Mulqueen who was probably as drunk as he was. Sweet Sixteen – that was it. Finbarr Fury's hit. One of his all-time favourites. No wonder his throat was sore. If Fury had heard the mangling the two of them had done on it, he would have battered them with his banjo. After that – it was all a blank. He slowly got up and went into the bathroom and turned on the shower. He pulled down his boxers and kicked them off and then stood for a full ten minutes under the cascading hot water until he felt his skin begin to shrivel. Only then did he turn off the water and step out. He hadn't even covered the bandage which was now sodden and wrinkled. He got a finger in under it and worked it down his leg and over his foot and threw it into the small bin. He examined his thigh. There was still a bit of light bruising and you could still see the five little red dots where the needle had been inserted but other than that, it looked fairly normal with the swelling completely gone. He grabbed a towel and dried himself and then went back into the bedroom and put on fresh clothes, his mind still trying to figure out the mystery of his missing jeans and crutches. Not to mention his wallet. That contained his police identity card, credit cards, blood donor's card, driving licence and if he remembered correctly, about two hundred euro, less of course, whatever he had spent in McCluskey's. He knew that eight out of ten people who found it would return it intact – there was enough identity stuff in it – but with his luck, it would probably be found by one of the town's toerags and if that was the case, he could whistle Dixie until the cows came home if he thought he would see it again. His doorbell rang.

Freda Bannon stood on the step, his crutches in one hand, his jeans – looking pristine and neatly pressed – folded over her arm. She grinned at him. 'How's the head, Scobie? I'd say you've a whole clatter of lambeg drums hammerin' away in there.' She shook her head. 'You were fuller than a bingo bus last night in McCluskey's. I've never seen anybody as pissed.'

He smiled sheepishly. 'Night's a bit of a blank all right, Freda. I'm nearly afraid to ask, but where did you find me jeans and crutches?'

She grinned again. 'You really don't remember, do ya?' She took his wallet from her pocket. 'And you haven't even asked about this yet. Jesus, Scobie, you really were bad.'

He took the wallet and stuck it in his pocket and then looked at her, his look slightly embarrassed. 'I didn't ... you know,. do anything I shouldn't have last night? You kno ... we didn't do ...'

She burst out laughing. 'You think because I'm bringin' you back your pants, that you and me did the belly flop together last night? Ah, that's priceless. Wait until I tell Orla. She'll wet herself laughin', she will.'

He smiled. 'Sorry, Freda.'

She gave him a playful punch on the arm. 'I'm not sayin' I wouldn't jump at the chance, Scobie, but the way you were last night, there was as much chance of that happenin' as Handy Andy stitchin' up the hole in his trouser pocket. You really can't remember?'

He shook his head. 'No, Freda. Why don't you come up and I'll make us a cup of tea and you can fill me in on the gory details.'

'Have to get back, Scobie. Today's one of our busiest days.' She left the crutches against the wall and handed him his jeans. 'When Orla and meself arrived in McCluskey's, yourself and Charlie Mulqueen were sittin' with yer arms around each other and murderin' Sweet Sixteen. And if that wasn't bad enough, that one that works as a secretary in Creufields joined ye and the three of ye stood up and did another massacre job on Scarlet Ribbons. Yerself and auld Charlie are no Finbar Furey. But I'll say this, yer woman can hold a tune. And she'd have held you too if you'd let her. Anyways, to cut a long story short, someone passing bumped into her and she spilt her glass of red wine on your jeans. Timmy O'Shea came in to pick up a fare and Macker asked him if he would run you home first. Timmy asked me to give him a hand. I told you on the way that we'd clean your jeans for you.' She laughed. 'I meant you could drop them in to us the next day but you insisted on taking them off in the taxi and givin' them to me. We found your keys in your jacket and we both helped you upstairs. We forgot the crutches. We left you snoring on the couch. And that's the story, Scobie. Now – I'll leave ya and love ya.'

'Thanks a million, Freda. I owe you.'

She turned and patted his arm. 'And ye needn't worry, Scobie. Neither Timmy or meself will tell anybody about your striptease in the taxi. Or that you wear Bart Simpson boxers. Wouldn't like to ruin your reputation with that bit of news.'

She grinned at him again and then went off down the street.

He carried the jeans and crutches back up and left them on the couch and then grabbed the parcel from Rome and went back down and out the door. His leg was feeling much better and if he favoured it a little, he could walk almost normal. He headed for Supermacs.

Tina Dolan was behind the counter and she gave him a wide smile when he walked in. He sat down at one of the empty tables and waited as she came over. 'Breakfast is finished, Scobie. But seeing as it's you, I can get one of the lads to do one for you if that's what you want. It'll take a few minutes though.'

He shook his head. 'You're all right, Tina. Think I'll head to the Cloisters and have a dinner there. Need something substantial.'

She grinned. 'A hard night so was it?'

'That's what they tell me anyways. Sit down for a minute.'

When she was facing him, he pushed the parcel over to her. 'Your key to the frosty Mrs. Ward's wooden heart.'

'Oh God, Scobie!' she exclaimed, excitement in her voice. She quickly opened it up. The cover on the bible was soft leather with a large papal crest and 'Holy Bible' etched underneath in gold lettering. She opened it up. The pages were soft and almost silken and on the first there was a handwritten inscription with the papal seal underneath.

The inscription read

Kathleen Ward
A good and faithful servant of the church
Remembering you always in my prayers.
Iosephum Cavelli – Bishop of Rome

Tina looked at him, her eyes sparkling. 'I don't know how to thank you, Scobie. I know she's just going to love this. I know she will.' She stood up and came around and gave him a quick peck on the cheek. 'You'll be top of my wedding invitation list.'

He grinned at her. 'I'll look forward to that, Tina. Just don't expect me to dance with your mother-in-law.' He stood up. 'Well time to rock and roll. I'll see you, Tina.'

She gripped his arm. 'I really am grateful, Scobie. And as I promised, there's a free breakfast for you any time you come.'

He rubbed his stomach. 'God, I don't know about that, Tina. If I take up that offer, I could turn into another Moby Dick Larkin. Let's just play it by ear, okay?'

'Okay, Scobie. Whatever way you want to play it. I'll see you. And thanks again.'

He went out and stopped outside the door. McCluskey was sweeping up the cigarette butts from in front of the bar. He saw Gerry. 'You're alive then.'

Gerry walked over. 'I am, Macker. And thanks for getting me home last night. Sorry if I was a bit out of order.'

McCluskey laughed. 'Arra you're all right, Scobie. But next time you and Charlie decide to do a duet, do me a favour and warn me. I can stick on the old ear defenders then.' He swept the last few butts into the dustpan and gave the path one last swipe of the brush. 'You coming in for a pint?'

'Well I was going to the Cloisters for a bit of dinner,' Gerry said.

'Come on in. I've an auld stew on and there's loads in it. And sure you can have a pint while you're waiting.'

'Okay,' Gerry said. 'But just the one.'

McCluskey laughed. 'The day Scobie Tierney has just one pint and walks away, that's the day I'll hand in me licence.'

Gerry followed him in.

He knew he was right.

*****

Made in the USA
Columbia, SC
08 December 2017